The S

Stuart Seaton is a f
and manager, a tele
and scriptwriter, and a broadcaster. He
among the country's best-known agricultural
journalists.

Available in Fontana by the same author

Inheritance

STUART SEATON

The Successors

FONTANA/Collins

First published by William Collins Sons & Co. Ltd 1986
First issued in Fontana Paperbacks 1987

Made and printed in Great Britain by
William Collins Sons & Co. Ltd, Glasgow

Few authors are self-sufficient.
I am not. And without the help,
understanding and patience of my
wife, *The Successors* might never
have emerged from their
Inheritance; or at least would
have taken a great deal longer
about it. So this is for Audrey.

S.S. 1986

PROLOGUE

The Citroen turned off the road which ran close to the sea between St Maxime and Cogolin, past the old farmhouse and the stone barns, and pointed towards the hills. Behind lay the flat marshland at the western end of the bay of St Tropez; ahead, beyond the hills, the Maure mountains were hazy grey against the unbroken blue-white of the sky.

The road wound north-west, into the searing sunlight of the late afternoon. The driver pushed dark glasses higher on his nose, narrowing his eyes.

Presently he turned into the foothills, towards the village. The windows of the car were down, but the air outside was too hot for movement to bring much relief. Across the sloping fields nothing stirred except a lone buzzard wheeling slowly, hunting the walls and ditches, dark wings tilted against the brilliant sky. As he followed the twisting road the driver could see the jumble of grey-walled houses and, above, the gaunt tower of the ruined castle. A car rounded a corner in front and he slowed, edging past it carefully, for the road was now little wider than the two vehicles and the hedges were high and growing wild. Then he was into the village and saw the church.

He stopped on a small levelled car park, and the heat closed in on him, stifling. He listened. The whole village slept as the sun slid slowly down towards the mountains. He swung his legs out of the car and stood up, looking around. The houses were dark, and there were cracked walls and weeds in the guttering. But flowers grew in window boxes and small trees climbed beside them and bicycles leaned against corners. The village was not dead after all.

He turned towards the church. It was low, with a squat tower, all grey stone and cement and incredibly ancient. He thought he had never seen such an ancient church. Slowly he walked uphill towards it, his shirt dark with sweat against his back in the shimmering heat. His footsteps seemed loud, echoing from the walls. Still he was the only thing moving.

He was in his early thirties, with black hair and a clearly-cut

7

face. He carried no spare flesh and his leanness made him look taller than he was. When he reached the church he stopped and looked around at the village, as if remembering once-familiar things; staring from one building to the next and along the sloping street. Then he faced the church again.

The cracked and iron-bound door was closed. He fingered it; and pushed gently. It swung away, creaking. Beyond was blackness. He took off his sunglasses and stood just inside the doorway, letting his eyes adjust; deep-set dark eyes, nearly as black as his hair.

The church looked even smaller inside than out. Thin shafts of light from the window slits picked out shadowy pews; stone pillars melted into the dimness. A single window at the far end illuminated the altar and its simple silver cross. The building smelled of old wood and damp stone; a thousand years of oldness and dampness. But it was cool; welcome after the brassy heat outside.

His footsteps made a dull, flat sound against the motionless air. He shuffled forward, unsure of the rough stone floor scarcely seen beneath his feet. When he stopped the silence surrounded him, pressing in. He shivered suddenly; turned and walked back to the door and outside, shielding his eyes with a hand as he pulled the sunglasses from his shirt pocket and put them on.

The graveyard was a distance away. As he neared it he saw that much of it was overgrown. Grey stones leaned from the sun-scorched grasses. Many were too old to tell him whose lives they recorded; wind and rainworn, the inscriptions had finally yielded to the dull green lichens.

But then he saw that part of it was tidier. The grass had been cut within recent weeks; stones stood upright and some were clean, with inscriptions he could read without stooping. He moved slowly between them. A small lizard scuttled away into the grass and the cracked earth.

He was reading every inscription now, his head moving from side to side as he went along the path. At the end he turned on to the grass and began to work his way back between the next rows of graves, head down, dark eyes watchful.

Then he found the stone he sought.

It was plain granite; a simple oblong little more than two feet high. He stood still, looking down at it; took off his glasses and crouched, reading the inscription. 'Beneath the cloak, a good man,' it said. And the name: that was what he had come to see.

He was still staring at it when the sun, lower in the sky now, threw a moving shadow across the stone, and the single word 'M'sieur?' was accusing. The man at the graveside twisted, started, and pushed himself upright.

The figure was medium-height, solid-shouldered, wearing faded denim trousers and an old shirt; around forty and brown-haired, with a greying moustache above a strong jaw. The eyes were steady, narrowed in the glare; then, suddenly, widening.

The younger man stared back, for seconds, in dawning astonishment, taking in the face and the trickle of sweat which ran down one temple. Behind him a car engine started in a narrow street, the sound muffled by the heat and the high stone walls. Two seagulls glided across the sun. One cackled suddenly. A breath of hot wind stirred, and then the black-haired man breathed: 'My God, Paul – Paul Cardin –'

The other was shaking his head slowly, wonderingly.

'Ricard – of all people – you, here? I can't believe it.' Little more than a whisper; then in a burst of delight: 'But this is wonderful. I saw you looking at the grave. I had to know who would look so closely at this one grave. But – you? You have come back?'

'Yes. I came to see it. I've come a long way. But – why are you here?'

'I live here. We've all come a long way.' A broad hand wiped sweat from a broad forehead. He was grinning, excited now. 'I didn't know you had survived. And now you're back. The Wolf of Ste Baume is here again. Everyone remembers you. Come to my house. I'll tell them all you're here.' He grasped the black-haired man by the elbows, squeezing his arms. 'We shall have the biggest party of the year. How long can you stay?'

'As long as you'll let me. Well, a couple of days, anyway.' Then a glance down at the grey stone and its inscription, and the pleasure faded. 'What happened to him, Paul? Why is he buried here?'

Cardin took the younger man by the arm and they turned away. Suddenly he was uneasy.

'It's a long story.' He was staring away across the rough fields, down towards the haze of the distant Mediterranean. 'Perhaps we should talk about it later.' He looked doubtfully at his companion.

The younger man checked; stood still. Cardin turned slowly, reluctantly. The hot wind stirred the parched grasses at their feet.

'Tell me why he is buried here.'

Cardin shrugged. He looked towards the church as if asking forgiveness.

'We brought him here, after it was over. They had put him in an unmarked grave. But we knew where it was. We had heard that he deserved something better.'

'An unmarked grave? In God's name, why? How was he killed?'

Cardin said simply: 'They killed him.' He hesitated for seconds before he added softly: 'We thought it was because of you.'

Silence then, except for the hot wind in the nearby trees. Silence; until the dark eyes closed and the whispered words, 'Oh Christ, I was afraid of that,' were in English.

Cardin stepped forward quickly; gripped his companion's elbow.

'Let's get away from here, and away from the sun.' He gestured across the cemetery. 'He is not the only person to talk about. There's so much to say, so many people to see. We'll talk through the night, eh?' He pulled at the elbow, leading the way, his excitement thrusting anxiety aside.

The younger man allowed himself to be propelled along the path, reacting to Cardin's enthusiasm, relaxing. He put a hand on the thick shoulder and his mouth widened.

'Right through the night, Paul. And take me to some of the others. François, Marcel, Claude –' He checked; glanced sideways. 'And your wife? How is she?'

'She is very well.' If Cardin noticed the slight hesitation he did not show it. 'We have two children now. She will be so happy that you are here. She has never forgotten what you did – that she's alive only because of you.'

'We helped each other. All of us.' A quick shrug. 'It will be good to see her again. And the others.'

They walked on, into the village and the welcome shade of the old walls.

The seagull, still circling the ruin of the castle, cackled again; then screamed once as it dipped towards the graveyard.

1

He flew the little Puss Moth steadily westwards at 3000 feet, close to the beaches where the early holidaymakers walked huddled in heavy coats, eager to catch the chill beginning of spring. Some turned their heads at the sound of the aircraft's engine and glimpsed the wings against the blue of the sky and the white canyons of distant cloud. But he was not looking down at them, for his eyes were on the grey sprawl of the city of Exeter eight miles ahead through the transparent disc of the propeller. Then he was looking to the right, and nearer, searching for the junction of two roads and a railway line parallel with one of them. His mouth widened in a grin of pleasure. He had held a private pilot's licence for a mere eight weeks but he had navigated solo out of Exeter up to Cullompton, then to Ilminster and south to the coast at Lyme Regis before turning back to Sidmouth, and had hit every point on his flight plan exactly. Now, before returning to Exeter, he was going to fly over his own small piece of the green and brown patchwork stretching below him.

He was Richard Haldane, eighteen years old, student in modern languages at Manchester university, and heir to 2000 acres of Devonshire farmland with his twin Robert and elder sister Ruth. That March day in 1936 they and their mother and their advisers were to meet formally for the first time since the death of their grandfather five weeks before, to formulate a business plan. But Richard had left early for his flight, confident that the freedom and adrenalin-spurting excitement which came from his new-found gift of wings would leave him clear in mind and spirit and ready for whatever the later talking might bring.

He saw the roads and the railway line just where he had expected them to be, and his hands and feet moved smoothly and the earth tilted below him. He slid down towards it, the aircraft vibrating slightly as it passed through a drifting shred of cloud, moisture condensing on the windscreen and then whipping away in vanishing streaks. Ahead now he could see the village of

Roxton straggling on either side of its main street and the tower of St Thomas's Church at one end of it. He held the steep turn, eyes flicking across to the altimeter, ears listening to the engine note; glorying in the swinging horizon and his power over transport through the limitless air.

At a thousand feet he levelled out, searching to the east of the village, finding the big house and the farm buildings sprawling alongside.

He throttled back, turning round the house, seeing its redbrick façade and stone-framed windows and the ivy surrounding them, its wide roof and lofty chimneys: Roxton Grange, with its sixteen rooms and great hall, heart of the estate which stretched around it and provided a living for thirty-five men and their families, tenant farmers and farm workers alike. Close by were the grey and brown stone buildings of the home farm with manager Martin Calder's house overlooking one end of the big yard around which the buildings clustered. He flattened out of the steep turn and saw beef cattle, like a child's tiny toys, crowding around a paddock gate close to the buildings. Beyond, the fields stretched green interspersed with patches of red earth newly ploughed and ready for spring cereals and early potatoes. He saw the dark spread of Morton Wood where he had played as a child and, further away, the land and buildings which made up the seven tenanted farms. He could see the grey dots of sheep, and in the valley the ribbon which came off the River Otter in a wide stream meandering through the fields and providing easy watering for the stock.

His grandfather's land; and for a moment the excitement of flying was submerged in sadness, for he had loved the old man who had dominated this place through his own short life and for so many years before he had been born. But Richard was a realist; he had already come to terms with Randolph Haldane's death, and the sadness passed as he pushed the throttle lever forward and raised the engine cowling and saw the land dropping away as he began to climb above the distant silver finger of the Exe. As he went he glimpsed the house again and saw a figure standing on the carriage drive. He was too far away to recognize it, but he still raised a hand in a symbolic wave from his lofty, superior, vibrating eyrie.

2

Harvey Roach said: 'The king is dead. Unfortunately we cannot say in the same breath "Long live the king". We must make interim arrangements. We have to appoint regents.'

Roach was a solicitor of the old school, given to allegory and the expansive phrase. He sat now at one end of the blackened oak refectory table in the big hall of Roxton Grange and surveyed his companions: Diane Haldane, her twenty-two-year-old daughter Ruth, twin eighteen-year-old sons Robert and Richard, and Conroy Jones, accountant to the Roxton estate and its long-time financial adviser.

'Your father-in-law,' Roach said to Diane Haldane, 'was an extraordinary man, known and respected throughout this county. He was one of our most progressive estate owners.'

Diane, fair-haired, still trim and youthful at forty-seven, watched him; half resigned, half exasperated. Why did he always have to lecture? Everyone knew the remarkable strengths of Randolph Haldane. His death had shocked them all, despite his eighty-five years, for he had seemed immortal.

'Let us remind ourselves of his life,' Roach droned, 'so that we may better interpret his purpose. He was a man of great courage who had been an adventurer in an age of adventure. He had survived it all; and always, let us remember, with one purpose. . . .'

The voice chanted on. And Diane remembered, for once Randolph had had a son. She had married him in the far-off days before the war when it had seemed that Edwardian Britain might be preserved forever. Ranulph: the son worthy of the father; strong in body and spirit; a leader among leaders. But he had gone with so many others, down into the mud of Flanders, and only her father-in-law's strength had saved her from all-consuming despair. From that dreadful moment so long ago in 1917, and despite his sixty-seven years, he had set himself the dual task of becoming surrogate father to his son's infant children and of holding together the inheritance which would have been Ranulph's and which he had then determined should be passed intact to his grandchildren.

Through the depression of the 1920s and now the economic

disaster of the 1930s he had given the family tireless leadership and spirit which had even survived the death of his own wife. Then, suddenly, on a cold February day, he had died as he might have wished, walking across the home pastures towards Morton Wood, with his beloved land around him; yet with his ambition unrealised, for his heirs were still too young for ultimate responsibility.

Diane looked at them. Too young – and perhaps too individual; for they were Haldanes, and the blood did not accept compromise kindly.

Roach's voice dragged her back to the day's business.

'Our purpose now is to interpret his wishes and safeguard the livelihoods of everyone who depends on this estate until you, his grandchildren' – he nodded across the table at the three youthful faces – 'have gained enough experience to succeed him in your own right.'

He paused, shuffling papers. The old clock against one panelled wall ticked slowly, solemnly, in the silence. Diane glanced at her sons. Both watched the solicitor: mirrors of each other, but not precisely, as if the glass were tilted a little. The black Haldane hair and dark deep-set eyes were the same, and so was the strong jaw. But within there were contrasts which emerged subtly in their faces. Richard's quick, easy leaning to mockery which was often more humorous than unkind lurked in the curve of his mouth, and there was a strange compulsion in his gaze which he had inherited from his grandfather and which reflected perception and criticism beyond his years; while Robert bore a ruthless streak and a razor tongue which found reflection in eyes which narrowed quickly in anger and a mouth which hardened frequently in intolerance. Physically they were strong and aggressive when provoked, but Robert was the first to raise his fists while Richard was more cunning and at school had been regarded as the more deadly. And for twins their attitude to each other was uncommon, for they were frequently in dispute and had been so all their lives, often relying ultimately on the tact of their sister to smooth differences and restore harmony.

Roach said: 'Many years ago Randolph Haldane decided that come what may his grandchildren would have to be capable of succeeding him by 1940, when Richard and Robert will be twenty-three and Ruth twenty-seven. As you know, his will provided

14

generously for you, Mrs Haldane; otherwise the estate will then be owned jointly by you three young people. And you have the comfort of knowing that your grandfather had so arranged affairs that death duties will be within Roxton's capacity in spite of agriculture's sorry state. Meanwhile, until you have achieved the ages he laid down, your mother will have executive powers. None of this is news to you, but it is pertinent to remind ourselves of it now.'

He nodded towards Conroy Jones, who was as slight and balding as the solicitor was big and bushy-haired. Jones accepted his cue, his bright bird-eyes darting around the table.

'My function is simple,' he said. His voice had an edge which matched the sharpness of his gaze. 'I and my partners have been accountants to this estate for fifteen years and I pride myself that I understand the business well. I promised Randolph I would continue to advise you to the best of my ability for as long as I may be required, and I will be proud to do just that.'

'I know it,' Diane said. She was unnaturally sombre in her formal grey suit and white blouse. 'And I'm grateful. I'll welcome your help.'

Jones's nod was a single, quick movement of his head.

'Whenever you wish, Mrs Haldane. But don't under-estimate yourself. You may not have been born to the land but you know a lot about this business. And Martin Calder is proven as a home farm manager. I think the machine will go on working fairly well.'

Diane thought: Now – this is when it must happen; from this moment there must never be any doubt. He's being condescending, Roach is preaching to me, and the children are hearing it.

She said: 'I intend that it should work very well. I have already discussed certain matters with Martin, and while he may not be over-happy about working for a woman I think he will accept it in time. In any event I'm confident that when I hand over this estate it will be in every respect as good as it is now. I shall hold management meetings each Monday morning at ten o'clock with Martin, my family when they're available and, I trust, with the advantage of your presence, Mr Jones.'

The silence lasted a mere three or four seconds; but to everyone around the table it felt longer. They stared at her, startled by the challenge in her voice. Jones blinked rapidly; then repeated his single nod.

'It will be my pleasure. Every Monday morning. That's an excellent start –' his pause was fractional '– if I may say so.'

'We won't be much help to you.' It was Ruth, with her shining dark hair and her mother's generous mouth which always seemed about to smile; but not at this moment, for she wanted to smother the stirring tension. 'I'm at Cambridge, Robert's at Reading, and Richard's two hundred and fifty miles away at Manchester. So except for the vacs you'll have to hold your meetings without us. We must do our best not to lose touch.' Her eyes questioned Diane. 'Especially if you plan any changes.'

'Not at the moment,' Diane said firmly. 'But when I do I'll talk to the three of you about them on the telephone first.'

Robert said: 'I won't allow myself to lose touch.' If he was responding to his mother's provocation he did not show it, for he addressed them all equally. But his voice was as hard as his eyes. 'Though I must say I'm concerned that grandfather has forced us to wait so long before we're allowed to take over. He always encouraged us to understand everything that went on here. I'm sure we did, too. I may have things to learn, but by the time I finish at Reading I'll be ready to take my full responsibilities. I think grandfather was too cautious, and with respect to you, Mother, I regret it.'

'I think he was wise,' Ruth retorted. 'If we make mistakes now, we could spend years putting them right. Agriculture is in such a financial mess that there's no room for errors, even small ones. I know that when I've qualified as a vet I'll still need to study estate management if I'm going to be useful here. And I won't qualify for another two and a half years.'

Robert said curtly: 'You're speaking for yourself. I chose agricultural science because I knew it would benefit me directly and quickly. I'll know when I'm competent. And it will be before I'm twenty-three.'

'Your grandfather's instructions are quite clear,' Roach began starchily, but Robert snapped back at him: 'I know. That doesn't mean I have to agree with them.'

'You have to accept them,' Diane said. She did not raise her voice, but her annoyance was obvious. 'And this is not the moment to debate his wisdom. Although we all know awareness of his age must have been a factor in his decisions, I think you should regard it as a tribute, Robert, that he felt you would be competent by the time you're twenty-three. You'll still be a very young man, you know.'

Robert flushed and his mouth tightened.

'We must agree to differ, mother. I'm sorry; I have to say what I think. I thought this meeting was to give everyone a chance to do that.'

'It is,' said Diane. She was now so much in command, and knew it, that she did not need to show further impatience. 'And we shall all continue to say what we think. What about you, Richard?'

Richard looked back at her. Then his gaze shifted, from face to face. Ruth thought: he looks as if he's trying to read our minds, and thinks he's succeeding; and how much older than Robert he seems, just these past weeks, since Grandad died. The dark eyes met hers and, for an instant, communicated humour to her; a secret, sardonic humour she knew lurked in him. She was close to Richard; closer, she was sure, than Robert was; but still not very close, for Richard guarded his innermost self and she thought no one would ever know it. Perhaps Richard himself did not know it yet.

His eyes moved on, to his brother now, and no one spoke. Jones watched curiously. He felt he understood the turbulent, abrasive Robert; but Richard was another matter.

'I was wondering.' The voice was quiet, almost gentle, as Richard leaned back in his chair. Momentarily he glanced towards the ceiling, and it was as if he looked for something; and then acknowledged it with a small lift of his eyebrows. 'If grandfather is still around somewhere, and can hear us now, I wonder what he thinks.' His eyes circled the table again. 'Six of us deciding how we can do something he did all by himself for most of his life. If he's listening, I hope he has time to be patient with us.'

Roach said sharply: 'There are many things to discuss, Richard. I hardly think we are wasting anybody's time.'

'Not wasting it, Mr Roach.' The hint of a tolerant smile. 'Just not extracting the last ounce from it. And you knew grandfather – he always did.' He glanced up at the corner of the ceiling again, and Ruth suddenly wanted to giggle as she saw her brother's eyelid flicker in what might have been a wink.

Jones saw it too, and said warily: 'You intrigue me, Richard. Do you really believe your grandfather might be listening to us?'

'That's nonsense,' Diane said sharply. 'Of course he doesn't.'

17

'You can never tell,' Richard said in his easy voice. He turned in his chair, looking around the lofty hall, towards the wide stairs, the big window, the door to the carriage drive outside; then on to the dark leather armchairs, the long sideboard where his grandfather had kept whisky and cigars; and finally to the big stone fireplace. He looked intently at that for several seconds and, slowly, they all turned to it. Then Diane betrayed herself with a quick intake of breath, and he put a hand over hers and said: 'No, mother. I don't think he's here.' His near-black eyes were gentle on her blue ones and she could not look away from him. 'But just for a moment I think we all imagined we saw him. Because that's where he stood, so often, when he discussed things with us. I just hope that the thought will remind us, if we're somewhat less than good-tempered, that he left unfinished business which is a considerable burden for us all.'

They were quiet then; until Conroy Jones said: 'That was an interesting speech, Richard. I think your grandfather would have appreciated it.'

'I doubt it,' Robert snapped. He was staring angrily at his brother. 'I thought it was another of your flights of fancy. Like your trip this morning. I must say I hope your new hobby isn't going to cost too much. Flying is an expensive indulgence, and our finances are far from sound.'

Richard raised an eyebrow.

'Don't let it worry you, brother. I use my own money – my own small legacy from grandfather. Just like the one you had. And I'll use it with or without your blessing.'

'That's enough.' Diane moved in swiftly. 'Save your disagreements for another time. We have important things to talk about. If you boys want to stay, you're welcome. But don't chip at each other, or I'll ask you to leave.'

They stayed, as Conroy Jones produced the records of farm and estate management, livestock and crops, rents and wages, building repairs and land ditched and drained; the complex detail of the battle to make the estate and the home farm profitable in the midst of an intense agricultural depression. They made decisions, they edged cautiously towards changes; and they accepted Diane's leadership. Yet when it was over she felt depressed, for she had seen yet again the cracks in the family's façade. Her hold on the estate was for less than five years. When it was over the boys who snapped and snarled at each other now would be men, and their quarrels would shatter their legacy. There had been Haldanes at Roxton since the 1700s. But not for much longer.

She had once voiced her fears to her father-in-law. She remembered him, cigar jutting from his hard mouth, nodding thoughtfully. He had said: 'I can't contradict you. But tell me what else I do – at my age. We can only hope that maturity will bring them closer together.'

No, she thought; it will not. The temperament which had carved out Randolph Haldane and her long-dead husband dominated her own sons now; and maybe it lurked in Ruth as well, hidden and waiting. Rebellion, obstinacy, challenge and courage. Dangerous virtues, in uncertain combination.

She could control them for a time; but only for a short time.

3

Mosley's blackshirts were marching. They came down Exeter's High Street on a Sunday morning, boots ringing on the roadway, faces hard behind a figure in a black uniform with a peaked cap angled arrogantly above a lean face and thin moustache: fifty assorted men pretending to be ruthless troopers in a dictatorship with a posturing, ruler-backed knight at their head.

They were leaving the city's heart where Mosley had harangued a small crowd, his ragged army drawn up on either side while a supporter sold the British Union of Fascists' newspaper *Action*. It was a weekend scene familiar around the country as the blackshirt leader rallied support for his conviction that in all Europe only Adolf Hitler, master of Germany, held the solution to economic troubles; that Russia and Jewish-led international business were the enemies of the people; that National Socialism was the salvation of a struggling, confused Britain.

Richard and Robert Haldane leaned on their Morris eight and watched him go; watched the thin, sceptical crowd disperse under the impartial eyes of the two policemen who had stood, side by side, in silent supervision of the gathering.

Robert said: 'He's very persuasive – and crazy, I think. How the hell did he get his knighthood?'

'I don't know.' Richard shook his head. 'But I reckon if he was plain Oswald Mosley instead of Sir Oswald the press would pay less attention to him. He's noisy, but not much else.'

'He has a bigger following than you think,' Robert retorted. 'A lot of people are pro-Nazi. It's a reaction against the communists. And any loud-mouthed orator can whip up anti-semitism in a crowd.'

'Maybe.' A dismissive shrug. 'I still think we give him and his kind too much credit. And Hitler too, for that matter. If we just built a few more aircraft and another couple of battleships we could afford to turn our backs and let him rant to himself –'

He checked, staring at the scattering crowd; then stabbed out a finger.

'Rob. Over there. Five or six to Mosley's right. That's Sam Salford.'

Robert stared, then nodded. His eyes narrowed.

'I wouldn't have believed it. One of our own men, strutting around in their damn' black uniforms. I'll fire the bastard. As soon as he gets back, I'll have him out.'

Richard looked at him curiously.

'Come now, brother. Surely we don't sack people because of their political views. That's what Germany and Russia do.'

'Naziism isn't politics,' Robert snapped. 'It's a destructive creed. Its aim is a one-party state. Have you read about the concentration camps? The bully boys and their guns rule over there. If Sam Salford believes in that, I don't want him at Roxton.'

They stood in silence, watching the black-clad men around their leader; then seeing them split up and walk away until only half-a-dozen were still standing in attendance.

'His bodyguard,' Robert muttered. 'A very rough bunch, according to the papers. And Salford's still hanging around. Maybe he wants to be one of them.'

Richard turned.

'Forget him. It's nothing to do with us. Mother would never agree to sacking him because of his politics.'

Robert opened the car door and slid behind the wheel. Richard put one hand on the radiator, vaulted over the front of the car in sudden exuberance, and climbed in beside him.

'I think it has something to do with all of us,' Robert said as they settled. 'If we were less tolerant we wouldn't be regarded as a push-over.'

'We boost their egos.' Richard sounded bored. 'I've told you before: ignore them and they'll become that much less important. I don't think Germany's the menace Churchill makes out. I know the Nazis are a nasty lot, but as long as they only kill Germans it's not our affair.'

'They reintroduced conscription last year,' Robert said, as he started the car. 'They didn't do that to kill Germans.'

'The French have had conscription for years.' Richard grinned at him. 'We don't get excited about that.'

'All right – what about their occupation of the Rhineland? Hitler calls it re-militarisation, Churchill calls it invasion. Either way it's a threat to other countries – including ours.'

'The Rhineland was German already. We took it off them after the war. Can't exactly blame them for wanting it back.' Richard grinned again. 'Now stop preaching and find a pub. I want a beer before we go home.'

They drove off, heading eastwards out of the city until they reached a roadside inn, one of their favourite haunts when they were at home from university. There they parked the car, ducked through a low doorway into a long mock-Tudor bar, and ordered beers.

As they hitched themselves on to stools at one end of the bar and looked around at the dozen or so men scattered through the room, Robert said: 'What are we going to do about George Walton?'

Richard inspected his beer.

'Leave him alone. He's doing no harm.'

'He's running the farm down,' snapped Robert. 'He's the worst tenant we have. His triennial review is due in two months. I'm in favour of doubling his rent. It's ridiculously low, even by today's standards. If we push him hard enough he'll have to get out.'

'And then what? We can't get anything out of him for dilapidations – he's flat broke. So we would have to spend money on the place before any one else would tender for it. I don't want to put any capital into it at the moment.'

Robert gulped his beer impatiently.

'And I don't want to see any part of our land neglected. He's lazy and he's ignorant. It's time we got rid of him.'

'He's a harmless old peasant,' Richard said easily. 'And he has a haridan of a wife. What would he do if we threw him out?'

'That's not our worry. I'm going to urge mother to force him out.'

'She won't.' Richard shook his head and grinned. 'She may have become a lot tougher since grandfather died, but she's not as ruthless as you are.'

Robert eyed him. Suddenly his mouth was tight.

'Business is ruthless, especially in times like these.' His voice was low and hard and clear. 'And this matters – a damn' sight more than wasting our time watching brainless thugs parading behind that jumped-up actor Mosley, and you flying aeroplanes and studying languages when you ought to be concentrating on agriculture. You've no sense of priorities; and neither have I, hanging around here.' He snatched up his glass and drank half a pint of beer without a breath.

Along the bar, behind Robert, three young men who wore black shirts and trousers and had been talking loudly about Germany's thriving industries, were suddenly silent. Richard watched them and said quietly: 'Don't choke yourself. And keep your voice down. You're attracting attention from some of the brainless thugs.'

Robert glanced over his shoulder and snapped: 'So what? Drink your beer. I'm going home.'

Richard shrugged, but he still watched the silent trio. He picked up his glass, drained it, slid off his stool and followed Robert along the bar. They passed the three motionless spectators at little more than arm's length; three black shadows with white faces and hard eyes in the dimness of the room.

They walked across the small car park to the Morris. As they reached it Richard looked back. The three dark-clothed young men were standing outside the door, watching them. Now, away from the interior of the bar, he saw them clearly. All were strongly built, one taller than the others. Their hair was close-cropped and their faces shared the coarse ugliness of aggressive intent spawned from ignorance. He said quietly to Robert: 'Your brainless thugs are still with us. And I think they're angry.'

Then, without a word, the three rushed, spreading out to come in from the centre and both sides.

It lasted less than fifteen seconds. Robert met the tall man head on, ducking his swinging punch and hitting him with great force beneath the heart, then following up with a flurry of short-armed close-range blows; Richard catapulted himself off the Morris between his two assailants, grabbing an outstretched fist and spinning one round to shield himself briefly from the other as he slashed with the blade of his hand across the windpipe of the man he held before swinging him away and lashing out with his foot into the second man's crotch. His first victim retched, clutching at his throat, helpless as Richard kidney-punched him viciously then whirled with another kick, this time to the head, as the other man came back within range. He reared backwards and Robert, leaving the tall man crumpled and groaning on the ground, met him from behind with a two-handed chop to the neck.

Breathing hard, the twins looked at each other, then at the three figures struggling on the ground in their agonies. A slow grin spread across Richard's face as he said: 'We may not always agree, brother, but there are some things we do remarkably well together.' Then they darted to their car, wrenched open the doors and left the car park in a shower of loose stones from their spinning tyres.

For half a mile neither spoke, until Robert, working hard at the wheel of the little car, said: 'What do you think of the blackshirts at close quarters, then? Do you still think we give them too much credit?'

Richard braced himself as the Morris swayed through a corner.

'For violent men they weren't very effective,' he said. 'And since they're incapacitated why are you driving like a lunatic?'

'The landlord might have seen what happened. If he telephones the police I think we should be well away from there.'

'We are,' Richard said. He leaned back in the little bucket seat. 'Now take it easy. You're disturbing the peace of the countryside.'

*   *   *

Diane said: 'Why didn't you go to the police yourselves? The men attacked you. Now if they complain, you could be in trouble. You ran away like a couple of criminals.'

23

'They won't complain. That sort wouldn't like to admit that two well-dressed strangers beat the living daylights out of three of them.' Richard reached across the luncheon table for salt, then added: 'I must admit they took me by surprise. Robert said something scathing about Mosley and his mob, but he didn't even know they were there – they just overheard us.'

'That's the measure of them,' Robert said. 'And did you notice they didn't speak – no threats, no challenge? They just came out of the pub and rushed. In the world they want they'd be in uniform, swinging truncheons on every street corner and belting into anyone who said a wrong word. Perhaps now you'll take them more seriously.'

Richard raised an eyebrow.

'Do three voiceless thugs make a political creed more dangerous? Revolutions need brains as well as brawn.'

'Mosley is highly intelligent,' snapped Robert. 'And the papers hint that he numbers some influential people among his friends – including, in case you hadn't noticed, our new King Edward.'

'I had noticed.' Richard was still indifferent. 'Either way, what we saw this morning was hardly a political meeting – just a small crowd listening to a good orator surrounded by a rabble in black clothes. No, brother, it doesn't prove a thing – except that more than three are required to put the Haldanes on their backs.' He grinned at the thought.

'Stop arguing,' Diane told them. 'And try to keep out of trouble. You were lucky. You could have been badly hurt.'

'But we weren't,' Robert retorted. 'And it's of no consequence. Much more important was the subject of our conversation at the time – George Walton and his rent review. Are you going to try to force him out?'

Diane stared at him.

'Certainly not. I know he's a poor tenant. But he pays the rent we ask. If we force him out, what will happen to him?'

Robert stabbed at his plate with a fork.

'Why should we care? His land isn't earning to potential and we're the sufferers. I know standards have fallen. Nobody can afford to farm as he'd like to. But if everyone farmed the way Walton does the estate would soon be bankrupt. I want to talk to him. I think we should give him a straight warning and double his rent to show we mean it.'

'Leave him alone,' Diane said. 'We're not increasing anybody's rent. No one can afford it. George Walton will be treated the same as the rest.'

'You're too easy-going,' Robert said. 'And grandfather was too lenient with people like that, as well.'

Richard said: 'He wasn't lenient. He understood people. He saw the estate as an entity which had to accommodate some degree of weakness as well as strengths. He certainly didn't see everyone as an automaton working just to pay the highest rent he could extract – which is your attitude, I suspect, dear brother.'

'I see it as a business.' Robert's mouth was hard. 'There's no room for sentiment in business.' He turned to his mother. 'Let me talk to him. If you never allow me to become involved with the tenants, how do you expect me to be ready to take full responsibilities? We've a right to ask him about the condition of his land and his stocking rates and the state of the buildings.'

'No one disputes that,' Diane said sharply. 'But I don't want him threatened. I know you too well, Robert.'

But an hour later he had extracted her consent that he should see George Walton, and stood in the yard of the run-down farm looking at peeling paint on barn doors and smelling decay where there should have been the freshness of clean buildings and well-swilled byre and dairy. Around the corner of the brick barn he could see part of a hay swath turner. It should have been ready for hitching behind a horse, for on a good farm the earliest hay crop was not more than a few weeks away, but one of the shafts was splintered. Alongside it was a four-wheeled cart with a broken axle. Then he turned. George Walton was standing at the house door, watching him; paunched and round-shouldered, balding with a long fringe of greying hair which blew up now in tattered strands in the wind. He wore a collarless shirt, thick trousers secured with a wide-buckled belt, and heavy boots.

'Afternoon, Mr Robert.' He eyed his visitor cautiously. 'Having a look round, then?' He thrust an old briar pipe into his mouth.

'Yes. And not liking what I see,' Robert said curtly. 'This place is in a mess, George.'

Walton shuffled towards him, pipe clenched between uneven teeth.

'It's not bad, sir. Just a few things needing to be done. I'll be

25

getting round to'm afore long.'

Robert walked across to the barn and pulled open the small door set within one of the large ones. He sniffed the air, staring in the dimness towards the old hay stacked at one end. Behind him Walton peered anxiously. Robert crossed the barn and thrust a hand into the stack. He moved three feet along and pushed his hand inside again. Then he faced Walton.

'It's mouldy. It's not even good enough for bedding. You ought to get it out of here.'

He pushed past Walton, out into the yard again, and walked along the byre wall to the Dutch barn at the far end. A quarter of the space under the high roof was occupied by old hay, tumbled and ragged, a mixture of dirty grey and brown. Robert did not even have to approach it.

'This stuff isn't worth keeping. It doesn't look as if it was ever stacked properly: which means you were running a big fire risk. My advice is to get rid of the lot and give your new crop a chance – and to stack it well.'

Walton pushed his pipe into a pocket, averting his eyes.

'Aye, Mr Robert. I'll look to it.' He glanced back towards the house as if anxious to ensure that they were not being watched. As Robert started to move towards the byre he said: 'Be you looking for something, sir? Anything I can show you?'

Robert turned back to him.

'Your rent review is due in two months. I need to see this place so that I can make up my mind what to do. My mother and family want my report.' His voice was brisk and hard-edged.

Walton stared at him, slow alarm on his face.

'You ain't thinking of raising it, sir? Not in these hard times, Mr Robert? I'm making next to nothing on milk, and you know what beef is fetching. Them calves'll be worth little enough when I sell 'em. Corn ain't worth growing, 'cept for feed. I'm selling a few eggs, but they only buy me baccy. I'm hardly paying m'way as it is –'

'You pay less rent than any other farm on the estate,' Robert snapped. 'You're neglecting the place. I'm going to walk round and see how far the neglect has gone.' He moved briskly into the byre, and Walton trailed miserably along in his wake.

Half an hour later he had gone, and as George Walton shuffled back towards the house the back door opened and he saw his wife on the step, big hands on wide hips, aproned skirt tight around ample thighs, heavy breasts thrusting against a stained woollen jumper. Her fleshy face was hostile and her hair untidy.

'George? Who was that? Who's been here?'

He winced at the sound of her strident voice.

'Mr Robert. From the big house.'

'What for? What did he want?' She marched across the yard towards him.

'He just came to – to look around. Said he hadn't bin here for a time. Wanted to see the buildings and the land –'

'You're a liar.' She peered at him, thick legs straddled. 'He wouldn't waste his time. He came for more'n that. What did he want?'

He looked at her, and now he was weary and his round shoulders slumped.

'It's rent review time, luv. Y'know – three years. He came to look –'

'Oh, bloody hell. And you had to show'm what it's like.' She swung round and began to stamp back towards the house, calling as she went: 'The whole place is a bloody disgrace. Next thing they'll find a way of getting us off. And if they put up the rent we'll have to go anyway. Oh, bloody hell –'

He watched her, and the wind blew his thin hair across his head and the hand he raised to his face was shaking. The back door slammed and he blinked and jerked as if he had been struck.

*   *   *

Robert stood in the drawing-room doorway and said: 'It's a shambles. So is he. He's in such a mess that he doesn't know how to get out of it. If I hadn't looked around he could have lost his new hay crop and we might have had two barns burned out by the end of the summer. The land is in poor heart, his cattle are indifferent and obviously not milking well, his feed store is dirty and rat-ridden. There's no reason why we should put up with a tenant like that.'

Diane looked at him in silence for seconds, then levelled a warning finger.

'But we shall. And I'll tell you why, in case you haven't heard the story. He was a fairly good farmer once. But there was a

27

tragedy. They had a late child, around 1926. A boy. One day George borrowed a tractor. He'd never driven one before. He took the child with him, sat him on his knee. The boy slipped and fell under one of the rear wheels. George had a total breakdown, and his wife turned against him. He neglected everything after that. It's all been very sad. That's why I don't want to make things worse if I can avoid it.'

'That's very noble of you, mother,' Robert said. 'But this is a business.'

'And we must never allow sentiment to stand in the way of profit.' It was Richard, sauntering into view behind his brother; and clearly at his most provocative. 'George is a peasant. Throw him off, I say. The next man will at least keep the place tidy, even if he won't be able to make a lot more money. But then he'd have to make more money, wouldn't he – or we would throw him off too. Perhaps it's a good job there's nobody to throw us off, because we aren't making much. But we're not peasants, like George. We can't have peasants in these days of modern farming –'

'Shut up.' Robert pushed himself away from the door as if he wanted to distance himself from his brother. 'If you've nothing constructive to say, keep quiet. You talk like –'

'I think you should both keep quiet.' Diane's voice cut between them. 'The way you behave with each other, I can't see much hope for Roxton's future when you come to take charge of it.'

'We shall leave all the decisions to Ruth, while we fight.' Richard waved a hand airily. 'We'll fight each other, we'll fight blackshirt thugs, he'll fight peasants, I'll fight tyrannical landlords – not us, of course, because Ruth could never be a tyrant – and if Hitler has anything to do with it we'll probably both fight Germans –' He broke off, and suddenly he was no longer flippant. 'Sorry, mother. That wasn't funny. I apologise.' He turned quickly to Robert. 'Come on, Rob. It's time we went.'

He walked out without looking back. After a quick glance, Robert followed. They crossed the hall and went through to the front door; then stood together on the wide drive, uncertain replicas, black hair stirring in the wind. Robert produced cigarettes; threw one to Richard, who found a match. Slowly they walked off towards the farm.

It was later, when Richard had returned to the house, that

28

Robert saw Martin Calder leaving one of the farm buildings, and raised his voice. 'Martin: I want to see Sam Salford, in the office.'

Calder walked over and said: 'He'll be in any time now, for milking. Can I help?' He was tall and big-shouldered, in his late thirties and with a pleasant open face and calm voice. He had been home farm manager at Roxton for five years and was universally respected by the men.

'No – except by bringing him to me as soon as he shows up. I want you to hear what I have to say to him.'

Calder's eyes were steady on the young man's face, but he said nothing except: 'Surely, Mr Robert. I'll do that.'

Five minutes later Robert barked 'Come in' to a knock at the office door, and saw Sam Salford there, with Calder behind him. When both were inside he said: 'I was in Exeter this morning, Sam, and saw you taking part in Mosley's rally. Normally I don't give a damn about a man's politics. But blackshirts are a different matter. Does your wife know what you do on a Sunday?'

Salford blinked. He was around Calder's age, solidly built and square jawed, and was clearly startled by the young man's aggression.

'She knows I go to meetings, Mr Robert. Ain't no harm in that. A man can do as he likes, I reckon.'

'He can't if he's in Hitler's Germany,' Robert snapped. 'Just remember that. And remember something else; if I ever see you in that black uniform on our farm, or hear of you preaching Naziism here, I'll fire you on the spot. Clear?'

Salford took his time before he replied. Then, slowly but obviously, his shoulders straightened and his face stiffened.

'Begging your pardon, sir, a man's beliefs is his own private affair. But I'll not talk about 'em here.'

'Good. Get back to work, then.' Robert waved a dismissive hand and Calder opened the door. Salford knew when to keep quiet and, stony-faced, nodded and left. Outside he looked hard at the farm manager but Calder gestured towards the farm buildings and said: 'You'd better do as you're told, Sam.'

He watched the labourer walk with long, deliberate strides across the drive to the paddock fencing and the white gate which marked the boundary between the gardens surrounding the house and the farm, then glanced back momentarily at the office door. Dear God, he thought; having a woman giving orders is bad enough. But what about that one? What the hell will he be like in another few years? This place is in for ructions, all right.

4

It was now July, the long summer vacations had begun, and Richard was flying his favourite club aeroplane, the white Puss Moth, from Exeter to Hurn for a light aircraft rally, with Ruth as a passenger.

This was her first flight and as they passed over Dorchester she was still tense, although her eyes were shining with excitement as she looked out at the blue-grey English Channel to their right and the hazy land ahead, and felt the aeroplane move against the occasionally-shifting wind and then the seat belt tighten across her lap as they passed through an air pocket.

She looked round the small, spartan cabin and the array of dials and switches, and raised her voice against the engine noise.

'I'd never imagined how detached one could feel. It really is another world.'

He glanced sideways at her and grinned.

'That's why I like it. I can forget everything else: the estate, and studying, and fighting Robert, and the price of beef and when we can afford to replace one of the tractors. Nothing seems to matter when I'm up here. I just concentrate on flying and making sure I get where I want to go.'

She looked at him curiously.

'Do you worry about things? I thought you never did.'

Again the characteristic grin. He pushed a lock of dark hair away from his forehead.

'I don't worry. There's no point – it doesn't help. But I do ask myself questions. Like whether I should be spending three years learning French and German.'

'I thought you enjoyed it. You're so good at it.'

'Oh yes, I'm good at it. I'll get a good degree. But I wonder sometimes if it makes sense. Robert's doing ag science and you're going to be a vet. You'll both know a hell of a lot more than I will when it comes to running Roxton.'

He leaned closer to the side window, studying the ground three thousand feet below, watching for landmarks, comparing them with the map on his knee and the line drawn across it. The sun was bright over the sea, and the heat from the land beneath them was creating mild turbulence. The aircraft sank a little and he moved the stick slightly as the left wing dropped a few degrees. The wing came up again.

She said: 'Do you think about what you're doing? Or is it habit now, like changing gear in a car?'

He shook his head, still looking for landmarks.

'In the air you need to think all the time. Only fools don't think. And aeroplanes bite fools.'

She did not laugh, because he was serious. Instead she said: 'You never had doubts about your course when you chose it, did you?'

He shrugged.

'We all enjoy doing things we do well. And you know French has always been easy for me. German's not much more difficult, either. So maybe I'm lazy. Or maybe I don't want to spend the rest of my life at Roxton.'

She stared at him. It was the first time she had heard him say that. Sometimes she had wondered, when he had seemed less enthusiastic than Robert over a home farm problem, or a decision on spending money here or saving it there; but then Richard could be so difficult to understand.

'Rich – do you really mean that? Do you want to get away?'

His eyes flicked across the artificial horizon and the altimeter, then out over the engine cowling and ahead. There was a heat haze now and the air was increasingly bumpy, although the Puss Moth was riding it well.

He said, half to himself: 'Twelve minutes, and we should see it.' Then he glanced across the little cabin. 'Do I want to get away? Sometimes. And more often since I went to Manchester. But I don't know where I want to go. I'll come away from university with an excellent command of French and a fair knowledge of some interesting French literature; able to speak reasonable German – and I won't have any idea how to put it all to profitable

31

use. That's why I'm asking questions.' He checked the line on his map against the compass heading and steered five degrees to the right. Now he was looking for Poole harbour and Bournemouth beyond, and his mouth widened suddenly when he glimpsed the outline of the great inlet and then the dotted yachts on the glassy water and two small coasters against a quayside. Then Bournemouth was emerging from the haze and he began to search the sky for other aircraft, knowing that traffic around Hurn would be heavy. As he did so he said: 'Do you want to spend all your life at Roxton? Working with Robert, and with me if I'm still around, running 2000 acres of farmland, dealing with tenants and with farm workers, trying to make it all pay in the face of whichever depression is current? Does it interest you enough to become your whole life's commitment?'

'I'll be a vet,' she objected. 'I hope to be in practice –'

'Right. So it won't be your whole commitment. And what happens when you marry? Your husband might work in London, or anywhere. Then guess what? You might even want your money out of the place: cash in your hot hand so that you can live in another world. Ever think of that?'

She was quiet then, watching the coastline slide below them, watching her brother's hands on the controls, watching the edge of the New Forest appear, feeling the wings rock a little in the hot air; knowing he had touched the flaw in her grandfather's plan. It was a familiar flaw to her, for she had thought about it many times.

He could see the airfield now, and glanced left and right behind, searching the sky for other aircraft as he began to turn. The Puss Moth carried no radio, and landing was a matter of knowing airfield rules and keeping a sharp lookout for traffic.

He settled now at 2000 feet on the 'dead' side of the airfield, searching for the signal square on the ground telling him the wind speed and landing area. He caught sight of a biplane ahead and settled in behind it at a respectful distance, starting to lose height; and then saw the red aircraft. It was a Percival Gull, flying faster than they were but on the same course, two hundred feet above them and little more than three hundred feet to the left. Its low wing seemed to be masking the pilot's view of the Puss Moth for, as Richard watched, it drifted nearer.

'Look at that blind fool.' He jabbed a finger towards it. 'He's closing on us.' He eased the engine revolutions, dropped his right wing with a little left rudder to side-slip away; then levelled off, opened the throttle and turned fast to the right, banking steeply. Ruth clutched in alarm at the side of the cabin but his grin was reassuring. They had both lost sight of the red aircraft now, and he held the Puss Moth in a tight turn, gradually making height. The horizon swung around them, trees and fields below and the coast beyond, then the New Forest heathland; until he was back in the landing circuit and saw the Gull, tiny in the distance and close to landing.

He said grimly: 'I'll take him apart when we get down. He wasn't keeping his eyes open. He should never have been there, overhauling us. He should have dropped in behind. He must be out of his mind.'

'Don't be angry.' She put out a hand to touch his. 'Don't start the weekend with a row. He must have made a mistake.'

'Mistakes kill people in the air,' he said. But he did not argue further, for he was concentrating, turning on to his final approach. The red aircraft was ahead, touching down. He held off, raising the nose a little, adjusting the flaps, watching his airspeed, feeling the controls heavier as the stall came nearer, slowing; then momentarily opening the throttle for a little extra lift, and they were over the boundary hedge and low, and the landing was good and smooth and they were taxiing and bumping as he held the stick hard back with just enough engine speed to take them on towards the parking area.

Thirty or more aircraft were there already, and a white-coated steward was marshalling the newcomers into lines. The red aircraft moved ahead of them, down between two rows, and turned sharply alongside another aeroplane. Then it was Richard's turn to park beside it, nose to a fence. He gave the throttle a last blip as he eased forward, then closed it and cut the switches. The propeller slowed and stopped, the fuselage vibrating as it did so; then there was silence after the noise of the last hour.

Richard said to her: 'There you are, ma'am. How was that for a first flight?'

She laughed, knowing that he was pleased with himself.

'Lovely. If you get an instructor's licence I'll let you teach me.'

'That's a deal,' he said. He checked over the switches, then pushed open the door and swung himself out. He walked round the nose of the Puss Moth, opened the door on the right of the aircraft and handed Ruth from her seat. Then he turned towards the red aircraft and the two young men who had just left it, leaned against the Puss Moth's fuselage and stared at them openly until they became aware of him and one nodded a greeting.

'Morning. Good trip?' Tentative, curious under Richard's eyes; a short, wiry man with good features and brown wavy hair, an expensive leather jacket and wide-legged trousers which almost concealed his white kid shoes.

Richard said: 'Until we went into the circuit here. Then some fool in a red Gull cut across us. He must have been blind in his right eye.'

The wiry man's cautious cordiality faded.

'I don't know what you're talking about. I didn't see you –'

'That was obvious. If I hadn't slipped away sharply and gone round again you could have downed us both.'

Then Ruth moved forward and put a hand on his arm.

'Don't, Richard,' she said quietly. 'No harm was done.'

Her slender presence and dark eyes eased the tension as both men from the Gull reacted to her. The wiry man said: 'Thank you. Maybe we'd better talk about it over a drink. I'm Nick Telford. This is Kurt Edelmann.'

Edelmann stepped forward. Like his companion, he was in his middle twenties, but taller and fair-haired, with a narrow face and fine-cut features. He half-bowed stiffly from the waist to Ruth; an abrupt Continental-style token.

'I am most pleased to meet you.' A deep voice; easy English but clearly a Germanic accent. He extended his hand. Ruth smiled and responded.

'Ruth Haldane,' she said. 'My brother is Richard.'

Nick Telford said cautiously: 'Hullo, Richard.' He pushed out his hand in a peace offering; and suddenly Richard grinned and said: 'Five minutes ago I wanted to hit you. Now I'll settle for that drink.'

They walked away from the aircraft together, the two pilots falling naturally into step and Kurt Edelmann and Ruth following and quickly establishing a link when Edelmann told her he would be at Cambridge in the autumn on a post-graduate course from Heidelberg after a degree in economics. He was Austrian, and like Ruth had just enjoyed his first flight.

34

In the bar Nick Telford bought drinks as he and Richard compared flight notes and the Hurn landing procedure without rancour, and then went on to discuss the merits of the Puss Moth. When talk turned to the Gull Richard said: 'That's a very expensive aeroplane. Not many clubs can afford one. Don't tell me you own it.'

'No such luck.' Telford shook his head. 'But the next best thing. My father has a third share in it. So when I'm a good boy I get to fly it. The old man is fairly well heeled, I'm glad to say.'

Later conversation revealed that Telford's father was a merchant banker and an ex-RFC pilot from the 1914–18 war, while Nick Telford himself was a journalist with the *Daily Express*. 'Sadly impecunious, old boy, I can tell you,' was his comment; but, clearly anxious to make up for his error on the landing circuit, he nevertheless ordered a bar lunch for four.

After that they spent the afternoon together, sitting on the grass and watching a flying display by the famous Alan Cobham air circus; and at the dinner dance that evening they shared a table and Edelmann danced several times with Ruth.

Richard watched them idly and said to Nick Telford: 'Kurt's a good looking devil. I think he's made a hit with my sister.'

Nick nodded. He looked thoughtful.

'You'd better tell her to be careful. He's a very single-minded man and not easily denied.'

'Ruth's old enough to look after herself,' Richard said. But his eyes were steady on Edelmann as the couple danced.

They stayed up until two in the morning, laughing and joking as they joined with others in childish but hilarious games which kept the hotel management in apprehensive attendance. Then before lunch the next day they wandered together around the aircraft park, talking to pilots and passengers, inspecting aeroplanes, comparing notes and experiences until, in the early afternoon, Nick announced that he would have to leave.

'Things to do, old boy, you know,' he said. 'It's all right for you – the easy student life, and all that. I've a living to earn tomorrow, and I'm supposed to be on call from midnight. Let's keep in touch.'

Kurt bowed over Ruth's hand and said: 'I am here for another week only. Then I return to my home. But I will telephone to you before I leave, and then I will see you in Cambridge in the autumn, yes?'

'I'd love that,' she said. 'I'll look forward to your call.'

Richard and Ruth watched the red Gull taxi away, and stood on the grass until it was airborne. Then they wandered back towards the control tower and he said: 'I guess we might as well go too. I'll check the weather forecast.'

She looked at him curiously.

'Nick didn't do that, did he?'

'No. But that's his affair. I like to know what's happening in the wide world.'

She squeezed his arm and said: 'I think you're a very careful pilot. I'm glad you are.'

He looked sideways at her.

'I just like living. Do you like Kurt Edelmann?'

She showed her surprise as she said: 'Yes. Do you?'

'Sure. On the surface. But it's rather different for me. I didn't dance with him.'

'Oh, you fool.' She laughed. 'It would have stopped the party if you had.'

'It certainly would if he'd held me like he held you.'

'Stop mocking me,' she retorted. 'I enjoyed it. You should have found a girl-friend instead of talking aeroplanes and newspapers all night with Nick. Why are you being protective all of a sudden?'

'Because Nick seems to think I should be. And he knows Kurt better than you do,' he said over his shoulder as he walked into the control tower building.

* * *

Conroy Jones said: 'None of the tenants has had a rent increase since 1930. Since then the price of every commodity except milk has fallen. That's a problem for them. But it's a problem for you, too, because not only has the cost of inputs risen – machinery, fertilisers, livestock feed, labour and the rest; but taxation has moved against you. Compared with five years ago you are paying four per cent more of the estate's reduced income in taxes. And your liquid capital is down to a quarter of what it was ten years ago. So like it or not, you will have to restructure your rents. The next triennial review is George Walton's. If you don't raise his rent, how can you raise others later on? You can't go on cushioning them. And I can tell you that some of the other estate owners are moving the same way.'

'What about landlords who have been allowing tenants to farm rent-free, just to keep the land in order?' Richard asked.

'It won't go on,' said Jones. 'Before I came here I telephoned four land agents for advice, and the message is clear.'

Robert said: 'You know my views. Walton is only paying ten shillings an acre. Even these days we shouldn't be letting any of our land for less than a pound, and the best farms should pay three. Walton's rent should be a pound and I vote we raise him to that figure.'

'You'll drive him out,' Ruth said. 'There's no way he'll make enough to support that.'

'That's at least what the farm's worth,' Robert retorted. 'So that's what we should charge. If Walton can't pay, someone else will. We're not running a charity.'

'Then let's find out exactly what we need instead of talking about what we should get,' said Richard. 'We've been living from year to year for too long. That's what happens in severe depressions. It's time we changed. We need a five-year financial projection.'

'Well, well,' Robert mocked. 'I thought you didn't understand anything unless it was in French. How come this sudden appreciation of agricultural economics?'

'Robert!' Diane rounded on him. 'This is a business meeting.'

Conroy Jones moved in quickly with a diversion.

'Estimating returns five years ahead is impossible. But there are hints that we've passed the worst. One of our problems has been cheap food from eastern Europe's miserable peasants. But Germany's buying more of it now – in exchange for industrial products. So eastern Europe is becoming more and more dependent on Hitler, and their ability to re-arm is limited to weapons and machine tools the Germans want to send them – which boosts German trade in spare parts. It's a fascinating jigsaw, but at least there might be some benefit for British farming.'

'Fascinating, and frightening,' Richard said. 'It shows what we're up against: not just Germany's arms but her accumulating economic strength – while we're producing platitudes and

37

America is so isolationist she might as well be on another planet, except for the way she disrupts the money markets.'

And so the meeting degenerated into a political discussion, although Jones was satisfied when he went away to draw up a questionnaire for a five-year development plan and, almost as an after-thought, they decided to raise George Walton's rent to a pound an acre. Walton was called to the estate office to be told the news by Diane, who insisted on doing it herself rather than leaving Harvey Roach's cold letter as the only notification. Walton took it without expression, but his face was grey beneath the weather-beaten skin when he left, and he sat in his battered Ford van outside the office for several minutes before he drove away.

5

Richard stretched his legs beneath a table in the Old Cock Tavern in Fleet Street, drank some beer, and said: 'I think I could be interested in newspapers.'

'Very interesting things, old boy,' Nick Telford told him, waving a hand. 'They don't pay a fortune in salaries. But there are compensations. I thought you were up to your ears in the family estate, though – farming and all that.'

'I'm not up to my ears in anything except French and German at Manchester. It's what happens afterwards that's concerning me.'

'You don't want to stay at Roxton?'

'It won't work,' Richard said. 'Mother has the last word now. But it's temporary. One day there'll be Robert, Ruth and myself. There's no chance of Robert and me working together amicably for long, and who knows what Ruth's future is? I reckon grandfather's dream is going to turn into a nightmare. Robert is the only one who really wants to commit to it, and he won't be able to afford it if Ruth and I pull out.'

'So you're looking for a career elsewhere.' Telford studied his beer. 'I've been in newspapers since I left Oxford. Two years with the *Daily Despatch* in Manchester, then this job with the *Express*. I'm twenty-six. Before I'm thirty I want to be news editor or foreign editor or maybe even night editor. And it's possible. Age isn't a barrier in The Street. Even experience isn't everything. It's the magic thing called flair. The ability to think of the right idea, the right headline, the right angle to a story; to get it faster than the opposition or show somebody else how to. Successful journalism isn't about writing. It's about initiative and originality. You've got to be willing to send your mother to gaol if it makes a good story, and never mind too much about the truth – if the facts aren't good enough, bend something a little. It's exciting, old boy. And if you're in the right place at the right time you can travel round the world. I've been to most of the European countries already. And you'd get a start, I reckon. You're educated, you've the right personality, you're aggressive, you fly aeroplanes, you speak French and some German, and you look and act seven or eight years older than you are.'

Richard drank the last of his beer, took their glasses to the bar and had them refilled, settled at the table again, and said: 'I don't want to send my mother to gaol, or invent something to make a story better, or think about sensational headlines. I want to see what's going wrong with the world and tell people about it. We're drifting into war, and still most people don't seem to realise it. I don't think Hitler's the threat we're told he is, in spite of all the talk about Austria. He's a dictator, he's a liar, and he's killed a lot of Germans. But does he really want war with Britain and France? More importantly, do the German people want it? How German are the Austrians – and the Sudetenlanders? Are they as German as the Rhinelanders, or do they have different loyalties? Until we know that we can't know if they'll accept German domination. And what do people here and in France understand about it? Nobody's asking the questions which matter, and ignorance will make war inevitable. I want to be able to ask them.'

'So you want to be off, doing the foreign stint. Maybe you'd make it. But you'd have to do time on the beat first – pounding the streets, doorstepping, digging the dirt, learning the alphabet. By then, if we're going to have another war, I'm afraid it may have started.' Nick drank some of his beer and scowled at the froth on the glass.

Richard nodded moodily.

'I think you're right. I have a terrible sense of urgency – a feeling that something very interesting is going to happen to me before long. I can't talk to Robert, because there's no debating ground between us. And I can't talk to mother, either, because my father was killed in the battle of Cambrai in 1917 and it distresses her to discuss war. I can talk to Ruth, but she doesn't feel passionately about it. I argue about it in college, but all I get is a collection of pseudo-communist distortions from people who think students have some sort of duty to be left wing and worship Mother Russia.'

Nick grinned at him quickly.

'Absolutely right, old boy. It was just the same when I was at Oxford. I was that terrible thing, a Conservative student. I didn't want to argue politics much, but as soon as some of the others realised I was on the right they wouldn't leave it alone. Petty-minded, dear lad. Best ignored. Most of 'em will grow up one day, albeit a bit late. Have a fag.' He thrust out a packet of Players.

'The only thing I'll regret will be the house.' Richard took a cigarette and lit it. 'You must have a weekend with us and see it. The family's been there for nearly two hundred years. It's a great old place. I wouldn't like to see it sold. But one day I think the whole lot will have to go. We'll just break up as a family otherwise. It would be better to sell, divide the cash, and go our separate ways but still be friends at a distance. Anyway, I'll be away from it for a year – I'm going to Paris in October. The Sorbonne. It's a great chance.'

'You'll find plenty of lefties there,' Nick chuckled. 'That's where they breed 'em. I don't think they've got over the revolution yet. Unreliable lot. Easily led. Bit prone to the old mob rule, you know. Must be the Latin temperament. But the girls are something. Very liberated. Went to Paris in the spring, then down to Cannes after a society floozie who was making the headlines. Found her, too – living with the butler from the family mansion who'd also disappeared. Good story. Picked up a French lady in Paris and took her south with me. She taught me things that would have been entirely beyond my dear mother's imagination. A very hot number, I can tell you. I was with her seven nights, and it was a different position every night. And all on expenses, too. Well – I had to have a guide and interpreter, didn't I? Oh yes – you'll enjoy yourself in Paris. But watch out for the social diseases, *mon ami* – the French invented them.' He finished his beer with a flourish, stood up and clapped Richard across the shoulder. 'Tell you what

– I'll show you round the office – news room, wire room, foreign desk and all that. If the editor's around you might even get a chance to have a chinwag. C'mon.'

They went out into Fleet Street, down towards Ludgate Circus and the *Daily Express* offices. Richard did not meet the editor, but he had a long conversation with the foreign editor, watched news stories coming in on teleprinters from the agencies, saw staff stories being handled ready for the next day's issue, photographs being selected and sized ready for page layouts, headlines being written and discussed.

When he came out he went up the street to a coffee shop and sat by himself for an hour, thinking. It was as if a crystal ball had been handed to him; and, no matter how vaguely, he could read it.

6

By the next summer, and for the first time in its recorded history, the Roxton estate was in debt.

The proposal was Robert's, and he had little difficulty in persuading his mother and Ruth that there should be major changes. Martin Calder was enthusiastic, Conroy Jones had no objections; but Richard, away in Paris, opposed the principle of borrowing to finance expansion while the depression continued.

The plan was to sell the traditional Dairy Shorthorn herd and replace it with tuberculin-tested black-and-white Friesians, the breed which was expanding quickly because of its heavier milk yields; and TT milk earned an extra penny a gallon. At the same time buildings were to be altered to meet new hygiene standards and accommodate more cattle, a new tractor was to replace two horses, neglected pastures were to be drained to enable potatoes to be grown on a worthwhile scale, and estate buildings repaired to provide tenants with better revenue opportunities which would support higher rents.

To supplement the small amount of available capital, a bank loan would pay for a third of it; a minor debt when set against the size of the business, but the agricultural depression remained severe and all borrowing was regarded as a high-risk venture. It was enough to present the family with its first big policy division.

Richard, sharing a two-roomed flat in Paris with Grant Hollis, a post-graduate reading philosophy and the son of the president of an American newspaper and magazine company, felt he was now too far away to influence his mother. He knew that Ruth was pre-occupied with friends at Cambridge and suspected that Kurt Edelmann was prominent among them; whatever the reason, she spent little time at home other than for veterinary practice, and Richard's frustration grew as he sensed that despite Diane's firm leadership she was falling gradually under Robert's persuasion. Of the loan he told her on the telephone: 'It offends me, and I'm sure it would have offended grandfather, because the climate is still wrong for spending. I would rather wait another year and then reconsider.'

At one point he wrote to Robert and accused him of gambling on a war restoring farming's stability, but then thought better of it and tore up the letter. So the plan went ahead; and in the locality eyebrows were raised, for years had passed since the last time much money had been spent on any of the farms in the area.

In Roxton's village store where, aided by the quick tongues and sharp ears of owners John and Edna Moorcock, all things were known and discussed. Martin Calder bought his week's supply of tobacco and said to Ned Baldock who had the joiner's shop near St Thomas's church: 'Hear that stuff about civil defence on the wireless last night, Ned?'

'Yes. I heard'm. Waste o' time, young Martin. Waste o' time. There won't be no war. You'll see.'

Calder shook his head gloomily.

'Germany's bent on it. I reckon we've got to get ready for it. If that Churchill's right we haven't got an air force and we've only half an army. But at least we can start learning what to do if there are air raids.'

'Air raids?' Ned Baldock growled scathingly. 'In Roxton? Why th'ell would Hitler drop bombs on Roxton? Don't be silly.' He turned to the bald-headed John Moorcock. 'What about you, John, then? D'you reckon you'll be a target?' He cackled and wiped his moustache with the back of his hand.

Moorcock leaned on the counter. He was a heavily-built,

round-faced fifty-year-old and had been a signaller in the 1914-18 war.

'Dunno. But old Hitler's got thousands of planes, the papers say. So they could get anywhere, I suppose. And how can they see where they're dropping their bombs? They're miles up.' He jerked a thumb skywards. 'Miles. It'll just be bad luck if one's got my number on it – or yours. But I suppose we're better off'n being in London or Plymouth or them places. Wouldn't fancy me chances there.'

Baldock stuffed thick twist into his pipe and scowled at it.

'Bloody warmongers, the pair o'you. It's folks talking like that as makes war. If everybody said there won't be one, the politicians'd have to take notice.'

'I can see old Hitler taking notice o' you,' grinned Calder. 'I can hear him saying to Goering "Better not start anything – that Ned Baldock don't believe in it". Anyway, you can please yourself. If there's a meeting I'll go and listen. More we know, better we'll be.'

'Propaganda,' Baldock grumbled. 'Bloody politicians and their propaganda.' He put a match to his pipe and stumped out in a cloud of foul-smelling smoke.

Moorcock grinned as the doorbell tinkled its farewell to the indignant joiner.

'Bad-tempered old sod,' he said without acrimony. 'How's things upalong, then?'

'All right, I suppose.' Calder propped himself against a corner of the counter. 'Mrs Haldane seems to be managing. Better'n I thought, I must say. And I've learned one thing – you don't argue with her over-much.'

'What about all the work there's going to be there?' Moorcock demanded. 'All them buildings an' things. Must be going to cost a fortune. Didn't know even your place could afford that sort of thing these days.'

Calder shrugged. He was cautious, for he knew that anything said in the Moorcock's shop would be known around the village within a week.

'It's been at a standstill for a long time, like everything else in farming,' he said indifferently. 'And we're not the first to bring in Friesians instead of Shorthorns.'

'I know that,' Moorcock retorted. 'But what about the buildings? I hear old Ned's got enough work to keep him in beer for three months. What's it all going to cost, then?'

'Dunno,' Calder said. He eyed the shopkeeper critically. 'Least, I'm not telling. It's got nothing to do with anyone else. Mrs Haldane'd sack me if she thought I'd been telling folk about the business.'

'How d'you like working for a woman, then?' Edna Moorcock pushed through the door from the room at the back of the shop, wiping her hands on her ample skirts. She grinned widely. 'Bet that's cut you down to size, Mr Calder.' She cackled.

'Better'n working for you, Mrs Moorcock,' Calder retorted cheerfully. 'Don't know how John here sticks it. He must have a hell of a life.'

'He does,' the woman said, grinning again. 'I see to that – '

'Shut up,' Moorcock growled in mock anger. He turned to Calder again. 'How about the Haldane kids? We don't see much of 'em now.'

'At college,' Calder said. 'But I think Robert will be the important one. The girl's going to be a vet, so mebbe that'll be useful. But t'other one, Richard, is a bit of a mystery. I don't think he'll stay around. D'you know he flies a plane, down at the aero club?'

'Heard so.' Moorcock sniffed disparagingly. 'Must have more money'n sense. Rather it was his neck'n mine.' He looked up as the door latch clicked, the bell rang, and two women came into the shop. Calder straightened, nodded in farewell, and went out. Across the street which divided Roxton into two halves he saw the Reverend Philip Smallwood and raised a hand in greeting.

'Morning, vicar. How's the church fund, then?'

Smallwood smiled. He was pleased that someone should remember the fund.

'Not a lot of progress, I'm afraid, Mr Calder. We still need over a thousand pounds to finish making the tower safe. Then there'll be other work to do.'

Calder said: 'Better get it done before a war comes. There'll be no money and no time then.'

'Good gracious, Mr Calder.' The vicar's smile disappeared. 'Let's not talk about such a thing. We must all pray that our leaders' efforts to preserve peace will be successful. Mr Chamberlain is a wise and Christian gentleman, you know.'

Calder thought: He's a soft old fool who believes everything

Hitler tells him. He said: 'I'm sure he is, vicar. But I still think you should raise the rest of the money as soon as you can.'

Smallwood eyed him.

'I hear your employers have been able to find some money,' he said resentfully. 'You've a lot of alterations starting soon, I believe. It makes me sad that we can't find just enough to repair the church.'

Martin Calder felt angry. He knew the Moorcocks were the village news agency, but to hear the vicar gossiping about his employers' affairs suddenly offended him.

'There's a difference, vicar,' he said abruptly. 'We have to earn it before we can invest it. Nobody gives us anything.' He turned away, ignoring Smallwood's indignation, and went on up the street. He wondered if German bombs would one day knock down the vicar's church altogether.

As he passed the school he saw children playing in the yard between the road and the old brick building; seven-, eight- and nine-year-olds, shouting in shrill excitement as they chased each other or kicked a football. He always felt a twinge of regret when he saw children playing, for he and his wife were childless. He turned as two boys stretched out their arms and made engine noises in their throats as they ran round each other. One made a rattling sound with his tongue as he swooped on the other and shouted: 'I'm a fighter and you're a German bomber and I'll shoot you down.' He made the rattling noise again.

Calder checked, watching. Suddenly the home farm improvements and the vicar's church tower did not seem so important. The sun still shone over Roxton. But it was not warm any more. And a new experience came to Martin Calder: the secret grief he had shared with his wife was gone, and he was glad there were no children of his own to witness what was to come.

*   *   *

Richard was in London, but neither his mother nor his brother and sister knew. He had crossed by the Saturday morning Calais–Dover ferry and early in the evening he walked up the drive of a substantial detached house on the edge of Berkhamsted, rang the bell, and was greeted by Nick Telford.

'Ah, *mon ami – comment allez-vous?*' Nick's accent was

deliberately appalling, and he grinned hugely as they shook hands. 'Glad you made it, dear boy. You're one of the first: chance to meet the old man before the rush.'

Richard already knew that the 'old man' was Graham Telford, London chief executive of the American-owned Swift Montford Merchant Bank and Investment Corporation; and as he handed his coat to a black-clad maid he looked across the hallway and saw his host stride into view.

'You are Richard Haldane. I guessed it.' Telford's voice had a cutting edge which made it seem louder than it was. 'Glad to see you here. I've heard a great deal about you from Nick.' His handshake was hard but his eyes were warm. Richard liked him instantly.

Then he was guided into a high-ceilinged lounge where he met Telford's wife Margaret, grey-haired and slightly built like her husband and clearly equally accomplished in the art of making a guest comfortable; and with her Michael Hendricks, foreign editor of the *Daily Telegraph*. And with Nick at his elbow Richard realised it was Hendricks's presence which had been the spur for his own invitation. The journalist was a lean, prematurely grey forty-year-old with a trim beard which added drama to his thin face and sharp eyes. He responded willingly to Richard's questions about his profession and argued eagerly about Germany and her relations with Austria and Czechoslovakia; about Mussolini's Abyssinian adventure and Italy's increasingly close support for Hitler; and about MacDonald and Baldwin, Churchill and Chamberlain, and the neglect of Britain's armed forces.

After that, with more guests arriving, talk turned to the current of pacifism and appeasement which ran through Britain and went deep into the streets and factories and the crowded houses in the smoky cities; and the contrasts on the Continent where men and women could not shelter from foreign armies behind the sea shores of an island. And Hendricks catalogued the strength of the Czech army and the natural barriers along the frontier with Germany: factors which might prompt Hitler to take Austria first and so provide himself with a new gateway to the Sudetenland industrial towns where most Czech arms were manufactured.

Then the subject was communism and Russia's conflicting attitudes to Germany on the one hand and the allied nations of France and Britain on the other; the strength of communism in

46

industrial France and the significance of that in her ability to defend herself if Hitler should attack with a Russian peace pact at his back.

Throughout, Richard argued vehemently, and Hendricks showed his interest in the young man from rural Devonshire who had combined his language studies at the Sorbonne with a passionate inquiry into motives and fears on the streets of Paris; and, as Margaret Telford called her guests to the buffet table in the adjoining room, he said to Richard: 'If you decide to travel when your studies permit, and you're interested in commissions, I'd like to hear from you.'

It was then that a bell pealed in the hallway, and Nick sidled up and said against the hubbub of talk: 'Last guests arriving, old boy. Knew they'd be late. But perhaps that makes the surprise all the better.' He grinned, and guided Richard through the crowd to the door, positioning him so that he could see Graham Telford greet Kurt Edelmann, and Ruth.

'Hope you don't mind,' Nick murmured. 'I told you we'd be happy if you'd stay the night. That was before I thought it would be pleasant if Kurt and Ruth joined us. Now you'll have to share with Kurt: we're running out of rooms, dear lad. All right?'

'All right?' Richard turned and stared at him; then looked back along the hallway. 'Yes. Of course. I'll sleep in the kitchen if you like.' He heard the tightness in his voice and made an effort to relax, aware that for him the stimulating evening had suddenly become confusing. He watched Nick stride away and shake Kurt's hand, plant a quick kiss on Ruth's cheek, and then point towards him. Ruth stared incredulously; then laughed in quick pleasure and ran to embrace him.

'Rich – what on earth are you doing here? You should be in Paris.' She turned swiftly. 'Nick, you didn't tell me.'

'Thought you wouldn't mind a surprise,' said Nick. 'It just seemed a good idea at the time.'

Now Richard was shaking Kurt's hard hand and heard himself saying: 'I'm just as surprised as you are. Nick said this would be an interesting party, but he didn't tell me how interesting.'

Kurt said: 'I am happy to see you again, Richard. I hear about you all the time from Ruth. She talks always about Roxton and you.'

Graham Telford guided them towards the dining room and the

long buffet table, saying: 'You have had a long drive from Cambridge. You will be ready to eat. Help yourselves to wine: you too, Richard. I hope you are enjoying yourself.' He moved closer to Richard and lowered his voice. 'Nick told me of your interests. I thought you might find something in common with Hendricks. You have been talking with him for a long time. I hope it's been useful.'

Richard turned and met the banker's sharp gaze.

'It's been a special occasion. I'm grateful to you.'

Telford walked with him into the crowded room; then said: 'I hope you were not too surprised to see your sister – and Kurt.' He added the Austrian's name carefully, and his meaning was clear.

'Surprised to see Ruth?' Richard's eyes were steady on Telford's now. 'Yes. But pleasantly so. I'm very fond of my sister. I don't know Kurt very well – although I believe she spends a lot of time with him.'

'So Nick tells me,' Telford said. 'Anyway, you'll have a chance to learn something about him tonight. I believe you're sharing a room.' He turned quickly, pointing to the table as people crowded around. 'Don't get left out. Find a plate and help yourself.'

Richard nodded and edged forward, looking at the laden table but thinking about Graham Telford and Kurt and his sister. Telford had told him clearly that he was uneasy about Edelmann. And Richard was confident that the banker knew his message had been received and understood.

They spent the rest of the evening with other guests, talking inconsequentially; with Richard and Ruth enjoying each other's company, Kurt Edelmann chatting with everyone, and Nick dispensing alcohol as if prohibition were to start the next day. Then, around midnight, farewells were said and soon Richard, Ruth and Kurt were left to enjoy a late cup of coffee with their hosts. Graham and Margaret Telford extended the utmost cordiality to the Austrian, and Richard found himself wondering if he had imagined the significance of the short exchange he had shared with Nick's father; until, as they left for their rooms, he saw again the sharp glint in Telford's searching gaze, and his eyes were hard in return.

The room was small, with twin beds at either end, a dressing table between, a small wardrobe and a handbasin in one corner. Richard took off his shirt, slung a towel across his shoulders and washed quickly. As he straightened he heard Kurt say: 'You are a strong man, I think, Richard. Very strong.'

He turned. The Austrian was sitting on his bed, clearly appraising his companion.

'Strong enough for most things,' Richard said shortly.

'You are also a hard man, able to – as you say in this country – take care of yourself.' A statement, not a question.

Richard shrugged. 'Usually. Why?'

'I am interested,' Kurt said. 'In Austria we value such things. Austria has seen many changes. We are at a crossroads, and have always been so, never knowing which road to take. Under such circumstances only the strong survive. It is important for a man to be strong, in body and spirit. Do you agree?'

'It helps. I don't think about it.' Richard gave a final dab with the towel and hung it on a rail beside the wash basin.

'You should. Strength is important – for a man, and for a nation.' Kurt was watching him, seeking his responses. 'That is why we all worry so much about Germany. She is strong.'

'Do you worry about Germany?' Richard sat on his bed and unlaced his shoes.

The Austrian nodded.

'Of course. But not only about Germany. About the uncertainty, also.'

'Do Austrians think Germany will invade?'

'Some do; some do not.' He waved a hand vaguely. 'It is difficult to tell what Hitler wants. He says so many things.'

'He says that Austrians are really Germans and should be given the chance to join the fatherland. Do you think they should?'

'A vote? Do you mean they should vote? Perhaps. The will of the people is important.'

'Is it not the most important thing of all?' Richard was no longer easy and indifferent.

'Usually. But sometimes the people are misled. It is difficult to decide what is truth and what is propaganda.'

'Goebbels is very good at propaganda,' Richard said. 'He is the best propagandist in Europe. Hitler is lucky to have him. Do you think Austria should become part of Germany?'

Kurt said: 'Austria is confused. I am confused also. Germany is economically stable; Austria is not. Germany is strong; Austria has many strong men, but they are often in dispute and our country is weakened.'

'So Germany might be good for Austria,' Richard said quietly. His dark eyes were black now, and his stare unblinking. 'Tell me about your friendship with Ruth.'

For seconds Kurt was silent. Then he shrugged.

'I had expected such a question. It is understandable. We are very good friends. We spent much time together. She is beautiful, and I respect her.'

'I'm glad you respect her. Would you like to marry her?'

Kurt lay back on his bed, his head turned sideways so that he could still see Richard. He seemed to hesitate before he said: 'I cannot answer that question. She must decide what our future relationship is to be.'

'Of course. But you have your own views – and wishes.' A challenge now; flat and quiet.

Kurt stretched his arms around his head, then relaxed.

'I cannot answer. Not to you. It is a question I can answer to her only. Perhaps if you ask her if she wishes to marry me she would reply in the same way. It is a matter for the two of us.'

'And for me also.' Still quiet, but hard. 'I am very fond of her. She does not have a father. Perhaps you would like to regard me as a substitute; one who has the same concern as a father –'

'But you are younger than she.' Kurt raised his head and his voice sharpened. 'You cannot assume such a responsibility.'

'I can,' said Richard. 'And I do.'

*   *   *

After his year in Paris, and just when she was expecting to hear that he was coming home, Diane received a letter from Richard.

'You may find this is something of a shock; a disappointment too, and I apologise in advance for that.

'In short, I have decided to give up my university studies.

'The atmosphere of university, the attitudes of some of the tutors and many fellow students I have found irritating. I have felt mentally suffocated and have become angry with myself for tolerating that. People are so blinkered; so unable to understand what is happening in Europe and what it means to us. Everyone should have ideals, and pacifism is noble –

50

but totally unreal in the face of harsh physical threat.

'I had hoped that a year out of the country would provide a different dimension. It has; but not of the sort I had foreseen.

'The Sorbonne is just like other universities. There is an obsessive cynicism about politics and the establishment, and a blind conviction that answers to our problems may be found either by turning the other cheek or by adopting some sort of Russian-communist society.

'But Paris is another matter. The excitement of being in a Continental country at this dangerous time is overwhelming, and I have found it impossible to continue my studies while so much is going on outside.

'People are crying for information. The lessons of Spain and Abyssinia, of the Rhineland and the German Jews are there to be learned yet are obscured by the machinery of state, by compliant civil servants, by politicians, by a frivolous Press – and by obsessive propaganda from the bearded wonders of the extreme left.

'As you know, my flat-mate is Grant Hollis. Herbert Hollis, his father, is president of an American newspaper company. He has become interested in my views and my impatience and has offered me a retainer and prospect of useful fees if I write for him about the European situation. He said he wants the reactions of youth as seen by youth rather than by established and cynical journalists. He also agrees with me that if I am to start I had better do it now, for by the time I finish my studies it is likely to be too late.

'In addition, the Daily Telegraph has promised other commissions if I am able to approach Europe's confusion in a different and informative way. I have, therefore, decided to become a freelance foreign correspondent and to live for a time on my wits. I now speak French well – I am bound to say much better than most students of my age – and have a sound knowledge of German. So I am basically well equipped to move around.

'I cannot sit by and watch Europe destroying itself without at least trying to convey in my own small way the views of ordinary people. I think it is especially important that the American public is properly informed, and so does Herbert Hollis. That, he says, is why he has hired me. It is flattering and exciting. I hope you will not criticise me too harshly for responding to it.'

After she had read the letter carefully a second time, Diane called Robert who had just completed his second year at Reading, held it out to him, and said: 'You must read this. It affects us all.'

Robert's verdict was immediate. He scanned the pages quickly, threw them on the nearby table, and exploded: 'The fool. The bloody fool –'

'No, Robert.' Diane's voice cut through this. 'No one swears in this house, and you know it. I'll have your apology for that before you go further.'

He looked at her, tight-mouthed; struggling to hold his temper in check. Then he shrugged.

'All right. I'm sorry. But this is incredible. He's throwing everything away – for what? How can he influence anything?'

'He can't,' she said. 'It's the involvement which attracts him. He wants to see and hear and be part of it. Do you think there'll be a war, Robert?'

He was staring at the letter. He had crumpled the edges of it as he had read it.

'Yes. I do.' He turned and walked over to the window; his face shadowed against its brightness. She watched him, and waited, until he said: 'Maybe he's right. Maybe we don't know enough about what's happening to ordinary people. We know all about the politicians. But how much of what they say is the truth? How much do we really understand?' Then he turned suddenly and strode back towards her. 'But he's given up everything. He'll have no qualifications. If he finds he can't make a living what's he going to do?'

She said: 'He knows he can come back here –'

'And do what?' Robert was exasperated again. 'He can't run this place. He just doesn't know enough. He's not interested.'

'He will still hold a one-third share in it when the time comes. Don't try to dismiss him. You can't. And I don't believe you want to.'

'I want to see him contributing,' Robert retorted. 'Roxton will need effort from all of us to make a success of it. If he'd abandoned his languages to study agriculture I'd welcome it. But this baffles me.'

She said firmly: 'You'll have to get used to it. I'm disappointed. But Richard is a maverick. He will never conform. I don't think he knows what he wants to do with his life. But I have to tell you I don't believe he wants to spend it here.'

Robert stared at her, as if the words had startled him. Then he lowered himself slowly into an armchair, leaned back and nodded.

'I've wondered about that for a long time – and if you had realised it. The trouble is that he and I can't talk intelligently. He won't discuss things seriously. So I can't ask him. It would only end in a row.' He looked at her. 'What do we do?'

'Nothing,' she said. 'I'll reply to his letter, and advocate caution. He'll expect that; and he'll ignore it. Then we'll go on doing what we're doing now, and hope that Richard finds his way to whatever he's looking for.'

7

A distant bell rang: two slow strokes of sound which floated away in the night above the frost-rimmed roofs. Ruth Haldane pulled the sheet and blankets closer around her bare shoulder, keeping out the January chill. But she felt warm and comfortable inside, and her mouth moved in a small smile in the darkness. She could hear Kurt's deep breathing and, because her eyes were accustomed to the dark, could detect the outline of his head and his fair hair on the pillow next to hers.

She had known him now for eighteen months. Known him? Sometimes she wondered if she knew every corner of his mind. Sometimes, indeed, she was sure she did not. Yet did anyone know everything about another person – absolutely everything? Probably she and Kurt were the same as every other couple. She loved him, and was sure of his love for her. Physically she felt she knew him totally, and enjoyed him more intensely than she would have thought possible. And they were good friends. He laughed a lot, was generous and considerate, most of the time he was easy-tempered, and they had many common interests. She did not understand much about the further political studies on which he was now concentrating, any more than he understood her veterinary world. But that hardly mattered.

She turned her head towards him. The risks of their relationship were obvious; but they were as careful as they could be, and she derived secret satisfaction from her defiance of convention. I'll make my own rules, she told herself, and thereby yielded to the provocation of Haldane blood; yet was unaware of it.

Would she marry him? He certainly wanted to marry her. But she held back, for now it was 1938. Germany's threats to Austria were constantly in the news, and the danger of war seemed to grow by the month. Kurt did not seem to take it as seriously as she: perhaps that was a mid-European attitude, bred of generations of men and women who had lived through political turmoil, military threat and conquest. He wanted to settle in his own country rather than Britain, she knew; and she had never been there. How could she decide until she knew what Austria and its people were like, and how they saw their political future? She would have to go there; and soon.

Supposing she liked it, and said she would marry him? In a year's time she could be living there. He would finish his course next summer, and knew that two jobs were being held open for him in Vienna: one in government, the other in the university. So the wedding might be quite soon. And her own studies? Kurt wanted her to give them up, but she recoiled from the prospect. Perhaps, once in Vienna, she would be able to resume them . . .

Yet, what then – if Germany annexed Austria, as the newspapers forecast? What then, for her? What if Churchill and others were right, and war came?

She shivered suddenly, turned onto her side and pressed her body against his. He stirred in his sleep and she whispered: 'Darling. Talk to me.' He moved, and she sensed rather than saw his eyes open. Her hand caressed his face, then slid down across his chest. He half-turned towards her and she murmured: 'Kurt – are you awake?'

His voice whispered back: 'Yes, of course. You woke me.'

'I'm sorry,' she said. 'But I want to talk. Will you take me to Austria? To meet your parents? And show me Vienna?'

He nodded. 'If you like. But why now – in the middle of the night?'

'I was thinking. About us. I don't know what your country's like. If Hitler invades it, what will happen? I want to know. You never really tell me what you think.'

He turned over to face her.

'I think this is not the time to discuss world politics.' But his voice was easy, joking. 'How can I ever understand a woman who wakes me in the middle of the night, not to make love but to talk about Hitler and invasion?'

'Don't laugh at me,' she whispered. 'I have to know. Because of us.'

He was silent for a while, his breath warm against her forehead.

'I don't know what might happen to my country,' he said eventually, now fully awake. 'Germany and Austria are not so different. Our languages are almost the same. We are the same people, at heart. Austria is already tied to Germany financially. I guess we would hardly know the difference.'

'But Kurt – Hitler's a dictator –'

'He was elected,' Kurt said. 'Ninety per cent of Germany voted for him.'

'The papers say there was intimidation,' she said. She was moving away from him, distancing herself so that she could argue without the distraction of his body and the stirring of his desire against her. 'It didn't sound like democracy –'

'It isn't like Britain,' he said sharply. 'The National Socialists aren't perfect, but at least there's not much unemployment, and these days not many people are starving. Germany has made an enormous economic recovery. I don't think Austria would suffer if we became part of Germany –'

He checked, sensing her withdrawal. One hand sought her breasts and caressed her gently. 'But don't let us argue. We'll go to Austria, then you can see for yourself. Let's take a few days off. You can say you aren't well. Your tutors will never know. If it's so important to you we can do it as soon as the weather improves. My parents wish to meet you. What do you say? I'll buy the tickets. Get a passport – and let's go.'

She relaxed. That was what she wanted – the chance to see for herself. No one knew what would happen in the future. But at least she would be able to see the present, and the people.

His fingers were persuasive, coaxing. She felt herself stirring inside. It was always like that; he knew how to break down her reserve; how to overcome her doubts. She moved her head, searching for his mouth, feeling his tongue. Her body pressed against his, encouraging him, welcoming him. Austria and Germany and Hitler slid from her mind.

8

Now it was March and the season was early. During the winter the Dairy Shorthorn herd had been dispersed at an indifferent sale, the main byre had been extended, and Martin Calder had bought eighty promising Friesians grading up to pedigree status. Once February had gone the weather was dry and, despite the cold soil, early cultivations began to prepare the land for spring sowing of cereals and additional potatoes. The new Friesian cattle had been housed on their arrival in January, but as the good weather continued so prospects improved for an early turn-out onto the first tentative grass growth and a crop of rye grown for grazing. That would bring welcome relief from the burden of heavy feed bills, and Martin predicted: 'If it goes on like this we'll make the best start we've had for several years.'

A hundred and thirty miles away in Reading Robert worked, thinking about Roxton, relating his studies to the estate with a single-mindedness which still surprised his tutors; yet with a growing unease about the future. He could not forget for long the relationship between his sister and the smiling, confident Kurt Edelmann, or the virtual disappearance of Richard who was writing home about working in Paris, Czechoslovakia and Austria and had had articles in the *Telegraph* on the Nazi Party's closing grip on the Austrian police. Robert knew that neither Richard nor Ruth had much interest in Roxton now, and that the problem they represented was beyond his ability to resolve. One day they would be entitled to a share of the estate equal to his own, and the division would shatter it. He was alternatively furiously angry, frustrated, and sad.

Then, on Monday 7th of March, he was called to the telephone and heard his mother's voice.

'It's Ruth,' she said; and her anger and anxiety came across to him clearly. 'She's taken off. Left her studies. She's gone to Innsbruck with Kurt to meet his family. And she's lied. She's told her tutors that she's ill and has to come home for a week. I don't understand, Robert. Why couldn't she wait until Easter?'

Robert's knuckles were white as his fingers tightened around the receiver and he snapped: 'Because she's a fool. Dear God, I thought we had enough trouble with one member of the family. But this surpasses everything. Did she tell you she wants to marry him?'

'I asked her. She said she's trying to make up her mind. That's why she has to meet his people and see what Austria is like. And we can't stop her. She rang from Dover. They're half-way across the Channel now.'

Robert took a long breath and said: 'Is she pregnant? Is that why they're in such a hurry?'

'I asked her that, too. She said not.'

'Thank God. That's a complication we can do without. But it makes the whole thing even more stupid. She must be out of her mind to go at a time like this. No one can guess what's going to happen between Germany and Austria. There won't be a war, because the Austrians have nothing to fight with. But it's still not the time for Ruth to behave like a love-sick tourist.'

Diane said: 'She's hopelessly under his influence. He's such a strong character. I can understand why she's attracted to him, but I don't like him. He's too smooth, too confident, as if he believes he has the answers to everybody's problems but he's keeping the secret to himself.'

'He keeps far too much to himself,' Robert growled. 'I've tried to talk about Germany with him, but he ducks the subject. I don't know what motivates him – except, obviously, a desire to marry her. And I can't think what we can do about it, except stay here and fume.'

'And worry,' Diane told him. 'He could be taking her into real trouble.'

'There's no immediate danger,' Robert said. 'No matter what happens there'll be no shooting.'

'Maybe. But think of the future. If Germany annexes Austria and then we go to war with Germany, Ruth will be in a nightmare position if she marries Kurt. It's unthinkable.'

They talked on; pointlessly, for there was nothing they could do except wait. Then Robert went back to the library where he had been researching, and at lunchtime Diane turned on the radio for a news bulletin.

The first item was from a BBC correspondent in Vienna who reported that the Austrian Government was expected to announce a plebiscite on whether the country should be absorbed by Germany. It would be at short notice, for the vote was likely to be heavily in favour of continued independence and Hitler would not like that. There were fears in Austria that the German army would move to stop this last, desperate attempt by Chancellor Von Schuschnigg to mobilize public opinion in his country's defence.

And within a few hours Ruth would be there.

9

The sunlight slanted between the buildings, arches throwing black shadows over pavements, Gothic and baroque stone in carved conflict above. A thin spring wind came down the valley, over the shops and houses and traffic, fluttering the long flags with their black swastikas on every street corner. To the north the grey Nordkette range was high and jagged against pale blue sky and scattered clouds, seeming to crowd in close above Innsbruck in the clear air.

Richard Haldane drove his battered black French-registered Citroen Light 15 slowly along the Maria-Theresien-Strasse, among the cars and vans and clanking trams. At every corner he saw black uniforms, always in pairs; black shirts and breeches, shining jackboots and peaked caps. People scattered along the pavements, hurrying, seeming to ignore the troopers. Richard stopped at a pavement edge, went into a shop, and bought a street map of the city. Then he drove away from the centre until he came to a quieter length of road between scattered houses and small shops. There were no troopers here. He parked the car and studied the map.

'Don't take risks,' Diane had said. 'But if you can find her and speak to her, it will help her to know you are there, waiting to bring her home as soon as they'll let you. You'll be all right with your credentials, won't you?'

'Yes,' he had said, without any idea whether he would be all right or not. 'Of course. I'll find her.'

It was an abrupt end to a long telephone conversation which had started when Diane had traced him to an hotel in Colmar where he was waiting for instructions from the *Telegraph* to cross the German border into Freiburg and then make his way to Austria, reasoning that someone crossing from Germany into Austria was less likely to attract attention at the moment than if they tried to enter from any other country. Richard was one of a team of freelance correspondents backing up senior staff writers who were already there, reporting on the German invasion of Austria.

But instead of receiving a call from the *Telegraph*'s foreign desk in Fleet Street, he found himself listening to his mother's news that Ruth was in Innsbruck and that it had taken thirty-six hours of frantic telephoning and being told by harassed operators that lines into Austria were disconnected before she had contacted her at Kurt Edelmann's home. Then she had learned that Ruth was under house arrest after a street incident. The police were making inquiries about her and would not allow her to leave the country until a decision had been made by 'higher authority'.

Diane had told him: 'Robert has spoken to the Foreign Office. They were sympathetic but not very helpful. They said there was a lot of tension but that it would soon die down and they felt sure she would be all right. Do you think that's all we can do, Richard? You know the scene so much better than we do.'

And Richard had said: 'That's not all we can do. I can go for her.'

He had not considered his own motives. He had been aware only of astonishment that Ruth should have placed herself at risk, and of cold anger that Kurt Edelmann should have been the instrument. Then he had thrust the questions away and had concentrated on the task. It was simple: Ruth was in trouble, and he would help her. He had often thought that she, not Robert, should have been his twin. Sometimes they were extraordinarily close, with an unvoiced intimacy and instinctive understanding: a

59

wordless communication of minds and strengths. It had been so since childhood and had translated easily through adolescence to maturity. He remembered their easy, honest conversations about school and ambition, about being fatherless, about frustrations and happiness; about sexual awareness and experiment, too, without trace of embarrassment. And Ruth had told him of her relationship with Kurt Edelmann when she had told no one else; the telling, she had said, had been her comfort and help.

Now he was in Innsbruck. He knew the Edelmanns' address, and that was all. He had no plans, except to find the house, march up to the door, and ask for Ruth. But instinct was telling him to survey the ground first. He studied the map, found the road he sought, and traced his way towards it, noting landmarks.

The area was pleasantly residential, although little more than a mile from the city centre. The houses looked as if they represented money. He drove slowly, watching for numbers on gates and doors.

Then he saw it: a chalet-style house, maybe four bedrooms, half an acre of garden, two big trees at the front, a twenty-yard drive to the door, flowers hanging in baskets, well cared-for lawns. Peaceful and ordinary, he thought; occasional cars and vans passing, a few well-dressed people walking, two children playing nearby. No troopers here; no sign of supervision.

He drove on, turning when he could and coming back, passing the house again.

Then he drove into the city centre by a different route, looking again for landmarks and for troopers, eventually parking the car off the Herzog Friedrich-Strasse and walking into a café. He wanted time to think.

A dozen or more men were there, and several women. A waitress took his modest order. When he spoke her eyes flicked momentarily as she heard his foreign accent, but she did not comment. She was his own age, neatly dressed and pretty. She served others, then came back to his table in a corner of the half-timbered, rather dim room. He smiled at her and said: 'Innsbruck is quiet today. I have only just arrived. Is it always quiet?'

She returned his smile cautiously, setting a plate on the table.

'It is quieter than usual, I think.' Her voice was cautious, too.

The buzz of conversation around the room made it easy for him to speak without attracting attention.

'Perhaps people are staying at home – because of what has happened?'

She was clearly uneasy.

'I don't know. Where do you come from?'

He was about to say 'I'm British'. Instead he said: 'I've come from Switzerland. I have business here. But it may be difficult now to see everyone I want to see. Do you think so?'

She glanced warily around, but no one was listening.

'It depends whom you have to see, I think. Perhaps in a few days it will be different – better.'

'I hope so.'

She turned abruptly and walked across the room to another table. She is afraid, Richard thought. Perhaps they're all afraid; of the troopers and the flags. Or perhaps they're not all afraid like this girl; there were a lot of Nazis in Austria, and he had talked to some of them on a previous visit. They would not be afraid.

He watched the waitress as he ate his cream strudel and drank rich coffee. But she was avoiding his eyes and eventually he left the café, crossed the street and bought a copy of *Der Angriff*, the newspaper of the Nazi Party in Germany. It was dated the previous day and its front page carried a four-column picture of Hitler acknowledging the crowds in Vienna, and German troops being handed flowers. The story told of an excited welcome for the Führer and the soldiers, of the resignation of Chancellor Von Schuschnigg, of the virtues of the Nazi Seyss-Inquart who had been appointed in his place (on Hitler's orders, although the paper did not report that), and of the need for the country to remain calm 'at this exciting moment in Austrian history'.

Richard walked slowly into the wide Maria-Theresien-Strasse. The sun shone on the mountains, so near to the north. He walked towards St Anne's column with the tramlines tracing iron patterns around it, looking at the shop windows. Food, furniture, clothes, a chemist and a sports shop. One window offered cloth – suit lengths and ready-made suits. Painted in crude white across the centre of the window was a big five-pointed star, and below the word 'Jude'. Over the window was inscribed the name of the owner: Anton Freund. The shop door was closed and there seemed to be no one inside.

Further along the pavement two troopers stood, watching the shop, looking at him, noting his pause at the window. They seemed to flaunt their swastika armbands. He walked slowly towards them, deliberately passing close so that he could see their faces clearly. One was thirty or so, round-faced beneath his peaked cap with staring blue eyes and down-turned mouth. The other was young, Richard's age, thin and mean. Both carried pistols in their belts and swung wooden batons from their wrists. He had a sudden mental picture of three men in black rushing towards him from a pub doorway in far-off Exeter.

He crossed the street. A shop window had been broken and clumsily boarded. The boards carried the painted star, like that on Anton Freund's shop, and the same word below it.

He went on, beneath the grey stone façades. Then he saw a bookshop and newsagents and, at the door, a man in the familiar uniform, corporal's stripes on his arm. A surge of resentment ran through him. The soldier was there to keep people out of the shop. I'm here legitimately, Richard thought; at the moment, anyway. Why the hell should I be kept out? He made to walk past the trooper into the shop and the man moved in front of him.

'What do you want?' Harsh voice, North German accent, hard eyes beneath the cap.

Richard returned his stare and said: 'A newspaper.'

The corporal jerked a thumb at the paper in Richard's hand.

'You have one. Why do you want another – from this shop?'

Richard looked past the uniform into the shop and saw other uniforms. He lifted the paper, turning the front page towards the guard.

'This is yesterday's. I want today's – from any shop.'

The man looked down, saw the masthead *Der Angriff*. When he looked back at Richard he had relaxed.

'You read the best paper. All right. You may go in.'

Richard nodded curtly and went inside. He was glad his accent had not aroused the man's curiosity.

Four troopers were examining books on shelves which ran on either side of the shop, forming a corridor. On the floor was a pile of books. As he watched a sergeant took a book from the shelf and threw it on the pile. Richard kept away from them, picked up a copy of *Der Angriff* from the counter and offered money to the man behind it. He was tall, thin, balding; wearing a shabby blue suit. And he was very frightened. His eyes bulged and sweat ran down his face.

Out on the sunlit street Richard nodded again to the corporal and crossed the wide pavement. Several people walked past, apparently unaware of the small drama in the bookshop. Unaware? Or perhaps just sensibly looking away, he thought. His chest was tight and tension ached in his thighs.

Then he saw the great banner. It hung across the grey baroque face of the Landhaus: a giant stylised German eagle holding a swastika in its talons, and below, the inscription – 'Ein Folk, Ein Reich, Ein Führer'.

He looked up at it, fascinated by its effrontery, its cynicism, its brutality. On either side the long black flags fluttered with their circled swastikas. Behind him, in a small shop, a man sweated as he watched his books selected for destruction. Further away other shops were empty and condemned by the scrawled 'Jude'. People passed, and now he saw their fear, in downcast eyes and quick, nervous steps; tangible fear, multiplying. He could smell it. He walked back to his car, remembering the hard eyes beneath the peaked cap at the bookshop door and the face of the man inside. Ein Folk, Ein Reich. His mouth tightened. Ruth was in this city, and she was afraid.

It was time to go.

He drove past the chalet-style house, slowing as he checked again for signs of surveillance and finding none. At the end of the road he turned left, then found he could go left again into a narrow lane which ran behind the houses. He thought: I don't know why I'm doing this; but a little caution can't do any harm. He passed behind the Edelmanns' house, then found a short cul-de-sac alongside the garden of the next house and reversed into it, tucking the car tightly against a low wall. Then he walked back the way he had come and approached the house between the two trees and up the drive.

The door knocker was a brass image of an old man's face, with thin cheeks and wide-set eyes. Momentarily he thought of his grandfather as he lifted it and heard the hard sound echo into the house. Then a middle-aged woman stood there holding the door only half open. She was dark with greying hair surrounding an angular face and large attractive eyes; wary eyes.

'I'm Richard Haldane,' he said in German. 'I'm here to see my sister, Ruth.'

The woman's hand pushed the door forward a few inches,

63

narrowing the gap. Her face was a defensive mask.

'That may not be possible. I think she may not be here –'

'She's here,' Richard said flatly. 'She's under house arrest, so she'd better be here. Kindly permit me to see her.'

A man's voice came from within the house.

'Who is there, mother?'

Kurt Edelmann. This was better. At least Kurt would not try to lie to him.

The woman turned her head, looking briefly over her shoulder.

'Will you come, please,' she said quietly, and then Kurt pulled the door wide and saw Richard.

For seconds they stared at each other; then the Austrian stepped past his mother and extended his hand.

'This is a surprise. I did not expect to see you here.' He spoke in English. His voice was level and not unfriendly, but his wide mouth did not smile.

'I'm sure you didn't,' Richard said. He shook hands briefly. 'I've come to see Ruth.'

'Of course. Please come in.' Kurt turned to the watching woman. 'Mother, this is Ruth's brother Richard.' He had reverted to his own language. 'We must make him welcome.'

The woman smiled mechanically. Richard followed Kurt into the dim wood-panelled hall and from there into a living room with more wood panelling and chintz-covered furniture.

From one of the chairs Ruth came to her feet, and her eyes opened wide when she saw the visitor.

'Richard – my dear Rich –' She ran to him, and he saw a purple bruise across her forehead and a scab over broken skin beneath her hairline. He took her by the shoulders and kissed her briefly on the cheek. His voice whispered in English: 'Who did that to you?'

'It's a long story. I'll tell you presently.' Her eyes were big and round and shocked. 'Why are you here? What's happening?'

'I came to see you,' he said curtly. 'I don't know what's happening. But I'm going to find out. Are you still under some sort of restriction?'

She stepped back, recoiling from his harshness.

'Yes. The police told me to stay here. If I go out they'll arrest me.'

Kurt Edelmann and his mother were watching them. Richard's

glance embraced them both and he said in German: 'I haven't time to waste. Tell me what has happened, please. Why is Ruth in this situation?'

Kurt came further into the room, crossed to Ruth's side and put a protective arm around her shoulders. She did not reject him, but neither did she respond.

'The circumstances are difficult,' he said. His blue eyes were guarded. 'The political situation is – volatile. Do you understand me, or would you rather speak English?'

'I understand. Go on.'

'No.' It was Ruth. She stepped forward, as if putting herself between the two men. 'I'll tell you.'

Richard heard footsteps and turned to see a man of sixty in the doorway. Edelmann senior, he thought. The same straight fair – now greying – hair, high and wide forehead, blue eyes and long nose. But not the same guarded, steady eyes; apprehensive eyes, rather – eyes that were older than the face. Richard did not wait for introductions. He extended a hand, said: 'Richard Haldane, Ruth's brother. You're Herr Edelmann.'

Edelmann nodded, accepting the proffered hand.

'Yes. We did not expect you – a visitor from England, at this time –'

'I'm here to help Ruth. I understand she is in trouble. I need to know what it is. And quickly, please.'

Ruth was staring at him. Dear heaven, she thought – how he's changed. He was always confident; but now he's so strong, so aggressive. And so calm.

Kurt was saying: 'It was unfortunate that I should bring her here at this time. We could not have known what was to happen, of course –'

'Why are the police interested in her?' The voice was low and level and tight.

Ruth said: 'Richard – let me tell you.'

He looked at her, with her bruised forehead and harassed eyes: and he looked at the three people watching him: the uneasy, anxious parents and the smooth, evasive son.

He said in English: 'All right. You tell me. But not here. In the garden. Where we can talk privately.'

'That is not necessary.' Kurt's voice was suddenly rough-edged. 'We are all Ruth's friends. I wish to marry her. I love her.

There are no secrets –'

'I'm not interested in secrets. I just want to talk to her privately.'

No one spoke. Then Ruth nodded briefly, glanced at Kurt and said: 'It would be better – easier for us to talk – for me to explain. Please don't be angry.'

She turned and walked to the door at the end of the room and Richard followed her. In the doorway he checked and glanced back.

'I'm in this country legitimately,' he said in his flat, confident voice. 'Don't attempt to telephone the police. It'll only get you into trouble. The German army knows I'm here.'

He closed the door and Ruth whispered: 'Richard – is that true? You've been to the military?'

He shook his head and gestured, and she led him across a kitchen and through a screened stable door into the garden at the rear of the house. There he said softly: 'It's not true. But it'll keep them quiet for a few minutes. Now tell me quickly.'

She took a long breath, looking at him wonderingly. Then she began to walk slowly away from the house and he fell into step with her. The lawn was soft beneath their feet.

'I came because he was pressing me to marry him. I had to see what it was like here. I loved him, Richard. Please understand.' She appealed, touching his arm, and he nodded, noting the past tense.

'I understand. What has happened since Sunday when the Germans came?'

'On Sunday we stayed in the house, listening to the wireless.' Her voice was small and tight. 'Kurt's parents were worried. But he wasn't. That was when I started to grasp just how pro-German he is – has always been, I suppose, although I hadn't wanted to recognise it. On Monday he said "Let's go and see what's happening." I trusted him. We went into the centre of the city. There were troopers and police everywhere, and flags being put up, and loudspeakers on the corners of buildings, and army vehicles. Some shops were open. Then something happened. Troopers were chasing several people. An old man fell down and when he started to get up a trooper clubbed him. He was close to us, and he was crying and bleeding. He was nearly as old as Grandad. I ran to him. The trooper pulled me away, and then he hit me.' She fingered the bruise, blinking quickly to resist tears. 'I fought him. I was frightened. And angry. Then Kurt dragged me away, telling the man I was English and didn't understand. Within a minute there were more troopers, then the police. They looked at my passport and asked questions and pushed me. I was silly. I argued with them. There was a big crowd around us. They put us into a van and brought us here and questioned Kurt's parents. They seemed to be satisfied with what Kurt told them and went away. But an hour later a policeman came back and ordered me to stay in the house until they had made inquiries about me. I've been here since.' The tears came faster than the blinks and ran down her cheeks.

He said: 'Is Kurt worried? Or does he think they'll forget it in a few days?'

She dabbed her eyes. He glanced at the house and saw a face at the kitchen window.

'He thinks – I was wrong to – to resist the trooper who hit me – and then to argue. He says they're paranoid. He says they'll either deport me quickly or – or send me to gaol for a month. A lot of people saw what happened and heard me criticizing. Kurt's father says they want to make an example of people to frighten others. People are being taken away and beaten, to frighten other people.' She looked at him, straight-shouldered now, and the tears were gone. 'I think that could happen to me.'

They were facing the house. He could see the woman watching them.

'Do you want to marry him?'

Without hesitation she said: 'No. I thought I did. We – we're lovers. But I couldn't marry him now. There's something about him I don't understand.'

'Then I'd better get you out of here.' He said it without hint of drama; almost conversationally.

She stared.

'How could you? It's impossible.'

'If there's any risk of you being dragged into a police station and beaten up, it's got to be possible. There's not much danger. The army's only in the cities and big towns. They haven't been here long enough to become established elsewhere. And a lot of people are welcoming them, so they won't be over-anxious.' He swung suddenly to face her, and his eyes held hers as if the contact were

67

physical. 'Trust me, Ruth. I've spent months talking to people who know what these men are really like. I've been here before, and to Czechoslovakia, and to Germany itself. I've talked to refugees – Jews and others. The story's always the same: what happens depends on individual SS officers. They can do anything they like. You could get badly hurt. Your British passport won't save you – they've nothing but contempt for the British. We've Chamberlain and rest to thank for that. So go into the house, pack a small overnight bag – and only a small one because you may have to carry it a long way – put on the stoutest shoes you have and the warmest coat, grab your money and your passport, and get back downstairs as fast as you can. And I mean fast.'

One hand covered her mouth and her eyes were big and frightened.

'Rich – I didn't tell you – they took my passport away.' A whisper, with panic in it.

For five whole seconds he was still; frozen. Then he said: 'That's bad. They'll take you to the police station to reclaim it, and they'll knock you about before they hand it over. That's the standard form. All right. We leave anyway. C'mon.'

He led her back to the house, squeezed her hand once, and pushed her through the kitchen to the stairs, whispering, 'Quickly, now.'

In the living room Kurt Edelmann and his parents rose to their feet: one hostile face, two apprehensive ones.

Richard said: 'I'm sorry if you feel I have been rude to you. Ruth is leaving with me. Now. I'm not taking her away from you, Kurt: you can rejoin her in England whenever you like. Your personal relationship is not my affair. But I am taking her to safety.' He was speaking in English and he saw the puzzled, worried faces of the parents, and ignored them.

Kurt snapped: 'Don't be a fool. You're putting her in far greater danger. If you're caught you'll be in tremendous trouble.'

'In my judgement she's already in danger. You know what happens when they take away a passport – before they hand it back. Right?'

Momentarily Kurt flinched, and Richard knew he had his answer. But the Austrian said: 'I can protect her. I have already argued successfully for her. If I hadn't she'd be in custody after hitting that trooper. Did you know she hit him? And then insulted

68

Nazis and Hitler – and a lot of people heard her? In the circumstances those were serious mistakes –'

'And it would be an even more serious mistake to leave her here now.' Richard's voice was ice. He said in German so that the parents could understand: 'We shall leave. If we are picked up within the next four hours we'll know you have reported our departure. Then two things will happen: Ruth will know you have betrayed her, Kurt. And I will come back here when I am released, to see you all again. Or if you're in England I'll find you there, Kurt.'

He said it so quietly that the message was lost for seconds. Then the woman made a small sound in her throat, and Kurt's face flushed and he said angrily: 'Don't threaten us, Richard –'

'I do not threaten. I tell you what will happen. Now tell me: do you intend to betray the girl you have loved, the girl who has been into your bed, the girl you have said you want to marry?'

They stood, an arm's length apart, challenging, defying, asserting. And Richard's strange hard eyes cut into Kurt Edelmann and he turned away; first his head, then a step sideways and back. He went to the window, looking out across the garden, and said: 'No.'

Then Ruth came into the room. She wore a tweed coat with a scarf and leather gloves and low-heeled shoes, and carried a small case. Her face was pale and her eyes betrayed tears she had shed while she had been upstairs.

Richard said, still in German: 'We need half an hour to reach the railway station, then three hours to get where I want to go. After that you can do what you like. Tell them you've just discovered she's left – anything. And one more thing. I lied to you. The military don't know I'm here. So you don't have to say anything about me if you don't want to.'

'How are you going to get to the station?' It was Kurt's father.

'That's my concern. I have a friend. That's all you need to know. Ruth – let's go.'

For an instant she hesitated, looking at Kurt. Then she held out a hand and he touched her fingers and said quietly: 'I'll see you in Cambridge.'

She nodded, and Richard took her by the elbow and steered her into the kitchen and then to the garden and down to the hedge and the fence he had already noted, and through a narrow gap at one end of it, pushing saplings aside, and they were in the road at the back of the houses. He took her case and they walked in silence to the cul-de-sac and he unlocked the car.

As he started it she whispered: 'I thought you said we were going on a train.'

His grin was humourless.

'That was a precaution. We're not going near the station. And I haven't any friends. Not here, anyway.' Another sideways grin. 'But don't worry. I don't think they'll report us until late tonight. By then we'll be out of reach.'

He drove out into the road, turning away from the house, and accelerated.

'If we're stopped, leave the talking to me. This is a French car, and I shall speak French. No German will know I'm not a Frenchman unless I have to show my passport. We'll bluff our way out, somehow. But I don't think we'll be stopped. There are cigarettes on the shelf. Light one for me. Help yourself if you want one.'

They avoided the centre of Innsbruck, driving alongside the river with scattered traffic around them. She lighted two Gauloises and gave one to him. Her hand was quivering.

'Where are we going. Please tell me.'

'To Nauders. South-west of here. A hundred miles, I think. Part of it is a good road, part isn't. There'll be other traffic for most of the way, so we shouldn't be too noticeable. The Swiss border is very close to the road near Nauders. We'll leave the car there and cross on foot. It will be rough mountain walking all night, probably through snow. If it gets too rough we'll stop and wait for daylight. But we'll get over: it's wild country and there aren't many man-made barriers. Or so I'm told.'

Presently, with Innsbruck behind them and Telfs ahead, she turned to him and said: 'Why did you do it – come for me – risk yourself?'

He glanced sideways at her.

'Would you take a risk or two for me?'

'Yes. You know I would.'

'Then don't ask damn' fool questions.'

She flushed and looked down. Her fingers were twined together tightly on her lap, and he reached out and covered them with his hand. When she looked up he was smiling at her.

'I'm sorry if it won't work out for you with Kurt,' he said gently.

She shook her head.

'So am I. But I've come to terms with it. At least I think so. But I have loved him – I suppose I still do.'

Ahead two grey lorries appeared. Richard said, 'Relax,' and drove steadily. The leading lorry fluttered a swastika from a mudguard. Then it was past, and the second one too, and Richard watched them recede in his mirror.

'How long have you been lovers?'

She looked away, out of the nearside window.

'Since last summer. I told you – remember?'

He nodded. 'Yes. You told me. I was thinking about myself, really.' He glanced at her quickly. 'It's strange. I've never made love to a girl. Never been to bed with a girl. What's it like?'

She turned to look at him, hiding her surprise. Suddenly his superb confidence, his maturity so much beyond his years, had eroded, and he was young and inexperienced and inadequate.

She said quietly: 'I don't know what it's like for a man. I only know what it's like for a woman. And I can't describe it. It consumes you. But I don't know how a man feels.'

His hand found hers again, as if he needed the reassurance of her touch, and she squeezed his fingers, and then traced lines between them, gently, slowly.

'When I find out I'll tell you,' he said. He looked at her. Then he took his hand away and put it back on the steering wheel and said: 'I'm sorry. Let's talk about something else, before I make a dreadful fool of myself. You're – disturbing me, sister.'

For seconds she was silent, not looking at him. Then she said distantly: 'It's the tension. I'm the same, when you touch me. I'm sorry. I shouldn't say that, should I? I should be ashamed. But I'm not. Not with you. We're very much alike.' A hesitation; then, 'Thank you for coming for me. I'll remember it always, whatever happens.'

He shrugged, glancing cautiously at her, trying to break the spell, but not thinking of anything to say.

She tried: 'What about the future – after this? There'll be a war now, won't there?'

He nodded. 'Certain. We have to fight. It's the only way to stop what's happening. If we do nothing the whole of Europe will go, one country at a time. There'll just be Britain left – a little offshore island. Then it will be our turn. We daren't let it get as far as that.'

'It's awful. The last war killed father. And millions more. Now it's going to happen again. And this is a terrible evil. Have you heard the stories about the concentration camps?'

'Yes. I've interviewed people with relatives in the camps. People too terrified to tell me their names. But it's not only that. It's a thousand things. We have to stop it. We have to get ready for it, before it's too late.'

Ahead the mountains of the Tyrol rose in serried white peaks, climbing up forever under cloud caps. The car jolted and swayed on the indifferent road surface. Richard was driving very fast.

'What will happen at home, do you think? To Roxton?'

He reached across for the Gauloises and pushed the packet towards her.

'You mean when we decide we want to take our money and run?' Flat calm and matter-of-fact, as if it were the most ordinary question in the world. It should have shocked her, to hear it so coldly, so abruptly; but it did not.

'Yes. That's what I mean. Have you really worked it out?' She shook two cigarettes from the pack; put them both in her mouth.

'In money? Not in detail. But I've thought about it.' He waited for her to light the cigarettes; took one from her. A car appeared ahead, travelling slowly in their direction. He checked his speed, looking for an open stretch of road so that he could overtake.

'I remember when we were kids – I was fifteen or so,' he said. 'Grandfather told us how he had willed the estate. He said it would be up to us to make a success of it. It didn't occur to him that we might not want to.'

She looked at him and marvelled again at his maturity, and the change in him.

'What do you want, Rich; for yourself?'

'I still don't know.' His voice was remote, as if he was only half-concentrating on the words as he studied the winding road and the car ahead. 'I've guessed what my share of Roxton would be, if I pulled out. It's a lot of money, even though the land market is so poor. Once, I think it gave me a feeling that I didn't need to work. But that went. And I don't know what happened then. I became utterly impatient with university. It seemed so trivial, so juvenile, compared with what's happening outside. I know I gave up my chance of a degree. But I don't regret it. What I'm doing now is an adventure. It's exciting; everything is a challenge. Perhaps if things were different I would want to go on doing it. But that is passing, too. I'm still looking for something. But it isn't Roxton. How about you?'

She played with her cigarette, watching the road; stiffened slightly as he pulled out suddenly and accelerated past the slower car.

'I said we are alike. I've been the same. I'm studying for a career. There's always the feeling, though, that it isn't terribly important – that I could have a lot of money, if I claimed it; and that one day I will claim it. The thing with Kurt showed that to me. Yet we both know the other part of the story; what it will mean to Roxton. And to Robert.'

They sat in silence then, for a long time; watching the road and the river alongside and the flat valley fields, listening to the old car's engine. Traffic was light and there were no Germans; not even in Telfs through which they passed easily and anonymously.

Presently, as they drove towards Imst, with high snow-topped mountains now crowding on either side of the valley, he said: 'There's going to be more to do than spend money, Ruth.'

'What good will a vet be when the war comes?' she asked. 'I ought to do something more useful.'

'No.' He shook his head. 'Nothing will be more useful than farming. Food will be scarce when the imports stop, just like last time. Farmers will need vets. There'll be a big expansion – more stock, more crops. The government will be crying out for it. Robert will have a big job on his hands.'

'Unless we pull the rug from under him,' she said quietly; and they were silent again.

Imst was ahead of them. Richard slowed, keeping strictly to the speed limit. If they were to find trouble it would be here, he thought.

Two policemen stood at a crossroads. They looked at the car, then away. Traffic was sparse. At six in the evening the sun had gone behind the snow-covered slopes of the mountains. They crossed one side of a square. There were fountains and statues and the houses had rounded window grilles. They passed below the great Gothic church with its giant statue outside. He pointed to it and said: 'St Christopher. He's supposed to look after travellers. I hope he's watching us.' She forced a smile but did not reply.

73

On the cobbles two German troop carriers stood; half-tracked vehicles, grim and purposeful, long and sloping at the front with two rows of open seats behind the driver's cab and a machine gun mounted at the rear. But there were no men with them. Richard drove very carefully, very correctly. He could feel himself sweating. Cars were parked, others moved in front of him and behind. Four soldiers in grey uniforms crossed the narrow street ahead. They were laughing. Traffic thinned between the buildings and fields appeared. They were on the Landeck road now.

Without looking at her he said: 'Stop worrying. We're okay.'

She glanced at him but said nothing.

They were still following the valley of the Inn. The fast-flowing water was grey-white. The valley was narrower, with pines climbing up the steep mountains. He turned on the car's sidelights, glanced at the mirror; said: 'Oh Christ. Don't look round.'

Two motor cyclists were behind, coming up fast. Grey uniforms, grey steel helmets; travelling fast. Richard drove steadily. The road was winding and narrow and the valley sides were threatening in the failing light. The soldiers slowed behind them, riding abreast.

'Light a cigarette for me.'

She did so. Her hands shook slightly. He took the cigarette from her and slanted it from the corner of his mouth. He hoped it looked casual; unworried.

The motor cycle engines rose in pitch and one machine pulled out to overtake. As it drew alongside the rider looked sideways at them. Goggles hid his eyes. In the fading light his uniform looked black; forbidding. He accelerated, crossed in front of them, slowed a little. There were more bends ahead. The second rider stayed behind. Another bend. They drove, escorted, for half a mile. Then the road straightened and the second rider picked up speed until he was alongside. He turned his head. Richard lifted one hand in casual acknowledgement. The man nodded, waved once, overtook and pulled level with his companion. They rounded the next bend side by side. Then they began to draw ahead. Richard slowed slightly, watching them go. He said: 'There. I told you not to worry.' His knuckles were white on the steering wheel.

'Oh God, please help us; stay with us.' He hardly heard her whispered words.

A car's lights were ahead, approaching. An ordinary car, a civilian car. It passed noisily.

Richard switched on his headlights and eased his back against the seat.

'I'm not going to pull the rug from under Robert.' He said it conversationally, as if there had been no break in their talk. 'And I don't think you are, either.'

She looked at him, startled, trying to recollect; fighting down her fear.

'If Roxton stays in one piece it will be more efficient,' he said. 'Farming will need all the efficiency it can find. Let's keep it in one piece, for the present at least. We can come to an arrangement with Robert, when the time comes. Nothing is going to matter now, except fighting – this.'

She nodded, confused and wordless.

They crossed and recrossed the river over narrow bridges as they approached Landeck, the small industrial town where the Arlberg road met the Inn valley. Another danger point, he thought; there could be a road-check here. But he said nothing. Above, perched on a rock, was the black outline of the great medieval castle, frowning down on them. There was little traffic in the narrow streets – and no soldiers. They turned left, staying with the river on their right, leaving the town, driving as fast as the road allowed, along stretches cut into rocks above the narrow valley floor. The snowline was closer on the slopes above them. Once she said, 'This would be beautiful in daylight, if we had time to appreciate it. Now it frightens me.' But he only grunted in reply, concentrating on driving in the gloom, the great range on their right black against the clouds and the last of the day. Pfunds was ahead, straddling the river, the little windows of the houses like yellow eyes as they approached. They drove slowly along the narrow street, seeing a few people but no traffic.

'I don't expect we'll see any troops now,' he said encouragingly. 'They won't have had time to get here.'

A heavy lorry trundled towards them and edged past, and then the little town receded and they entered the narrow, grim gorge leading to the Finstermuns pass, the headlights picking up rock that towered upwards, jagged and forbidding above the dimly-seen trees on either side and the snow above.

He drove for ten minutes then, abruptly, turned off the road onto a narrow track between dense pines. The valley sides reared up in the darkness. He turned off the lights, opened the door. Cold air hit them.

'I think this is about as far as it's wise to drive,' he said. 'We can't be far from the border.'

She put out a hand to check him.

'Rich – how did you know about this road, and where to stop? And what about the car?'

He grinned humourlessly, feeling the snow-chilled air in his lungs.

'I knew about this place because when I started the work I'm doing now, an old-timer took pity on a green youngster and told me that it was always wise to know a few back doors in case things got rough. I know two ways out of Czechoslovakia and three out of Austria. This is one. But it's all theory. Now we're going to find out if it really works.'

He slid out of the car, opened the rear door and pulled a warm overcoat off the seat; put it on. Then he crammed a cap on his head, dug under the driver's seat and produced heavy boots. He grunted in the cold air as he put them on and laced them tightly. All the time she stood beside him, watching in the dimness. Then he looked at her and said: 'You've nothing to cover your head. Wrap your scarf round it. Keeping your head warm is important.'

Without a word she did as she was told, tucking the ends of the scarf firmly down inside her coat collar. He inspected her and nodded his approval.

She said: 'And the car, Rich? What happens to it?'

He leaned forward and picked up a torch from beside the driving seat; closed the door quietly. He stood for seconds, listening. Then he put an arm around her shoulders.

'It's my present to Hitler,' he said. 'Let's say I swopped it for you. Now we'll start. First we walk, then we climb.'

10

On the table was a buff-covered booklet entitled 'The Protection of Your Home Against Air Raids'. Beside it lay a leaflet with the words 'Masking Your Windows' at the top. They were not new; but now somebody had brought them out again, for yet more study.

The tired, sad voice of Neville Chamberlain pronounced verdict and sentence. They listened, trying to remember the phrases as if it were important to do so.

'I am speaking to you from the Cabinet Room of number 10 Downing Street. . . . the British Ambassador in Berlin handed the German Government a final note stating that unless. . . . I have to tell you now that no such undertaking has been received and that consequently this country is at war with Germany. . . . it is evil things we shall be fighting. . . . I am certain that the right will prevail. . . .'

The national anthem was a thin, lonely sound through the small loudspeaker of the radio set. Robert waited until the final chord before he leaned over and, slowly, turned off the set. They all stared at it: Diane and Ruth sitting close together on the settee; Mary Pritchard, the housekeeper whose buxom presence was the domestic hub of Roxton Grange; and Robert himself.

Then, in a small, clear voice, Diane said: 'So Ranulph died for nothing. I'm glad he cannot know.'

Ruth touched her in sympathetic understanding, and Mary pushed herself up out of the chair.

'I'll make some tea,' she said. She could think of no other way to contribute to the awful moment.

'No.' Robert dragged his gaze away from the silent radio. 'Later, Mary. At the moment – something stronger.' He walked over to the sideboard and poured four large whiskies. When he had handed them out he said: 'Here's to happier times. They'll come. Eventually.'

The women stared at him. None of them had drunk neat whisky before. But they responded to him. In spite of his youth, he was the leader now; and suddenly they were aware of it. For better or worse, what happened to Roxton from this moment would be first and foremost Robert's responsibility. And they knew he was not afraid of it.

He looked across at his mother, anxiety showing.

'I'm all right,' she said. 'Don't worry. I won't make a scene.'

He said, with a gentleness which was surprising for him, 'I never thought you would,' and then drank the rest of his whisky quickly before he turned away and stared out of the window.

Across the lawn and the garden the poplars rippled against the breeze. Two rooks swooped low across the lawn like miniature black aeroplanes. Beyond the white gate the farm was quiet. He heard the women moving, and wondered again that his mother was so controlled. She had come to terms with the inevitability of war, as most people had; she was already a member of the Women's Voluntary Service and that afternoon would be down in the village receiving evacuees from Southampton. But he had been aware of her private agony through the last struggling years of peace, and although he had no memories of his father he was sufficiently perceptive to understand at least some of the reasons.

On the other side of the white gate he saw Martin Calder crossing a yard to one of the barns. Martin would also be in the village after lunch, and Robert would be with him, for both were wardens. They had been to lectures together and had practised fire-fighting with buckets of sand and stirrup pumps, learning how to use dustbin lids to protect themselves as they tackled dummy incendiary bombs. Would dustbin lids help against real incendiary bombs? Maybe at Roxton they would never have to find out. Maybe the adhesive strips of paper across the windows and the dyed calico blackout curtains on wooden frames were unnecessary. But they were there, and light bulbs had been removed from the farm buildings and replaced with oil lamps which were easier to shield, and there were small stocks of flour, sugar, tea and tinned foods in the cupboard, and a new tractor in one of the barns in case it was a long time before the factories made other new tractors.

He felt rather than heard Ruth beside him. He looked round. His mother and Mary had gone and Ruth was holding the whisky bottle. He stared, questioning, then held out his glass and she poured some of the liquid into it, then into her own glass.

She said quietly: 'We forgot something, Rob. We forgot the most important toast.'

It shocked him. He turned with her, and they both looked at a photograph on the table. We've got to be ready for it, Richard had said. There he was, in the picture frame, uniformed, ready for it; ready for war. And the war had begun.

'I don't know if there is a God,' Ruth said. 'But if there is, I hope he has time to look after Rich.'

For a moment they stared at the photograph. Then Robert held out his glass and said: 'I'll drink to that. Here's to you, brother.'

He put out a hand and, for a moment, rested it on Ruth's shoulder as they both drank.

*   *   *

Grasses stirred in the wind and the sun shone on the rolling Wiltshire countryside. Above the Bath road the giant white horse carved into the chalk bowl of the hill looked clean. Beyond it a small monument crowned the crest, pointing a finger skywards. On the road below a blue Austin saloon came up from Calne and turned left, down the lane towards the cluster of buildings. It carried Royal Air Force number plates.

From a window of the mess Richard watched its approach. He felt sorry for the driver who must have missed the drama of the Prime Minister's declaration of war. Richard had stood with the other young men who were learning to fly Tiger Moths here at Yatesbury, listening to the old, weary voice, and they had all stiffened to attention when the national anthem had been played.

Then Steve Mitchell, who had been a partner in a bright public relations agency in London and was a couple of years older than Richard, punched him lightly in the ribs and said: 'That's it, then. In six months we'll be in action. I'd rather it was six days.' And Philip Fletcher, who had joined the RAF straight from university, grinned and said: 'Hell's bells, give us time. None of us has gone solo yet. Except Richard.'

Richard shrugged in acknowledgement. Initial flying training had become a formality for him. The instructors had to make sure he flew to their own exacting standards; but he had a lot of flying time to his credit and he hoped to be posted away from Yatesbury within a week now, on his way north to Sealand and intermediate training.

He hoped he would get a weekend at home between courses.

He would like to see how Robert was making out; although he had no doubts about it, for since he had come down from Reading, Robert had ensured that everyone knew he was not just a youngster fresh from university but the future master of Roxton; or one of them, at least.

The blue Austin stopped outside the mess and Richard saw the Chief Flying Instructor climb out. Squadron Leader Howard Grant, a Royal Air Force veteran of forty, was the man who would decide if Richard was to leave the initial course earlier than the rest.

Beyond Grant the Tiger Moths were lined up: yellow biplanes with open cockpits, waiting. They were forgiving aeroplanes, which was just as well in view of the way some of the pupils handled them. Richard loved them: the open cockpits lent an exhilaration to the business of flying which the old Puss Moth had lacked.

He remembered flying over Roxton, surveying the estate from the air; then telling Robert that although one day he and Ruth would probably pull out and leave him to it, now it would not be for a long time.

Ruth's Austrian adventure and Kurt Edelmann had been responsible for that. Kurt had returned to Cambridge a week after Richard and Ruth had found their cold, exhausting way out of Austria in March 1938, but he had then seen Ruth only rarely until, with a doctorate to his credit, he had gone back to his own country. Afterwards they had heard nothing of him.

Richard had gone on working from Paris, earning a meagre living but enjoying it; until the invasion of Czechoslovakia and the Munich crisis. Then he had tried to join the RAF and eventually had been accepted into the Volunteer Reserve, waiting impatiently until, in March 1939, had come the letter he had sought.

Now he was here at Yatesbury, in the heart of the gentle Wiltshire countryside, and there was war. The mess was buzzing with youthful excitement; but somehow he did not share it. He stood a little apart from the others, even apart from himself, as if he were without form, secretly observing Richard Haldane and the flamboyant Steve Mitchell who had driven racing cars at weekends until three months ago and Philip Fletcher who had married the lovely dark-haired Jan two weeks before, and the rest. His secret self looked at eager faces and shining eyes and heard laughter and boastful slang, and remembered jackboots in Austria and the Jewish refugees interviewed by the real Richard Haldane and the tanks he had seen roll into Czechoslovakia and a terrified shopkeeper in Innsbruck. He thought: Why are we treating this like a game when it's the gateway to hell? How many of us will be alive in a year's time? And yet the real Richard Haldane was not afraid.

'Gentlemen, your attention please.' The CFO was in the doorway, hatless, his greying temples catching the sunlight from the window. 'You've heard the declaration of war. We knew it was coming, so it changes nothing, except that we have to hurry a little more. We'll start flying at noon. The harder you work now, the quicker you'll reach a squadron.'

The conversation bubbled again as Grant left, and everyone moved towards the door. Richard went with the rest, exchanging banter, until he was outside. Then, somehow, he was by himself; crossing the tarmac towards the yellow biplanes, still and resting in the Sunday sunlight but smelling of petrol and oil and well-used machinery and doped fabric. He looked up at the scattered cumulus clouds and the pale blue of the sky and thought it was all like yesterday. The hangars were the same, and the trees, and the distant sound of a car on the Bath road. He was the same, and the yellow Tiger Moths. Yet there was war; war in the summer silence with a lark singing somewhere. It should not feel like this. It was too peaceful, too ordinary. A great question stretched ahead of him and he could not even begin to understand it, let alone answer it on this solemn, memorable day, the third of September 1939.

He reached forward and touched the wingtip of the nearest Tiger Moth. At least that was real.

*   *   *

They had come on the train from Exeter: thirty confused, appre-hensive excited children, the youngest aged seven and the oldest twelve. They had left Southampton early that morning, carrying their cases and their bundles, each with a label tied to a coat collar or a cuff. Two school teachers shepherded them now into the hall beside Roxton's church, following the half-dozen women who wore WVS armbands and smiled cautiously at the assorted waifs.

The scene was being repeated in many parts of Britain as evacuees left the cities which were considered prime air raid targets and sought temporary homes in quieter places.

Edna Moorcock from the all-purpose shop along the street sat at a trestle table looking at lists of names on sheets of paper. She did not expect it would take long to allocate the children to their new homes, for there were sufficient volunteers and the anxious foster-parents had been interviewed.

The hall was crowded by those same volunteers, mostly couples except where the men were on their way to the wardens' post in the scout hut conveniently situated beside the Rising Sun nearby. They inspected the children, mentally rejecting the ragged ones with running noses and hair obviously cut at the kitchen table; seeking out the neater, better-presented children, who, they reasoned, might at least be clean.

One of the children was crying; a thin mousy-haired eight-year-old in a faded blue dress which hung below the hem of a threadbare coat. The older child next to her said loudly: 'Shurrup, Mabel. There's no good squawkin'. You ain't hurt.' The crying child stuffed fingers into her mouth and stifled the sobs, eyes downcast as Diane crossed to her and said gently: 'Come on, Mabel, cheer up. It's going to be all right. You see.'

Mabel sniffed, turning her head away. The older child looked up at Diane with bright impertinent eyes and said: 'You havin' one of us, missis?'

Diane had already promised to take into Roxton Grange four girls from the newly-formed Women's Land Army. She shook her head.

'No. Someone else is coming to stay with me. But you'll have a good home –'

'What're you doin' here if you're not havin' one of us, then?' the girl demanded. Her bright eyes were hostile now.

'I'm helping,' Diane said. 'You look after Mabel and be kind to her.' She walked along the line of children and heard the child snap to her distressed neighbour: 'Belt up, you sniffin' little bugger. If you make a noise like that no one'll have you.'

*　　*　　*

In the scout hut eighteen men perched on hard wooden chairs

facing Jeffrey Aston who was landlord of the Rising Sun and had been appointed Chief Warden because he had been a sergeant major in the '14–'18 war. Beside him was Sergeant Colin Bamford of the county police force.

A wiry young man with prematurely grey hair, Bamford said: 'We will have two men on duty every night. When they're alerted they will contact all other wardens who will rendezvous here and will then patrol their sectors. A duty warden will remain at the post to provide liaison. Mr Aston will work closely with police headquarters and will have complete authority. His deputy will be Martin Calder of Roxton Home Farm.' He nodded towards Martin who sat beside Robert at the back of the hall, and the others murmured their approval.

'How long will it be before we get uniforms?' someone asked, and Bamford said: 'You'll have to make do with armbands for a start. But don't let that lessen your authority. First and foremost that applies to the blackout. Don't put up with any argument. And don't hesitate to report anyone who refuses to accept your instructions.'

'It's going to be difficult reporting friends,' John Moorcock said. 'And customers.' He grimaced.

'I have just as many friends and customers as you have,' said Jeffrey Aston. 'We'll have to learn to be tactful. I don't think there'll be much trouble.'

'You'll have trouble from some,' Bamford said grimly. 'This area is likely to feel a long way from the war and there'll be folks who won't take kindly to being told what to do. Just remember that your friends and customers could be responsible for the deaths of a lot of people if they don't accept discipline. And another thing.' He looked around the serious faces. 'Keep your eyes and ears open all the time, on duty or not. I don't want to start any spy scares, but it's as well to remember there are still a few people who think old Hitler's not a bad sort of feller.'

The meeting went on for another hour. Then, when it broke up, Bamford said quietly to Robert: 'I'd like a private word with you, Mr Haldane.'

They walked out into the late sunshine, away from the others. When Bamford was satisfied that no one could overhear them he said: 'You have a man working for you called Salford.'

Robert eyed him warily.

83

'That's right. What's on your mind.'

'I think you know. We have the names of people who have been members of the British Fascist Party, including Salford. He's been active, attending meetings, speaking at some of them, selling the newspaper *Action*. This weekend, all over the country, leading members of the BFP are being rounded up and will go into internment while we check them out. Salford doesn't quite come into that category, but we still think he's worth watching. So I'm asking for your help. Neither you nor I know what goes on in a man's mind. So please keep your eye on him. If you see or hear anything which concerns you, no matter how trivial it might seem, get in touch with me immediately.'

'Of course.' Somehow Robert felt he resented the sergeant's warning, although he knew the man was doing no more than his job demanded. It seemed like an interference in Roxton's affairs. 'Though I doubt if there's anything to worry about. I can't imagine Sam Salford as a spy, even though I once wanted to sack him for being a Mosleyite.'

'Spy, potential saboteur, a whispering propagandist – or a loyal citizen,' said Bamford. 'Nothing's impossible. Do the other men know he's a Fascist?'

'Yes. And they don't like it. They'll watch him.' Robert took a long breath. 'It somehow brings the war a bit closer.'

'It may be closer to all of us than we think,' Bamford said solemnly. He looked at his watch. 'I'll get back to the station. There's a lot more work to do before my duty'll be over for today. And I want to get to a radio so I can hear the news at six o'clock. Find out what's been happening everywhere else – and especially if there've been any air raids. The sirens sounded in London this morning, you know, although nothing happened.'

*   *   *

Richard turned the Tiger Moth onto the final leg of his approach. He could see the Chief Flying Instructor's head in the cockpit in front. It was the first time Grant had flown with him. They had been airborne for half-an-hour and he knew he was under close scrutiny.

He eased the throttle. The upper wing shielded his eyes from the sun and he could see the small airfield ahead and the buildings away to the right of the engine cowling. Three hundred feet and it was a good approach. He thought the whole flight had been good and hoped Grant felt the same about it. There were cattle in a field close to the Bath road below and for an instant he wondered what was happening at Roxton on this first day of the war. Robert was in charge now, in spite of their mother's presence, and Ruth would keep an eye on the stock when she was not working for the Exeter veterinary practice where she was a new assistant. That was a useful arrangement; but most of the responsibility rested on Robert. It was a good thing Martin Calder was so competent.

He was too low. He opened the throttle and as the engine responded raised the nose. Damn. Grant would have noticed that. He checked his airspeed and trim and held his approach across the radio school buildings, across the narrow lane leading to Yatesbury village, across the hedge boundary to the airfield, throttling back, twenty feet, ten, stick back, wheels jarring then running as smoothly as the grass allowed, tail just off the ground then touching. A good one.

He taxied round to dispersal, switched off, watching the propeller as it stopped, and released the harness which held him down in his seat.

As they walked side by side away from the Tiger Moth Grant said: 'Not bad, Haldane. Your experience shows. But don't get over-confident. What happened on the final? I thought you'd gone to sleep.'

Richard said: 'Sorry, sir. I was distracted for a moment.'

'Distracted?' Grant raised an eyebrow. 'I hope you never use that as an excuse when you bend an aeroplane – as you surely will if you lose your concentration on the landing circuit.'

'It won't happen again, sir.' Richard looked straight ahead.

'Good.' Grant was curt. He glanced at his watch. 'We've just missed the six o'clock news. But no doubt everyone will bring us up to date.' He was silent for a moment as they walked, then added: 'I'll check through your flying programme for next week. Then I think we'll send you off to Sealand. We've got to push our way through pilot training as fast as we can, and I think you're wasting time here – when you're not being distracted.'

* * *

85

Late in the evening a wind came up from the Channel, along the estuary of the Exe and then inland over Roxton. Ruth sat on her bedroom windowsill, watching the last light of the day and the clouds moving across a low moon, gradually obscuring it. Somehow it was symbolic: the lights were going out everywhere.

She had spent the afternoon with the practice's senior partner on a Woodbury farm where a Shorthorn heifer had been in trouble at calving. 'Our job doesn't stop just because a war's started,' he had said, in half apology for calling her out on that special, dreadful Sunday. But the calf was born dead and she was depressed as well as tired.

Downstairs she could hear Robert moving. She had gained a new respect for her turbulent brother that day. Since his return from Reading he had matured quickly, and now the last traces of youth seemed to have left him. Their mother might still have the ultimate authority, but the decisions would now be Robert's and Diane would let him run ahead of the pack, for he was fit to lead in this new, uncertain, fragile world.

And Richard? His future was the most fragile of all. The unspeakable did not happen only to others.

She remembered him now, as she often did, in Austria: his strength and courage, and the way she had followed him without question. She remembered, too, how he had verbally scourged her once they had reached the safety of Switzerland, and her shame as she had wept under the lash of his tongue, for she had known that his anger was justified. She had loved Kurt; but it had been a blinding, subversive love.

Kurt. Where was he now? Eighteen months ago, her lover; now her enemy. Everybody's enemy, and especially Richard's. He would be in uniform, being trained to kill all the Richards in the world, while Richard was learning how to kill all the Kurts. Perhaps one day they would meet on a battlefield. It was a horrible, frightening fantasy, and she shuddered as she dragged her mind away from it.

Beyond her room an owl hooted as the night closed in; a distant, echoing sound across the trees. She opened the window to listen, and heard the stillness of the dark. Was everywhere so still, waiting for the storm?

It was the end of the first day of the war, and she marvelled at the peace across the hidden farmland.

11

The snow of 1940s early weeks was the worst for a decade, holding back farmers' efforts to prepare the land for spring sowing. It blanketed Northern France, too, and there was little serious fighting as the armies faced each other across a bitter landscape. In the air there were occasional raids on coastal towns and a few inland as well, but casualties were light, while RAF bombers spent some of their time dropping propaganda leaflets on the Germans. Only at sea was there the sort of war which had been expected, but the censored reports of shipping losses and the limited introduction of food rationing failed to persuade many people that serious shortages were likely.

But politicians and senior civil servants were alarmed. After years of low prices, few farmers believed that the slow improvement in the value of their products would be maintained, and so many were heavily in debt that the task of organising expansion was daunting to anxious Ministry of Agriculture and Food officials. So War Agricultural Executive Committees had been set up, with powers to dictate ploughing and cropping programmes. They were the Government's strong arm in the countryside, with the ultimate sanction: they could authorise a farmer's removal from his land if they judged that he was failing to manage it efficiently.

The arrival of the chairman of the county War Ag – as it was already known – at Roxton Grange was therefore not a moment to be taken lightly. His name was Bennett, he carried the courtesy title of Major from the 1914–18 war and wore a crisp military moustache to reinforce it, he owned three thousand acres of land near Plymouth; and he came straight to the point of his visit.

'We have been studying the performance of one of your tenants, a man named Walton,' he said. 'We are much concerned. His is not a big farm, but even eighty acres can't be neglected. And the whole place is in a poor state. You must be aware of that.'

'I am,' Diane said. 'He is the only tenant with whom we have a problem. And I knew the Ministry was taking an interest in the farm.'

'Good,' said Bennett briskly. 'So you won't be surprised to know that we feel we must serve ploughing orders on him and then supervise him. We could do it directly, but I thought it would be courteous to talk with you about it first.'

'Thank you,' Diane said coldly. 'Show them to me and explain them, please.'

Bennett did so; and then Diane swept the papers back into their envelope and slid them into her handbag. To the surprised visitor she said: 'Thank you, Major Bennett. I shall discuss these with Mr Walton this afternoon. Since the land is ours I think it would be better if it were done that way – don't you?'

Bennett stared at her. He was clearly not used to being addressed so curtly by a woman.

'If you wish, Mrs Haldane. I would have thought it would be easier to have a member of the committee visit the farm – an independent voice and one with external authority, if you understand.'

'I understand perfectly, Major. But since I own the land I think my authority will not be questioned. I'll telephone you tomorrow.' She smiled brightly and rose to her feet, giving Bennett little option but to leave.

But when he had gone she said to Robert: 'This is unfortunate. Somehow it reflects badly upon the whole estate. That's why I want to handle it myself.'

'Wouldn't it be better if you let me do it?' Robert looked doubtful.

'No.' Her voice left no room for argument. 'You will bully him. I think he has to be led – forcibly, perhaps, but led nonetheless.'

Two hours later George Walton sat in the estate office as she said: 'It amounts to this: of your eighty acres, you must plough thirty before the end of March. Ten must go down to new grass as a start towards better hay and grazing, and the rest sown to cereals. As soon as the weather improves Robert will walk over the land with you and help you to decide exactly what to grow and where.'

Walton scratched his head and said stubbornly: 'I still don't understand. What difference does it make to anybody else what I grow?'

'It makes a difference to the country,' Diane said patiently. 'It's difficult to get imported food through the U-boat net. We have to grow more at home, on every farm.'

'Then why don't they pay us more?' Walton rumbled, with an

unexpected show of spirit. 'I've spent ten years without two pennies to rub together. Why should I jump to it now, just because the flamin' politicians have got us into a war?'

Diane said: 'Like it or not, we're in a war, and the law's been changed. You can be compelled to do as they say, Mr Walton. They can even throw you off your farm if you don't, and I won't be able to stop them. But I'm sure you don't want to resist this. We need every bit of food we can get. You'll play your part, won't you?'

Walton stared at her, but the rebellion was already fading. He shrugged his rounded shoulders.

'I suppose so. But grass grows itself on this farm, Mrs Haldane. It has to, because I've no cash to pay for fertilisers, so there's only the muck from the cattle. And I don't grow corn because I can't afford to, and no contractor'd come here at harvest without being paid in advance, and that ain't possible. Where'm I going to get the money for all these changes, then?'

She stood up, preparing to leave.

'From the bank, Mr Walton. Banks are being encouraged to lend to farmers. It's a vital part of the war effort. You won't find much trouble getting the cash, I'm sure.' She said it as gently as she could.

Afterwards George Walton showed the ploughing order to his wife who said: 'Borrow from the bank? She must be bloody joking. I don't care what the government says, no bank's going to lend you money. She doesn't know what she's talking about.'

He looked at her and the hurt showed in his eyes, although she was incapable of seeing it. She did not know what it had cost him to admit to his landlord, and a woman at that, that he could pay neither for seed nor fertilisers, let alone harvesting. And if he had told her she would not have understood, for she thought George Walton had long lost the last shreds of pride.

*   *   *

The snows had melted when Pilot Officers Richard Haldane and Nick Telford met in a Lincoln pub, bought pints of beer and toasted each other. Richard had come from Yorkshire where his Hurricane squadron was based, and Nick from one of the bomber stations near Cambridge from which he flew twin-engined Wellingtons. It was their first meeting since the end of their flying training.

'Five ops,' said Nick cheerfully. 'Great fun, old boy. Though on two trips half the bomb bay was full of leaflets telling the Jerries what naughty boys they are and how we're ready to forgive them if they get rid of Hitler and surrender. Who ever thought that lot up should be made to fly out and drop the bloody things.'

'Where've you been?' Richard was clearly envious.

'Hamburg twice. Easy trips – straight in from the sea, hit the docks, then get the hell out again. Bit of flack over the target, but not too hairy. The other three were the Ruhr – Essen and Dusseldorf. God only knows what we hit or where the damned leaflets landed. Couldn't see a thing, old boy. The bomb aimer put up a show of doing things according to the book, but I didn't believe him and he didn't expect me to. Cloud and rain and ice on the wings. Glad to get back, I can tell you. And what are you doing, being a glamorous fighter pilot?'

'Damn all,' Richard said. 'There's no glamour, that's certain. I've applied for a posting to France, but nothing's happened. Stuck up there on the Yorkshire moors, cold as charity, and no action to warm things up. We do a patrol every day, but it's only to stop us getting bored out of our minds. But I have seen one Jerry. That was a funny feeling.'

'Did you get him?' Nick showed excitement.

'No. Junkers 88 – too fast for the Hurricanes. Three of us were scrambled because there was a plot. We flew up and down the coast for half an hour, then we saw him. The flight commander said tally-ho and we went after him. I thought: This is it, Richard. This is what they've been teaching you to do. Shoot the bastard out of the sky before he can do whatever he's been sent to do. Didn't occur to me until later that if we'd got close enough he might have been shooting at me, too. But we didn't get close. He saw us and put his nose down. For a twin-engined job those 88s are quick, I can tell you. But at least I can say I've seen a German aeroplane.' He grinned.

'And what about the social life, old boy?' Nick drank some of his beer. 'Plenty of north-country popsies?'

'Not one.' Richard shook his head in mock despair. 'At least, no one worth a second glance. We had a dance at the station just before Christmas. You should have seen the talent. I was in bed

90

before midnight – and by myself.'

'Still virginal?' Nick raised an eyebrow. He lit a cigarette and passed one to Richard. 'My, you're taking your time, dear lad.'

'I suppose you're going to tell me you're bedding a different wench every night,' Richard said agreeably, 'and expect me to believe it.'

Nick finished his beer, slid the glass towards the barman, and looked pained.

'Would I lie to you, *mon ami*? No, I have to admit things are a bit monkish at the moment. Some nice skirt in Cambridge, but nothing has responded to the old Telford charm. I think I must be saving myself for your beautiful sister. Have some more beer.'

Richard stared.

'Saving yourself for Ruth? What's that supposed to mean?' He nodded to the barman who refilled his glass.

'Just what I say. Shouldn't have told you, I suppose. When are you going to invite me down for a weekend so that I can renew the acquaintance?'

'You can invite yourself.' Richard was studying his companion curiously. 'I'll tell mother you want a break in the country the next time you get a forty-eight. She'll be delighted, whether I'm there or not. But I didn't know you were pining after Ruth.'

'Pining? I'm not sure. Say interested, old boy. Do you mind?'

'Don't be an ass. But why now? You could have shown it earlier, you know.'

Nick sighed and placed his hand over his heart.

'I was smitten from the first moment. D'you remember getting out of that kindergarten aeroplane of yours at Hurn and all but challenging me to a duel? God, I thought you were an arrogant bastard, showing me up in front of a stunning girl like that. You were right, of course – I'd been flying that Gull as if it were a dustbin. But you didn't have to tell me.' He was grinning now at the memory. 'Anyway, by the time I'd finished trying to be civil to you, that execrable swine Kurt had thrown his hat in the ring and she'd picked it up. He was such a smooth, handsome sod I didn't stand a chance then. And even after Austria I didn't know for certain she wasn't still seeing him. But I confess I've never forgotten her.'

'Then you'd better tell her so and see what happens,' Richard said. He studied his cigarette and added: 'I wonder what

91

happened to Kurt.'

'In uniform, old boy. Like all good Germans and Austrians. What else?'

'Yes. I suppose so. What a hell of a change in everything, since that day at Hurn.'

'Does Ruth ever talk about him?'

'No. It's a part of her past she's not very happy about.'

Nick reached for his beer and watched Richard over the rim of the glass.

'Good,' he said. 'I'm glad to hear it.'

12

The spring had gone, and with it the last vestige of what had become known, through the strangely-quiet winter, as the 'phoney war'. The German army was in Norway and the British response had been shattered; Denmark had been occupied with scarcely a shot fired, Holland had crumbled, then Belgium; and German tanks had swept round the corner of the supposedly impregnable Maginot Line of gun emplacements and concrete corridors and had descended upon France with a fury which destroyed resistance. Paris was open to the invaders and the British army was trapped against the coast around the little town of Dunkirk. In the first few days of June 330,000 men were brought back by a rescue armada of private launches, fishing boats, merchant ships and warships; but they came without equipment, their morale was destroyed, and Britain's defences were limited to a navy with ocean-wide responsibilities and an air force short of pilots and aircraft.

Throughout the country a civilian volunteer force was raised. But few had rifles, for there were not enough for the army's needs, and there were no vehicles except for private cars running on a meagre ration of petrol, and bicycles.

There was only fear; and, growing out of it, a desperate determination to fight on with whatever was left.

When thirty men paraded on the school playground at Roxton

they carried broom handles as weapons so that they could be taught the elements of soldiers' drill. Rising Sun landlord Jeffrey Aston was given temporary charge of them, recalling his army days of twenty-five years before, and found the experience depressing.

Down the street in the Moorcocks' village store, joiner Ned Baldock stood at the window, watched the marching men, and said: 'Bloody fools. Broom handles. They'll be a lot o' use when Jerry comes. Lambs to the bloody slaughter.'

'They'll have guns soon, and be taught to use 'em.' Edna Moorcock's voice was tart. 'And what d'you mean – when Jerry comes? He's got to cross the Channel first. And he can't swim it.'

'He's got plenty o' boats,' Baldock growled. 'His own, an' Dutch an' French boats now. The army couldn't stop him in Belgium. Why d'you think it'll be able to stop him when he gets here, then?'

'The navy'll stop him afore he gets here,' John Moorcock declared, but Baldock retorted: 'What about them bloody dive-bombers – Stukas? They'll sink everything we got.'

The door bell rang and all three turned to inspect Sam Salford from Roxton home farm. He hesitated, conscious of their stares, then pushed into the shop.

'Ten Woodbines, John,' he said, nodding towards the tobacco shelves. 'An' I want four dozen three-inch screws – bit o' maintenance at the farm.'

Moorcock reached for the cigarettes, then walked round the counter to a shelf piled high with small cardboard boxes.

'Gettin' difficult to get, screws is,' he said, rummaging. 'But I've got some, somewhere.' He jerked his head towards the window. 'Bin watching 'em marching about, then?'

Salford hitched at the broad leather belt around his strong waist.

'Only for a minute. They're not very good at it yet.'

Baldock sniffed and wiped the back of a hand across his straggling moustache.

'You'll know a lot about marchin', I suppose.'

Salford did not turn round. He watched Moorcock opening boxes as he searched for the right screws. When Baldock repeated the question he said, still without turning: 'Not much. You don't have to know a lot to see they're only learning.'

Moorcock's glance at Baldock was a hard warning. He said: 'Let's hope they get rifles afore long, and enough ammo to practice with. Hitler'd be laughin' fit to bust if he could see'm.'

''Spect you're laughin' too, Sam,' the joiner said provocatively. He pulled a curl of twist from a greasy waistcoat pocket and began to cut a slice with his penknife.

This time Salford turned.

'Not me, Ned. I don't think it's funny.'

Baldock put away the knife and searched for his pipe. Moorcock found the right box of screws and began to count them aloud. Baldock produced his pipe, blew into it, and said: 'Thought you might, you havin' learned marchin' with them Fascist fellers – Mosley an' all.'

Edna Moorcock picked up a cardboard display from the counter and moved it, trying to divert attention to herself. Her husband counted up to forty-eight and began to put the screws into a paper bag. He glared at Baldock who rubbed the twist between his hard hands. The doorlatch rattled and the bell rang, and the vicar came in. Moorcock looked relieved and the Reverend Smallwood beamed in response to his hurried greeting. Salford paid for the screws and the Woodbines, put them into his pocket and moved towards the door.

As he passed the joiner he said: 'I learned a lot. But I've learned a lot more since.'

Baldock jeered: 'Whose side are you on now, then? Where's your black shirt'n trousers –'

The last word exploded in a gasp and his pipe dropped from his mouth as Salford hit him just above the waist, very hard; then stood, threatening, inviting the joiner to retaliate. But Moorcock came round the counter remarkably quickly for a big man, shouldered between them, and shouted: 'Get out – the pair o' ye. There'll be no fightin' in my shop. Go on – out –' He pulled open the door, took the breathless Baldock by the shoulder and bundled him through, then turned back to Salford.

The farm worker stepped out of reach. His eyes were hard and his fists clenched at his sides.

'Don't you touch me, John Moorcock,' he growled. 'I've no quarrel with you, an' don't want one. You ask me to go, an' I will. But keep your hands away.'

Moorcock hesitated.

'All right, then. But you'll have to go.'

Salford nodded. He went through the door without a backward glance. The Reverend Smallwood took off his glasses with a shaking hand.

'Goodness gracious. What was that about?'

Edna Moorcock stared out of the window, trying to catch a glimpse of the two men, and snapped: 'Sam Salford was one o' them blackshirts afore the war. Fascists – like Hitler. Ned was needlin' him about it. I got no sympathy with either of'm. Ned's a defeatist, preachin' gloom an' how Hitler's going to beat us. We'd be better off without both of 'em in the village.'

Outside the joiner clutched his stomach, marched up to Constable Charlie Danson who lived at the local police station, and began to complain. Sam Salford watched him for a moment, then turned up the street and stood outside the school railings as the newly-recruited volunteers struggled to follow Jeffrey Aston's barking commands.

The incident cost the farm worker a ten-shilling fine for common assault, publicity in the local newspaper and a sharp rebuke from Martin Calder to whom he said: 'It's the same everywhere, Mr Calder. People keep on sniping. It's no use telling'm I changed me mind when the war started. No one listens. I just lost me temper.'

Calder said: 'You've got to show them you're patriotic, Sam. They'll not believe you otherwise.'

The following evening Salford went to the Rising Sun and asked Jeffrey Aston if he could join the volunteers. Aston welcomed him and told him to turn out the next Tuesday night. But before then he spoke to police headquarters in Exeter and, when Salford attended, told him stiffly that he could accept no more recruits for the time being. Afterwards he rang Sergeant Bamford who said: 'You did right to mention it to me. We can't have fellers like that getting their hands on guns.' To which Aston responded testily: 'That's an academic observation, Sergeant. None of us can get our hands on guns.'

The next day Sam Salford went into Exeter and volunteered for the army. He was the first Roxton estate worker to do so; the rest were content to accept their occupations as being reserved from military service.

13

Richard had flown into RAF Hanford at three o'clock on a June afternoon in a brand new Spitfire. He was followed down by Steve Mitchell and Philip Fletcher whom he had first met during initial flying training and who had caught up with him on the Hurricane squadron in Yorkshire. The posting south to Sussex had meant unexpected promotion to Flying Officer for him, but he had been well aware as he had circled Hanford that his landing would be under scrutiny from critical ground staff who would have the job of maintaining his aircraft.

Now, coming back across the airfield towards the dispersal area, moving the long nose of the Spitfire from side to side so that he could see ahead, he spotted an empty bay and made for it, watching the ground crew back away as they saw his intention. He brought the machine round with a flourish, one wheel locked and a small cloud of dust rising from the tail, and stopped directly in front of the bay and precisely in the centre. He disconnected his radio-telephone leads, cut the switches, released the straps over his shoulders, picked up his map and extracted himself from the cockpit.

As he swung down on to the wing and dropped to the ground he found himself facing a Flight Sergeant who held a clip board. The man was tall and granite-faced, twenty years older than Richard.

'Afternoon, sir,' he said. He glanced at his clipboard, then at the Spitfire. 'Two-three-two –' checking off the number '– you must be Mr Haldane, sir.'

Richard pushed his helmet off. He was still a little deaf after the flight.

'That's right, Flight. And what's your name?'

'Robbins, sir. Welcome to Hanford.' The hard mouth did not smile. 'That was a neat arrival, sir. Only trouble is – this is the CO's bay. He's airborne, testing his kite after a little trouble we had this morning. He'll be back any minute.' His grey stare encompassed the sky.

Richard eyed him. He knew a rebuke when he heard one; and how to deal with it.

'All right. I'll move it,' he said. He held out his helmet and map. 'Hang on to these. Get me a trolley-acc, sharpish, and show me which bay doesn't belong to the CO.'

Robbins stiffened.

'Not necessary, sir. I'll have it moved.' He swung on his heel and bellowed: 'Atkins – Barber – get this kite over to number six. Fast.' His eyes swept across the field, seeing two more aircraft taxiing in. 'And those two are at the far end. But keep well clear until they've stopped. They don't know our drill.'

The two men scampered from the side of the bay as Richard walked away from his aircraft. Robbins did not follow him, so Richard paused, looking back. Mitchell and Fletcher were close now, and their snarling Merlin engines made normal conversation impossible, so he extended a hand and crooked a finger. For a second Robbins hesitated; then walked across.

Richard raised his voice: 'My kit is following by rail. But there's a small hold-all in the cockpit. Have someone bring it to the flight office, please. And Flight' – Robbins heard steel in the voice and stiffened – 'I'm sure your drill isn't unique. We've probably encountered it somewhere already.'

He walked away. Robbins swung to supervise the handling of the Spitfire and shouted orders to more men as the other aircraft came to a stop. When he turned back he found a corporal beside him.

'New arrivals, Flight?'

Robbins nodded and his grey eyes glinted.

'Yes. Brought their own aircraft, too, which simplifies things.'

The corporal watched Richard's receding figure.

'Wet behind the ears, Flight?'

Robbins looked down at him and, for an instant, the granite mouth widened in the touch of a grin.

'No. Ex-Hurricane squadron up north – 13 Group. Don't know how much action they've seen. But I'll tell you one thing for nothing. That one –' he nodded after Richard '– is a good pilot and a good officer. Don't chance your arm with him. If he lasts long enough we'll know he's here.'

*   *   *

Now four weeks had gone and it was six o'clock on a fine morning in July. Richard lay awake, watching the brightening curtain across the window of the room he shared with Steve Mitchell.

Philip Fletcher had spent the night off the station with his wife.

Mitchell was still asleep; but then he had got through six pints of Fox and Pheasant ale the night before, so Richard thought he was entitled to an extra ten minutes.

Distantly he heard a Merlin start up. The night maintenance shift must have been working on it in one of the big hangars. He pictured the airfield scene, with the mist rising slowly, urged away by the light in the eastern sky; the shapes of aircraft in the dispersal areas gradually forming and becoming solid, though silent yet; the blister hangars where the simpler repair and maintenance jobs had been done. Men would be moving soon, walking or cycling to the flight huts and dispersals, dark forms through the mist, calling and quipping to each other as the sun edged above the horizon.

Another fine day. The German attacks, spasmodic a month ago, were taking on a regular pattern. And they were building up their strength. Yesterday he had flown with the squadron into a formation of forty Dornier bombers and an equal number of escorting Messerschmitt fighters. The second Hanford squadron, using the nearby satellite airfield, had followed them in: twenty-four against eighty. Jerry had lost nine for certain; they had lost four. Three of the pilots had baled out and were back on the station with various minor injuries. Only Larry Allan had bought it. He had gone down a flamer. Richard had seen the Spitfire explode before it hit the ground. He grimaced now as he pushed the bedclothes back. Larry had been one of the veterans of the French campaign with five kills to his credit and then another six on his new squadron; a tough pilot, and ferocious in a scrap. Not now, though.

Richard began to dress. Six kills on the squadron. He had four of his own now. Four in four weeks. Not exactly breaking records. He remembered the first, flying at 25,000 feet over Hampshire as wing man in a vic led by the CO. Squadron Leader Keith Sandham looked after his new pilots and his final words to Richard before take off had been: 'Stick to my tail like glue. And watch your mirror because your life and mine depend on it.'

They had come down out of the sun on to twenty more Dornier bombers and a small fighter escort up above, and he had stuck to Sandham's tail as they had flashed through the formation, seeing the skipper firing at a Dornier and smoke coming from it, getting closer to German aircraft than anything he had imagined up in Yorkshire, sitting hunched in the cockpit with a dry mouth and fast-beating heart, dragging the Spitfire round in a tight turn as he followed his leader. Then Sandham climbed hard and flipped over on his back, and Richard lost him. He went over himself, searching the sky; and suddenly there was a Messerschmitt crossing in front of him, half a mile away.

He pulled round after it, pushing the throttle through the gate, cutting across the radius of the German aircraft's circle. He had been told a Spitfire could out turn a Messerschmitt and now he found it was true, and the range was abruptly down to 400 yards, then 300 and 200, and he was cold and detached and held his fire until the Messerschmitt's wings filled his gunsight. Then he pressed the button in a long six-second burst and the Spitfire shuddered under the recoil of the eight machine guns in the wings and there were pieces coming off the other aircraft and white smoke as it spun away frantically. He went after it, forgetting about his mirror, forgetting about everything except the turning, twisting aircraft in front. It drifted across his sights again and he got in a quick burst of fire, and the white smoke was thicker and there was oil in it, and then a flash of flame and the Messerschmitt went straight down. He rolled so that he could see it, and glimpsed the brilliant orange mushroom as it hit the ground far below.

And all he could think as he regrouped with his squadron confused minutes later was: I killed a man. Oh Christ, I killed a man.

Since then he had killed other men, but he no longer thought about it in those terms. He was shooting down aeroplanes which carried bombs which killed people on the ground, and other aeroplanes sent to protect the bombers. Winston Churchill had said the battle of France was over and the battle of Britain was about to begin. Well, it had begun, and he was part of it, and he hated German aircraft and the men inside them.

He looked down at the snoring Mitchell, jabbed his finger into the man's solar plexus, and said: 'Come on, you lazy sod.' Then he went out of the room to shave.

Philip Fletcher was in the mess for breakfast. Richard thought: What a hell of a life. Last night in bed with your wife, this morning turning up for work, devil's work; and if you're still alive when the sun goes down maybe you go back to her and the warmth of her

99

body and her unvoiced dread. He would stay single while this lot went on.

He winked at Philip as he passed.

'Morning, old mate. Your lady well and sparkling, as ever?'

If Philip had spent the night away with a popsie the question would have been ribald. But it was different when a man was married, even if for only a few months. And Jan was a super girl.

Philip, fair-haired, compact and confident, said: 'Positively blooming. She sent her love to you – although I cautioned her about it.'

'I shall cherish it,' Richard said as he attacked his bacon and egg.

Presently they were joined by a bleary-eyed Mitchell, then the skipper himself. Other pilots and non-flying officers drifted in and out, and the sun was bright yellow beyond the windows, and the Tannoy crackled into them.

'Squadron at readiness. Squadron at readiness.'

They sat for seconds, staring at each other. Then Sandham looked at his watch and said: 'My word, this is an early start. We'd better see what it's all about, gentlemen.' A deceptively calm man, invariably courteous; a natural leader whose battle skills had been forged in the confusion of France and whose fourteen victims and DFC medal ribbon were evidence of it.

They snatched last gulps of coffee and followed their squadron commander through the door.

Outside everyone in sight was running – jogging down the main road towards the airfield, scrambling after pick-up trucks and vans as they swept past, or grabbing bicycles and pedalling furiously. On the airfield engine covers were whipped off, cockpit hoods slid back. Men swung up onto wings, climbed into cockpits; unlocked controls and threw out the locking struts; operated priming pumps to push fuel to the engines, flicked on magneto switches and pulled control columns hard back while other men pushed trolley-accs – portable starter motors – up to the long noses of the Spitfires and plugged in thick black leads. The men in the cockpits pressed the Spitfires' starter-buttons, signalling with their hands as those on the ground pushed the buttons on the trolleys. Propellers moved, gears banged, cylinders fired and blades spun as the aircraft shook themselves awake. In the cockpits several men primed again, and then the engines were alive, one after the other, with great slamming surges of sound and the propellers becoming grey blurs and blue smoke jetting from the exhaust stubs against the cold morning air.

At the controls the aircraftmen set the warm-up revs, watching the dials as the first of the pilots' vans appeared, men dropping off and running into the flight huts. Here and there a machine was tested for mag-drop to ensure that the two sets of plugs were firing correctly: four men used their weight by draping themselves over each of the tailplanes while the fitters in the cockpits opened the throttles to maximum, watching the rev-counters. The noise was hellish.

Then, slowly, it all began to die away. One by one the engines stopped. The pilots, leads of their helmets dangling, walked out of the flight huts. Some crossed to their aircraft, checking, talking to the fitters; others stood in groups, glancing occasionally at the clear morning sky, wondering where the plot was that had sparked all that activity. Somewhere Jerry was airborne. Everything now depended on the targets.

After a while Richard went back to the flight hut, looking for a chair and a newspaper. The coldness which clamped a hand on his stomach whenever the Tannoy sounded had gone, as it always did when he got to his Spitfire. Other pilots joined him. Someone looked for Jane in the *Daily Mirror*, then passed the strip cartoon around; someone else asked for help with a crossword clue. Flight Sergeant Robbins was in the doorway of his office, and Sandham crossed over to check details of overnight maintenance and the repair of two aircraft damaged yesterday; then came back, lighting a cigarette. Twelve months before he had been a non-smoker. Now he got through thirty a day. It happened to them all.

One of the WAAF riggers was watching Richard. He was aware of her, shapeless in her overalls but with neat dark hair and a pretty face. Her name was Mary Barker, and she was never far away when he climbed into his aircraft. On some days she was allocated to it and she held the straps for him and helped him settle in the cockpit. She never spoke out of turn, but her eyes rarely left him, and he did not know how tense she was until he came back.

'Stand by. Squadron stand by,' the Tannoy blared.

The pilots looked at each other. No desperate urgency, probably. Take-off might come in two minutes or twenty. Richard walked to his machine, and it was Mary Barker standing beside it.

101

He said cheerfully, 'Morning,' and she said, 'It looks as if there's a flap on somewhere, sir.'

He climbed into the cockpit and she handed him the straps carefully, pulling them over his shoulders. He locked the straps and plugged in the R/T lead. She leaned across the windscreen and gave it a final polish with a handful of clean cotton waste before closing the door for him. He grinned at her and she said, 'Good luck, sir.' He thought she meant 'Take care,' but she dared not say that. He nodded and said, 'Thanks,' and she dropped off the wing root.

Someone moved a trolley-acc and plugged in the lead. Now there was only the waiting, and that was the worst part.

It went on for ten dragging, gnawing minutes until Flight Sergeant Robbins suddenly darted into view at his office door, waving his arms, and the Tannoy's harshness was lost as the starter-motors turned and the propellers revolved and the engines fired in gushes of savage sound. Chocks were jerked away and the machines began to move, bumping over the grass, turning, riggers hanging on to wingtips to help them round and then watching with eyes screwed up against the blast of the slipstream and ears singing as the sound battered back at them.

Sandham was out in front, his two wingmen taxiing into position on either side. He looked round, checking, then watching the control tower and seeing the green flare and holding up his hand for the others to see before pushing the throttle forward. The squadron went with him, engines bellowing, wheels bumping, tails rising, twelve aircraft snarling across the grass and lifting, wheels retracting, noses skywards, leaving emptiness on the airfield and unbelievable stillness and quiet.

LACW Mary Barker stared at the horizon as if she could still see the aircraft, until a corporal passed her and said, 'Come on, ducks, wake up. We've got a lot to do,' and she nodded distantly.

Robbins went back to his office and said to the engineer officer: 'That's the earliest start-up yet, sir.'

The engineer officer, who had spent twenty minutes in the control tower listening to reports of plots showing the build-up of German formations over the French coast, said: 'It is. But we'll have to get used to it. There are some busy days ahead.' And because he knew what spare parts the stores contained and, more importantly, what they did not, and how long it was taking to get new parts which were needed to keep damaged aircraft flying, he had to fight down the apprehension which lurked somewhere in his chest.

He turned to the window and stared out across the summer sky towards the east where the squadron's twelve pilots were already in visual contact with two other squadrons as they climbed to 25,000 feet and beyond, searching for the vital height advantage over the as yet unseen enemy.

Richard heard his flight commander quip on the R/T: 'Blue leader to Falcon One. Looks like a big party. After all this trouble I hope the guests arrive on time.' Sandham's voice came back: 'Falcon leader to all sections. Don't worry. There'll be plenty of guests. Keep watching out.'

Almost immediately the R/T crackled again, and the controller's voice was crisp and businesslike.

'Control to Falcon leader. Good morning. We have some business for you. Many bandits approaching Worthing. Angels twelve and twenty. Vector one six one. Buster.'

Sandham waggled his wings and the squadron shifted course behind him, throttles wide in response to the 'buster' instruction.

'Falcon leader calling. One six one. Buster.'

Richard shifted his gun-button safety catch and leaned back, forcing himself to relax, feeling the Spitfire rise and fall in the slipstream from the aircraft ahead. Here we go, he thought. See if you can make it five. Or even six.

*   *   *

In the next four weeks he aged four years; or was it more? He saw friends obliterated when their aircraft exploded, heard one scream over the R/T as he fought to get out of a flaming cockpit and failed, brought his own Spitfire back to base again and again with bullet holes stitched in lines across wings and tail. Once, after a cannon shell had exploded somewhere behind his seat and left him with hardly any controls at all, he came into land, yawing badly, undercarriage legs jammed up inside the wings, but fortunately still with usable flaps. The Spitfire went down on its belly, skidded for over a hundred yards across the turf, propeller buckled, air intake crushed underneath, pieces flying off. His shoulders were battered by the straps which held him to his seat, fumes rose around him from the smitten engine, acrid and choking, until suddenly all was still and it was a stillness he could hear as he sat in the cockpit trying to drag his mind to recognise that he was still alive, and hearing men outside as they clambered up to him. 'Are you all right?' Then, 'Come on, sir – get out – she could still go up.' Hands reached for him and he heaved himself up and out of the cockpit, down on to the wing. Then his feet were on the ground and his knees gave way and he was face down on the grass, for no reason he could understand; for in the crisis and fear of the landing he had forgotten the shell splinter in his right leg and the blood soaking into his trousers and the pain.

He had survived it, and much more, and was still flying; and from that very day as a flight commander, for Alan Drummond who had travelled across the world from Australia for what he had described as 'the shooting season', and under whom Richard had flown all the time he had been with the squadron, had gone down in a great air battle that morning and, still in what was left of his Spitfire, was buried twenty or more feet down in a Hampshire field. Richard assumed his mantle.

The first thing he did was say to Sandham: 'I want to talk about tactics, skipper. I think we ought to fly in units of four instead of vic-threes. We're too rigid. Too exposed.'

And Sandham had said: 'All right. Other squadrons are thinking the same way. We'll talk tonight.'

And so he had taken off again, leading Philip Fletcher on his port wing and a new pilot, fresh in only three days from training, on the other side, and wishing he had a fourth man to weave across the tails of all three so that they could concentrate on the attack without worrying about being picked off from behind.

Half an hour later he took his small formation up in a tight climbing turn to get above a group of escorting Messerschmitts, leaving the bombers to a Hurricane squadron down below. As he did so they began to break, for they had seen him, and he kicked the rudder and pushed the throttle through the gate and hurtled in amongst the enemy, selecting a target as it pulled up hard in front, firing a quick burst, seeing Philip at the edge of his vision and his guns firing too –

'Blue leader – behind you – break – break –'

He thought it was Sandham's voice but could not be sure. He went wing over, then stick back, searching his mirror, finding nothing, turning his head frantically, and seeing pieces flying off Philip's aircraft close in on his left, crazy tumbling pieces as the world spun beneath him and then above him, and a great flash as the Spitfire alongside blew up.

He heard his voice: 'Oh no, please God, not Phil.' But it was Phil, and the pieces were dropping lazily from the swelling mushroom of smoke as the flame died and there was nothing left inside the mushroom.

His discipline came back and he searched for the new pilot who had been on his starboard wing and found him turning, rocking, not knowing which way to go, and closed on him and called him up and led him back into the cauldron. But all the time a corner of his mind said if only I'd had a fourth man, another wing man to keep his eyes skinned for the bounce. . .

When they landed he walked stiffly away from the Spitfire, ignoring Mary's 'Not a scratch today, sir. Good show' and leaving her staring after him, her eyes hurt just for a moment, as he stalked to the flight office and waited for Sandham to land.

He said in a flat, calm voice: 'Fletcher's bought it, skipper. Blew up. We were bounced.'

'I know,' Sandham said. 'There were two of them, like hawks. I saw them.'

Richard remembered the warning shout. He said, in the same calm voice: 'I'm the one who has to tell her. As soon as we've finished for the day. Okay?'

A nod. 'Yes. If you want to. It isn't an easy thing to do.'

'I know,' he said. 'But it has to be me.'

Later he reached the small hotel near Hanford where Phil and Jan Fletcher had taken a room at a rate which left the owner no profit at all, and climbed the stairs. At the door he hesitated, just for a moment; then knocked.

When she opened the door she stared at him, and his carefully prepared words deserted him as he saw the dawning in her eyes, for there could be only one reason why a silent, grey-faced Richard would call on her at that time of day. She was petite and dark with big expressive eyes and a small nose, and he saw her begin to shake her head as if the gesture would ward off the inevitable.

Then she whispered, 'Phil. Oh, Phil,' and he put out his arms to her and she came to him, her head against his shoulder. He felt a quiver run through her but for a time she made no sound.

It was the worst moment of his war.

* * *

But now he was a Flight Lieutenant who had shot down twelve enemy aircraft and damaged many more and Sandham told him he had been recommended for a DFC. So when Jan Fletcher had been taken away by her parents to grieve in the small Warwickshire village which had been her home before Phil had come along, he turned the page of his memory, as they all did, and started again with the few old friends who were left and the new ones who came in, almost day by day, to take their places.

So he was at least as interested as the rest when a notice went up in the mess announcing that a repertory theatre company currently playing in Southampton prior – war exigencies permitting – to a short London season had been invited to visit Hanford where they would perform extracts from three plays. And it was also decreed that, afterwards, officers would host the players for drinks and supper.

It was the popular consensus that the weather on the day could not have been better: thick, low cloud blanketed the southern quarter of England and much of northern France. The Luftwaffe could have taken off; but navigators could not have found their targets, nor their bases afterwards, so they stayed at home. For the defenders the respite was desperately needed, and at Hanford the approach to the evening's entertainment the more leisurely in consequence.

The station theatre was crowded when the visitors began their performance with the last act from a Coward play, followed by an extract from a Priestley comedy and, finally, two acts from *The Merchant of Venice*.

Richard enjoyed the Coward, not least for a tiny gem of a supporting role by a tawny-haired actress whose compelling eyes and fine, slender features sent him searching through the programme the moment the play was over. He found her name: Elizabeth Kent. He thought: I'll see her at the party afterwards. And the prospect was disturbing as well as exciting.

He was disappointed when she did not appear in the Priestley, but sat tensely in his seat as the show ended with the final acts of

The Merchant of Venice, for he had already noted that she was Portia. He loved Shakespeare, but now was impatient for the ending of the play, scarcely hearing the other players, concentrating on the face, the voice and the easy movements of the girl with the gold-flecked hair. He wished that, just for a moment, she would look across the footlights at him instead of always at Shylock, Antonio and Bassanio; then scoffed at the thought, telling himself that she was probably the producer's wife – or the mistress of half the male company. Weren't actresses like that? Anyway, she would be fun to meet.

The cast and their two producers came into the mess and were greeted formally by the Group Captain; eight men and seven women who, after their reception by the senior officers, dispersed slowly across the big room, from one group to another. And here Richard knew was his dangerous moment, for as a mere Flight Lieutenant he would not be expected to interrupt if the lady who was his target was in conversation with anyone of senior rank.

. He watched her as she came closer, and marvelled. Her hair, which was indeed touched with lights sometimes gold and sometimes shining bronze, held a hint of indiscipline in the way it fell across her forehead and on to her collar. It was not untidy; yet it was careless, as if she trusted it to form its own patterns and was content to permit it some eccentricity. Her eyes were wide-set and large and serious, yet with a hint of humour lurking; and her mouth was wide too, expressive and confident like her jaw, balancing cheekbones which were high and clearly formed. If he had expected glamour and formality in her dress he would have been disappointed, for she wore a check open-necked shirt under a comfortable fine cord jacket and above a slender-fitting skirt which graced her movements through the crowded uniforms. He was breathless; then was annoyed that he should allow himself to be so impressed, so captivated. A voice in his mind said she's an actress, not a goddess; yet he knew that, whatever the label, she was in his eyes the most exciting woman he had ever seen. And another voice said you'll get one chance, one second of a chance, and if you don't nail her then she'll be gone because half the men in this room want her.

She and the company's leading actor, a grey-haired fifty-year-old who had played an extravagant, compelling Shylock to her Portia, were under the escort of a Wing Commander who caught

Richard's eyes, turned them towards him in the crowd, and said: 'Come and meet Flight Lieutenant Haldane, who has just been made a Flight Commander and will shortly be wearing the ribbon of the DFC. Michael Peters and Elizabeth Kent.'

He shook hands with Peters first, finding the grip firm and cordial. Then he turned to the girl, and her eyes were hazel and flecked with golden lights like her hair and were clear and questioning, and he took a long breath and said softly, 'Oh upright judge; oh learned judge,' and bowed.

The Wing Commander raised his eyebrows; Michael Peters tilted his head curiously; and Elizabeth Kent held on to his dark gaze and responded quickly: 'Thyself shalt see the act; for as thou urgest justice, be assured thou shalt have justice, more than thou desir'st.' And Richard came back instantly: 'Oh learned judge.' He swung, pointing at Peters. 'Mark, Jew: a learned judge!'

Then she laughed; not at him, but with him, and with Peters and, finally, with the Wing Commander who joined in the amusement because he felt it was courteous to do so.

The others were still laughing when she said, just loudly enough for his ears and no others: 'At least I know somebody stayed awake right through the show.'

'Awake?' he murmured. 'No – electrified. And now I shall be devastated if you leave without telling me the story of your life.'

The Wing Commander intervened, sensing something of the exchange even if he had not heard it fully above the conversations around them.

'I didn't know you were so accomplished,' he said to Richard patronisingly; then to his guests: 'There are still a lot of people to meet –'

His hand reached for Elizabeth Kent's elbow as if to guide her away but she turned, avoiding the touch.

'I'm sure you won't think I am rude if I say that just for a few minutes I'd rather stay right here,' she said, in a voice which gave little room for argument. 'I've met a lot of people already, and it's been a tiring evening.' She turned to Peters. 'You go on, Michael: you're better at it than I am, anyway.'

She bestowed her warmest smile on the startled Wing Commander, who forced a shrug as Peters nodded.

'All right, darling. You stay and talk to your new Gratiano.' And to the Wing Commander: 'Now do me a favour, dear chap –

introduce me to one or two of your delightful lady officers.'

Then the crowd moved, and Peters and the Wing Commander were gone, and he was staring at her in wordless surprise as she said: 'I had to get rid of him, the pompous idiot.' She glanced around. 'Your Wing Commander, I mean.' She mimicked, 'I didn't know you were so accomplished,' then laughed into his eyes. 'I can't stand sarcasm. It must be dreadfully hard for men like you to put up with men like him.' She touched his sleeve and moved closer to him. 'Talk intimately to me. We're about to be interrupted, unless you put up a convincing performance.'

He suddenly realised how tall she was: only a couple of inches less than his own six feet. He stood facing her; and then reached for her hands and held them both. She came closer still.

'I'm not very practised at intimate conversations, Miss Kent,' he said softly. 'But if I keep talking like this do you think people will imagine we're old friends having a glad reunion?'

'Old friends – or even old lovers.' Her fingers squeezed his and she kissed him quickly on the nose, her eyes searching his face. 'And I think the danger has just walked past.' She freed her hands with some difficulty, laughing at him again. 'Don't make a meal of it. I need a drink more than anything else at this moment. Can you get one?'

He shook his head, not moving away from her.

'If I go to the bar you will be submerged immediately beneath a struggling male mass and I shall never see you again. I can't allow that – you haven't even started to tell me the story of your life. So we'll have to wait until we catch a steward's eye.'

Across the room he saw an empty chair, and suddenly took her elbow, threaded her through the crowd, sat her firmly in the chair and perched on one arm in a position which effectively shielded her from all but the most determined intruder.

She looked up at him, appreciating his strategy, and said: 'Full marks for initiative, Flight Lieutenant.'

'Richard,' he said; and added, 'please: it's so much easier to say.' He stuck out an arm suddenly, catching a steward's sleeve, and turned to her.

'A John Collins, I think,' she said, then added mischievously, 'Richard. You could never have played the Third. You're not quite wicked enough. But dangerous, I think. May I have a sandwich, too?'

109

He nodded to the steward, then said to her: 'Chapter One of the life story first. Where do you come from – Elizabeth?'

'The South West,' she said. 'I'm a Devonian.'

He stared down at her.

'And where from in Devonshire?'

'Newton Abbot. My father's a doctor there. Have you ever heard of Newton Abbot?'

'Yes. Have you ever heard of Roxton?'

She brushed a lock of hair away from her forehead.

'I've heard of it. It's a village near Exeter, somewhere. Why?'

'I live there,' he said; and suddenly they were laughing together, saying what a coincidence it was, and did he know this place, and did she know that, and how long was it since they had been at home, and how the war had changed things. The steward came back and he took a plate of sandwiches and gave it to her, and held her drink for her while settling his own pint of beer on the floor at her feet. She asked him about people around the room and he bent his head close to hers so that he could tell her things he might not have wanted others to hear, and her eyes held on to his and he knew now there was a waiting and a watching there, and that she was looking for his own waiting and watching, and seeing it.

As soon as he could he said: 'You don't wear a ring. Does that really mean you're not married.'

'It does.' She was amused by the directness of his question. 'And you?'

'No. But what about Michael Peters? He called you darling. Are you his lady?'

She took her drink from his hand, looked down at it, and murmured: 'You really shouldn't ask questions like that.' Then she saw the disappointment shadow his face, and relented quickly. 'Don't be silly. Everybody calls everybody else darling in the theatre. Of course I'm not his lady. Nor anyone else's at the moment.'

He laughed at himself then.

'Sorry. I asked for that. How long have you been acting?'

'Four hard years. Though how long it will go on, now, I don't know. I'll probably finish up joining something. And what were you before you were caught up in all this?'

'Foreign correspondent for newspapers and magazines. Thumbing it around Europe – very precarious way to earn a living. Though probably not as precarious as the present one.' He grinned, then checked. 'I'm sorry. It was meant to be a joke.'

She said: 'Yes. I understand. How long have you been at Hanford?'

'A couple of lifetimes. About eight weeks, actually. When will you have your next night off?'

'My next –? Oh, Sunday, I suppose.'

'That's no good. I can't buy you dinner on a Sunday. There's nowhere open these days.'

'You could buy me a drink,' she said, and he put a cigarette packet on her knee, gave her a pencil, and said: 'Write down your 'phone number for me.'

She did so, observing: 'It's only until next week. Then we go to Reading. After that, unless the backers change their minds, it will be London.'

'Richard, you cunning old devil – introduce me to the beautiful lady.' It was Steve Mitchell, two other pilots at his side, grinning down at them as he pushed between people, manoeuvring so that he could inspect Elizabeth.

'Go away,' Richard said. 'You're interrupting a very private conversation. And the lady doesn't want to know you.'

She looked up at their enthusiastic faces and could not resist them. 'Oh, come on, Richard. I'll have to endure it some time. Tell me who they are.'

'All right.' He stood up. 'Meet Ken and Johnny. And he –' he gestured with his pint glass towards Steve '– he's the one who snores.'

'The one who – what?' She dissolved into laughter. 'I can't call him that. What's his name?'

'Steve. And he does snore. I share a room with him. You should hear the way he snores – no, on second thoughts you shouldn't. Just take my word for it.'

They fell into rapid-fire banter and she shared it; and they loved her for it, crowding round her as they were joined by others. It went on for half-an-hour as she became the focus of attention for a dozen men, not one of whom troubled to conceal his admiration, all of whom vied for her personal attention. Yet throughout Richard felt not a quiver of unease, for every two or three minutes her eyes flickered across to his and spoke silent words as if they

111

had been friends for a long time and had a special understanding. So when it was time to go, it was the most natural thing in the world that somehow she should be beside him again. Her arm slipped through his, and Mitchell and the others saw it and took just that one step away which signified their recognition, even though they all escorted her to the door and out into the night.

A coach was waiting for the visitors and as farewells were called they climbed aboard. But she held back in the crowd, and his hand found hers as he said: 'I'll ring you, Elizabeth.' He did not have to ask if she would see him again. 'And thanks. I've enjoyed every moment.'

Her eyes were on his in the dark and among the people as she said close to his ear: 'My very private friends call me Lisa.' She pronounced it Leesa. He thought it was a magic sound, and kept close to her.

'It's beautiful. Good night, Lisa.'

Their fingers drifted apart, reluctantly. She went to the coach, and Steve Mitchell cheered her and others joined in as she waved and disappeared into the dark interior.

Later that night, as Steve fell into his habitual snoring sleep, Richard lay on his narrow bed and remembered her voice. He was irritated that he could not now recall every line of her face and every fleck of her eyes. But her voice was clear in his mind, and the way she said 'Lisa', and he knew that if he never saw her again he would remember it for ever.

And in her small room in the private hotel where the company was staying she lay awake, and her eyes traced patterns on the ceiling and every pattern made some part of his face; and she knew that whatever happened in the future, after tonight her life could never be the same again.

*　　*　　*

The next day the low cloud had gone and the Germans changed their tactics and began to attack the RAF's airfields. Richard flew in the morning, but the squadron failed to achieve the interception intended by control and they landed later, frustrated, and sat on the grass close to the aircraft, waiting for the next alarm. A NAAFI van came round and they bought sandwiches and tea and listened to the one o'clock news. The high cumulus clouds left

112

over from the previous day dispersed and the sun was hot. Some of the ground crew played desultory football, and the pilots read and dozed. Then, at three o'clock the field telephone rang, someone picked it up, yelled 'Scramble – squadron scramble!' and everyone was running.

Before the first Spitfire engine had started they heard the sirens from the nearby town and were startled. This was new. Then the shattering thunder of the Merlins drowned out everything else and no one on the airfield heard the tannoy bellow: 'All personnel not directly concerned with flying operations and anti-aircraft defence take cover. Repeat, take cover.'

The Spitfires moved away, jockeying for take-off positions, swinging in small clouds of dust and smoke as the green went and they were away across the airfield, three on three on three on three, airborne, wheels tucking away, climbing, turning together, reforming into three groups of four, the din of their departure receding until the ground staff began to hear the Tannoy again, and Flight Sergeant Robbins cupped his hands and shouted: 'Well, don't just stand there. That means you – the lot of you – at the double.'

Ten miles away the squadron turned to meet a group of fast Junkers 88 bombers flying low after finding a way round the Portsmouth anti-aircraft guns, but Sandham saw the high escorting Messerschmitts poised and the bombers got through as the fighters hurled themselves at each other, vapour trails coiling across the sky.

In ten minutes three of the defenders and five of the Messerschmitts had gone down and the fighting had spread across miles of sky, so that by the time the order was given to return they had been away nearly an hour.

With a leaking glycol tank and a coughing engine, Richard was one of the last to sight Hanford, and the columns of smoke rising from the remains of a hangar and from the brick and wooden buildings of the camp itself. Ahead he saw a Spitfire landing close to the boundary hedge and realised that the airfield itself was gouged, with great holes where there had been unbroken grass tracts. His engine was over-heating badly and he came straight in, following the previous aircraft's line, listening to the Merlin's distress, thankfully feeling the wheels jar as he touched down, his head on one side as he looked past the oil-covered windscreen,

113

slowing on the brakes, cutting the switches as the fumes rose in the cockpit.

It was not until he had left the aircraft that he realised the full extent of the damage; and somehow it brought the war closer to him than ever. Until that moment the fighting and the fear and the death had been in the air; a mile, three miles, five miles high. Now it was at Hanford, and bodies were lying on the grass and on the concrete roads, and buildings were twisted and smashed and smoke stung his eyes as he saw the rescue workers with desperate blackened faces, and it hurt terribly because Hanford had been home and somehow a refuge at the end of each savage day.

It hurt him even more when he found that the mess had been destroyed, for that was where he had met Lisa, and part of his memory of her seemed to lie in the smoking wreckage.

*   *   *

Early the following Sunday night he walked into the bar of a Winchester hotel, just six hours after baling out of his wrecked aircraft. He had been attacked by two Messerschmitts, and as he had twisted and turned frantically in response to their combined fire, and had felt the cannon shells and machine gun bullets strike the Spitfire, his mind had pleaded: Don't let me die now – I can't die now – I have to see her tonight –

Then flame had licked back from the engine and he had rolled the shattered aircraft, heaved back the hood, and struggled clear of the straps and the cockpit. As he did so one of the Messerschmitts had flashed by close to him, and he had straightened his body and spread his arms and legs to balance himself and had fallen ten thousand feet before opening his parachute, for he was terrified of being machine-gunned while hanging in the harness. And as he had plunged downwards his racing mind had repeated her name, over and over, until he had judged it safe to pull the handle which opened the 'chute.

He had been lucky, landing in an open field in a standing corn crop which had cushioned his fall a little, and finding farm workers running towards him. Within half-an-hour he had been able to telephone Hanford, and an hour after that a van had been driven out to pick him up.

114

Now he looked at Lisa coming to meet him across the hotel lounge and thought how strange, how unbelievable, was the transition in such short time from all that fear and confusion and mortal danger to the calm of her hazel eyes and the pleasure in her voice as she said: 'Richard – I'm so glad to see you again.'

He let an hour go by before he told her about baling out, and then wished he had not mentioned it when he saw distress tighten her face. He rushed the conversation on to other things and she let it go; but, he knew, she did not forget.

That moment apart, it was the most relaxed, comfortable, heart-warming evening he could remember. They talked and laughed and whispered confidences, and were serious and careless and serious again, and he knew she loved every minute of it just as he did, and it was as if they had known each other for a year.

But it had to end. She had to catch the last train back to Southampton, for he had too little petrol to take her there in his old Ford saloon and then get back to Hanford afterwards; so at ten o'clock they stood on the railway station platform with a train grinding and hissing to a standstill beside them and the smell of smoke in the air. Carriage doors banged and feet scraped and scrambled and voices called; and suddenly he kissed her on the mouth, not passionately, not urgently, but with total ease and familiarity as if they had all the time in the world for that kiss and all the others they knew were to come.

She pressed her cheek against his and whispered: 'You're very special to me. Take care, if you can.' Her hands found his and they held on to each other for seconds before she turned and climbed into a carriage and the train took her away in a confusion of noise and steam and rhythm.

*   *   *

Two weeks later he made three telephone calls from the temporary mess at Hanford. To his mother he said: 'I'm coming home on a spot of leave, so dust the bedroom.' To Nick Telford he said: 'You've finished your tour? Great – let's get together with the girls.' And to Lisa: 'I haven't had to do anything to fix it. Events have done that for me. But I want your undivided attention for two weeks.'

Then he went to help Sandham pack up the affairs of what was left of the squadron, for now only four of them were survivors and the RAF had decided there was no point in sending in any more replacements; it was better to pull them out of the battle and post in a new squadron to take over.

Their kit was despatched by road, and in the early afternoon they walked out to dispersal. The Group Captain and the Wing Commander were there; and others, too, including Flight Sergeant Robbins and many of the men and women who had kept their patched aircraft flying through the desperate weeks. They stood in an informal group, and the Station Commander shook each of them by the hand: Sandham; then Richard, for he was next in seniority among those who were left; then Steve Mitchell and the young pilot named Ken whom Lisa had met when she had visited Hanford.

All the others were either dead, or in hospital.

Robbins spoke to them, his grey face still hard but his eyes quiet. Some of the others among the ground crew exchanged a word as well; yet others stood back, for the aircraft they had serviced and the men who had flown them were not there.

Then the trolley-accs were wheeled up and Richard found LACW Mary Barker waiting on the wing of his aircraft.

She said: 'I'm sorry we shan't see you again, sir.'

'Don't bet on it.' He grinned at her. 'Bad pennies keep turning up.'

He climbed into the cockpit, taking the harness straps from her, saying, 'Thanks,' and feeling slightly awkward because of the way she looked at him.

'Do you think they might send you back here, sir?'

'Got a feeling about it,' he nodded. 'When we've been reformed, I know the CO will want to bring us back if he gets a chance.'

She stepped away, calling: 'I hope so. Good luck, sir.' Then she slid down off the wing, and he checked his watch. Three minutes before scheduled take-off. Not bad. They had to get clear before the new squadron came in. It was going to be a copy-book hand-over.

He saw Sandham raise a hand, signalled to the riggers and pressed the starter button. Then he was opening the throttle and the four Spitfires moved together, clear of the blast pens, clear of the flight huts, clear of the watchers, turning out with Sandham up in front. The green went from the control tower and the throttles were pushed wide and they were away in the dust and blue exhaust haze and the bellowing snarl of the Merlins, across the grass and lifting, climbing against the sky. Then Sandham took them round in a tight turn and brought them back, close and in perfect formation, low across the airfield, rocking his wings in a final gesture; and the Group Captain saluted.

After that there was the empty silence as the spectators turned away; until Robbins, conscious of the Station Commander's presence, twisted round towards the ground crew and shouted: 'Right. That's your fun for today. You've got thirty minutes to get this place looking like a show case. At the double, now.'

*   *   *

Three days after that Richard caught a train south to London, met Lisa on Euston station, and together they went to Berkhamsted and Nick Telford's home. Lisa had had no trouble getting away, for the Blitz on London was now beginning in earnest and the backers had withdrawn support for her play. She was, in the language of the theatre, 'resting', and for once did not complain, for there was the prospect ahead of two unbroken weeks with Richard.

Nick, after completing the recognised tour of thirty bombing operations, had already been at home for a couple of days and had slept away most of them. Now he showed no sign of lingering tension, and in his company Richard quickly felt the strain and the fear and the tragedies of his days at Hanford begin to lift from him.

Then they were on the train again, the three of them, heading down to Exeter; and it was Ruth who met them on the platform, and Richard grinned with pleasure when he saw the way she and Nick greeted one another, for he knew Nick had been visiting Roxton during the summer, and why.

They dined together that night, with Robert and Diane; and Richard was delighted with their reception of Lisa and the way she slipped so easily into their company. She and Robert swiftly became good companions, for despite their temperamental differences the twins remained mirrors of each other, and Lisa enjoyed the novelty of having two almost-identical men at her side.

But, secretly, Diane was concerned as she detected Robert's growing reserve and knew he sensed the gulf between himself and the others. They were couples, close and becoming closer; the men leading dangerous lives, Richard with a medal for gallantry and an exquisitely attractive girl, Ruth hand-in-hand with her flamboyant bomber pilot. Diane saw Robert glance at them sometimes; and read in his eyes a hint of disappointment in himself.

Finally she spoke to Richard about it.

'It's not just that he's by himself and you and Ruth are not; it's the basic difference between himself and you, his twin. He's a civilian while you're away in uniform. And you've become a glamorous figure in some people's eyes: a pilot with a medal. I think he feels inferior. And yet there's nothing he can do about it. The authorities wouldn't accept him if he tried to join one of the services. He's registered, but they've just ignored him.'

'And quite right,' said Richard. 'What he's doing here is far more important than anything he could do in uniform. He should be satisfied with that.'

Afterwards, though, he made an effort to include Robert when he and Nick went out with the girls; yet just as often Robert excused himself. He was running the estate with infinite enthusiasm and energy, and also spent two evenings a week on rifle and grenade practice with the Local Defence Volunteers whose organisation had just been renamed by Churchill as the Home Guard – and had been given arms. Like everyone else, Robert took the threat of invasion seriously, and his awareness was heightened when he learned that Richard and Nick had to make daily telephone checks back to their stations and were prepared to return at a moment's notice.

But Nick treated it all as a joke, and Richard did not refer to the war at all if he could help it. With Lisa and Ruth they were out every day, walking on Dartmoor, leaning on railings and looking at barbed wire-strewn beaches, haunting a handful of favourite pubs, laughing and living every minute.

One night they went to a dinner-dance at a Torquay hotel where there were now a good number of permanent residents for whom the place had become a luxury refuge from the realities of war. Lisa, like many actresses, was also a trained dancer, and knew the steps of the latest American jive dancing which had scarcely been seen yet in Britain. So when the four-piece band began a fast Benny Goodman jazz number she said to Richard: 'Come on – let's wake this lot up. Let me show you something new.'

She did: and the sight gradually cleared the floor until they, with Nick and Ruth and another uniformed couple, were the only ones left. She whirled round him, skirts spreading, eyes shining; leaning back at arm's length, using his hand as a pivot, going through a routine of excitement which communicated to Richard as he became her foil and her balance. She turned beneath his arm, behind his back, fingers locked then hands changing as she circled and spun to face him again, her feet moving in fast rhythmic patterns; and the band responded, hammering out the tempo, driving the riffs, extending the number until exhaustion brought it to an end and they collapsed into their chairs, laughing as much at the astonishment of the other diners as at their own pleasure.

But at other times they were quiet and private, walking across the home farm or sitting in separate rooms in the house, whispering their dreams, touching and teaching each other; and Robert kept tactfully away, working in his study, leaving them to their new companionships and their secrets.

It was during such an evening, when there were only two nights left before it all had to end, that Nick and Ruth came into the drawing room where Richard and Lisa sat in the half-dark, her head against his shoulder, her legs drawn up close to him on the settee.

Nick said: 'Are we disturbing you two?'

Lisa turned, sleepily, to look at them.

'No. Come in.'

He crossed to a cupboard, poured drinks, and handed out the glasses. Ruth settled in an armchair and Nick perched beside her.

'It's all over on Thursday,' he said.

'It had occurred to us,' Richard said quietly.

'For the last night,' Nick said, 'we're going up to a little hotel I know near Lincoln. It's only ten miles from my station – and only about twenty from your new base, Richard. Do you two want to join us?'

Richard and Lisa exchanged glances. He saw the answer in her eyes and nodded.

'Sure. Why not?'

In the dimness Nick glanced across at Ruth. She was concentrating on her glass. He hesitated, watching her; but she did not look at him.

He said: 'There's just one thing, old boy. We might as well tell you now.' He took a long breath, then rushed on: 'We've come to – an agreement. We're booking a double room.'

Richard's fingers moved through Lisa's hair. He could feel her warmth against him.

'Good for you,' he said easily. 'I hope the walls are sound-proof.'

Ruth laughed; a small, embarrassed sound. Nick said: 'Absolutely so, old lad. Place is built like a fortress. Couple of hundred years old. Stone everywhere. Could have an orgy there, and no one'd know.'

'Just as well,' Richard said. But Ruth interrupted: 'Does it make any difference? Do you still want to come?'

He looked down at Lisa and kissed her on the forehead.

'I expect so. We'll let you know.'

Ruth said, with sudden candour: 'I hope you come with us. We could make it a party – book rooms next to each other.' She laughed quickly, looking at Richard, wanting his approval.

'We'll talk about it,' Richard said. Then he grinned. 'But whatever we do, I'll give you a toast.' He stood up, brandishing his glass. 'Here's to a sleepless night and an easy conscience in the morning.'

They all laughed then, and he detected relief in Ruth's voice as they responded to him, and in her eyes when she saw his hint of a private wink. Then he glanced at Nick and said, 'Happy landings, old mate,' and turned away suddenly because at the edge of his vision there was a great mushroom of oily smoke and an aircraft was destroyed in the flame at its heart and he saw Phil Fletcher's fair hair and handsome face until it all disintegrated and there was Jan in the doorway of her room; and he drank quickly, fighting down the image and the shock, seeing Nick and Ruth hugging each other, then Lisa close to him and her big eyes reading his and the sudden anxiety in them. She did not know what he had seen, but she had glimpsed his fear in the fading daylight, and now she reached for him, her face against his, trying to protect him from it, trying to wipe it away. Nick and Ruth were laughing, raising glasses, oblivious of everything except each other, and Lisa

120

whispered: 'Richard – my love – what is it?'

He held her close and whispered back: 'Nothing now. Nothing. It's gone. You sent it away.' Her hair was across his face and his fingers held it there, and his mind said Oh God, was that me, or was it Nick, because it was one of us, and Phil came back to tell me. He reached for Lisa's hand and said: 'Come on, let's walk round the garden before supper.' And to Nick: 'Don't get too involved. We'll be back.'

Outside they crossed the carriage drive and went through the little gate which led into the walled garden beside the house. The air was still warm after the day. They walked right to the end of the garden before she stopped and faced him, holding his hands tightly.

'Tell me. Please. What happened?'

He said: 'I saw a ghost. It happens now and then, to people like me and Nick and the others. It just appeared at the wrong moment, that's all. It's difficult not to – remember things, occasionally. I'm sorry. I hope I didn't spoil it for Ruth and Nick.'

'No. They didn't see. But I did.'

He slid his arm around her shoulders, pulling her close.

'You know me better than I know myself.' He put his face against her hair so that she could not see into his eyes, and was quiet for seconds until he whispered: 'Never leave me, Lisa.'

She turned quickly away from him, pressing her back against his chest, her face hidden from him.

'You would have to send me away.' Her voice was a breath against the night air, and he heard it catch in her throat. 'Please don't ever do that.'

He slid his arms beneath hers, around her, and his hands cupped her breasts. They were small and firm and he felt a shiver run through her, and knew she was crying. She put her head back against his shoulder, and he said softly, 'Send you away? Could I send away my reason for living?' And there were tears stinging his own eyes, for he had seen a ghost and he did not want to go with it, now that he had found her.

She twisted suddenly to face him, and her mouth sought his; and then wonderingly, her fingers felt his face, and she said, 'Oh, my love; we are part of each other, aren't we?' Then she clung to him fiercely and whispered: 'Don't let's go with them. Take me somewhere else. It will be the most private, the most precious thing we shall ever do. I don't want to laugh about it and tell jokes. I want it to be the most secret thing, that first time, so that there are only the two of us in the world.'

And he thought: Please God, let it last a little while; and then all in the same moment, a terrible urgency gripped him, and whatever was left for him had to be achieved and enjoyed and treasured while there were still senses to record it and memory to keep it, and he took her face between his hands and whispered: 'I will take you to a secret place. No one will know where we are or why we have gone, and afterwards we'll never tell and it will always be our private place, our first time place. But I will do it only if you make me a promise.'

A trick of the evening sky turned his eyes into dark mirrors, magnet mirrors which drew her, captured her; and she breathed: 'You know I will.'

His fingers caressed her hair. 'Promise yourself. If I live long enough, promise that you will be my wife and I may be your husband for all our lives. But try to understand that I can't do it yet. Men who go to war should not take wives, my love. Will you take me, and be my own; and yet wait for me?'

She raised her hands and covered his, holding them against her face, her eyes searching.

'Darling – why? In six weeks you have changed my life. I would marry you now, tonight. Or wait for you for ever. But why, why must we wait?'

He looked at her, and for an instant her face was Jan's and he closed his eyes to shut out the change and whispered: 'Please be patient with me. I just don't believe it's right, when so much can be destroyed, so quickly. But never doubt me. Please promise you never will.'

Still she searched his face, struggling to understand, wanting his contentment as well as her own; then, so gently, kissed him and said: 'I promise that; and that I am yours and that nothing, neither time nor place nor life itself, will change that.'

* * *

The next morning Ruth and Nick started on their journey to Lincoln, and Richard and Lisa travelled with them as far as Hanford where Richard had left his car when he had flown out with the remnants of his squadron. Before their departure they stood in the big hall of the house, and Robert said: 'Lisa, come to Roxton to see Ruth and me any time you feel like it. We'll keep a room with your name on the door.' And to Nick: 'I don't have to invite you back – Ruth will look after that. Take care. I'll just keep the old business going.'

Then they were gone, the four of them in Nick's old Alvis, travelling together to Hanford where Richard and Lisa got out at the gates of the RAF station.

'Sure you won't stay with us?' Nick asked. He grinned. 'We could compare notes over breakfast. It would be the most interesting meal of the year.'

But Richard shook his head.

'Not this time, *mon ami*. We'll fix it for another day. Enjoy yourselves.'

As they drove away Nick reached across and squeezed Ruth's hand.

'I wish they'd come,' he said. 'They're such good company. I'm surprised, really. I thought we might have tempted them, you know, over the last hurdle. D'you think they'll stick together?'

'Sure of it,' she said. 'They're as close as we are. But they haven't known each other as long. I suppose they need more time.'

Later, Richard drove his Ford along the same road, and Lisa said: 'Where are we going?'

'To a place so secret that even I don't know where it is,' he said; and they laughed, content with their private world.

Three leisurely hours later they drove over the River Avon into Stratford and Richard stopped in front of a black-and-white timbered hotel which had stood there in another guise when Shakespeare had died in the New Place nearby. He went inside to the reception desk and said to the clerk: 'Do you have a double room available for tonight?'

She was sixty, grey-haired, and wore spectacles low on her long nose so that she viewed the world with permanent disapproval; but that melted as she surveyed his uniform, the pilot's brevet and the small medal ribbon beneath it, and she said: 'Yes. One night only, sir?'

'One night only,' he said, then added: 'May I see the room, please?'

The disapproval returned, for continental habits were unacceptable to hoteliers in Britain, with or without a war. But he bestowed his most charming smile upon her, and she looked at his uniform again and nodded.

'I'll call the porter,' she said. A minute later Richard followed the ageing servant – the younger men who had once worked there were in one or other of the armed forces – across the entrance hall, up a flight of stairs, and along a narrow, uneven corridor between oak panelled walls.

The room was adequate, neatly furnished and well carpeted. But it was unimpressive and contained two single beds. So he shook his head and said: 'I'm sorry. It isn't big enough. Let's go back and talk to the receptionist.'

At the desk once more he said easily: 'I would like something bigger, and essentially with a double bed.' He leaned towards the lowered spectacles, and added confidentially, 'You see, my wife and I have not been married very long. I'm sure you understand.'

She looked at him, blinked twice, then nodded curtly.

'I have another room. But it's more expensive. An extra five shillings.'

'I'm sure it will be worth it,' Richard said, and departed on a further tour of inspection, this time to approve and return to the car to collect Lisa and their two suitcases.

As they approached the reception desk together he whispered: 'Keep your glove on your left hand. I think she's rather old-fashioned.' And Lisa whispered back mockingly. 'I'm sure she'll never suspect.'

The eyes looked over the spectacles and examined Lisa minutely. But she returned the stare with her warmest smile, and Richard signed the registration form with a flourishing 'Flt Lt & Mrs Richard Haldane'. Then he took the key, shook his head as the ancient porter offered to carry the cases, and led the way towards the staircase.

As they disappeared the porter said: 'What d'you think, Mrs Morgan? D'you reckon they're married?'

The spectacles slipped further down the nose.

'Probably not,' she said. 'But he's in uniform. He deserves whatever he can get. She's a honey, isn't she? And did you see? He's got a medal ribbon.'

She looked across towards the stairs, and her gaze was almost cordial.

Upstairs, Richard and Lisa stood together in the room and looked at the small leaded windows, and then the wide bed; and he reached for her hand and said quietly: 'Now we're here, I don't know what to say.'

She slid her hands up around his neck, and he buried his face in her hair. Her voice was muffled against his ear.

'Don't say anything. Just hold me. For ever.'

*   *   *

Later they walked along the river bank, watching the swans gliding on the water and duck flighting in through the trees alongside the theatre. It was quiet as the sun went down, with only the distant murmur of the town and the occasional growl of a vehicle crossing the bridge, and they felt alone even though there were other couples nearby. They wandered slowly through the theatre gardens and along towards the church with its tower rising beside the river, and found the door open so went inside to look at Shakespeare's grave. Then they returned, hand-in-hand, talking a little but more often in absorbed silence, drifting with the time which was all that stood between their contentment and the wonder awaiting them in the wide bed behind the leaded windows in their first time place.

14

The harvest of 1940 was a near record, and nowhere more so than in the South West. Roxton's increased acreage of wheat and barley was yielding well as the first of the crops were cut and stooked, and Robert was glad Martin Calder had the help of the Land Army girls who were now a respected part of the farm labour force.

But agriculture was still not equipped to handle harvests of that year's size and there was a welcome, too, for the men and women

– and the children who were given special leave from school – who responded to national appeals and came out of the towns to help. They were mostly unskilled, and many abandoned the work as soon as they found it was tough and demanding; but there remained a nucleus who were a valued addition to the hard-pressed permanent staff, and there was almost a holiday atmosphere on the estate farms as everyone helped everyone else and the corn was gathered while the fine weather held.

But further east the great air battles raged and the harvest was won while the machine guns rattled overhead and the vapour trails curved across the sky and the bombs fell as the German air force made its final, desperate attempt to gain that prerequisite for invasion – mastery of the air along the south coast.

It was at the peak of one such battle that two Hurricanes drove a Dornier bomber away from its protecting fighters over Dorset and pursued it westwards. The German pilot zig-zagged as he lost height, trying to turn out to sea but being harried and forced back as his machine was hit repeatedly by the Hurricanes' fire.

Martin Calder saw it as he drove a tractor and laden trailer back towards the farm buildings where a rick was being built. He had heard engines, and looked up beyond Morton Wood to see a twin-engined aircraft flying low and trailing smoke. Then he heard a distant staccato rattle and saw a fighter curve in across the tail of the bomber, followed closely by another. He stopped the tractor and stood up on the seat to get a better view, calling to two men and a Land Army girl working nearby.

A mile away Ned Baldock drove out of the village on his way to a Roxton estate farm where the tenant was adding a lean-to to a byre and needed professional help. These days Ned did most of his travelling around the village on a bicycle, keeping his small petrol ration for journeys to the surrounding farms. Now he steered his two-cylinder Jowett van into the lane which cut behind Morton Wood just as the crippled Dornier lifted over the trees. He peered out of the window of the van, staring incredulously, and swerved in his excitement so that the van's nearside front wheel caught the rough grass at the side of the lane. Two seconds later the vehicle's radiator was buried in the hedge, and Ned was clutching the steering wheel and cursing. Then a Hurricane flashed low overhead, a burst of machine gun fire crackled across the fields, and Ned jumped from his van and stood at the side of

126

the road, raising his fists to the sky and shouting: 'Bloody idiots – flying like lunatics – take your bloody war somewhere else – leave folk in –'

He got no further, because the panicking German crew had released the only bomb remaining in their aircraft as the pilot pulled into a frantic climb to give them a chance to bale out. The bomb came down like a torpedo, hit the corn stubble in the field from which Martin Calder's team had just cleared the stooks, skidded along the greasy surface, bounced over the hedge and exploded against the Jowett.

There was only just enough of Ned Baldock left for the Reverend Smallwood to bury two days later. He was the village's first victim of the war.

In the field Calder threw himself from the tractor as the bomb exploded, then scrambled to his feet and, followed by the others, began to run towards the smoke and the wreckage beyond the hedge.

But then the Land Army girl shrieked: 'Mr Calder – look – look –' She was pointing upwards and he twisted to see the Dornier, much higher now, turning across the sky with flames jetting from one engine, and a parachute blossoming behind it. Then, with a roar, the aircraft blew up, and again Martin and his workers were flat on their faces, covering their heads, then jumping to their feet, staring at the parachutist a thousand feet above them.

Calder shouted: 'Get back to the farm. He'll have a gun. Come on –'

He jumped on to the tractor, the others scrambled up on to the trailer, and he drove the quarter mile back to the farm faster than he had ever driven a laden tractor in his life.

At the farm he shouted to one of the men: 'Get my gun. It's in the kitchen.' Then he ran round to the Grange and was met by Robert at the estate office door.

Breathless, he said: 'German parachutist, Mr Robert – coming down this side of Morton Wood. His plane was shot down. We'd better get guns.'

Within the minute Robert, armed with his small-bore rifle, and Martin with his shotgun, were on the tractor, driving across the paddock behind the barns, while a shaking Mary Pritchard telephoned the police.

As they bounced over the fields Robert shouted: 'We don't

take any chances. The papers say these chaps give up straight away. But there must be some who'll make a break for it if they can. So don't risk yourself until we know what we're up against.'

They could see the wood now, but there was no sign of the parachutist. So they abandoned the tractor and walked forward, moving away from each other, until suddenly Martin stopped and pointed.

The grey-white canopy was draped across the lower branches of an oak at the edge of the wood. And from two hundred yards away they could see that no one was attached to it.

Robert pushed a cartridge into the chamber of the rifle and thumbed the safety catch clear. He turned in to the edge of the wood, seeing Martin moving now along the hedge side across the field. He walked quickly and quietly, from one tree trunk to the next; and then saw Martin raise his arm, pointing.

Rifle across his body, Robert moved forward; and saw a grey figure slide between two trees forty yards away.

'Halt!' His voice echoed away into the wood, and a startled pigeon called and flapped through the leaves. Then there were only the summer sounds.

Quite calmly, Robert raised his rifle, pointed it at the spot where he had last seen movement, and fired.

The explosion cracked and the bullet ripped through the foliage. As silence returned he pushed another cartridge into the breech and shouted again: 'Halt!'

The warning was enough. Slowly a figure materialised beyond the leaves, and Robert saw that the hands were raised. He watched, motionless, as the man moved forward; saw Martin running, crouching as he did so, across the field, shotgun pointing. The German was closer now, and Robert could see his uniform, and that one trouser leg was torn up to the knee. He held the rifle steady and let the German see him. The man stopped, hands raised higher. Robert called: 'He's in front of me, Martin. Cover him from your side.' The German looked round, startled; saw Martin with his shotgun beyond the nearest tree, and stood still.

Robert moved forward. He held his rifle in one hand and pointed to the man's belt.

'The pistol. Take it out and drop it.'

If the man did not understand the language, he understood the gesture. He kept one hand raised, lowered the other slowly and

128

unbuttoned the holster flap at his waist, took out a pistol and offered it, butt first, on the palm of his hand. Robert stepped forward, reached, and took it. The man raised his hand again.

It was only then that Robert looked at his face and saw blood running down one side from the edge of the flying helmet, and the frightened eyes. Suddenly he felt sorry for him.

He pointed the rifle towards the open field.

'That way,' he said; and followed the German clear of the wood, across the front of Martin's shotgun.

He said: 'Keep your gun ready, Martin. But I don't think we'll have any trouble.' Then he nodded to the German and said: 'Come on. Let's get you to a doctor. Your bit of the war's over.'

Later he said to Diane: 'The curious thing is that I was prepared to kill him, if he'd tried to escape. I wouldn't have thought I was capable of that. I suppose we don't really know what makes us tick until something like that happens. But in a way I'm glad I was the one to find him. At least I proved to myself that, given the chance, I could probably face the things Richard faces.' He grinned quickly. 'Preferably with Martin alongside.'

Diane looked at her son and, once again, felt secret concern for him.

'And why not?' she asked. 'Whatever Richard does, you could do just as well.'

But Robert shook his head.

'I couldn't fly aeroplanes,' he said. 'I'm just the farmer of the family. Today's bit of action will be the last excitement I'll see in the war – unless the bastards invade. It's the luck of the draw. I'll just go on rusticating and running the business until my dear brother and sister want their money. Then – we'll have to wait and see.'

Very quietly Diane said: 'Will they really want to get out?'

'I'm not sure about Ruth. But Richard will. We talked about it. It isn't that he's no longer interested. He asked questions about the tenancies and the labour force, and how profits have been changing from one commodity to another, and the way the new Government regulations affect us. But he admits he wouldn't be able to manage the home farm, and that he wouldn't want to. He just doesn't want to anchor himself in a corner of rural Britain.'

'So you'll have to be prepared to pay him out,' Diane said. 'But you'll be able to afford to. It's tragic, but if this war goes on for another two or three years farming will make more money than it could ever have made in peacetime with the imports flooding in. The Government has had to let us accumulate capital again, otherwise we couldn't produce the extra food. I think you should try hard to build up a good financial reserve. Then when Richard wants to pull out you won't have to borrow a fortune to find his share.'

Robert nodded. 'It might work. As long as Ruth doesn't want her share at the same time. But I think it won't be long before she marries Nick, and then she'll almost certainly want to get out when the war's over.'

But afterwards he cautioned himself: don't try to work things out. The war is going to last a long time, and there's no knowing what things will be like when it's over, or how we will all react. The only thing certain is that they will be different.

*   *   *

Richard flicked his R/T switch and snapped: 'Blue leader to blue three. What the hell are you doing out there? I said fly tight. That means so I can reach out and touch your wing. Now close up.'

The Spitfire flying on his right and just behind wavered. A voice said: 'Blue three to leader. Sorry. I was picking up some turbulence –'

'Then fly through it,' Richard snapped. 'Let me see the whites of your eyes.'

He watched the other aircraft edge closer. The pilot was Ted Collins, only three weeks out of training; a nineteen-year-old who still seemed to regard a fifty-foot gap between aircraft as a formation essential. Richard lifted one gloved thumb as the other aircraft closed on him slowly. Under his breath he muttered: 'Come on, man. Closer. Don't be bloody scared of it.' Then he snapped aloud: 'Turning left – go.' He rolled, opening the throttle a little, and took the formation of four round in a tight turn, watching Collins who was on the outside and now should have crossed behind them to the opposite wing, but obviously had not reacted quickly enough.

He said: 'Blue three. Where the hell are you? Pedal, man, pedal.' And he tightened the turn further.

He had been up with the flight for half an hour, and would be

flying again after lunch. It had been like that for three weeks.
German air activity in the area had been minimal and the
reformed squadron had been able to concentrate on working up to
a pitch of flying efficiency which had startled the newcomers,
including two Frenchmen who had waded off the beaches of
Dunkirk back in May. Richard had a rapport with them because
he spoke their language and knew their country, but they were
allocated to a flight which at that moment was being led by
Sandham himself in a series of low-level passes over the beaches
and cliffs north of Scarborough.

Soon after they had joined the squadron Richard had sat in his
CO's office and said: 'Why don't you give the Frenchmen to me?'

'I'd be glad to,' Sandham had told him. 'They give me no end of
trouble. I can't stop them talking in their own language when
things get exciting.'

'That's what I mean. I can understand them.'

'You might, but the others couldn't. They have to learn
English, and R/T procedure, and they won't if they think their
flight commander knows what they're nattering about. You know
as well as I that everybody has to understand everybody else when
we get back to the real thing.'

'All right. I'll give them language lessons. See if that helps.'

Now, three weeks later, Sandham had told him that the Frenchmen were at last beginning to learn verbal discipline; Steve
Mitchell, promoted and commanding C Flight, reported good
progress with his three new pilots; and Richard himself was
satisfied that B Flight would make a good fighting team in spite of
Collins's nervousness in close formation.

He reported as much to Sandham when they sat together in the
bar of the local pub after dinner that evening; and the squadron
leader looked at him curiously.

'So why do you chase them so hard?'

'Because their lives may depend on what I teach them.'

'I've been watching them,' Sandham said. 'Last week you took
Mitch and his men up with yours. I sat right here in the bar
afterwards and heard them talking. They're scared of you: scared
of the way you make them fly close up like pieces of a jigsaw
puzzle, then break them fast and reform tight within seconds;
scared of the way you take them wave-hopping and hedge-
hopping. Leadership's one thing, but you're flogging them.

131

What's eating you?'

'Nothing,' Richard drank some of his beer. 'I just want them to stay alive. However scared they are of me, they'll be twice as scared when Jerry gets at them. At least I only shoot them down verbally.'

Sandham fished in his pocket for cigarettes.

'All right,' he said. 'Forget it. How's Lisa?'

'Pretty good.' Richard took a cigarette from the proffered packet. 'She's up in Edinburgh in some Maugham play. Gloomy stuff for war-time entertainment, by the sound of it. But things are getting more difficult. So many theatres have closed. She thinks she may have to give it up before long.'

'What will she do then?' Sandham offered the flame of his lighter. He was watching Richard through the smoke as he lit his cigarette.

'Nursing. She wants to do something useful. And her old man's a doctor, so it's understandable.'

'She still won't be anywhere near you, unless you're very lucky.'

Richard said shortly: 'Can't help that, Keith.'

Sandham studied the end of his cigarette, then glanced up at his companion.

'You could, you know. If you wanted to.'

Five or six men came into the bar, noisily. They called to the barmaid, joking with each other. One said: 'Where's Colly?' Another retorted: 'Sulking, probably. Did you hear the roasting he got –' Then he saw the two men sitting in a corner of the room and checked, signalling a warning to the others.

Richard watched them and said to Sandham: 'I don't know what you're talking about.'

'You do.' Sandham raised his empty glass in a signal to the barmaid. 'I was there at Hanford when you met. I've never seen two people hit each other straight between the eyes the way you did. And you changed from that day, very much for the better. You spent your leave with her, you telephone her every night, I see you reading letters every day which can only be from her. Yet suddenly you're a miserable bastard. Are you going to tell me about it – or shall I tell you?'

Richard inhaled sharply from his cigarette.

'Look after your own business, Keith.'

'It is my business. You're my senior flight commander. If you have something on your mind I want to know what it is – before they send us south again.' He watched the barmaid bring two pints of beer along the bar, paid for them, then turned his quiet, direct gaze back to his companion. Richard sampled the beer and said nothing.

Sandham said: 'For Christ's sake, Richard – why don't you marry her? She could be here, living in the village, close to you. And when we're posted she could stay with you, move anywhere in the country with you. As the wife of a serviceman she wouldn't be subject to conscription –'

'Shut up,' Richard said; yet without anger, as if he did not want to dispute Sandham's view. He looked round the room, searching for a new topic of conversation.

'I won't.' Sandham shifted forward in his chair. 'Because you worry me. And I'll tell you what's eating you. You won't marry her because you think it's wrong to get hitched when we're in the middle of a war. Yet you want to marry her, and she wants to marry you. For God's sake, how stupid can a man be?'

Richard's head jerked round and his dark eyes shone in the scattered light from the electric bulbs overhead.

'It's not stupid. You know what it does to a girl when her husband is killed. It's far worse for a wife than it is if they're not married. Dear Lord, you've written enough letters when chaps have got the chop, and seen their wives, too. So have I. Remember Phil? I went to tell Jan. I'll never forget. It isn't right for a girl to have a husband doing what we're doing, and to live close to the station so he can go home to her like going home from work. Because one day he won't go home. And that's far worse than just being the girl-friend and spending a few nights together and –'

'You're wrong.' Sandham stabbed his finger in the air between them. 'I'm married, and I can tell you how Marj feels about it. If I go, she'll be glad we've had the things she'll be able to remember –'

'It's not the same for you,' Richard retorted. 'You didn't have a choice. You were married when this lot started. I know I'm right –'.

'You don't. That's your trouble. That's why you're so damn' bad tempered. You're afraid of marriage; and you know there's a flaw in your reasoning. A wife knows that if her man gets killed, at least she's been a part of him. There's no substitute for it.'

'And that's why it's worse for a wife than for a girl-friend.' Richard jabbed the remains of his cigarette into an ashtray and ground it against the glass. Then, still looking at it, he said: 'I'm going to get the chop, Keith. Sooner or later it'll happen. That's why I can't marry Lisa, no matter how much I want to. And I can't tell her that.'

Sandham said carefully: 'We all feel like that sometimes. We all know we have to be lucky as well as clever. Stop thinking you're different.'

'Different?' Richard looked at him almost scornfully. He picked up his beer glass and drained it, pushed a lock of his black hair away from his forehead, and reached for another cigarette from the packet on the table. 'I'm not different. I'm like all the others – Larry, Johnny, Shorty, Phil, Foxy, Alan, and the rest. Maybe they didn't all know. But I do. Now let's talk about something else.'

He lit his cigarette, and Keith Sandham thought it was probably his tenth of the evening. Then he waved to the barmaid for more beer. Sandham shrugged. He had confirmed his suspicions. And he knew there was nothing unusual about Richard's view of marriage. A lot of men shared it, just as an equal number held the opposite opinion. But the conviction with which he had spoken about his own death was a different matter. When men talked like that, they took themselves one step closer to the brink. Sandham thought: I'll have to look after him. And I'd better keep away from the subject of marriage for a time. Let's hope others do the same.

* * *

Thirty miles away Nick Telford, newly promoted to Flight Lieutenant, limped around training circuits with fledgling bomber pilots and agitated unsuccessfully to get back to an operational squadron. Meanwhile, on one or two nights every week he and Richard met at a half-way pub to drink beer and swop stories about their frustrations.

And it was on one such evening, only three weeks after Richard's conversation with Keith Sandham, that Nick waited for him at the bar of their favourite meeting place with bright eyes and

134

a grin which spread across his face as Richard came in through the door.

They shook hands in greeting and Nick said: 'I have news for you, old boy. Great news. Stand by to set up the drinks.'

Richard looked at him suspiciously.

'Scrounging again, Telford? And so early in the evening?'

'You're going to drink my health – and, in absentia, that of your dear sister. We're getting hitched the next time I can get leave. I've just spent a fortune on the telephone to fix it.'

Richard said: 'You secretive old devil.' He fought to show the pleasure that was expected of him; the pleasure he felt for Nick and Ruth; the pleasure that, just for a few seconds, was spoiled by his own private conflicts. It was the briefest struggle; but it went deep and it hurt while it lasted. Then he grinned widely and pumped Nick's hand. 'I can't claim it's a surprise. It's been bloody obvious for a long time. Great stuff, *mon ami*. Hey – that's worth a drop of the hard stuff, if they've got any.'

He leaned on the bar, bought two large whiskies; then, clutching one in his hand, said: 'Here's to you, you old devil – and my poor misguided sister who deserves a better fate.'

They drank, laughing at each other. Then Nick said: 'One other thing. You're best man. So you'd better lay on some sort of leave when I get mine.'

'I'll be there, whenever it is – if I have to fly there. When d'you reckon?'

'Christmas, give or take. Even if I haven't finished playing nursemaid to the new boys, there'll be a spot of leave due then. And what about Lisa? Ruth wants her to be bridesmaid. She will, won't she?'

'Of course she will. She'd love it. Tell you what: drink up and we'll go and 'phone her. Tell her the good news. Come on.'

They swallowed their whisky, went outside, found a telephone box and just managed to catch Lisa in her dressing-room before her stage call. Then, after ten minutes' excited, wise-cracking conversation, they hung up, shook hands enthusiastically with a policeman who happened to be passing, and made their way back to the pub where they bought drinks for a dozen startled locals before finally settling in a corner to catch their breath.

It was only then that Nick looked at his companion in sudden curiosity and said: 'Hey – I've just thought of something. When

are you and Lisa going to do it? What are you waiting for? Do it
when we do. Make it a double, old boy. That would be fantastic.
A wizard party. . .'

His voice trailed, and he hesitated; unsure of himself, for
Richard's face was carefully expressionless. Then he added
lamely: 'Sorry, mate. I just thought it would be a good idea. Hope
I haven't said the wrong thing.'

'No.' Richard shook his head. He played with his glass on the
table; then abruptly felt for cigarettes in his pocket, concentrating
on the task. 'It's just that – well, I don't see things in quite the
same way.'

He found the cigaretes, offered one to Nick and accepted a
light. Then, through the smoke, he forced a smile.

'Sorry if you didn't get quite the reaction you expected. And I'd
better tell you the truth. I don't believe in war-time marriages.
Every man to his own views. I respect yours and I don't want to
argue about it. But neither of us is a good life insurance bet at the
moment. When you marry Ruth you'll both have my heartfelt
good wishes and I hope to God you're still alive when this lot's
finished. I have a feeling I won't be. No –' he held up a silencing
hand '– don't make a speech about it. I said I'd tell you the truth. I
just believe that when I get the chop Lisa won't be hurt quite as
much if we're not married. The wedding will have to wait. Now
for Christ's sake let's talk about something else.'

Nick took a long breath; then nodded. He knew when to keep
quiet, so he concealed his concern and led off into a series of hair-
raising stories of circuits and bumps in the very second-hand
Wellington bombers being used for advanced flying training. Not
once during the rest of the evening were weddings mentioned, and
by the time the two friends met again any lingering embarrassment between them had evaporated, so that plans for Nick's
marriage were discussed with maximum enjoyment.

A week later Lisa's Edinburgh play ended its run and she spent
a night with Richard on her way across the country to the BBC's
Bristol studios for a part in a short radio serial. Inevitably they
talked about the wedding, and Richard told her of his conversation with Nick, omitting only any mention of his personal premon-
ition. She was calm and matter-of-fact about it, giving him no hint
of her secret disappointment and longing, staunchly maintaining
that they should live by his beliefs, for she knew they were not

uncommon among RAF aircrew. But later, as they lay in bed, there was a hint of desperation in her loving, and an almost frantic need for the satisfaction he had learned to give her, for it consumed her, and in the exhaustion and peace which followed she could forget.

*   *   *

Nick's leave came in the week between Christmas and New Year, and the wedding was arranged for New Year's Eve, a Monday – an odd day to get married, everyone agreed, although it was the best they could manage. But it appealed to them both that their wedding night should provide – in Nick's words – a wizard way to let the New Year in.

So there gathered at Roxton Grange Graham and Margaret Telford, Lisa's parents Lawrence and Christine and her younger sister Tricia and, of course, Robert, who was now effectively master of Roxton, for Diane's tenure as executrix had ended. Like most war-time weddings it was intended to be a modest affair, but there were family friends to swell the gathering, Richard had brought Steve Mitchell and Keith Sandham with his wife Marjorie, while Nick had his own supporting contingent. The hostess was Diane, catering with the aid of a food ration coupon pool to which everyone had contributed, while Graham Telford had dipped into his still considerable cellar to provide the wine.

At St Thomas's Church the congregation was swelled by many villagers, every tenant farmer on the estate, even including George Walton and his wife, and most of the home farm workers; and there was the novel sight of the bride being given away by the twin of the groom's best man.

It was a situation which appealed to Nick, whose speech was unanimously voted the most hilarious of the day. But later Richard reserved a special moment of drama for himself when he rose to announce the end of the reception's formalities; but then added: 'Before we break up, I want to snatch a moment of this happy occasion for myself, and for someone else. Nick has given his own present to the bridesmaid: now I have one.'

He walked along the table to Lisa, exchanging a wink with Nick who was the only other person to know what he intended to do. When he reached her he stood behind her chair and rested his hands on her shoulders. She looked up at him, her eyes shining as he said: 'A few days ago Lisa and I went shopping. This was the result.' He held out one hand to show the diamond and sapphire ring which had been concealed in it. Then, as the applause began, she stood up beside him and offered her left hand and he slipped the ring onto her finger, and drew her close and kissed her and whispered: 'For all my life, Lisa.' And for a moment she hid her face against his neck so that she could compose herself before she was able to look at the people who surrounded them and respond to their enthusiasm and good wishes.

Later, before the afternoon light began to fade down towards the year's ending, it was Robert's turn to play host as he took the guests for a tour of the home farm; and found himself cornered by Graham Telford who revealed an intense interest in the financial structure of farming even if he had little understanding of its practicalities. He asked questions about the capital and running costs of machinery, why four horses were still on the farm, the rate of milking and the cost of using buildings for winter-housing beef, relative labour costs for different enterprises, returns on crops compared with invested capital, the economics of tenanted farms, and much more, until Robert looked at him curiously and said: 'You sound as if you're preparing a take-over bid.'

Telford laughed and leaned comfortably on the top bar of a gate.

'A money man's instincts, that's all – prompted by a tinge of envy.' He pointed across a wintry paddock towards the rolling fields and the dark outline of Morton Wood in the distance. 'When I look from my windows at home I see half an acre of reasonably neat garden; from my office window in the City I see a blank wall of another building – if it's still standing when I get back – and bombed rubble further along the street; and I measure success in the figures which denote my handling of other people's money. You have a major business – 2,000 acres, tenanted farms, employees, capital investment, production schedules, buying and selling: yet it's all integrated with an environment which must be worth far more than can be contained in any balance sheet. I suspect you are embarking on a life which will bring you a satisfaction which has always eluded me.'

Robert said: 'I enjoy it. I've done so since I was a child. And it's rewarding now to see everything improving after the disasters of the past. The future is uncertain because of the war, and because I don't know what either my brother or sister intend to do when it's over. But in the meantime I am the family's business caretaker, and it's satisfying even if it's unglamorous.'

'It's essential,' said Telford, 'to the country and to your own future. If Richard doesn't come back here I shall think he's mad. Ruth's position now is different, and we shall have to wait and see. But she retains a great interest in Roxton; and in case you don't know it, that is being fuelled by Nick who is fascinated by everything here. I think your sister's wedding has lessened your worries about the future.'

'I hope you're right,' Robert said. 'Because if both Ruth and Richard want to get out, the family partnership would have to be dissolved and I would have to sell a lot of land to pay them out. It's not a prospect I like to think about.'

'Then don't,' Graham Telford said. 'Your job is to produce as much as you can and hope your tenants are doing the same; and to re-establish your finances so you can withstand future pressures. That's big stuff, Robert, without worrying about a future you cannot predict; and if I had control of it I'd think it was a fascinating job, too.' He looked at his watch. 'Come on. The happy couple will be leaving soon. Let's go and give them a send off.'

15

Major Bennett said: 'I have to discuss this with you, Mrs Haldane. The farm is yours and the man is one of your tenants. Our actions will obviously affect you.'

It was the spring of 1941, food rationing had tightened as German U-boats sank increasing tonnages of Atlantic shipping, and pressure on farming to boost output was growing. But Diane made no secret of her hostility.

'You are talking to the wrong person now, Major.' Her voice was chill. 'The estate is owned by my family. Robert, will you take over, please?'

'Of course.' Robert looked warily at their visitor, whom he

139

regarded as pompous and officious. He was also secretly conscious of his own youth and inexperience, for Bennett oozed confidence and superiority. 'George Walton has been our worst tenant for years. I confess I wanted to force him out before the war, but my mother decided otherwise and I'm sure she was right. The man has an unhappy history.'

'I know the story,' Bennett said brusquely. 'But the Ministry won't accept excuses. If land is not being farmed well the farmer has to be dispossessed, and as chairman of the executive committee in this county it's my unpleasant job to sign the necessary papers. Walton's case has been examined in the greatest detail. We've had advisory officers there, they've studied his cropping and his livestock, they've inspected his accounts, they've sampled his soil. The recommendation is that he has to go. Good land is being under-farmed and the country can't afford that.'

Robert's mouth tightened.

'You don't have to read me a lesson in patriotism,' he snapped. 'I know what's needed.'

'Then perhaps you will be prepared to acknowledge that he has to go,' Bennett said. He took a folder from his briefcase and flourished it. 'If you will kindly read these papers, we can then discuss anything you don't understand.' He put an open file on the table between them.

Robert looked down at the documents; then up at the grey-haired man who sat behind them with his crisp moustache and cold, superior eyes. Anything you don't understand. The chairman of the all-powerful committee, the ex-officer from the first World War, the big land-owner, talking to the youngster scarcely out of college and struggling to manage his little estate. Anything you don't understand. Robert glanced at his mother, and suddenly she saw a spark in his eyes which was reminiscent of Richard, and even of Randolph before him.

He said: 'I'm sure I shall understand every word of them. But I have no intention of signing away a man's tenancy until I'm satisfied that your conclusions are reasonable and that the evidence indicates a comprehensive investigation. So leave the papers with me. When I've read them and made any necessary checks of my own, I'll be in touch with you.'

'There is no possible alternative to dispossession,' Bennett said. He was frowning, for the young man sat opposite to him was not reacting as he had expected. 'We do not approach these matters lightly –'

'Neither do I.' Robert's voice was icy. 'Especially when I know that at least some of the evidence in that file –' he tapped the papers on the table '– has probably been gathered by people who have never farmed commercially in their lives, no matter what their academic qualifications. So until I've read them and spoken with Walton myself, we can make no further progress.' He stood up, clearly inviting Bennett to leave. 'I'll telephone you within a week.'

Bennett shrugged, snapped the catch on his briefcase, and rose to his feet. His face, usually as grey as his hair, was slightly flushed.

'As you wish, Mr Haldane,' he said stiffly; and walked briskly, shoulders squared, to the door.

When he had gone Robert stood for a moment, staring at the floor, forehead creased; until Diane said: 'I want to fight him. Can we?'

He looked up at her. She was bright-eyed and angry.

'I don't know,' he said. 'But I'm going to try – not for Walton's sake but for ours and our future relations with the Ministry. I've got to show him that I'm not here to be trampled on.'

She looked at him, for seconds; and her slow smile was confident.

'This place is in good hands,' she said softly.

*   *   *

Simon Metcalf's thick-lensed, heavy-rimmed spectacles dominated his face, which was round and pale beneath a bald head. He was manager of the Exeter branch of the Midland Bank, and he was not enjoying his conversation with the young man who represented one of the area's substantial private land holdings. He said stiffly: 'I cannot possibly discuss Mr Walton's affairs without his express authority. Indeed, had you not been aware of it already, I would not even have admitted that Mr Walton is one of our clients. I appreciate that you are his landlord, and you obviously know that I have been consulted by the Ministry of Agriculture and am aware of certain – ah – problems. But I can't go further than that in Mr Walton's absence.'

'All right,' Robert said patiently. 'Then let me put a circumstance to you. There is a tenant farmer who is in an impossible position. He has no money and cannot borrow because no one will lend to him. Yet without money he cannot farm the land he rents. Everything he has is run down and neglected and he has given up the fight. His landlord is concerned that the land should be well farmed and is anxious to avoid a Ministry dispossession order. But in order to do so he has to find a way to give the tenant a fresh start which will make him credit-worthy and will satisfy the Ministry that there is some future for the farm under the existing tenancy.'

'The description of affairs is your own, Mr Haldane,' Metcalf said cautiously. 'But I understand it. What comes next in this – ah – theoretical exercise?'

Robert said: 'You will not loan money unless you are satisfied that it is reasonably secure. Correct?'

'Basically, yes.'

'Let us return to our imaginary characters, then. The landlord believes the farmer might still make something of himself, and the estate saved from the embarrassment of having a tenant dispossessed. In his view the tenant needs money for basic re-equipment, the purchase of seeds and fertilisers, and the replacement of his worst stock. It might amount to £1500, perhaps as much as £2000. If the landlord guaranteed that amount, and produced a schedule of expenditure and estimated revenue, and evidence that the farm would be supervised for an agreed period, would a banker who was familiar with both parties be prepared to loan?'

Metcalf took off his spectacles and polished them energetically on a white handkerchief, blinking at his visitor.

'If he was satisfied with the control of the loan – I expect so. Obviously a guarantee from a substantial landowner would be a major factor.'

'I'll come back to see you tomorrow,' said Robert, and left.

The next morning he called at Field Foot Farm and said to George Walton: 'Get into my car and come across to the Grange. I want to talk with you.'

Walton looked at him, hesitated, then drew himself up.

'I'm in trouble with them Ministry fellers, Mr Robert. Is that right?'

'You're in big trouble,' Robert said brusquely. 'Let's get across to the office and talk about it.'

142

They talked for two hours; then Robert telephoned solicitor Harvey Roach and accountant Conroy Jones, and finally rang Bennett.

'I've studied your papers,' he said. 'You were quite mistaken when you said there was no alternative to dispossession. The Ministry's concern is that land should be well farmed. It's mine also. Therefore I'm taking over supervisory control of Field Foot Farm for the next two years. The estate is standing guarantor for a loan to George Walton to put him on his feet again, and everything he does will be monitored here. Ministry ploughing orders will be scrupulously observed, and productivity will be raised at least to the county's average for similar land. Our solicitors will put the details in writing immediately.' He paused, then added sarcastically: 'We can then discuss anything you don't understand. Good afternoon, Major.'

He put the receiver down and looked at his mother who had been sat in the estate office with him.

She said: 'Robert – I'm proud. Not because you've cut the Major down to size. Because I know that you're glad you've saved George Walton.'

*　　*　　*

As Diane and Robert reflected on their brush with authority, her other son was sitting in the cockpit of a Spitfire three miles above the coast of Normandy. Below him a squadron of twin-engined Blenheims flew steadily through heavy flak as they bombed the docks at Cherbourg; and ahead Squadron Leader Keith Sandham called on the R/T: 'Falcon leader to all sections. Keep a sharp lookout. The opposition can't be far away.'

Within thirty seconds another voice crackled in the earphones:'Yellow three to Falcon leader – bandits three o'clock, angels twenty.'

Away to their right the rest of the wing responded to the same alarm and thirty-six fighters turned towards the enemy, throttles hard through the gates, climbing to meet the attack.

Richard led his flight round, closing on Sandham, calling: 'Blue leader to blue four – keep weaving – watch out in case there's another lot somewhere.'

'Blue four to leader – okay, chief.' Ken Abrams' voice was flat calm.

The Messerschmitts were still a mile away when the Spitfires attained comparable height and turned again to keep between the defending German fighters and the Blenheims far below. Richard thought, not for the first time under the circumstances: What a hell of a change – now we're doing what they did only a few months ago.

Sandham's voice said: 'Normal attack, gentlemen, please.'

The squadron split as the three flights of four moved away from each other, re-forming in a well-drilled movement. They were flying across the line of the oncoming Messerschmitts which were now very close; and suddenly the guns opened up.

After the first attack it became a free-for-all, although Richard knew that Abrams was still with him, weaving, covering his tail as he pulled round hard to cut inside a Messerschmitt's turn. His hands were sweating and his heart was thumping hard against his chest, but he was not conscious of either, only of the aircraft ahead. He glanced once in his mirror, caught a glimpse of Abrams' aircraft, tried a short deflection burst at the German fighter and knew he had hit its outer wing, but then lost it.

He looked round, saw more aircraft and pulled towards them; and as he did so a Spitfire and a Messerschmitt collided head-on a quarter of a mile ahead. The two aircraft exploded in a brilliant flash and a black smoke cloud, pieces cartwheeling outwards. Richard's breath whistled through his teeth and he forced himself to look away, searching for enemy aircraft.

A long way to his right he saw two Messerschmitts locked on to a turning, twisting Spitfire, and he put his wing over and hurtled towards them, centring the nearer aircraft in his sights, coming in on a beam attack which the German pilot never saw as the Spitfire's eight machine guns scythed bullets along the fuselage. The Messerschmitt rolled slowly, crippled, smoke suddenly streaming, dropping away. Then there was flame in the smoke and part of the engine cowling fell off and now the dive was vertical and Richard pulled up steeply, looking for the other Messerschmitt but not finding it, or the Spitfire which had been so close to it.

Like many air battles, this one had spread across miles of sky, and it seemed a long time before Richard saw another Spitfire. He could see no enemy aircraft, nor the Blenheims which had been there below him only a few minutes before, although he knew that by now they were scheduled to be on their way back. So he eased his aching muscles, checked his fuel gauge, and slid in alongside the other Spitfire as both turned out across the Channel. The aircraft carried the insignia of one of the other squadrons in the wing, and he waved to the pilot and got a response. He searched the sky above and behind, but saw nothing; and then remembered the head-on collision. It had been too fast for him to recognize the Spitfire. Christ, he thought. What a way to go. The quickest there is. Just one great big bang, then nothing.

It was only when he landed that he found it had been Keith Sandham.

Steve Mitchell said: 'I saw him. Like slow motion. They started half a mile apart, lining up on each other, flying straight at each other. One of them started firing at about four hundred yards. I don't know which. Then – they hit and blew up. Oh bloody hell. I can't believe it.'

Keith. Skipper. He'd flown with him since the previous June. God knows how many sorties. His teacher, his leader, his confessor. His friend. Only Mitch had been his friend for longer on the squadron. Christ, it wasn't true. The skipper always came back. Quiet and confident, and always back there in the evening, buying a pint.

He'd have to see Marj. It would be like Jan all over again. Marj lived three miles away. She was the same as Keith: quiet, almost gentle. Yet practical. She knew; you could tell, talking to her. You couldn't be the wife of a man who had been CO of a fighter squadron for nearly a year without knowing it could happen; that it was almost certain to happen, sooner or later.

Like it would to him.

Another shattered wife. He could never have a wife, while this went on. Lisa understood. Oh hell. What a thing, what a bloody awful thing to happen.

He saw Marj that night. The Wing Commander had already told her. But she said she was glad he had come. He stayed with her until her sister arrived. Then he went back to the station and sat in his room and drank one whisky after another until he fell asleep.

The next morning the Wing Commander sent for him and said: 'Bad show yesterday, Haldane. Bloody bad show. There aren't many like Keith Sandham.'

He looked straight across the Wing Commander's desk and

said: 'There are none like Keith Sandham, sir.'

The Wing Commander nodded, accepting the rebuke. He was nearly forty years old, but he still flew on operations sometimes.

'Yes. You may be right. You knew him well; so you know he ran a good squadron. In the air and on the ground. You'll find him a difficult man to follow.'

'Sir?'

'I'm giving you the squadron. Not just because you're the senior flight commander. I like your style. So did Keith. He nominated you when the squadron was posted back here from 12 Group. I won't say congratulations, because in the circumstances you wouldn't like it. I'll just say good luck. And we all need some of that.'

16

Flight Lieutenant Nicholas Telford was singing, tunelessly but with enthusiasm. The French coast was behind, the English Channel beneath, and the Kent cliffs and beaches ahead. The four-engined Halifax was cruising smoothly at 10,000 feet, and every minute took him and his crew closer to their base and the end of their last operation of the tour.

He eased his back against the seat. It had not been a long flight: Cologne was one of the nearer targets for the night bombers. But it only took a couple of hours for his spine to start aching. Somehow the Halifax seat did not suit his anatomy. But now he did not care. One tour on Wellingtons; now a second on the big Halifax, complete, finished, ready to be pushed away into the recesses of the mind, only to be pulled out again in snatches of memory; and at a suitable distance from the flak and the night fighters. In half an hour he would be down. In two days he would be with Ruth. For two whole weeks he would be with Ruth, this April in 1942.

He glanced to his right at Joe Saxonby, the flight engineer. He was dozing, his head falling forward uncomfortably. Joe had a

146

wife and a twelve-month-old son. He also had deep scars around his right shoulder from shrapnel which had screamed through the cockpit on the second flight of the tour. Nick had picked up one of the metal splinters too; that was the cause of the scar running across his cheek. At first it had troubled him; but Ruth said it looked rather dramatic and gave him extra character. Momentarily he fingered it, and remembered fighting the wounded Halifax all the way back from Mannheim. Doug Fairley had been in the tail turret then; but he was dead when they landed, which was why Malcolm Walker – 'Johnny', inevitably, to everyone – was sitting back there now, still watching for German night fighters which sometimes patrolled up the Channel looking for returning bombers whose crews were relaxing too soon.

Peter Hatch, whom everyone called 'Nut', interrupted Nick's crooning, his voice harsh on the intercom as it always was.

'Hey, Skip, how about turning starboard on to three five two?'

Nut was the navigator, and he was guiding them safely home, as he always did. He had joined the crew after that second flight of the tour, for Robin Roberts who had been sitting at the navigator's table on that operation had had an arm severed when the flak had burst close to them, and was now back in civvy street.

Nick fingered his scar again. It had been the hairiest flight of all. The Halifax had been like a sieve when he had coaxed it down on to the runway. When he had inspected it later he had wondered how he had managed to fly it home. Others had wondered, too; which was why they had given him the DFC. Secretly he had been pleased about that; most of them were, if they got a gong, although no one ever admitted it.

They cruised on; seven men, listening to the engines, all conscious in various ways of a great and growing relief deep in their bodies. It was over; at least until the next tour, and maybe there wouldn't be one for them, for there was always a chance of an easier posting. Thirty flights was the usual tour. This time four of them had gone thirty-two. But this was definitely the last.

They were all alert, ready for the landing. It was still dark outside, although they could see the eastern horizon faintly, and there was thin cloud about; but inside the dials glowed and they felt affection for this great thirty-ton lump of metal which had kept them up in the air so often and for so long, and was bringing them back yet again.

Nick rolled into a turn, watching the thin beam of light which beckoned them towards their base; a lonely, welcoming light. Six or seven minutes flying time now. Then, the day after tomorrow, the peace of the Roxton fields. They would spend a few days there, then go up to London to see his parents, then back to Roxton again. April 1942, and there were still corners of the country where you could forget. He knew he was weary. But Ruth would put that right.

A girl's voice from the control tower was chanting the landing drill, telling him the height at which he should join the circuit, giving him his course. This was where you had to be careful, for there were other homing aircraft hidden in the darkness around, all heading for the same small strips of concrete. He steadied the Halifax, checking the instruments, dropping through the stack of unseen aircraft in his turn. He watched Joe moving the levers which lowered the undercarriage, and adjusted the trim, feeling the change in the slipstream as the wheels dropped from their housings; then adjusted the trim again as the flaps went down. The runway lights were clear now, and the four throttles boosted engine power for landing. The Halifax was crabbing slightly and he corrected it; then saw the lights at the end of the runway and settled the wheels down on to the concrete, feeling them jar, then grip, holding the control column back, seeing Joe close the throttles slowly, using the rudders to keep the nose straight on the runway's centre line. They were home, and it was finished.

When they had left the aircraft they all stood in a group beneath one wing, listening to the sounds of other engines above them. Then Nick said: 'That's it, then. Thanks, fellers.' And suddenly their relief erupted and they pumped each others' hands and slapped shoulders and grinned and joked, and promised themselves countless beers, and women, and forty-eight hours unbroken sleep, and nights on the town, until they scrambled into the crew van and went for debriefing and coffee and rum and then breakfast, staring round at the other faces, hoping to see everyone, laughing like schoolboys as they realised that all the station's aircraft had returned. That made their final flight of the tour even better.

*   *   *

Robert watched Nick come out of the byre after helping Martin Calder and the head cowman feed the dairy herd at afternoon milking, and said: 'You'll make a farmer yet. I reckon you can put the rations together as well as anyone on the place.'

Nick grinned.

'I have a feeling there's more to it than that,' he said. 'But it's great fun. It may be ordinary for Martin and his men, but it does me good.'

Robert nodded. He did not have to be told how much Nick had needed the therapy of relaxation augmented by a little work around the home farm. He had been shocked by his brother-in-law's changed appearance when he had started his leave, and the number of cigarettes he was smoking, and Ruth had told him quietly: 'He's terribly tense, Rob. This leave hasn't come a moment too soon.'

Now, ten days later, Nick's eyes were as bright as ever. His manner had become as careless and flippant as once it had been, and he and Ruth were immersed in each other.

They saw Lisa several times, for she was now a nurse at the city and county hospital. She went out for evenings with them; once Robert escorted her, and she found it intriguing to be in the close company of the man who was so nearly Richard's double even though his humour and interests were often in contrast.

But on the evening of the 4th of May she was on duty and had to decline an invitation to join Ruth and Nick at the house of the senior partner in Ruth's veterinary practice. His name was Colin Cawson, and he was a grey-bearded sixty-year-old bachelor who was delighted to show off his culinary skills and who had planned for his guests a meal which, in view of wartime rationing, was a tribute both to his ability in the kitchen and his black market contacts. He took a near-fatherly interest in Ruth and her pilot husband, and they looked forward both to his table and his company as they drove across Exeter to his old-fashioned house beyond the city's western suburbs.

*   *   *

As they knocked on the door, two hundred miles away a man wearing a blue-grey uniform with a jacket collar buttoned high at the throat and a peaked cap bearing an eagle emblem, knocked sharply on a table top. He rose to his feet as three other uniformed figures strode through a door and made their way to the front of a long room to face 108 men, also uniformed, some carrying clip boards and pencils, others lounging back on wooden chairs. All scrambled upright as the three men appeared, then settled again as one stepped forward and signalled with a curt movement of his hand.

He said: 'Good evening, gentlemen. Our business tonight will not take long. The operation is straightforward, and I do not anticipate that you will meet heavy opposition.' Oberstleutnant Hans Schulz was addressing three Staffeln which made up 11 Gruppe in Bomber Geschwader 27 of the Luftwaffe, at their base close to Caen in Normandy.

'Tonight's operation is a small one, but important nevertheless, with a specific target, and no other aircraft will take part,' he said, and then nodded to a tall fair-haired man who had been waiting quietly in the background and who now stepped forward easily, confidently, with scarcely a glance at Schulz. He was the intelligence officer of the Gruppe.

'The target is conveniently near,' he said, and rolled aside the large cover over a map and photographs which stood on an easel at his side. He pointed with a cane.

'Take off is at fifteen minutes after midnight.' He indicated the location of the Caen airfield. 'You will follow the course indicated over Cherbourg and then at minimum height steer five degrees east of north so that if, in spite of your altitude, you are detected on enemy radar, the impression will be that you are making for Southampton.' He tapped the map with his pointer. 'Here you will alter course to fly, again at minimum altitude to keep beneath the radar, parallel with the coast at a distance of thirty kilometres until you reach the mouth of the River Exe, and will then follow the river to the city of Exeter. Because you will be below the radar you should not be detected until you are close to it. AA defences are light, and while there is a night fighter squadron based at the RAF station east of Exeter' – again the tapping pointer – 'you should be over the target and away before the enemy realises what is happening. Your target is the city centre, and you will return at will once you have bombed, again flying as low as possible and keeping to the west so that you are as far as possible from the night fighter base.'

He then detailed the course, the order in which the aircraft were to approach the target, bombing patterns and the radio frequencies to be used, before inviting questions. The last, almost as an afterthought, came from a young Feldwebel at the back of the room.

'Herr Hauptmann – is there any military significance in this target?'

The fair-haired intelligence officer's mouth was thin and wide.

'The significance of this target is related to the significance of the German city of Lubeck to the RAF. If Lubeck, with its architectural beauty, was a legitimate target for enemy bombers, so Exeter is a legitimate target for ours. The British must understand the extent of their follies. Do you have any further questions, Feldwebel Hinze?'

The young man flushed and shook his head.

'No, Herr Hauptmann. None.'

Oberstleutnant Schulz nodded to another officer who gave the crews a short weather briefing, then gathered up his papers, stood up, clicked his heels and gave the stiff-armed Nazi salute, and moved smartly away towards the door followed by his Staffel commanders and Intelligence Officer Kurt Edelmann.

The crews then dispersed to make their final notes, and to eat supper as they waited for midnight and take-off, by which time Colin Cawson had satisfied his guests in Exeter and was relaxing with them over drinks and conversation which did not draw to a close until almost two o'clock, just as the first wave of Heinkels flew up the coast past Teignmouth.

Two minutes after Ruth and Nick left Cawson's house, the Exeter air raid warning sirens sounded.

Nick said: 'Listen. That's the second time in a week.'

'They dropped only a few bombs last time,' she said, and sounded worried. 'But one fell near the hospital. I wonder why they're coming back. There's nothing here of military value.'

'Nuisance. They just send out a handful of planes. Raids like that don't have to have military targets. Don't worry. This time they'll probably pass over and go for Taunton, or somewhere.' He grinned at her in the dark, and they drove on into the deserted city centre, peering through the glimmer cast by the masked headlights.

It was as they crossed the river into New Bridge Street that they heard the first aircraft engines; and suddenly Nick was uneasy. He wound down the car's window and listened. Ruth glanced at him questioningly.

'More than a handful up there,' he said; and his nerves jerked him in his seat as anti-aircraft guns opened fire somewhere south of the city.

Then, as they drove up the hill into High Street, they heard a shrill whistle, and in the faint glow of their headlights saw a figure which materialized into a policeman. As they stopped he ran up to the car and shouted: 'There's a bloody air raid – leave that thing where it is and –' Then he saw Nick's uniform and checked. 'Sorry, sir. But you'll have to take shelter.' He opened the car door and added: 'Come with me. I'll show you.'

Inside the car they exchanged glances, then Nick nodded.

'It might be sensible,' he said. 'Better get out.'

They abandoned the car and followed the policeman at a brisk trot up the street; just as Feldwebel Hinze, tense in the nose of a Heinkel 5000 feet above and with eyes glued to his bombsight, released two high explosive bombs followed by a load of incendiaries, chanted 'Bombs gone,' then added: 'That's something for Lubeck, you bastards.'

The first bomb fell behind St Stephen's church in High Street, bringing down part of the tower, the south wall and most of the roof, and Nick sprawled across the pavement, trying to protect Ruth with his body as the explosion shattered the night a hundred yards in front of them and debris cascaded and flame seared upwards as a gas main fractured. He scrambled to his knees and dragged her against the wall of a building just as the second of Feldwebel Hinze's bombs hit the back of it and blew it forward so that it fell in a roaring, scraping eruption of stone and brick and the shock wave hammered through it as it collapsed.

Further along the street, then left and right and behind, more bombs fell; first the high explosives, then the incendiaries, until the whole city centre seemed alight and alive with flame and smoke and rumbling debris. Then, abruptly, it was over and the throbbing engines overhead were gone, and the loudest sounds were the fire engine and ambulance bells and the shouts of the gathering rescue teams and, so faintly, the cries of those who were buried alive beneath the ruins.

The civilian defence and rescue forces in Exeter were facing

152

their first great test. There had been a few bombs on the city before. But this was different: this was mass destruction of the city's heart, and it would spread unless the fires were contained. Hoses criss-crossed the streets, flames lighting the faces of the men and shining on their helmets as they struggled to send their jets of water into blazing, tottering buildings. Away from the fires, rescue teams were formed and lights set up as shovels clanged against piles of debris and men began the grim, desperate, exhausting search for survivors beneath the rubble.

It went on through the night. Only the fire areas were beyond the reach of the rescuers, until the flames had gone and the ruins cooled. Elsewhere they fought their way through stone and brick and timbers and choking dust, their own lives at risk as debris shifted; stopping sometimes in response to shouted orders, listening in the tense silence for the hint of a cry; then digging again, carefully now, faces streaked with dirt, as the ambulance crews waited behind them.

In High Street the ruins sprawled on both sides. Someone brought up a mechanical shovel to clear rubble into waiting lorries. Near the scarred Guild Hall and the remains of St Stephen's Church men heaved stone blocks aside and struggled with splintered timbers as pale daylight filtered through the dust clouds. Then one of them shouted: 'Quiet – everybody quiet – I heard something.'

They stood, perched awkwardly on the ruins, eyes grey-rimmed. Someone signalled to the driver of the shovel and he stopped the great throbbing engine. Overhead a seagull called against the morning sky. They bent, staring at the debris. One man went down on his knees, his head turning first one way then another. Nearby, masonry shifted and scraped, and they waited for the stillness to return. Then the man on his knees said quietly: 'Here. Just here. Like – like mewing.'

They began again, but slowly; bricks and stone and wood moved cautiously; levering with spades and crowbars but using their hands to lift the rubble away.

Then they saw cloth. Blue cloth beneath the dust and grit. They worked faster, calling more men to help. A length of timber was moved, then more stones, and they had made a hole. Someone shone a torch in the half-light. There was a man, crumpled. In air force uniform. A rescuer wormed down, lifting out more bricks.

Arms stretched down to him. Slowly, grunting, they got hands beneath the man and, with infinite care, brought him up into the dawn.

A voice said: 'Oh Christ. He's dead.'

They laid him on the piled rubble and someone brought a stretcher. They could see the uniform now, and the wings on it. Then the ambulance men were there and they wrapped a cloth around him, and a voice cried from the hole: 'Come back – there's someone else –'

It took them five more minutes to lift her out. And as they held her, so gently, and saw her blackened face and hair, she moved her head and they heard the small sound they had heard before, and one of the men put his grimed cheek against hers and whispered: 'It's all right, m'love. We've got you now.'

But she did not move again.

*   *   *

It was over, and the little church was quiet again. He had returned to the house with the others after the service; but then had said to Lisa: 'Please excuse me. I want to go back.'

Now he walked through the lychgate, turned off the paved path leading to the church, and crossed between old stones. Ahead, in the Haldane family's corner of the churchyard, he could see a grave digger picking up a spade and making ready to shovel earth into the new grave. The man looked up at him, startled.

'Will you leave me, please? Come back in ten minutes.'

The voice contemplated no argument, and the man said, 'Yes, sir,' put down his spade and walked away, glancing back curiously before he rounded the corner of the church and pulled a packet of Woodbines from his pocket, lighting one against the cup of his soiled hand.

The wind was chill among the elms at the edge of the churchyard in spite of the fitful sunshine. He walked carefully round the open grave and the high pile of soil and clay, until he could look straight down and see the two coffins, side by side, and read the shining metal plates.

He stood still then; for a minute, two minutes, and longer. The peaked cap of his uniform was under his arm, and his hands were clasped behind his back. Strands of his dark hair blew across his

154

forehead, and once he brushed them aside. And all the time he looked down at the two coffins deep in the earth, and if anyone had stood close to him they would have seen a strange light in his near-black eyes and would have been fearful of its intensity.

Then he raised those eyes above the grave, and beyond to the trees and the sky, and his voice whispered into the wind and carried away on it: 'For each of you, there will be a thousand; and when that is done, I will take another thousand. You cannot be avenged; but if you can hear me, know that there will be revenge, and I will multiply it.'

And he stood in the wind and sun, and closed his eyes as the tears ran down his cheeks.

17

The Group Captain and the Wing Commander drove slowly along the perimeter track towards the watch tower. Overhead grey clouds reached from horizon to horizon, the ceiling was under a thousand feet and getting lower, and there was little wind to encourage hope that the weather might improve.

Ahead they saw a figure leave the control building and walk away towards the distant flight huts. The Wing Commander commented: 'Haldane, sir. Whenever we're grounded by the weather he hangs around, reading the met reports, waiting. He's like an explosion looking for somewhere to happen. All he wants is to get across the Channel on a rhubarb.' The word was slang for low-flying intruder raids by small groups of fighters attacking ground targets. 'He'll surely kill himself one day.'

The Group Captain stopped the car beside the watch tower.

'I know,' he said. 'I've read your reports. I've never seen a man react so dramatically to personal tragedy. And time doesn't seem to lessen it.'

'I don't think it will. He remains a first-class squadron commander and an exceptional pilot. But where he used to temper his aggression with discipline, he's now totally single-minded. All he wants is to be across there doing as much damage as he can – and, I have to say, killing as many people as he can. I think he also has the death wish; but he wouldn't be the first, after the length of time he's been on ops.'

'How do his men regard him?'

'Before the Exeter raid they admired him. Since then –' the Wing Commander hesitated momentarily '– some of them are afraid of him. He leads them into desperate situations sometimes, and if any man doesn't follow him totally, he savages him in front of the rest when they return. His own aircraft take a terrible hammering, but somehow he keeps getting them back; but he's losing pilots, and my view is that he's taking foolish risks with them.'

The Group Captain said: 'War is about taking risks. The trick is to know when they're worth taking. How long since he was on leave?'

'Six months, apart from the compassionate when his sister was killed and two or three forty-eights since. He's been out three times in foul weather against my orders, and when I've reprimanded him he's said "Do you want me to kill Germans, or not?" I've flown with him myself several times, and I don't mind telling you, sir – he scares me.'

The Group Captain did not have to remind himself that his senior Wing Commander had an impressive operational record, with medal ribbons to demonstrate that he did not scare easily.

'All right,' he said. 'We'll take him off ops. I'll have him posted – give him a rest, while he's still alive.'

'He'll fight you all the way,' the Wing Commander warned.

'He'll take orders,' said the Group Captain. 'I'll see if I can arrange one of the PR trips to America for him. Give him a new environment for a few weeks. I'll ring the Air Ministry tomorrow. He's earned something of the sort.' He looked hard at his subordinate. 'My impression is that he may have earned something else. Isn't it time he was put down for a DSO? His record is outstanding, whatever his motivation in the last few months.'

The Wing Commander looked pleased.

'I'd recommend that wholeheartedly, sir.'

'Good.' The Group Captain opened the car door. 'I'll put it forward. In the meantime – keep him alive, if you can.'

*　　*　　*

Richard lifted the Spitfire up over the beaches near St Aubin on the Normandy coast, at a point where he knew from experience there were no defending guns, then dropped down to tree-top height and streaked inland. Close behind flew Steve Mitchell, tucked in low and close to his leader's tail. Both aircraft were carrying drop tanks, a squadron experiment to increase the limited range of the Spitfire for intruder operations and a facility for which Richard had been arguing for months.

This was Mitchell's twenty-seventh birthday, and before take-off Richard had said to him: 'Let's see if we can find you a present, Mitch. A nice convoy would do fine.' Now he concentrated on following the aircraft just ahead, down between lines of poplars, up over electricity cables, past farm houses at chimney height, flat and low across fields at 280 miles an hour, watching left, right and especially above and behind, flying by instinct except for one eye on the compass and on the map tied to his knee, riding the turbulence, pulse rate up but steady.

Then Richard broke radio silence, for both knew that by now their presence would have been detected.

'Hard left, Mitch – a train.'

They tilted, and Richard's port wing seemed to clip a tree as a railway line swung into view. Half a mile ahead a train steamed, closed box-cars in a snaking line and Richard pulled wide so that he could rake the sides of the vehicles with cannon and machine gun fire. They flashed down the line of trucks, aircraft shuddering against the recoil of the guns, seeing flashes as their fire struck, and pieces of metal and wood flying, and one truck suddenly mushrooming flame. Then it was all behind them and they hurtled on southward, heading for a satellite bomber airfield between Caen and Le Mans.

They came upon it suddenly, just after they had jettisoned their extra fuel tanks; and the tracer climbed to meet them and the pom-poms opened up. Richard called, 'I'll take the ack-ack – you go for the rest,' and they diverged, Richard's guns hammering as he lined up on the defenders' sand-bagged positions. He sat hunched in his cockpit as he pulled round in a tight turn, seeing grey-clad figures running and tumbling. His mouth widened behind his mask and he whispered: 'You bastards.'

A gun on his right sewed a pattern of holes along one of his wings and he swung towards it, below hangar height, catching a quick glimpse of Mitchell's aircraft in a vertical bank on the other side of the airfield and fire suddenly belching from something on the ground before he lined up on the gun emplacement, then felt the Spitfire buck as a cannon shell exploded somewhere beneath it. He steadied it as he fired a short burst and saw two men catapult backwards and grinned his mirthless grin as he thundered over their shattered refuge. He turned hard, 200 feet up, saw Mitchell through smoke clouds, flicked his R/T switch and said: 'Okay. Stay with me. Let's see what else is around.'

He turned on to 170 degrees and throttled back a little to give Mitchell time to catch up; then heard the voice in his headset: 'Hey, boss' – in the air Mitchell always called him 'boss' despite their close friendship – 'what's the idea? Are you looking for a holiday on the Med? How much flying time d'you reckon before we turn round?'

Richard waved a gloved hand to the other pilot.

'Another few minutes. You never know how lucky we might be. They're not used to prowlers this far south –'

It was then that he saw the explosion; right at the edge of his vision, smoke and a flash and pieces of metal, out of focus, close beside him yet far, far away. Not Mitch, for he was on the other side. Then it was gone and his mind shuddered against an image of the long-dead Phil Fletcher, and the face distorted and dissolved into Jan's grief and then into Marj's grief too, and he wiped a hand across his eyes to blot it out and sat in the cockpit sweating and muttering, 'Christ, dear Christ – why now?' And then, 'No, please, don't take me now – I haven't finished –'

The two aircraft snarled on, low across fields, heading for Blois and the broad reaches of the Loire, and Mitchell said: 'Boss – if we don't turn now we won't make it.'

'Okay,' Richard acknowledged. He was still looking for targets, and still fighting down the memory of his private, dreadful ghosts. He went into a shallow turn, seeing another river ahead; refusing to let himself wonder why the vision had come to him again after so long.

Then his engine coughed.

He had not been watching his instruments. Now he saw that his oil pressure was low and the temperature high. The engine missed again; then a third time. And he remembered the cannon shell.

Quite calmly he said: 'Mitch, I may have a little trouble. I'm going up, in case the machinery stops. You stay on the deck – less chance of anything hitting you.'

Equally calmly Mitchell responded: 'I'll stay with you. Watching out for the one-nineties.' The Focke Wulf 190 was Germany's newest and most dangerous fighter.

Both aircraft lifted. But at 600 feet Richard's engine missed again, and badly this time, and Mitchell said: 'You have an oil leak, boss. Not dreadful. But not good, either.' He sounded easy, almost indifferent, as if they were talking about a scratch on the paintwork.

Richard pushed the throttle forward and raised the nose further, wanting more height so that he could bale out if necessary; then felt his speed dropping as the engine spluttered, and he knew he was not going to get the altitude he needed.

He was going down; there was no doubt about it. This was it. The end of the story. For a frightening moment panic gripped him, and he saw Phil Fletcher's face again. Then he pushed the memory aside, forcing himself to think; and remembered the second river.

It was still there, just below his port wing. He had crossed the Loire. So this had to be the Cher – the boundary in this area between German-occupied and Vichy-controlled France.

Without hesitation he went left, glanced up and saw Mitchell's aircraft swinging with him. He pushed back his hood so that Mitchell could see him and gave a repeated thumbs-down sign.

'I've had it, Mitch.' Steady, flat-calm; as if someone else were speaking. 'Don't hang around. Have a good party tonight. Tell Lisa I'll be okay. I'll find my way back. Be sure to tell her.'

Mitchell pulled wide of the stricken Spitfire and said: 'I'll tell her. To hell with the party. Good luck. Put it down gently, so you don't break any eggs. Take care, you old sod.'

The river was behind him now, and open country ahead. But there were trees; too many trees. Woods and scattered copses. Fields with trees around them and across them. Christ – how many trees? Did these bloody Frenchmen grow nothing but trees? Where the hell was he? It didn't matter, except that he was south of the Cher. And there was a field, long and narrow, with trees on either side and at the end; but a long field, and almost dead ahead. Two hundred feet, and the engine was banging and shuddering and doing nothing for him. He did not even look at the rev counter, or the oil gauges, because there was no point. The machinery was stopping and there was not a bloody thing he could do about it. Phil. Did you come to tell me? Don't call me yet, Phil. I haven't finished. And Lisa wouldn't like it. A hundred feet, less. What a bloody silly thought – Lisa wouldn't like it. Too high – flaps are down, but still too high. Oh Christ, don't let me overshoot into those bloody trees. Lisa, I tried but I just couldn't make it – I'm sorry –

Mitchell flew slowly up above, watching, fascinated and horrified, telling himself it couldn't be happening: not to Richard, because he was immortal, indestructible, the cold calculating one, the one who always came back.

But not this time.

The Spitfire was very low now, and Richard stalled it, with the control column hard back. He thought Oh God I left it too late I should have been down fifty yards back Lisa wait for me in case I get out of this. Trees hurtled on either side as the idling propeller hit the ground and buckled, then the air intakes and the underside grinding and cracking, and he was thrown against the straps and his head hit something and the trees ahead were too close and dark and he was going into them and he wouldn't get back to Lisa –

Steve Mitchell saw the Spitfire skidding and bucking, saw the tail break off; saw it slewing sideways as it ploughed on through a wire fence and into the wood and it was gone, and he said aloud: 'Christ, oh dear Christ, please stop it.' Branches waved and tossed, then were still. He turned steeply, watching all the time, no longer looking for Focke Wulfs, watching the awful stillness of the wood, circling and waiting, not knowing why: and then seeing, as if from another world, a great flash down there among the trees and a column of flame, then black smoke funnelling up and debris scattering through it as it spread over the place where Richard Haldane had gone.

*   *   *

He was the one to tell Lisa, on the telephone. He was as gentle as he could be, and when he had finished she was quiet; until he said: 'Lisa – are you still there?' And she replied: 'Yes, Mitch. I'm still here. What's left of me.' And he went on hurriedly: 'Don't give up. He could be all right. He's walked away from two crash-landings before. Hang on tight, girl. There's a good chance for him.' But he thought: You liar, you rotten lousy liar, you know he didn't have a chance, why don't you give it to her straight?

But he couldn't do that. Not to Lisa.

He gave it straight to the Wing Commander, though. He said: 'He hadn't a hope, sir. He went smack into the trees, then blew up. No one could have survived that.' And the Wing Commander said: 'We'll have to post him missing believed killed; at least until we get confirmation through the Red Cross.'

When Lisa told Robert she repeated Steve Mitchell's words again and again, as if doing so would make them come true; and she looked at Robert's dark hair and near-black eyes and the face that was almost Richard's and suddenly that was the worst moment of all, as if she were seeing Richard in a mirror but could only touch the glass and never reach beyond it, and she covered her face and wept. He took her in his arms to comfort her but being close to him was too much like being close to Richard and that made it unbearable. She pushed herself away but could not tell him why.

Later they told Diane and it was too close to Ruth's death and they had to call a doctor to sedate her, even though Lisa kept repeating Steve Mitchell's lies.

*   *   *

They stood in a group among the wreckage, shovels in hand, uniforms muddy. Overhead, branches moved in the wind and the sun filtered between the scarred trees.

The local Inspector of Police picked his way through the torn metal, then moved off among the blackened branches and scorched undergrowth to more debris and the two gendarmes examining it. With him went a civilian, dark-coated, with watchful eyes. He was the Gestapo observer attached to the police in the area: the normal situation in that part of France which the Germans had left under the control of their puppet Vichy government.

The inspector pointed.

'The engine block. And one of the wheels. God knows where

161

the other one is.'

The dark-coated man nodded absently. He held a stout stick which he had picked up at the edge of the wood, and he was using it to turn over pieces of twisted metal. He had been doing that since he had arrived, walking through the hundred-metre square of scarred woodland over which the wreckage was spread, prodding and peering. He had spent a long time looking at the remains of the cockpit section of the fuselage, part of which lay thirty or forty paces from the blackened area which must have been the heart of the explosion. He was wandering off in that direction again when one of the policemen prodded into charred metal nearby, picked something up and looked at it before walking over to the inspector. He held out his hand and offered an identity disc on a length of thin chain.

The inspector took it and studied it, holding it up to the light through the trees.

'Royal Air Force. Haldane R. And a number,' he said.

The Gestapo observer reached for it, read it himself, then put it into his pocket.

'Good,' he said. 'Now he has a name.' His French was fair, although with a marked accent.

The inspector said: 'What will you do – pass it to the Red Cross in Switzerland so that they can report him killed?'

The man in the dark coat looked at him coldly.

'Before I report a man killed I want to see a body,' he said.

The inspector shrugged.

'You'll look a long time for a body in this mess. The thing blew up. Look at the damage to the trees. All over the place. The pilot must have been blown into a thousand pieces.'

'Then why can't I find one of them?' The voice was as cold as the eyes.

The inspector shrugged again.

'There was fire. A great explosion. Then everything burned. You can see what happened. The trees are burned, and the bushes. Even the earth is burned. All blackened and stinking, everywhere. The bits of the pilot would have been burned as well.'

The Gestapo observer prodded away with his stick, and shook his head.

'All metal,' he said. 'Somewhere there should be pieces of a body. A finger or a toe, or a skull or an arm. Or a piece of flesh burned by the fire. But there's nothing. I agree that he could have been totally destroyed. But equally –' He shook his head again, still poking with the stick.

The inspector eyed him, trying to conceal his exasperation. He had always been careful not to quarrel with the men sent to make sure the police did their job the way the Germans wanted it to be done. But sometimes he found it difficult.

'So what are you going to do?' he asked.

'Not me. You,' the dark-coated man said. 'You start a search. If there was a miracle and he survived, he must be within a mile or two, minus a leg or an arm, and badly smashed up. But however bad he is, if he's still alive your men must find him, and whoever is sheltering him. They must be dealt with. In the meantime –' he pulled the identity disc from his pocket and waved it so that it swung on its broken chain '– I'll report that he's missing. And he'll stay missing until I see a body.'

He moved away, walking carefully through the scattered remains of the aircraft, prodding and peering. The inspector thought he was paranoid; like most of the Germans he had seen. It was the Resistance, of course. They knew it was there, in occupied France and in Vichy France, and they were afraid of it. Maybe this one imagined the Resistance had come along and spirited the pilot's mutilated body away for a secret burial in a churchyard. The inspector's shoulders moved in his habitual shrug. Maybe the Resistance had been here. If they had he would not ask questions. He liked to keep as far away as he could from the Germans and the Resistance. He liked a quiet life. Certainly he was not going to worry because a British pilot had been blown to bits.

18

Rain ran steadily down the small window. He lay on his back, watching it and listening to the wind in the trees which lined up like sentinels along the side of the old house and down the edge of the field behind it. He turned his head, looking at the cheap dressing table and the simple chair beside it. The walls were painted plaster; clean but crude in a pale pinkish shade that had seen better days. The single light bulb hanging from the centre of the cracked ceiling had no shade and hurt his eyes when it was turned on at night. The room was his shelter and his salvation; but he hated it, because he could not leave it and so it was also his prison.

He felt better today. But that was a relative matter: better today than he had been last week, better still than a month ago. He tried not to remember the way he had felt before that.

But at least he was alive. And the little wizened doctor who came to him secretly out of the village near the town of Loches said that one day he would be almost as good as new. It was just a matter of patience.

But Richard Haldane felt he did not have a lot of that left.

He stirred in the bed: gently, for his left leg was encased in plaster from foot to thigh, his left forearm was also in plaster, the deep lacerations down the right side of his body were tender even though the sixty-two stitches had been taken out a month or more ago, and his broken ribs snatched like a sharp metal band around his chest whenever he sat up. But he was no longer dizzy when he moved, and the doctor seemed confident that although his skull had been fractured there had been no damage to his brain.

The door latch clicked and he smiled at the rotund, grey-haired woman who looked at him anxiously.

'You are feeling better?' she asked, as she did every time she saw him. She came into the room, walking softly on the bare wooden floor as if afraid she might wake him.

'Better every day, Madame,' he said.

'I'll bring you some broth, and a little chicken.' Madame Marchand was the wife of a peasant farmer who scratched a living from twelve hectares of indifferent land and augmented its meagre return with the money he earned working in the village bakery at night; but she was also a countrywoman who had learned from childhood how to make good food from scarce material.

Richard said: 'I would enjoy that.' His smile was wider. 'One day, Madame, I will repay you for all this.'

'You will repay me on the day you are able to walk out of here. That is all the payment I need.' She came further into the room and closed the door behind her. 'Georges talked with someone in

164

the village last night,' she said conspiratorially. 'Someone who will help you when you are well. It's all arranged. And it will be a simple matter because you speak our language and you know our customs. We shall turn you into a Frenchman and neither the police nor the Gestapo will ever know you are anything else.' She patted him on one hand. 'I'll bring the food. Then you must rest again.'

She went out, still walking quietly, looking back at him with her habitual worried frown.

He closed his eyes. So Georges Marchand had been talking to someone. That was what he had promised. The escape network would look after him. They would take him south-west, through the Pyrenees into Spain, then down to Gibraltar. Others had gone that way. While the Germans left nearly half France unoccupied it was not too difficult.

But his injuries would have to heal first. Until then he was trapped in this little farmhouse, hidden away from the police and the German 'observers' who watched them, dependent entirely on Georges Marchand and his wife, on the village doctor, and on the silence of neighbours.

Georges had been the one to find him. He could remember nothing of it; nor of the crash itself or the final minutes of his flight. But they had told him the tale. Georges, visiting friends in a village seven miles away, had seen the Spitfire come down and had heard an explosion. He had hurried through the wood to find smouldering wreckage scattered through broken trees – and, to his amazement, the badly injured pilot lying behind a stout beech, still strapped to the remains of his seat and with pieces of the fuselage attached to the seat frame. The Spitfire had disintegrated as it had hit the trees, the cockpit section had split away and come to rest thirty or forty metres from the engine and fuel tank which had exploded seconds later, and the wings and the remainder of the fuselage had been torn and twisted into unrecognisable debris.

But Richard had been alive; unconscious, bleeding profusely from severe lacerations, with other injuries which Marchand could not assess; but still breathing.

Marchand had run to the nearby house and was joined by two men armed with hacksaws and axes. And as they had begun to cut Richard free and struggled to stop his bleeding, one had seen that a silver chain around his neck was caught in a metal spar and was cutting across his windpipe. Gently he had cut the chain, pulling it and the disc attached to it away from the unconscious pilot, and had thrown it into the debris.

They had worked for half an hour to free him; then had carried him on a make-shift stretcher to the house. If they kept him there they knew he would be found and, although one man had favoured handing him over to the police so that he might receive hospital treatment, Marchand had telephoned the doctor who lived in his own village and had then taken the unconscious man in his old van down narrow lanes and by-ways to his little farmhouse.

At first the doctor had shaken his grey head: the victim was too badly injured and would not recover whether he remained at the farm or was handed over to the authorities. But he had set the broken limbs and had bathed the lacerations and stitched them where he could, and had visited the farm every night for two weeks until Richard had regained consciousness and, slowly, had begun to recover.

Now he knew it was only a question of time. How well he would walk, how much use his left arm would be to him, remained uncertain. But he would recover. He had been uneasy about the loss of his identity disc, for if he was captured that would have been his safeguard; his proof that he was entitled to treatment as a prisoner-of-war. But it was gone, and since the wreckage would now have been cleared away there was no point in asking that someone should go back and search for it. Perhaps, when his escape journey began, the Resistance would not have wanted him to wear it. Anyway, it did not matter, and he no longer cared about it. All he had to do was concentrate on recovery, and hope he was not discovered by the police. He had been provided with a temporary identity card by an unknown friend of Marchand's, for which someone had come one night to take his photograph. But both he and his hosts were uneasy about it, for the photograph was so obviously that of a sick man. He was described on the card as a farm worker, and the story was that he had been injured in an incident with a bull. But it was flimsy and would not stand investigation if a Gestapo observer got hold of it. All he could do was stay in his little bedroom, and hope.

Once he had asked Marchand if there was a way for him to send a message back to England so that his family would know he was alive, but the farmer had shaken his head. 'We are too close to the

German-occupied zone,' he had said. 'We have to be very careful. The Resistance in these parts does not have the equipment to transmit radio messages to London. But don't worry. Once the network picks you up, someone will see that a message is sent. Be patient.'

So he stayed in his room and remembered Lisa, every hour and every day, until the plaster cast was cut away from his arm and he began to exercise it in spite of the pain from his ribs. Then the doctor took away the cast on his leg, and he was horrified to see how wasted it was, and how weak it felt when he tried to walk on it. But, with the aid of a stick, he could go outside, and the chill autumn air was wine to him.

With the freedom of movement his spirit returned, and he set himself a daily schedule of exercises. The doctor taught him how to massage his legs and, day by day, his strength came back. Madame Marchand became anxious that he was tiring himself, but he followed his programme with dogged determination: an hour's exercise, an hour's rest, an hour's walking around the little farm, two hours' rest, an hour's exercise, an hour's rest, then a short walk. In the evenings he rested again, but always exercised before he went to bed.

Early in November he was visited by a small, swarthy man who did not give his name but who said: 'I am told you are making good progress, m'sieur, and that by the end of December you may be able to start your journey – if you do not mind taking your stick with you, perhaps. We shall have the arrangements ready.'

But three days later, on 11th November, his hopes of an early escape were destroyed; for on that day the German army took control of Vichy France, and with the troops came new Gestapo personnel who did not pretend to be passive observers, and there were units of the dreaded SS to enforce the discipline of occupation. Many Resistance workers were arrested within the first week, for the Germans had been working quietly to identify them before the take-over; and for a time almost all activity stopped as people watched and waited for the initial fury to die. And Richard waited, for he had no alternative; passing time with his exercises and now with work around the little farm.

Through December and January his strength improved and he became an accepted part of the Marchand household, enjoying evenings playing cards and drinking wine with local callers, exchanging stories with them, noting that one of them was the swarthy man who had visited him in November and whom he now addressed, as did the others, as Marcel. At Christmas extra food was produced, for it was a point of honour to demonstrate that even the German army could not stand between French men and women and their devotion to the art of cooking and the serious business of eating and drinking.

For a while Richard even began to enjoy himself; except sometimes at night, when he would stand at the house door and stare up at the stars and wonder how they looked over Roxton and whether Lisa was watching them from her parents' home at Newton Abbot. Then he longed for her, and the sound of her voice and the silk of her hair against his face and the feel of her body; and the frustrations and impatience returned and he flexed his muscles and tested his strength.

It was late in February when the man called Marcel came to him, pulling his corduroy cap low over his shaggy hair and rubbing his fingers across the stubble on his chin as he said: 'It is nearly time, Richard. You will soon have a new identity card, new clothes, a ration card, and a new name. You will be Ricard Michel, a salesman selling shirts and ties for a manufacturer in Toulouse. An arrangement has been made with that manufacturer to ensure that your story will stand investigation. I will give you the details tomorrow, when I shall return with a photographer. This time' – he grinned and showed broken teeth – 'your picture will look more like a human being and less like a corpse.'

He came back the next day with the photographer; and also with the courier who was to escort Richard to Lyon. They introduced her as Yvonne Cardin; she was around thirty years old, dark and petite and attractive and, Richard judged from her confident voice and steady eyes, competent. Marcel said: 'Yvonne is an experienced guide. It is in your interests to do exactly as she says at all times. Your safety, and hers, depend on that. Now tell me how you feel. Are you as strong as you look?'

Richard said: 'Strong enough. My leg and my arm are sometimes weak, and now and then they ache. But they won't prove a handicap.'

Marchand told him: 'You have made a remarkable recovery, for one who was nearly dead.'

'Thanks to Madame,' Richard said. He turned to her. 'I cannot express my gratitude. But for a long time I have wanted to ask you one question: why have you done this? You have placed yourselves at great risk, you have taken a stranger into your home and nursed him as if he were your son, not for a few weeks but for six months. Why have you done this for me?'

The grey-haired woman wiped her hands down her pinafore. She thought for several seconds before she replied, and once looked at her husband for help but he seemed embarrassed and was silent. Finally she said: 'It is something you do without thinking at first. Then, after a time, you go on doing it because you want to. We have no children, but since you were brought here you have become to us as a child. So we have done it for ourselves as well as for you. And we have also done it for France, for you have to fight for France now. You must come here after the war, when the Germans have gone. But before then I hope you will fly over us many times, and that the Germans will fear you.'

He said softly: 'Madame Marchand, wherever I go the Germans will fear me. I made that promise to someone else. Now I can go on keeping it.'

*   *   *

On the day Richard was told he was soon to leave the farmhouse near Loches, Diane telephoned Lisa and said: 'I'm going to have a few days' holiday as soon as the weather improves. I'm trying to persuade Robert to join me. We both need it. And I'm sure you do, too. Will you come?'

Lisa thought how much better Diane sounded now: just in the last few weeks she seemed to have begun to fight back, to accept Robert's encouragement and strength.

'I'd like to,' she said. 'Where are you going?'

'I don't know. Somewhere in the Cotswolds, perhaps. It will still be too cold to stay on the coast, and in any case there's barbed wire everywhere. But do come if you can.'

'I will. I'll try very hard. Thanks, Diane.'

They chatted for a few minutes, then rang off; and Diane marvelled, as she had so often done in the recent past, at Lisa's calm and control. She knew, they all knew, that Richard must be dead. Sooner or later there would be confirmation. She felt better now that she had accepted it herself, for hoping when there was no hope had been the worst torture; and she was sure the same thing had happened to Lisa. Robert knew, that was certain. He had had a second meeting with Steve Mitchell just before Christmas. Diane did not know what had been said, but afterwards Robert's attitude had changed, and he had gently led them all towards acceptance of the inevitable.

But none of them talked about the medal, for somehow it seemed the saddest thing that Richard should have died without knowing. A DSO was a major award. The Group Captain had asked her if she would like to receive it, but she had refused. It would have been too much like a posthumous award. So the squadron had taken it, and there had been a small presentation ceremony which she had not had the courage to attend. Robert and Lisa had been there, and when they came back neither would talk much about it, except to say that the medal would be held among the squadron honours until Richard returned.

But they all knew he would not return.

19

Travelling to Lyon had been easy. Twice there had been checks on the trains, but their papers had provided good reasons for their journey and there had been no trouble. The first time apprehension had gripped Richard and he had felt himself sweating, but he had covered it by talking in French to the two soldiers and then listening to their conversation together in German without giving them any sign that he understood. The second time it had been less nerve-wracking, and now as they walked out of the Gare de Perrache he was almost sorry that the rail journey was over, for it had given him his first sense of freedom.

They walked north in fading daylight to the Place Carnot, and Richard passed the monument to the revolution without a glance although he badly wanted to inspect it. But he was Ricard Michel, a travelling salesman who would have seen all the monuments in Lyon many times, so he walked on, the petite Yvonne at his side, carrying his case of samples in one hand and their shared suitcase in the other.

Ten minutes later she turned into an elderly four-storey building, led the way up two flights of stairs and opened a door in a long corridor of doors.

'This is it,' she said. 'A bed-sitting room, a bathroom and a kitchen. It's home until we're told when to move on. Boring, and not very clean; but we'll make the best of it.'

There was food in the kitchen cupboards, and he watched her competent preparation of the meal, only then realising that he was hungry. They washed while they waited for the meal to cook, then sat on either side of a plain deal table. To his surprise she had found a bottle of wine, and they toasted each other.

'Is it always as straightforward as this?' he asked.

'We've only just started,' she said. 'Nothing is straightforward. Sometimes it seems to be, and that is when it may be the most dangerous. But this is a safe place. And our contacts are experienced.'

He looked at her curiously.

'May I ask the question you heard me ask Madame Marchand?'

'Why I do this?' She smiled. 'One of her reasons. For France. It may sound melodramatic. But if your country had been occupied, wouldn't you do it? It is the only way we can fight: through other people.'

He nodded towards her hands. 'You wear a ring. You have a husband. Yet you travel through France, at great risk to yourself, sharing a room with a stranger –'

He stopped, for she was shaking her head. She said: 'A room, yes. But that is all. It is my work.'

He nodded. He liked her directness, and her calm eyes.

'Of course. But many husbands would not like their wives to share a room with a stranger, for any reason. He must be very tolerant.' He was teasing her gently now.

'He is most intolerant – of Germans,' she said. 'He is a fugitive, like you. The German army has offered a reward for his capture. He is a Maquisard. You know what that is? A fighter, in the south, in the mountains. They have little to fight with; but one day it will be different. He is waiting for that day, and trying to train the men and the boys who are also fugitives, and those who are not but who are only waiting for the right time to take up guns. I will not tell you where he is, for it is better that you do not know. But we are nearer to him now than we were in Loches.'

'Will you be able to see him soon?'

171

'One can never tell. It is three months since the last time. We were in Paris. He is an explosives expert. He tried to blow up a German general in his car, but something went wrong. He escaped in a gun battle, and the Germans have sought him ever since.' She reached suddenly across the table, her hand resting over his. 'I pray that he will not be caught, for they will kill him if they can. But then –' she shrugged '– that is the war. He has killed Germans, just as you have. And he will kill more.'

'If I am lucky, I will kill more, too.' He said it quietly, and she saw something in his eyes she had not seen before.

'You have a special reason to say that.' She was watching his face, and her fingers were tight across his hand.

He said: 'A very special reason. But I have to forget it until I can get back.' Then there was the hint of a smile and the mood was changed as he freed his hand from hers and passed it over the top of his head. 'I hope they let me fly again after that bump.'

She was suddenly anxious for him.

'You feel all right? It has been a tiring day, and you have been tense. I could tell.'

'I feel very well,' he said. 'And I shall feel even better if we do not neglect your excellent meal.'

They ate then, and afterwards tidied the kitchen and extended the bed-settee. There were blankets in a cupboard and two pillows, and he dragged them out and spread the blankets across the bed. But he kept one back, and carried cushions across to an armchair in a corner of the room.

'You use the bed,' he said. 'I'll sleep well in the chair.'

She watched him arrange the cushions and the blanket, then said: 'You are the fifth man I have escorted in this way. None of the other four understood fully what our relationship had to be until I insisted, although they were all very polite. I suppose they were – tempted.' She looked at him with disarming honesty.

'I'm too tired for temptation,' he said. He took off his jacket, arranged it over the back of a dining chair, took off his tie and began to unbutton his shirt.

'You will be easy to live with, Richard. And we may have to live together like this for a number of nights. We cannot sleep in our clothes. So we must see each other not as a man and a woman, but just as two people.'

172

He said: 'Two people with a job to do.' He took off his shirt and folded it carefully, for it was the only one he had, and laid it on the table. When he looked round she had slipped out of her skirt and was unfastening her heavy cotton blouse. She wore nothing under it, but did not glance at him as she turned her back and took it off. He thought: thank God for a practical, no-nonsense woman. Then he took off his trousers, laid them across the back of a chair, sat in his make-shift bed and rolled the blanket around him.

She said, 'Good night, Richard, sleep well,' walked past his chair and turned the light out. He heard her come back again and, in the faint glow from the curtained window, saw her pale shape slide into the bed. He said, 'Good night, Yvonne,' and closed his eyes.

When he woke it was eight o'clock in the morning and she was already dressed. She came out of the bathroom, brushing her hair and smiling at him.

'You may stay in bed and rest if you wish,' she said. 'I will go out in a little while and arrange a meeting. Do not worry if I do not return until this afternoon. There is food in the kitchen and you will be all right as long as you stay inside.' She laughed quickly. 'You would be all right if you went out, I'm sure. You speak better French than half the people in this city. But you must promise not to take the risk.'

'I promise,' he said solemnly, and sat up in his blankets, watching her with undisguised admiration. He thought she was a remarkable woman.

She did not return until the end of the afternoon, and when she came in he knew at once that something had gone wrong.

'There has been a change of plan for you,' she said. She took off her coat and hung it in the small wardrobe in one corner of the room, then carried a bag into the kitchen, calling over her shoulder: 'I have brought more food. I had enough coupons for two small steaks, some vegetables and garlic. There is still wine in the cupboard, so we shall not starve.'

He followed her into the kitchen and leaned against the door, watching her.

'And why has there been a change of plan?' he asked.

She concentrated on unpacking the bag.

'Things often change,' she said. 'The network has to adapt to

173

circumstances. It is a game of – hide and seek, if you like. With the police and the Gestapo.'

He said: 'Stop hiding things from me. Remember I am not a stranger in this country. Tell me the truth.'

She inspected the steaks critically.

'I think you are a very capable man, Richard. There is something about you which gives me confidence, and we may have need to give each other confidence.' She turned to face him. 'The route we had prepared for you is closed. There have been arrests, and safe houses are no longer safe. There is great police and Gestapo activity here in Lyon. We have to leave tomorrow morning, and we will go to Avignon instead of to Clermont-Ferrand. From there we go to Aix and await new instructions. Our aim is still to get you across to Narbonne and Carcassonne and through the mountains into Spain. But now we have to go a long way round. It had been intended that I should pass you over to another courier at Clermont, but now I will stay with you as far as Aix. Does that satisfy you?'

'Yes. It will do for a start. Now let's make a meal. The steaks look good.'

She stood with her back to the small cooker, leaning on it, studying him.

'I think you are extraordinary,' she said. 'You know there is danger, yet you are not afraid. You are so calm. Do you have a lady in England?'

'Yes.'

'What is her name?'

'Lisa.'

'I think Lisa must be a special lady,' she said. 'And a most fortunate one. Come. I will teach you to cook steaks the French way, so that you can show her when you return home.'

'You forget I lived in France for a long time,' he said. 'I will teach you to cook steaks with a little touch of English panache.'

They joked their way through the preparation of the meal and the eating of it, enjoying the bottle of Medoc which had been in the cupboard, then passing an hour playing chess with pieces and a board they found in the wardrobe. After that they went to bed, but this time Yvonne insisted on sleeping in the chair; and again they were indifferent to each others' scantily-clad bodies as they undressed.

174

There was a heavy police presence at the railway station the next morning, but they boarded the train without incident. She bought the tickets with money she said had been given to her the night before and which, she whispered, had originated in London and had reached the area via a parachute drop arranged by a British agent.

In the afternoon they arrived in Aix-en-Provence. Before they left the station Yvonne sat on a seat near the entrance and motioned to Richard to sit beside her. After a few minutes a man walked slowly past, fiddling with a shopping bag, and a newspaper slipped from under his arm and fell close to them. Yvonne leaned forward, picked it up, and called: 'M'sieur – you should put your paper in the bag.'

The man turned, as if surprised; then walked back, took the paper, gave a small bow and said: 'Unfortunately the bag is full, madame, but I shall take more care of it.'

He walked slowly off towards the station entrance, and just before they lost sight of him Yvonne said: 'Come. He's our man. All we do is follow him.'

Fifteen minutes later the man led them into an old building which had been converted into apartments, up three flights of stairs, and into a small flat. He closed the door and held out his hand in greeting to Richard.

'I am sorry to be so secretive,' he said. 'But it is necessary. I hope you had a good journey.'

They shook hands, and he embraced Yvonne.

'A quiet journey,' she said. 'Is all quiet here?'

'Better than it was,' he said. 'We have had several difficult weeks. But now they seem to have lost interest.' He looked at Richard. 'I am told you speak French well.'

'I have lived in your country,' Richard said; and Yvonne added: 'He speaks excellent French. No German would know he is not a Frenchman, and some Frenchmen would not know either.'

'Good. In that case it will be an advantage if you come to the meeting we have arranged. Then you will see what everyone looks like. I will come back for you in an hour.' He turned to Yvonne. 'You will be free to return tomorrow.'

After he had gone she said: 'So it is tomorrow. I shall miss you. I would like to have stayed with you for the rest of your journey.'

He tweaked the end of her nose and grinned.

'My next escort will not be half as pretty, maybe even a man, and probably unable to cook,' he said. 'I think I shall refuse to go unless you come with me.' Then, abruptly, he was serious. 'Why are things so hot? That man was on edge.'

'It is the Gestapo,' she said. 'There have been several British agents and a parachute drop of arms. Also we think someone may have talked. The army has been strengthened all the way from Lyon to the coast, and the Gestapo has been very tough. It makes escape routes difficult to organise.'

He asked no more questions. But when the man returned and they followed him through the streets of the old town he was watchful, and flexed and eased his shoulder muscles again and again, ready for trouble.

The café chosen for the meeting was long and narrow behind its blackout curtain. At the end furthest from the street was a table partly separated from the others by an alcove wall, with a convenient escape door beyond it. Within the alcove it was possible for people to talk quietly without being heard elsewhere.

Four men were sat there, with glasses on the table. They were introduced to Richard by first names only; and when they realised he had a fluent command of their language they paid him no further attention but absorbed him into their conversation which, to his surprise, had nothing to do with the Resistance or escape routes for fugitive British airmen, but was essentially political: the organisation of France on communist principles once the Germans had been defeated. And that defeat was accepted as so inevitable that they did not seem to think it was worth discussing. As they talked they drank calvados or Pernod, and glasses were refilled again and again. Yvonne drank wine, but Richard asked for coffee which drew from Jean, who was obviously the leader of the group, the comment that it was 'a drink for the morning, Ricard – there are better things for later in the day'; to which Richard shrugged and said, 'I am not as well practised as you, and I don't want to leave with a headache.'

Then, after an hour, and with the daylight fading rapidly outside the café window, Jean interrupted the arguments.

'It is close to curfew time. The arrangements for tomorrow are settled. Martin will be your guide, Ricard.' He indicated a small, bright-eyed weather-beaten fifty-year-old across the table, whom Richard had already noted as the heaviest drinker and most vociferous debater of the group. 'Yvonne will escort you back to this café. At exactly nine o'clock Martin will drive up in a truck. He will stop to buy cigarettes. You will ask him for a lift towards Marseille. You may see others of us in the area, keeping watch. Just ignore us. Martin will take you to Marseille, and the next part of your journey will be arranged there. It is as simple as that.' He smiled broadly, nodded around the table, and stood up. Immediately the arguments began again, and continued as the group wandered through the now almost-deserted café, calling farewells to the owner, and out into the street.

Yvonne slipped her arm through Richard's and said: 'Come. We must walk quickly because of the curfew. The police are strict these days.'

Richard said quietly: 'What was that all about? It was not a meeting to discuss anything except politics. I did not need to be there, and neither did you.'

She glanced back. Three of the group were still standing outside the café and their raised voices echoed along the street.

'That is the way it is in Provence,' she said. 'They wanted to look at you, to see how much of a risk you posed. They are very nervous at the moment, but I think they were pleased with what they saw.' She glanced up at him curiously. 'Why did you drink only coffee? The wine was agreeable.'

'Because I thought at least one person in the group should remain sober.' He squeezed her arm. 'I don't think your two glasses will have done much harm, but I was being careful –'

He checked. She felt him stiffen as they walked and looked at him quickly.

'Is something wrong?'

'The man standing at the first-floor window above the clothing shop on the other side of the street was there when we walked the other way, an hour ago,' he said softly. 'Don't look – he's backed out of sight. But I saw him clearly, and it was the same man.'

'You have been observant,' she whispered. 'And I have been neglectful. You are going my job for me.'

'I feel uneasy. I've felt it since we arrived here. I think something is wrong.'

They walked on steadily. Presently she said: 'It may be nothing. Many people watch the street from their apartments, if they are bored.'

'That's right,' he said. 'It may be nothing. We should assume it is something. Can we approach our apartment building from a different direction?'

'Yes. The next street on the right. But we must walk quickly because of the curfew.'

They did so; came to the street on which the building stood, and paused at the corner. It was quiet. Three people were walking away, a car and a van were parked. The daylight had almost gone.

Richard said: 'The van is parked where a car was parked when we left.'

'Plain vans are dangerous,' she whispered.

They stood in the shadows. The three pedestrians had gone. Long seconds stretched one minute into another. Then Yvonne hissed: 'There's someone in the doorway of the apartments. I saw a movement.'

'It's a trap,' Richard said softly. 'Radio in the van to warn men inside the building when we approach. Remember the man in the window? Probably another link. I can't believe this is just for me. They can't know anything about me. It's bigger than that. I think this is the night they've picked to mop up the whole of your network in Aix.'

She pulled his arm.

'Come on. I know where to go – someone who is outside the network, but who will help. Then I'll try to warn the others.'

They turned together; to find a man facing them in the darkened side-street, five yards away.

Richard said, just loudly enough for the man to hear: 'M'sieur – come quickly – there is trouble.' He waved a hand to the man, then pointed back to the street they had been watching.

The man came forward. He was hatless, wearing a dark coat; medium height and strongly built. There was a gun in his right hand.

Richard said, panic edging his voice: 'Quickly, m'sieur – there is fighting. Are you the police? Shall I call the police?'

The man was within arm's length, his gun no longer pointing at Richard, his eyes looking beyond him. Richard took the gun in one hand and smashed the blade of his other hand across the man's throat, all in one fast savage movement which turned into a second as he pulled the man round, gun held aloft, and slammed his head back against the wall alongside. Then he had the gun, wrenching it clear of nerveless fingers, hammering it into the man's face then again into the side of his head above the ear, flinging him aside and grabbing Yvonne's hand and starting to run.

At the other end of the side-street she pointed to the left and he followed her, darting from doorway to doorway, then across a wide, empty street and down into an alley leading into other, narrow streets. For ten minutes they ran, from corner to corner, shadow to shadow, among old buildings, shops and offices crowded together, seeing no one, hearing car engines sometimes close and sometimes distant. Once they stopped, listening to shouts, but they were far away. He followed her round behind a church, stumbling over low railings, across waste ground and through the remains of a derelict building. There he held her back for a moment and panted: 'Do you really know where we're going?'

She nodded, clinging to him, catching her breath, whispering: 'Yes. I know. Not far now.' She clung tighter. 'You did well, then, Richard.'

'It got me a prize,' he said. He held up the gun so that she could see it against the faint light of the sky. 'I feel better with this in my hand.'

She peered at it and hissed: 'A Luger. German. French police don't use them. So he was Gestapo.'

'I never doubted it,' he said. 'Come on.'

Three minutes later they climbed a low wall into a yard beside a shed and a taller building beyond, and Yvonne knocked urgently in a series of coded taps on a battered door. It opened a couple of inches and she whispered into the crack: 'Yvonne Cardin. And a friend.'

The door opened wider and she pulled Richard after her into blackness. Shoes shuffled and the door closed. Then a light came on and a small man with a sharp-nosed, wizened face and totally bald head blinked at them. They were in a dusty, bare-boarded corridor.

Yvonne said: 'This is Richard. A British airman. His identity card says he is Ricard Michel. I've brought him down from the north. Things have gone wrong. Tonight we met Jean and the others. I think we were watched. The Gestapo was waiting for us after we left. Richard fought one of them and took his gun. Then we ran. I think they're on to the network. May I telephone?'

The wizened man nodded. He led them along the corridor and into a small office with an old, dirty desk and papers piled on it and on the floor. Cupboards against the walls revealed books and more papers. The man said: 'Be quick. And careful. The Germans are like hornets – everywhere.' His voice was high-pitched and cracked, like a rusty hinge.

She found a telephone among the piles of papers; dialled a number. They stood, watching her. She seemed to listen for a long time. Then she replaced the telephone.

'That was Jean's number,' she said. She sounded very calm. 'Someone picked up the receiver and did not speak. I could hear him breathing. The police must be there.'

The wizened man said: 'I'll make a call.' He dialled; said: 'Maurice? Charles. Have you heard the weather forecast? I think there is a storm coming.' He listened then, making grunting sounds; tracing a pattern in the dust on the desk top. Then he said: 'All right. Take care of yourself.' He put down the telephone and looked at them.

'There is trouble,' he said. He glanced at Richard. 'You have come at a bad time. There have been many arrests, and a gun battle outside St Mary Magdalene, on the Rue Chastel. The word is that someone has talked.' He said to Yvonne: 'I think you should get out of Aix quickly.' His lined face cracked into a smile. 'Fortunately you know where to go. But what do we do with Richard? Hide him?'

Just for a moment she hesitated; then said: 'Can you hide him here?'

The man said: 'Yes. I have done such things before, as you know.' He nodded at the silent man beside her. 'Does he understand us? Does he speak any French?'

In spite of the situation she laughed.

'He has lived in France,' she said. 'It is sometimes difficult to tell he is not French.' To Richard she said: 'This would be a safe place to hide. Charles would look after you well.' She said it as if she was reluctant to admit it.

Richard looked at the old man, then at the girl who had been his guide and companion for the past week. He still held the Luger automatic in his hand. He pushed it into his coat pocket.

'You are going to see your husband?'

'Yes. I shall try to do that. I knew you would realise what

180

Charles meant.'

His voice was flat and decisive. 'Then I shall come with you. I have been hiding for more than seven months. I am tired of hiding. And now I have a gun. When do we start and how do we get there?'

'It is not the place for a British escaper,' the old man said in his scraping voice. 'It is very tough in the mountains. They are fugitives, but they are also training to fight. That is their real purpose.'

Yvonne said: 'I think Richard could teach them something. You did not see the way he dealt with the Gestapo man a short time ago, Charles. Paul could not have done better.'

'That is the highest praise,' the old man said; but Richard interrupted him: 'You can stop discussing me as if I were an object to be picked up and put down. If you'll take me, I'm coming with you, Yvonne. If you won't, somehow I'll get to Spain on my own. I have an identity card and a ration card. I'll find a way of picking up enough money to keep me moving. There's nothing else to be said. What's the answer?'

She saw his near-black eyes and his hard mouth and remembered the way he had been in the street close to the apartment, and said: 'Paul will be glad to have you there. In a little while we'll find a new escape route for you. But for now – yes, come if you want to.'

The old man sighed audibly, then shrugged.

'You are a brave man. Also a foolhardy one. But I suppose you think you have little to lose. Maybe that is true of many of us.' He passed a hand across his bald head in mock despair and shuffled from the room.

She said: 'Don't let him fool you. He is tough, and resourceful. He dislikes the political in-fighting between the Resistance and Maquis groups, so he keeps himself to himself. But he has a quantity of arms hidden somewhere, and once the real fighting starts he will be a valuable ally. In the meantime he is loyal to my husband and his close friends.'

'That's fortunate for us,' Richard said. 'How do we get out of Aix?'

'In a box built into the floor of a vegetable truck,' she said, and laughed at his quick expression of distaste. 'It will not be comfortable. But he is a merchant, and he has a licence from the Germans to drive at night so that he can move food supplies between Aix market and the villages round about. It's very useful. He has used it several times to help Paul and his men.'

In the next five hours they had a frugal meal with the wizened man and dozed in chairs until he told them it was time to go. His movement licence did not allow him to set out from Aix before four o'clock in the morning, so soon after three he took them into the small warehouse next to his office and said: 'This is the truck. That is where you will hide. There's a switch in one corner which rings a bell in the cab, for emergencies. Please get in so that I can load up on top of you.'

The old Renault was an open truck with high sides, and built into the flat was a container which Richard immediately likened to a large coffin: seven feet long, three feet wide and two feet deep. Ventilation holes were drilled along both sides. It looked claustrophobic and uncomfortable but, after a glance at Yvonne, he hauled himself onto the flat and helped her up beside him. Then he sat on the edge of the recessed box and slid down into it, only then realising that an old piece of carpet had been laid at the bottom. It smelled of cabbages, but was otherwise apparently clean. Then Yvonne lowered herself in beside him, turning on her side so that she could face him. Above them the old man stood, peering down. Humourlessly he said, 'It will be uncomfortable, but others have survived it, so I suppose you will,' and dragged heavy boarding across to bridge the top and complete the floor of the flat.

In the darkness Richard shifted so that he could rest his head on one arm. He could feel her warmth, and her thighs against him, and said: 'Sorry for the intimacy. But I'm glad I'm not in here by myself.' His voice was muffled in the confined space.

'Me, too,' she said. 'And I'm glad it's you and not one or two others I've known. Let's call it a working bonus.' She forced a laugh.

For the next half-hour they listened to the bangs and scrapes above as the old man loaded the truck, then heard the engine start and felt its vibration, followed by a series of jolts as the truck began to move. After that it settled down to a steady, rumbling, swaying motion, with the engine noise loud but bearable. They were thrown together again and again, until Richard slid his arm around her shoulders and held her against him. With his mouth close to her ear he said: 'Is that better? Or would you rather try to keep away from me?'

'No.' She wriggled to get closer. 'It's much more comfortable.'

They lay like that, hardly speaking thereafter above the engine noise and the rumble of the suspension and tyres, for two hours which seemed more like two days, until the truck slowed and stopped. For several minutes they listened to the idling engine and, faintly, voices. Then they were jolted in their prison again as the vehicle manoeuvred, noises booming in a confined space until, with a suddenness which surprised them, there was stillness and silence, and they knew that they had reached their destination.

Some time later the truck had been unloaded, the boards were lifted, and they blinked in the electric light of a high-roofed shed. Stiffly, awkwardly, they levered themselves up while Charles surveyed them critically.

'You don't look too bad,' he volunteered. 'You'll feel better when you've had a drink. We had a good drive. There was a road block on the outskirts of Aix, but they waved me through. Someone there must have known my truck. They trust me, you see.' His lined face cracked in a cynical grin.

Richard dragged himself out of the box, then pulled Yvonne up beside him. They stood on the flat of the truck, dusting themselves down, looking ruefully at their creased clothing, exercising their limbs; then climbed down on to the floor of the shed. The truck's load of potatoes, cabbages and other vegetables was piled alongside. Richard looked up at the rooflights and saw that outside the night was fading.

He said: 'Where are we?'

'St Benoit,' she said. 'Fifty kilometres or so south-east of Aix. A very small village, a few poor farms, and the mountains. It is hard country, and the people are hard. They will not accept you easily. But take no notice. They will learn.'

They spent the day in a cottage along the village's only street. A middle-aged couple lived there, shabbily dressed, sombre and suspicious until they were told by Charles that Yvonne was the wife of Paul Cardin. Then they treated her deferentially, but still warily, and virtually ignored Richard. During the morning the man left, and they learned he had strips of land on the hillsides close to the village and was preparing to sow the spring crops. The woman said to Yvonne: 'There is food in the kitchen. Take what

183

you need. But remember we do not have much.' Then she disappeared upstairs to the cottage's bedroom, and they saw little of her.

Yvonne said: 'Now we wait. A message will have been sent. Something will happen soon.'

'And you will see your husband again,' he said. 'You must be very happy, after such a long time.'

'I am very happy,' she said. 'And happy that I may stay here for a while.' She looked up at him. 'I am also happy that you are here. I think we have come to know each other very well, Richard; and to trust each other.' Her smile was suddenly mischievous. 'Since I was married you are the only man except my husband with whom I have lain so close and for so long as we did last night.'

He was silent for seconds, looking at her. Then he reached out and, just for a moment, touched her cheek with his fingers.

'Don't ask me to do it again,' he said softly. 'I'm not made of wood. Next time it might be different.'

20

They had chosen Bath for their short holiday, because it was easy to reach by train – petrol rationing prohibited the use of a car – and because there were pleasant walks near at hand and it seemed far away from the war. Diane was staying for a week, but Lisa was unable to get more than four days' leave from the hospital, and Robert was reluctant to stay away from Roxton for long.

They spent a day wandering round the Roman sites in the city, another in the sparsely-stocked shops, and two days walking in the countryside nearby. Then, on the day Lisa was to return, Robert telephoned Martin and then announced that he would leave too. So they said their farewells and made their way to the station. The train, like most, was crowded, and they squeezed into a corridor and stood shoulder to shoulder with others as whistles were blown and steam hissed and they jolted into motion.

Then Robert said: 'I enjoyed it. Mother was right. We all needed to get away. I hadn't realised.'

She inspected his face and announced: 'You look better. Something about you – more at ease, I think. And younger, too.'

'Are you glad you came?' he asked.

'Yes. I've enjoyed the rest.' She looked at him and smiled. 'And the company.'

'Good. I was afraid it might have been too much of a family thing for you.'

'I am family,' she said. 'I've been part of your family for a long time. Just as much as if I'd married Richard. And –' she looked away for a moment, out of the window '– no one understands the way you do.' Then she pushed the thought away and brightened again. 'I thought your mother was great. She's really showing great courage.'

'So are you.' He said it so quietly that she hardly heard him above the noise of the train.

'I've been helped,' she said, 'especially by you.' The train rocked and somebody squeezed past, pushing them together. 'I'm sorry,' she said, 'but it's so crowded.' She steadied herself, one hand against the side of the corridor.

'We've helped each other,' he said.

They passed the rest of the journey discussing the Roman antiquities they had seen, and the countryside over which they had walked, and her nursing experiences and the changes on the estate; then, after the train left Taunton, found seats and dozed until they reached Exeter.

As they left the train Robert said: 'Shall we have a meal before we go our separate ways? It will probably only be a café, but it will be better than eating alone later on.'

She nodded, pleased. 'I'd like that.' And she fell into step with him as he took her suitcase and they walked up the hill to the city centre.

They sat at a corner table in a small prefabricated café in High Street and ate steak and kidney pie, laughing as they debated the contents and wondering if ham and dried egg – the only cooked alternative – would have been a better choice. Then Robert said: 'Instead of their watery coffee, let's walk down the street and find a drink we can enjoy.' So they strolled past the ruins which stood in mute testimony to the horror of the 5th of May 1942; passed without comment the place where Ruth and Nick had died, for they had taught themselves many months before to do that; and

185

on past the Guild Hall to an old inn where Robert bought their drinks and they perched on stools at the corner of the bar.

He said: 'I wish you would come and look at the farm sometimes. There've been a lot of changes.'

She played with the stem of her glass, watching her fingers as they moved around it.

'I haven't wanted to come. You must know why.'

He put out his hand to cover hers, just for a moment.

'I do know. And if you still don't want to, I'll understand. But we've come to terms with so many things. I thought that perhaps, after all this time, you might want to try. It would be a change from the hospital, and being at home.'

She stared down at her glass again. Then she said: 'Give me a cigarette, please.'

'Of course.' He concealed his surprise. Lisa smoked very little. He produced a packet of Players and she took one carefully, then accepted his light. He looked at her through the flame of the match and the curling blue-grey smoke, and saw the golden lights which flecked her eyes, and the anguish there.

'I have something to tell you, Rob,' she said. She was choosing her words, slowly and carefully. 'There's another reason why I haven't wanted to come to Roxton; not just because I would see Richard there, wherever I looked. There's something else. It's time I told you.'

He waited; wanting to help her but not knowing what to say. Another couple came in and began to debate their drinks. Further away two men laughed at a private joke. She studied her cigarette; then quickly inhaled from it.

'You've been my barrier, Rob,' she said. 'Your face, your hair, the way you walk, sometimes your eyes and even your voice. They're all Richard. It's like looking at his picture, and watching it move and hearing it speak, yet never being able to touch it. I know there are differences, but –' she hesitated, searching for words '– but time plays tricks with memory, and I forget some of them. It would have been so much easier if you had not been twins. But you're too alike.'

He took a long breath; then shook his head slowly, wonderingly.

'I didn't know. I should have realised. I'm sorry. But I'm glad you've told me. At least I understand.'

186

'I thought I would never be able to tell you,' she said. 'I didn't know how to. But being with you for the last few days has helped. You've started to be Robert, not just Richard's likeness. I meant it, on the train, when I said I'd enjoyed the company. Especially yours. So – yes please – I'd like to come to Roxton.'

He leaned across, took the cigarette from between her fingers, and tapped it into an ashtray.

'You were about to burn yourself,' he said. 'Thank you for telling me. I hope you'll come. Telephone me when you feel you'd like to. I'll look forward to it.'

21

Philip Wiseman, whose code name was Marius, sat on the Avignon train, smoking his way through the day's second pack of cigarettes. By the evening he would be into the third. But there was nothing unusual about that.

Wiseman was a 'pianist': Resistance jargon for a radio operator. He had been born in Brussels of a British father and a Belgian mother, and in 1938 had married a local girl. But in the spring of 1940 he had seen her, and their baby son, killed by a German fighter which had strafed a column of refugees trudging along a poplar-lined road into France ahead of the advancing German panzers. He had tried to bury the two bodies at the roadside, but there had been others with the same grim task, and no one had a spade; so in the end he had left them lying together under a hedge, the tattered remains of the child in his mother's blood-soaked arms. Wiseman had made his way west, right across northern France to Cherbourg, where he had bribed his way on to one of the last ships to sail to England before France collapsed. Then, after the tedious but essential formalities, he had gone to London and, through another Belgian expatriate, had eventually contacted the Special Operations Executive. That was how he came to be in France now, in the autumn of 1943, after being dropped by parachute near Lyon complete with the small suitcase which contained his transmitter. He had been there for three months.

He did not know how many operators were working in the Lyon–Avignon–Marseille circuit, but thought there were three. His job was to liaise with the main resistance group in Lyon, and to link with Maquis groups in the southern mountains. Now he was on his way back to his temporary Avignon base. His papers said he was a self-employed electrician, and his story was that he was looking for work. In fact he had been into the mountains east and south of Aix to meet the man called Paul Cardin, the leader of one of the most successful Maquis groups in the area. Cardin needed more arms and was in dispute with another group as to who should get the next consignment. That evening Wiseman would relay the details to London.

He would relay something else, too. He stared out of the train window at the barren countryside and thought about the man who had been at Cardin's side throughout their meeting; a man whom he now knew was an RAF Squadron Leader on the run, and who seemed to be an essential element in the Cardin group. Indeed, Wiseman was not sure whether it was the Cardin group any longer, or whether it had become the Haldane group, for Cardin referred several times to his companion, and appeared to defer to him on tactical matters.

An extraordinary man, Richard Haldane, Wiseman thought. The locals around St Benoit and the other mountain villages knew him as Ricard Michel and referred to him as the Wolf of Ste Baume, after the mountains on either side of which Cardin and his group operated. Wiseman thought Cardin probably encouraged the drama, for he was a skilled propagandist who knew the importance of morale among his men and the local populace upon whom they depended for their food and security. If he could boost it by building up the reputation of the man at his side, he would certainly do so.

But it was not just propaganda. Wiseman knew that Cardin's group was feared by the German army over a wide area, and that its reputation had grown rapidly after the man called Michel had joined it in the spring. It had been shrewdly managed in the field, and he suspected that the newcomer was behind that. The group never struck at targets within fifteen kilometres of its bases – and Wiseman did not know exactly where those were – and the Germans did not seem to know where they came from when they attacked railways, bridges and telephone lines. There had been hunts, and there had been reprisals in which helpless villagers across the mountains had been killed; and each had been followed by savage revenge against German troops, to such a degree that the reprisals had stopped. Wiseman had heard stories of Ricard Michel out at night, silently removing German guards so that explosives could be planted; and once leading a raid on the police headquarters in the nearby town to snatch back a Maquisard who had been captured and would have been handed over to Gestapo torture the next day. It was said that he enjoyed killing Germans, and Wiseman approved of that.

That night the Belgian had a job to do for the Wolf of Ste Baume, for just before he had left their meeting place he had been taken aside and told: 'My name is not Michel, as you may have guessed. I am Richard Haldane and I am a Squadron Leader in the Royal Air Force. I have been on the run for a year. You are the first radio operator I've met. I've no idea if my family knows I am alive, or if I've been reported killed. Will you please send a message to London to say I am alive? Is that permitted?'

Wiseman had nodded. 'Yes. I can do that. Write down your service number for me. I'll send it along with your name. That will ensure they find your family. Don't worry about it. I'll look after it.'

Now he was coming into Avignon, and he saw the great Papal palace rising above the walled town and the rivers beside it. He felt more comfortable here; out on the mountain slopes, with only the trees and the scrub and the rocks and the scattered cottages, he felt exposed. He was happier with buildings and narrow winding streets, for they provided more places to hide.

Clutching his bag of electricians' tools, he left the train, pausing on the platform for a moment to light a cigarette. At the barriers two soldiers were checking papers. He scarcely glanced at them, for he knew his were in order. Then he walked through the town to the empty two-roomed apartment which was always available to him when he needed to transmit.

Before he started, he took a cardboard box from an otherwise bare cupboard. He had left food in it the previous day, and now he was hungry. While he ate bread, paté and cheese, he pulled out his wallet and searched for the piece of paper on which Richard had written his service number. As he did so he caught sight of the photograph he always carried, and extracted it, propping it up on the table which, with one wooden chair, was the only furniture in the room.

It was a tattered picture of a fair-haired girl holding a baby. He looked at it for a long time. It no longer distressed him to see it; but it often helped him just before he was going to transmit, for that was the dangerous time and he sometimes needed extra strength that came with their memory.

Afterwards he opened another cupboard, took out the suitcase which contained his radio, and began to set it up. Outside the uncurtained window the light was beginning to fade, but he could see enough to get the equipment ready. He settled on the chair, lighted a cigarette, turned the dials, checked the frequency, looked at his watch to make sure he was within the time brackets set for reception, then began to tap out his call sign. When the signal came back telling him that he was being received he began to send his message. He could remember much of the code, but now and then consulted notes, concentrating on the task.

Outside, an unmarked van cruised quietly up the street; then it reversed and came back, slowly, finally stopping at the pavement close to the apartment block. If Wiseman had seen it he would have known immediately that it was a radio-goniometric van, used to trace the source of transmissions such as his. But his room was at the back of the block, and he could neither see nor hear it.

It took him nearly fifteen minutes to transmit details of the Cardin group's arms needs and to notify London of the local dispute, then to give further information about the proposed dropping zone for the next delivery. Fifteen minutes was reckoned to be twice the safe limit for continuous transmission because of the danger of detection, but he often accepted such risks. And now he still had not finished, and so sent the signal which indicated that he had a further transmission. Then he looked for the piece of paper on which Richard's number was written. He laid it on the table and began to tap out: 'Please note and pass to appropriate authority –'

'Police – open the door.' The voice was deep and harsh, and the banging was loud through the empty room. He snatched off his earphones and scrambled to his feet, facing the door in the dimness of the room. It shook as someone hammered on it with a fist, and the sweat started on his face.

Then, just as suddenly, he was cold and still. There were two ways out of the room: through the door and through the window. But beyond the window was a drop of twenty-five metres, and beyond the door were armed men. If he jumped from the window he would die, and the men would live. So there was no alternative.

He lifted a panel from within the case which had held his transmitter and took out the revolver which had been hidden there since he had left an RAF airfield in Oxfordshire a lifetime ago. As he did so a boot kicked the door and a panel splintered. He glanced at the table, saw Richard Haldane's number, and picked up the small piece of paper, pushed it into his mouth, chewed it into a ball and swallowed it. Then he saw the tattered photograph still propped up on the table and reached for it. He was holding it in his left hand, and the gun in his right, when the door crashed back and he shot the first man who tumbled into the room, then the second man too, before the third put three bullets through his chest and he spun backwards, the gun flying across the floor but the photograph still clutched between his curling, crushing fingers.

*   *   *

Paul Cardin was not tall; but he was square-shouldered and deep-chested and strong. He stood now on the slopes of a hill which ran down into a long steep-sided valley, stared across the rock-strewn descent to the road at the bottom, and said: 'The cover couldn't be better, both for the attack and the retreat.'

Richard leaned against a cork oak tree and nodded. Like Cardin, he wore battered, faded corduroy trousers, a woollen shirt and a leather jacket over it to keep out the late autumn wind.

'If the convoy is similar to the last we'll need to cover a two hundred metre front, with men on both sides of the road and a Piat at each end,' he said. The Piat was an anti-tank gun which was new to their arsenal, and both were anxious to try it against the armoured cars which escorted German road convoys. 'Let's mark out some vantage points.'

They scrambled down the slope, from rock to rock, tree to tree, hollow to hollow, until they reached the winding road. Then they worked their way along it and up the other side of the valley. Finally, as the daylight began to fade, they came back, climbing the valley side to their starting point and the stolen German army motorcycle which they had left against a tree. They mounted it, Cardin kicked it into life, and they rode away along the track which wandered across the hillside.

Half an hour later they pushed the motorcycle into a shallow cave, replaced the brushwood which concealed it, and started to walk the last two kilometres to St Benoit.

As they went Cardin said: 'It should be a good operation. And the men need it. They're restless.'

'If you can lay your hands on more plastic explosive we'll find plenty of ways to keep them busy,' Richard said.

'I'll get some,' Cardin grinned. 'And more detonators. It's all waiting down in the old factory at Aix. I'll have it back here in a couple of days.'

They walked singly then, for the path was narrow and rough. Richard looked at the Frenchman's broad back and thought he had met few men with whom he had a greater rapport. Nick, certainly – there could be no one like Nick; Mitch and Keith Sandham; and that was about all. Cardin took many risks, but he calculated them coldly and finely. He was a ruthless, single-minded fighter and a born leader; yet he retained a sardonic sense of humour not greatly different from Richard's own. The thirty or so maquisards whom he led treated him with unquestioning respect even though he kept out of their political discussions for, unlike the majority, he was not a communist. Richard thought himself fortunate to have become the confidant and companion of such a man.

And then he wondered, as he often did, how long it would go on; how long it would be before he saw Roxton and his mother and Robert, and Lisa. Especially Lisa. She was a beacon to him, through the days of hiding and in the cold nights and when he was afraid. At first there had been grim satisfaction in being accepted as part of a guerilla group; a chance to get close to his enemies and to vent his bitterness and his hatred. But now he was becoming restless, feeling he might get back home if he really tried, even if it meant going without guides. She was there, through all this time; and sometimes when it was still and he was by himself he could hear her voice. He still looked at the stars, as he had done back at the Marchands' farmhouse, and wondered if she was looking at them too; they were his link with her, because they shone and winked above them both. He wondered when she had first known

192

that he was still alive. Perhaps not until Marius, the radio operator, had sent his message. He had been saddened when he had heard that Marius had been killed. Paul had heard about it during a visit to Aix. Someone said the Gestapo had shot him, but that he had taken two of them with him. He could only hope that it had not been before his message had been sent. But Paul thought the shooting had been several days later.

He ought to try to move on. Yet it would not be easy. His friendship with Paul was close; and the subtle understanding which had grown originally between himself and Yvonne remained, to a degree which sometimes secretly concerned him. He had to acknowledge that there was a curious satisfaction in knowing what the mountain people and the Maquisards called him. It was unnecessarily dramatic, but at least it was a sign that others thought he was contributing to their communal struggle. And in a strange, masochistic way he enjoyed the wild life and the hard conditions. He had recovered well from his injuries and except for aches in his arm and leg was probably stronger than he had ever been. Oh well, he thought, we shall see; events were sometimes master of those who sought to control them.

They dropped down to the few houses which made up the village and split up, Paul going to the little farm where he and Yvonne had a room, and Richard to the cottage where he slept in a tiny attic.

The following day Paul left for Aix; and in the evening a German army patrol came to St Benoit.

Afterwards it was said they were just looking for a deserter, and that might have been so, for there were only four soldiers and a sergeant in a single vehicle and when they called at the little farm which was the first of St Benoit's small string of buildings they were not particularly aggressive. But unfortunately they found François there, and he was hot-tempered and tried to reach the Thompson sub-machine gun under his bed. So they marched him out of the house, and with him the deaf peasant farmer who owned the little holding, and put them in the back of the truck under the rifle muzzle of one of the soldiers.

The next house was where Yvonne and Paul had been living, and by the time Richard was alerted two hundred yards away they had her in the roadway, for they had found a small automatic pistol in her handbag.

193

The soldiers were now standing by the truck, rifles unslung, sensing that they had stumbled on more than they had expected. Richard could see them as he ducked between farm buildings, working his way nearer; but he saw no sign of the dozen other Cardin men who were hidden nearby, and he knew that the rest were scattered over several miles of rough country and beyond reach.

He was close enough now to see Yvonne. She was arguing loudly with the sergeant, clearly hoping that others would hear the disturbance. Then the sergeant hit her across her face and she spun away from him and fell; and Richard, who had picked up two grenades from his attic room as well as his Luger, pulled the pin on one of them and threw the grenade behind a low wall thirty yards from the soldiers and their vehicle. It exploded harmlessly but had the desired effect, for the men dropped flat on the road, twisting to face the direction of the explosion, then crawling round the truck, using it as cover, their backs to Richard. Yvonne rolled over and over away from them, one of the soldiers saw her and swung his rifle towards her, and Richard steadied his Luger against the wall of a cottage and shot him. Then he shouted, 'Yvonne – run –' and she scrambled further away, on her feet, falling, then on her feet again. At the same time François jumped clear of the truck, dragging the old farmer with him, and ran for the cover of a wall. A soldier fired and the farmer fell; then François vaulted the wall and Richard threw his second grenade, this time at the truck and the grey-clad figures around it. He did not see it explode; by then Yvonne had reached him and he had pulled her into the shelter of his wall, and they were running. Behind, after the grenade went off and the echoes had died, there were shouts in German and several rifle shots, and a woman screaming in one of the cottages.

It was six in the evening and the late autumn daylight was already half-gone; but they still had a nerve-shattering twenty seconds of open ground to cover before they reached a line of scrub trees. Then they checked, looking back, but there was no sign of the soldiers, although the shouting went on.

Yvonne hissed: 'There was a radio in the truck. Unless the grenade wrecked it, they'll have reinforcements within half an hour. We can't go back to see how the others are.'

Richard said: 'They'll all be ducking out now. We'll have to

194

look after ourselves. It's going to be a hard night. Come on.'

They set out through the scrub, uphill, quickly reaching rough country. They realised now they had little to fear from the survivors of the patrol which had entered the village; but equally they knew the Germans would soon have search parties strung out across the hills and that they had to move fast to escape the net. They had, however, the advantage of knowing the terrain intimately, and they made rapid progress until the darkness slowed them.

Their aim was to cross a narrow mountain road and make for still higher ground beyond it. Up there was a small cave and if they could reach that they should be far enough away from St Benoit and its surrounding hills to escape the search parties; then, when the daylight came, they could move on.

But the road was the danger. By the time they reached it there could be patrols out along it. So as they approached it they moved cautiously, stopping frequently to listen. The road ran along a ledge cut into the hill, one turn following another, and they did not see the headlights of the motorcycle patrol until it was close to them and they could not go back because the light would sweep across the open ground they had just crossed to reach the road. So they ran across it and threw themselves full length behind a rock outcrop and scrub trees as the first of the two motorcycles rounded the bend close to them and the headlights outlined the rock and the trees.

They lay side by side and Yvonne reached for Richard's arm and held it tightly with both hands while he levelled the Luger, watching the road and the patrol. There were four men, black figures etched against the lights as they passed slowly; two riders and two sidecar passengers each crouched behind a light machine gun. Richard thought: if I had a rifle I could kill all four. But he did not have a rifle, and in any case wanted the patrol to pass by without an incident which might lead to a search later. So they watched, pulses racing, muscles knotted and aching, as the lights and the sound of the engines receded, and they came out of their hiding place and scrambled in the darkness up the hill.

It took them an hour to find the cave. Had they not known the country so well they would never have found it in the darkness; but they went straight to it and pushed aside the low birch which grew conveniently across the entrance. It was six feet square and a little less in height, the floor rising rapidly to the descending roof at the back. They groped around, throwing out rock chippings, and sat down side by side, breathing hard.

For a little while they were silent, listening to the night outside; until Richard said: 'What will happen to those people in the village? The people in the cottages who let us sleep there and fed us?'

For a long time she did not answer. But he did not repeat the question, for he knew she had heard it.

At last she said: 'I don't know. It will depend on what the Germans find. They'll search every house. But except for François everyone had time to get away. If they all took their guns with them, there might be no proof. Except for Henri and Marie, where Paul and I were staying.' She was silent then, not wanting to talk about what might happen to Henri and Marie.

'François had time to get away, in the confusion,' Richard said. 'And the old man he lived with was shot, so the bastards probably can't touch him now.'

They sat for a time, thinking about it, and their own situation. They would probably escape. At dawn they would climb over the nearby ridge and in three hours would reach a village where Richard was known. There were people there who would hide them for a time. But they would not be able to go back to St Benoit, or the country around it. Everything would change now, even though the group would remuster somewhere.

Outside a night bird called, and Yvonne said: 'It's going to be cold. And neither of us is very well clothed.'

He put one arm around her shoulders, pulling her closer to him.

'It will help if we keep each other warm,' he said, and was glad to feel her against him, for he had been aware of the chill creeping through his body.

She put her head against his shoulder.

'I didn't thank you,' she said. 'For what you did back there.'

He said, in the flat, hard voice she had heard before when he talked about such things: 'I fought Germans. That's what I'm here for.'

She shook her head against him.

'You could have got out, on your own,' she said. 'Like the rest must have done. We didn't see anything of the others. But you came for me. I'd have been in Aix now, and tomorrow they'd have given me to the Gestapo.'

'No. Not unless they'd got to me first.' He whispered it, close to her ear. 'They won't take you away, Yvonne. Not while I still have a gun. I'd kill you before I'd let them get their hands on you.'

For a moment she held her breath. Then she shivered, and he tightened his arm around her.

'Oh God,' she said. 'You mean that, don't you? You really would.' Then she shivered again, and said, so quietly that he hardly heard her: 'And I'd want you to.'

The fingers of his free hand touched her face, caressing; and he felt her lips search for the palm of his hand.

'Dear Christ. What a hell of a world this is.' There was despair in his voice, and she had never heard him speak like that, and she turned her face up towards his.

And then he kissed her in the dark; gently, then urgently, in desperate longing. And they were lost, as if they had known it must happen and now they were faced with it there was nothing they could do except give themselves to it. The tension with which they had lived for so long, and the surging fear which punctuated it, and the agony of lost friends and of dreadful death and shattered life which surrounded them were suddenly submerged by flooding relief that they were alive and together and there would be tomorrow for them. Her shirt was unbuttoned and the breasts he had seen but had not touched in Lyon were there for his fingers and his lips, and her hand was struggling with the waist-band of his trousers, freeing it, searching for him, and his own was beneath her skirt, finding her as she whispered over and over into his ear: 'Don't stop – Richard – don't stop –' Then she was crying, sobbing against him, urging him, and they were one and he felt her immeasurable passion and then was swept away by his own and the wonder of her.

At the end she cried out again and again, and the rock walls muffled and distorted her frantic voice and he struggled back to awareness and truth, for in the dark and his distant memory it was Lisa's voice he heard in their first time place. He tried to push the weight of his body from her but failed, and turned his head away so that she should not feel his own tears and his agony.

*   *   *

197

The next morning they crossed the ridge and went down to the village, and Richard sent a messenger to Aix to warn Paul. But before they left the cave he took her in his arms and said: 'Perhaps last night was inevitable. Perhaps, even if circumstances had been different, it would have happened sooner or later, because there is something very special between us, and we've both known about it for a long time. But –'

He checked, for she put her fingers up to cover his lips, and her eyes were warm and comforting and wise.

'But it must not happen again,' she whispered, 'because there is Paul, and there is also Lisa although she is very far away. Promise me one thing only, before we return to the daylight and the life we left for just a little time last night: promise that you will never forget me.'

He held her close and said: 'That is the easiest promise I shall ever make. I'll never forget you.' For he knew that it was beyond his will to forget; and yet that remembering would be an endless private torture.

22

There were no Christmas bells pealing from the square tower of St Thomas's Church in Roxton village; nor had there been for four years, for church bells were the signal that Britain had been invaded and even though the threat had receded they remained silent.

But the decorations were out in the hall next to the church, because the Boxing Day celebration was a dance at the end of a week's Christmas fund-raising to provide what were euphemistically called 'Forces' comforts' – clothes, games, books and anything else which the civilian population imagined might improve the lot of local men away in uniform.

Diane had accepted responsibility for organizing the dance, and with 150 tickets sold was pleased with the prospect for the next few hours' entertainment and a profit for the fund; and Robert was delighted to see his mother involving herself enthusiastically in war effort work, even though he recognised that it was part of her

198

private defence against the impact of her loss.

There was nothing sophisticated about the occasion: just a village dance under wartime conditions which imposed severe restrictions upon everybody's relaxation and pleasure. Yet for Roxton it was one of the social excitements of 1943, and dresses and suits which had been preserved carefully and worn only on special occasions were pressed and prepared for this climax to local Christmas celebrations.

Diane's particular pleasure was the presence of Lawrence and Christine Kent; not only because she liked the easy-mannered doctor and his effervescent wife, but because she had become especially concerned to encourage the growing friendship between their daughter and Robert. It was her comfort to see the girl who would have married Richard becoming closer to her other son; and although she cautioned herself against trying to plan the lives of the next generation, she remained determined to foster the relationship.

Now she was pleased that Robert had invited Lisa and her parents to spend the night of the 26th of December at the Grange. Of course it avoided transport difficulties, since even a doctor had to be careful how he used precious petrol coupons; but Diane was well aware that Robert had welcomed the chance to have Lisa staying at the house. Since their spring holiday together Lisa had often been to the Grange and she and Robert had dined out on such meagre restaurant fare as was available. Yet she also observed Lisa's reserve, and shared the reason for it: the tiny, flickering hope that, somehow, somewhere, Richard might still be alive; for his death had not yet been irrevocably confirmed and without that confirmation, whatever other evidence there might be and whatever the dictates of reason, that hope had to be nurtured.

It was towards the end of the evening that Lawrence Kent and his wife talked privately with Diane. At a table in a corner of the village hall, with the noise of chatter and the moderately-disciplined efforts of a local dance band around them, they watched Lisa and Robert pass them on the crowded dance floor, and the doctor said thoughtfully: 'I'm glad to see they're good friends.'

'So am I,' Diane nodded.

Kent said cautiously: 'She still hopes Richard might come back, you know.'

'Just as I do,' Diane said calmly, 'however forlorn the hope. "Missing believed killed" is not the same as "killed in action". Robert can't bring himself to share the hope. I think Steve Mitchell had something to do with that, although Robert won't talk about it. But Lisa and I will go on hoping, until the final proof.'

'We have to hope,' Kent said. 'But we have to be realistic too, and I know you are. That's why I'm happy to see Robert and Lisa enjoying each other's company. I hope it pleases you, Diane.'

She leaned across the table and said to both of them: 'It delights me. I want happiness for my son as much as you want it for your daughter. If things are really as they appear, it would give us all pleasure if they found that happiness together.'

On the dance floor Robert said: 'Your dear parents and my mother have their heads very close together.'

Lisa glanced back over her shoulder and laughed.

'Diane's probably telling them how much money she's made out of the dance. She's done a marvellous job, you know.'

'It's a therapy,' he said quietly. 'Like your nursing. It takes up all the time there is.'

Her gold-flecked eyes were close to his dark ones as they danced.

'You're very understanding, Rob.'

'We all know the score, Lisa, and it's harder for mother, because of Ruth and because a war killed her husband, too. But let's enjoy Christmas.'

'Yes.' She squeezed his shoulder and glanced down at the necklet she was wearing. 'I've enjoyed it – especially this. Thank you again. I don't know how you managed to find anything so pretty. There's so little in the shops.'

'It's less original than your present to me,' he said, and grinned at her.

'And less trouble,' she said for she had given him a Labrador puppy to replace the old Roxton Grange dog which had died earlier in the year.

'I'll think of you every time he chews the furniture,' he said, and she rested her head against his cheek as they laughed about it.

At the end of the evening, when the dance was over and they had returned to the Grange and their parents had gone to bed, they stood in the big hall and he held out a hand to her and she

200

took it as he said: 'Lisa – thanks for Christmas. I've enjoyed it. Because of you.'

She stood close to him, tall and slender and serious, with her hair catching the light.

'It's been good fun, Rob.'

She was very still then, because his black eyes were talking to her and she understood them.

He said softly: 'I'm going to take a terrible chance now; because I have to, sometime, and now feels right.' And his fingers tightened over hers and brought her nearer and, very gently, he kissed her. It was the first time.

She did not resist; but her response was muted; not reluctant, yet not encouraging him. Then she put her head against his shoulder and whispered: 'Don't rush me, Rob. I can't forget him. I have to wait. Just a little longer.'

He released her hand and slid both his arms around her shoulders.

'I know that. And I accept it. But I love you, Lisa. When you're ready, I'll be waiting for you.'

She raised her eyes to his and, just for a moment, relaxed as she felt the pressure of his hands against her back and let herself be aware of his body against hers.

'I won't run away from you,' she said. 'I – I want to come to you. But give me a little more time.'

For seconds he held her before he kissed her again; once on the forehead then, without hesitation, on the lips. He let it last and she did not try to break away; rather, he felt the warmth of her welcome to him.

When they parted she said: 'Be patient with me, Rob. It's the only way.'

And so, cautiously, they made their pact with each other.

23

He lived through the winter in one farm house and cottage after another, high above the Mediterranean and south of the mountains over which he had been fighting before the patrol had come to St Benoit. Paul and Yvonne were never far away, and on the dark nights they gathered men around them and taught the techniques of sabotage and silent killing and the handling of Piats and explosives and sub-machine guns. Then, with the spring, the ambushes started, and trains were derailed and telephone wires laid in tangles across roads and the word went out that Paul Cardin and Ricard Michel were again leading the secret war against the oppressors, and that the Wolf of Ste Baume who killed with such bitterness and hatred had come to the Maures and the Estoril.

He saw Yvonne many times, and occasionally was alone with her; but not once did they yield to the temptation which lurked for them both, for she and Paul enjoyed their bed, while he lay in his own and remembered Lisa and then his betrayal was torture in his mind.

Meanwhile the Germans sought them. Somewhere in the mountains fringing the Mediterranean they knew there was a Maquis group which was more active and more effective than others; but they could not find its base, for it struck over fifty kilometres of coastline and inland to a depth of forty kilometres, and they had learned that reprisals against the villagers brought even more savage reprisals against themselves. But they were hard hit just at the time when British and American troops were expected to invade northern France and perhaps the south of the country as well.

In the mountains they heard that German security was under a new and more ruthless command, and that someone had been brought in from the north to lead the fight against them; but they shrugged it off, for such tales had been told before, and they had been hunted for so long that new stories were only old ones in a fresh guise.

Yet there had to be an end to it, and for Richard it came so simply that afterwards he found it difficult to believe.

It began on a day in April when they decided to blow up an electricity sub-station close to St Raphael. They chose the target because they knew a German army base was supplied from the station; and also because they had learned that military security operations in the area were now conducted from the town and it appealed to them that they should strike under the noses of their hunters.

It was a simple operation involving stealth rather than strength; one man to plant the explosives, another to act as lookout and to provide covering fire if it was needed. For three weeks, on the night chosen for the attack, informants watched the movement of army patrols and police and checked on nearby buildings and escape routes; then Richard went in armed with a machine pistol and grenades, and Marcel Dubois followed to demonstrate that he was as expert with explosives as was Paul himself.

But on the same evening Feldwebel Hermann Lange went to the house of his French girl-friend and said: 'I've found somewhere we can go.' He had half a bottle of cheap German brandy in his pocket and a blanket under his arm, and he led the willing girl to the shell of a long-deserted cottage on the edge of the town and within sight of the sub-station. They went inside half an hour before Richard came in from the surrounding countryside like a grey shadow and eased himself in through the unlocked door of the cottage, for it had been chosen as the point from which he should oversee Marcel's approach to the target.

From the darkness in the back of the cottage Lange saw the outline of a man at the empty window frame overlooking the road, put a warning hand across the girl's mouth, slid his pistol out of the belt which he had discarded earlier, and crept across the floor. He had taken off his boots when he had settled down with the girl, and he made no sound as he came up behind Richard and brought the barrel of the gun down savagely across the side of his head.

When Richard struggled back to awareness he was disarmed, his wrists were tied tightly behind his back with a thin belt from the girl's dress, and the Feldwebel stood over him with his levelled pistol.

Half an hour later he was in a town centre hotel which had become the German army's security centre, under the guard of two soldiers, and with Feldwebel Lange staring at him under the bright electric light.

'Your face is familiar,' Lange said in German. 'I don't think I have seen you before. But I think I have seen drawings.' He had clearly drunk too much from his brandy bottle and was struggling to discipline his memory.

Richard said in French: 'I am sorry. I do not understand.' He stood stiffly between the two soldiers, his wrists still bound, his head throbbing and a streak of dried blood across his temple and his ear.

Lange was still staring.

'You carried two grenades and a machine pistol, you have no papers, you were clearly involved in criminal activity. And you are tall with black hair and black eyes.' He was talking to himself as much as to the prisoner.

Richard said again: 'I am sorry. I do not understand. I do not speak German.' His mind had cleared now in spite of the pain in his head, and was saying over and over again: This is it. I've bought it. I should have checked out that bloody cottage before I went into it. Oh Christ. Unless I can prove I'm a British serviceman they'll shoot me. They might shoot me even so. This bloody sergeant might. He's drunk enough to do anything.

Lange thrust his face close to Richard's.

'I've sent for the officer in command,' he said. 'He'll be very interested to see you. And you'd better talk to him, before he hands you over to others who will make sure you talk. Oh yes, you'll talk all right.'

He turned abruptly and walked to the door. Then, as he opened it, he looked back at the prisoner, his eyes widening suddenly.

'Black hair and black eyes. And tall. My God –' his voice rose in excitement '– I think I've got one of the biggest prizes of the lot. I think this is the one we've all been looking for.' His arm came up and he pointed at the two soldiers. 'Guard him. Don't take your eyes off him. I think he's the one they call The Wolf.'

Richard stood still, his eyes fixed on the wall beyond the desk which dominated the small room. For a moment he felt sick. He had not known that the Germans had a good description of him. If they knew who he was and what he had been doing, no amount of pleading that he was a British serviceman entitled to be treated as a prisoner-of-war would help him.

He heard the door close behind him. The guards moved away, turning so that they faced him from opposite sides, their rifles across their arms. There was no help for him.

He stood like that for ten minutes, listening to his own breathing, trying to control his heartbeat, trying to ignore the pain in his head, trying to think, preparing his story. Then there were footsteps beyond the door and Lange's voice raised as the door opened: 'He tallies exactly with the descriptions we have been given, Herr Major. I'm certain he is the one.'

Footsteps in the room now. Richard stared at the wall, standing as if at ease on a parade ground, his bound hands behind his back, his shoulders square, his head up. There was a man at his side, fully as tall as himself, hatless and fair-haired. The man walked round him slowly, inspecting him, until they stood face to face and he looked into the blue eyes of Intelligence Major Kurt Edelmann.

For slow, dragging seconds they were frozen, expressionless, staring. Then Richard took a long breath and braced himself for the gamble.

He said in French: 'I do not understand the things that have been said to me. I do not speak German. I am a British officer in the Royal Air Force and am entitled to be treated as a prisoner-of-war under the Geneva Convention.'

Edelmann went on looking at him. Then he turned, went round behind the desk and sat down. He gave no sign of recognition as he said to Lange: 'Untie his hands.'

The Feldwebel clicked his heels and did so, rough fingers hurting Richard's bruised wrists. Then Edelmann nodded to one of the soldiers.

'Fetch a bowl of warm water and a clean cloth from the medical stores. If this man is to answer questions intelligently he must be made to feel reasonably comfortable. He is of no use to me with a bloody face.'

The soldier stamped his salute and went out. The remaining soldier raised his rifle fractionally, watchfully. Lange stood behind Richard, waiting. And all the time Edelmann stared, first at Richard's face, then at his rough clothes, then again at his face.

Eventually he said: 'Bring a chair for this man.'

Lange brought a wooden chair from somewhere outside the room and placed it in front of the desk. Edelmann nodded to it and said in fair French: 'Sit down, British officer who speaks no German.'

Moving stiffly, Richard sat down. He began to massage his wrists, then raised one hand and cautiously ran his fingers across the side of his head.

Edelmann said curtly, still in French: 'You are not hurt badly.' He looked up as the soldier returned with a metal bowl and a wide cotton bandage and reverted to German. 'Put it on the desk, beside the prisoner.'

The man did so, then returned to his previous stance, rifle crooked on his arm.

Edelmann said to Richard: 'You may bathe your head if you like.' He opened a drawer in the desk and pulled a small shaving mirror from it, pushing it across towards the bowl. 'There. Now you can see what you are doing.' Then he looked up at Lange and the two soldiers and said abruptly: 'Leave us. Stand guard at either end of the corridor outside. I will interrogate the prisoner alone.'

The soldiers changed grips on their rifles, stamped their feet and marched out of the room. But Lange hesitated.

'Herr Major,' he said tentatively, 'this man may be very dangerous. Would if not be better if I remained –?'

Edelmann silenced him with a quick hand movement.

'I am also very dangerous, Feldwebel Lange. Now leave us.'

Lange drew himself up, clicked his heels, barked: 'I am sorry, Herr Major.' Then he walked smartly from the room and closed the door quietly.

Edelmann leaned back in his chair, eyes unwavering on Richard's face. Then he reached for his belt, unbuttoned his pistol holster, drew out the weapon and placed it on the desk in front of him, the butt close to his hand.

'I am sorry I must take precautions,' he said in his near-perfect English. 'But I am sure you understand.'

Richard looked at the pistol. It was a Luger, like the one he had so often used. Then he met Edelmann's steady stare again.

'I would do the same,' he said, and was shocked because it was the first time he had spoken English for a year and a half. He licked his lips and added: 'I've just realised how unfamiliar I am with my own language.'

Edelmann's smile was a slight widening of his mouth; nothing more.

'I am sure we shall understand each other, whether we speak in English, or French, or –' the smile flickered again '– or German.'

'I expect so.' Richard glanced at the metal bowl, then reached

206

for it. He soaked a corner of the cotton bandage in the warm water, inspected his face in the shaving mirror, then began to bathe the blood-caked skin. As he did so he said cautiously: 'I had difficulty in believing my own eyes when I saw you here.'

'I have been here for two months,' Edelmann said. 'The army is not happy to have a Luftwaffe officer in charge of certain aspects of its security. But it is a job I was chosen to do.' He took a long breath. 'I must say our meeting is a remarkable coincidence. I was astonished to find that you were the prisoner everyone was so excited about. It had occurred to me once that the description we had reminded me of the old days when you and I knew each other. But I did not attach any significance to that. But now – here you are. Richard Haldane. The Wolf of the Mountains.'

Richard winced as he bathed the side of his head.

'Richard Haldane, squadron leader, Royal Air Force,' he said. 'I crashed in northern France in September 1942. I've been on the run ever since.'

Edelmann slid a packet of cigarettes from a pocket, selected one, then pushed the packet across the desk.

'Help yourself when you're ready,' he said. He lighted his own cigarette and added conversationally: 'You must have had a lot of help, to stay free for so long.'

Richard shrugged, still working on his face.

'You forget I speak French well,' he said. 'A few people have helped me with food and money, but I have never asked their names. Otherwise I have worked my way across France, stealing what I needed if I couldn't get it any other way. I was trying to get to Switzerland.' He dabbed his face with the bandage, then felt the swelling on the side of his head where Lange's pistol had struck him.

Edelmann watched him; then shook his head.

'I don't believe you,' he said. 'And neither will others. You were found with hand grenades manufactured in Britain, and a machine pistol which was German army issue and obviously stolen from a store or possibly a dead German soldier. You will have to tell me what you were doing in that cottage, and where you obtained your weapons, and where you came from, and the names of those with whom you have been associating: because I know you are the man whom the mountain peasants call The Wolf, and that being so I know you are one of the leaders of an

207

armed gang which has committed many crimes against the German military command and has killed many soldiers.'

Richard put down the blood-stained bandage he had been using on his face and reached for the cigarette packet. Just for an instant Edelmann's hand hovered over the Luger, then relaxed as Richard picked up the packet and drew out a cigarette. He slid a lighter across the desk.

Richard said: 'The only thing you know about me is that my name is Richard Haldane and that I come from a Devonshire village called Roxton and that before the war I flew aeroplanes for pleasure.' He lighted his cigarette and blew smoke into the air. 'To that knowledge I will add that I became a pilot in the RAF and attained the rank of Squadron Leader before I was shot down during an intruder raid on an airfield in northern France, since when I have been trying to avoid capture, which is the duty of every member of the armed forces, British or German.'

'Oh, dear God.' Suddenly Edelmann was exasperated. 'Richard – don't you realise what a desperate situation you are in? The State Security Police – the Gestapo – are looking for you. You are one of the most wanted men in France. And they will make you talk, Richard. They will make you tell the truth. They are ruthless, and they are efficient. Your only hope is to answer our questions, all our questions. You may think it means betraying your friends. But the alternative is such agony as you have never imagined, and death at the end of it.'

'You are not entitled to expect anything from me beyond my service number, my rank and my name.' Richard's voice was harsh in the stillness of the room. 'You know that. You also know it is an international crime to torture a prisoner-of-war.'

Edelmann leaned across the desk, eyes narrowed, face taut, mouth thin.

'The Gestapo doesn't give a damn about international crime. They will show you no mercy. You will have to tell them. Make up your mind to it. For your own sake, and the sake of your family.'

Richard drew hard on his cigarette, inhaling deeply; taking a long time to exhale. His eyes flicked once to the gun on the desk, just beyond the reach of his arm.

Edelmann said: 'Don't do it.' A simple, staccato order.

'And if I force you to shoot me, won't I be better off?' Whispered words. 'Won't that be better than the Gestapo?'

'It will not be better than telling the truth,' Edelmann rapped. 'At least you will still be alive.'

'Don't tell me bloody lies.' Suddenly the anger surfaced and the black eyes flared. 'If the Gestapo get me, they'll kill me no matter what I say. Unless you treat me as a prisoner-of-war, I'm dead. Now which is it, Kurt? Tell me.'

Silence then; and it seemed to go on for a long time. Then, slowly, Edelmann leaned back, and something in his face seemed to surrender; but not to Richard.

'I can do nothing,' he said. 'It is beyond my authority. My task is to take the offensive against anti-German activity; not to deal with the prisoners we take. Others have that responsibility.'

Richard drew in more smoke. He felt it bite into his lungs, and he needed the sensation. He knew he had lost. Edelmann would carry out orders. He had to get the gun; to die in this room, or trying to get out of it. He did not care which. Anything was better than sitting in a cell, waiting for the Gestapo to come for him.

'Let's stop arguing,' he said at last; and his voice was weary. 'You'll do as you must. But before you do, tell me how your family is faring. I met them once, as I'm sure you remember.'

Edelmann watched him, tensely, curiously. Then he nodded.

'Of course I remember. They are well, I think. I have not seen them for nearly a year, and they are getting older. They still live in Innsbruck. And your family?'

'I don't know,' Richard said. 'I have not been getting letters – remember?' He thought: he's still too near the gun; and I'm too far away.

Edelmann forced a smile.

'Of course. It was a silly question. But the last time you were at home –' he hesitated '– tell me how was Ruth then?'

The gun blurred at the edge of Richard's vision, and his black eyes riveted the man beyond the desk.

'Ruth is dead.' Jagged words, hurting as they fell into the room.

The skin crinkled at the corners of Edelmann's eyes. Suddenly he was sad, and he did not want to believe what he had heard.

'Dead, Richard? Ruth is dead? I am so sorry. I had often thought of her. But – I am so sorry. What happened?'

'She was killed in an air raid.' Richard threw the sentence across the desk; then leaned forward and stabbed the end of his

209

cigarette into an ashtray. The movement took him nearer to the gun.

Edelmann said: 'That is even worse: that it should have been the war. It was in London, perhaps? She had visited London?'

'She had visited Exeter.' Richard said it almost indifferently, for he was concentrating on the gun now, although he was still not looking directly at it.

It seemed a long time before Edelmann replied, and before Richard's mind focused on the effect of his words upon the Austrian; before he saw that the colour was draining from the face and it was grey, and the blue eyes were wider and shocked.

'In Exeter?' So quietly that Richard hardly heard him. Then: 'When was this? Please tell me the date.'

Richard was no longer thinking about the gun. He stared at Edelmann.

'It was in 1942. The 5th of May. The early hours of that day.' His voice was harsh again, for the memory stirred the hatred in him.

The blue eyes were on his face, but now he knew they were not seeing him. The wide mouth which had been so confident was slack, and a muscle jumped suddenly along the jaw. The last colour had gone from the cheeks; and then the eyes closed and Edelmann put a hand over them, and Richard saw that the fingers were quivering.

'I killed her, then.' The ghost of a sound, as if the words were hardly formed. And then again: 'I killed her.'

Richard was still, his mind struggling. Then reality snapped into him and, smoothly and easily, he leaned forward and picked up the Luger. Edelmann did not see him. He held the gun on his knee, just below the level of the desk, and said: 'What the hell do you mean?'

Edelmann's hand came down from his face. He did not seem to be aware that the gun had gone from the desk top.

'I planned the raid, Richard.' A hoarse whisper, haunted. 'I was intelligence officer of II Gruppe in Bomber Geschwader 27. We were told to destroy Exeter. It was my job to plan it. I briefed the crews – told them the targets – the bombing patterns –'

His voice died, his stare shifting to the desk then up to Richard's rock-carved face and black eyes filled with hatred.

'You did that? You, Kurt Edelmann, planned that?'

'Richard – not Ruth – it was just another raid –'

'You bastard.' Richard was straightening slowly, coming to his feet, the Luger levelled from his waist. 'You murdering bastard.' All the bitterness of the years wrenched the words from him. 'You were the one – as much as if you had dropped the bombs yourself. It was your plan. You killed her, and you killed Nick – you don't know that – you killed your friend Nick, too, because he was with her. He was her husband, and you killed them both, you bloody butcher, you bloody awful butcher –'

He stopped, because it was all too much, and there were no words foul enough or savage enough for his anger. There was only the man behind the desk with agony in his wide eyes, seeing his own death in the gun facing him. The hand holding the Luger was steady, but the mind that sent signals to the finger curled across the trigger was frozen in its fury; seeing nothing except the grey-white face and the lines etched into it, and the image of the girl he had loved from childhood and whose life had been crushed from her because this man had ordered it; and the loyal friend who had died with her. Then it all blurred and shifted and there were two coffins in a grave and silver plates on them and a Royal Air Force cap carefully placed as a reminder that the man who had loved this woman had been gallant and courageous through greater perils than that which had finally destroyed him.

Then it was that the finger on the Luger's trigger slackened, for the dreadful second truth came to him and surged up across the first that they were all killers, each no more and no less, and that Nick had bombed German cities and killed beautiful life-loving women and brave men and had not known their names any more than he himself had known the names of the men he had killed or of those destroyed by their deaths, or Kurt Edelmann had known the name of Ruth when he had sent his instruments of hell through the night.

And he whispered: 'Oh Christ, Kurt. Oh dear Christ, what have we come to?'

*　　*　　*

When they talked again, Richard still had the gun, but it pointed at the floor; and he sat, his shoulders slack, on the hard chair.

Kurt Edelmann said: 'We are the persecutors, and the perse-cuted. There is no help for us but that which we can find for

211

ourselves.'

Richard looked down at the gun in his hand and moved it slowly from side to side; almost as if it was a novel thing.

'Once this was my help,' he said. 'In my hand, or in the wings of my aeroplane. The only help I needed was in this. Now I feel that if I had all the guns in the world, they would not help me.' And he knew he was tired; for the first time since he had struggled back to life in a distant French farm house, he was tired beyond recall, and he wanted to sleep until the horror was over.

Edelmann lit a cigarette and held it out. Richard looked at it; then, slowly, reached for it.

'The gun you have now will not help you,' the Austrian said. There was no threat in his voice; only sadness. 'There is no way out of this room except through the door, and there's a guard at each end of the corridor. And beyond the guards there are more, and they all know I am questioning somebody. They are all alert. If you take me out as a hostage, you cannot avoid turning your back towards one of them. Then you will die.'

Richard looked at the gun again and said quietly: 'I would probably save somebody else's life if I used it on myself; in here.' He was resigned now, and cold inside. There was nothing else for him. 'If I don't, either I shoot it out in the corridor, or you give me to the Gestapo.'

He drew deeply on his cigarette, and watched Edelmann light one for himself. They sat, looking through the smoke; and Richard's fingers moved along the blue-black barrel of the gun.

'At least we understand a little of each other,' he said. 'It's taken us a long time to do that. Such a long time.'

Edelmann nodded. The colour had crept slowly back into his face; but it was an old face, a weary face.

He said, quietly and carefully: 'It has taken too long to learn; to know what we are, and where we are going. First Ruth – and now you? No, Richard. I cannot bring her back; but I can reach out to her, through you. I cannot get you out of this place, in freedom. But I can send you away in some degree of safety. The Gestapo shall not have you. You are a prisoner-of-war, and will be treated honourably.'

'You can't do that.' Richard shook his head. 'They won't let you.'

Edelmann waved him into silence, the movement of his hand

tracing a smoke pattern between them.

'You are Squadron Leader Richard Haldane, a British pilot who has been trying to escape to Switzerland since you were shot down,' he said. 'You had found an arms cache in the hills. There are many of them up there, hidden by the guerrillas. That was how you came to be carrying a gun and grenades. You are not the Wolf of the Mountains. You know nothing of the Maquis. Three weeks ago you were in Aix; before that you were in Grenoble for a long time, trying to get to the Swiss border, sleeping rough, but you were beaten by our security. You have told me this, even though you are not obliged to tell me more than your name and rank and service number. I believe you, for there is no evidence to the contrary.' He moved his shoulders in a shrug. 'Tomorrow I will send you to be a prisoner-of-war. And you will be alive.'

Richard said: 'They will not believe it. That Feldwebel will not believe it. The risk is too great: the risk to you.'

'It is the least dreadful of all the risks,' Edelmann said. 'Lange will do as he is told. If the Gestapo learns I have had a prisoner, they will not be allowed to suspect that he was other than an escaping British pilot. You have no choice, Richard. So please do not argue. And –' he hesitated, then said softly '– and trust me. In Ruth's memory, trust me.'

They smoked the rest of their cigarettes in silence, not looking at each other. Then Richard reached for the ashtray and, very carefully, stubbed out the remains of the tobacco. He took a long breath, closed his eyes for a moment, and stood up. Carefully he leaned across the desk and put the Luger on it, the butt close to Edelmann's fingers.

He said: 'As a British officer, I am in your hands.'

Kurt Edelmann pushed himself out of his chair. He picked up the pistol, slid it into its holster, and buttoned the flap. Then he came round the desk, and the two men faced each other; motionless until, as if at a signal, their hands clasped.

Edelmann said: 'One day you will come to see me; or I will come to see you. And we will have much to remember, for there is much that we have learned to understand. I say again, Richard: in Ruth's memory, trust me.'

24

Robert came down the wide stairs into the hall of Roxton Grange and nodded towards the radio on a side table.

'Anything important on the news?'

Lisa said: 'It's all important now. But nothing new since yesterday. The German army is just folding up. Either the British or the Americans will link up with the Russians tomorrow. It's nearly finished, Rob – it can't go on more than another few days.'

He crossed the hall and stared out of the window at the bright spring day.

'Five years,' he said quietly. 'Who would have guessed? And it isn't nearly finished, you know. There's still Japan. God knows how long that will go on. But at least it will soon stop in Europe.' He heard her footsteps, and held out a hand, drawing her close to him. 'It will seem strange to be able to make plans again, real plans for a real future.'

She watched a flock of starlings beyond the drive outside, without really seeing them.

'I haven't come to terms with it,' she said at last. 'I read the newspapers and I listen to the news and we talk about it at the hospital, and I know it's ending; yet somehow it isn't real.' She looked at him quickly, her eyes asking to be understood. 'I can't forget, Rob.'

He slid an arm around her waist.

'Neither of us will ever forget – Richard, or Ruth. But it may be easier to live with, once the war is finished. We have to plan our lives. They would both have wanted that.' He hesitated for a moment, then kissed her briefly on the forehead. 'And for me the most important plan is for our marriage. Everything hinges on that.'

'I know.' She rested her head momentarily on his shoulder. 'Once it's really finished, Rob. Once I can feel absolutely sure, and accept it – then we will. They – I suppose they will repatriate the prisoners quickly, won't they?'

'Very quickly. It will be an absolute priority. The armies must be over-running the prison camps now.' He said it confidently, yet impersonally. It did not occur to him that Richard might be in one of the camps and that if he came back he, Robert, would lose the girl with whom he was now deeply in love, for he knew his brother was dead. He had talked to Steve Mitchell who had held out no hope that Richard could have survived his crash. Mitch had said: 'Face it now, Rob. Don't go on torturing yourself. The Spit smashed itself to pieces in those trees. Then what was left blew up. No one could have come out of it. We haven't heard anything simply because Jerry would have had no means of identification. There would be nothing left. I saw it happen, Rob. I hate saying this to you, but it's better to say it than to tell lies. In any case, if by some miracle he had come out of it, Jerry would have reported him a prisoner. They haven't. I couldn't make myself say it to Lisa. But you'll have to get it across to her somehow.'

As gently as he could – and gentleness did not come easily to Robert's nature – he had tried to tell her, and she seemed to accept it. Yet all the time a corner of her mind had clung to the official word 'missing', rejecting the ultimate acceptance in the absence of the ultimate verdict.

She had come close to him, and she would marry him. He was sure she loved him, at least enough to make it work; but he also knew she had to let the enormous European drama act itself out to the final curtain call. Only when the last barriers had gone would she allow herself to accept that Richard had gone too.

Across the hall the telephone rang and he walked over to it. She watched him; heard him answer and start to discuss some farm problem with a Ministry of Agriculture adviser. She understood only a little of the subject, and turned back to the window and the spring sun beyond, picturing herself married to Robert and sharing this house and his business; and finding herself, as so often in the past when she had thought about it, strangely detached, as if she were an observer watching someone else.

She could see Robert now, at the edge of her vision, holding the telephone against his ear by cocking his head on one side and raising his shoulder. He was using both hands to emphasise his words, as if the caller could see him; a measure of his enthusiasm for farming and everything connected with it.

She would have to learn to share that; or at least understand some of it.

A strand of his black hair had fallen across his forehead. Richard's hair used to do that. And the wide-legged emphatic stance was the same. Sometimes, if the light was poor, there was so little difference between them; except in the voice, for Richard's had had a magic for her, a subtlety and a quality for which she had no words yet which remained in her secret memory even now, two and a half years after he had gone. When everything was very quiet she could conjure it from the past and listen to it; sometimes sadly but often thankfully, for the sound of him had been one of her great pleasures and she was glad she could remember it so well.

She no longer wondered what it would have been like to have married him, to have lived with him in a peaceful, permanent world. Robert was her man now; and for a moment she felt sorry for him. It was not the first time the feeling had come to her, for she had no illusions about their relationship. Robert was a substitute; a look-alike in the shadows; a compensation. She had come to love him, but remotely. He would not be difficult to live with, even though he lacked Richard's extraordinary, instinctive understanding of her and the magnetism of his gentle, mocking humour. Robert would be a comfortable companion; certainly not an exciting lover.

Sometimes she wondered what he would be like in bed. But she had never felt more than briefly tempted to find out. He had wanted it, certainly; but he had stopped seeking it now, realising that it would be too final for her while the last faint flame flickered. It was the ultimate giving and the ultimate taking, and she was not ready for it. Nor, she thought at that moment, would she ever be. It would happen, when they married, and she would want to enjoy it then for she would have crossed the great barrier and there would be nothing left to draw her back. But she knew she would have to struggle against the images of bygone nights and their limitless passion and possession, and she dreaded that in ecstasy she might call out the wrong name. She would have to school herself, as in so much else in the new world.

Poor Robert, she thought. And poor Lisa.

25

'Hey – British. Cigarette, huh?'

Captain Sokolov was three inches over six feet in height and built like a human bull. He leaned forward from the battered armchair in which he sat and threw a cigarette across to Richard, his flat-nosed face splitting into a heavy-lipped grin.

He was Richard's captor, and protector; and had been both for more than two months.

They were now in a half-ruined farmhouse in central Hungary, and the sequence of events which had led Richard there had begun four weeks after he had been escorted from St Raphael, under guard on his way to Germany. He had been taken by train to Lyon, then across to Strasbourg where he had been briefly interrogated by an indifferent German army major, and finally to a prison camp near Leipzig where he had quickly found that most of the other inmates were hard-core trouble-makers regarded by the Germans as dangerous. He had been questioned again, notes were made of his personal details, and he had settled in a crowded wooden hut with forty other RAF prisoners.

Immediately his fellow inmates learned that he spoke German he was in demand as a teacher, preparing several men for the next escape attempt. But the lessons were little more than two weeks old when he was summoned to the camp commandant's office and told he was being transferred to another prison.

He was taken away in a truck, guarded by a sergeant and a soldier. They drove for several hours, and he knew by the sun that they were heading east. At first his escorts refused to talk to him, but when they stopped for food he at last broke through their hostile silence and got an answer to his inevitable question.

'You are going to a prison camp near the Czech border,' the sergeant said. 'You must be a special case, Squadron Leader.'

'Why do you say that?' Richard asked warily.

The sergeant shrugged, making clear that the affair was none of his business.

'Because only special cases go there. It is not bad – not as bad as some. But not good, either. There are many nationalities there: military, and civilians also. All special. Don't ask me why. But take my advice: don't step out of line.'

That was all the information he got; but when he arrived at the camp he knew what the sergeant had meant.

It was just a group of buildings in a clearing deep in a forest; a central compound with the huts set around it, and the whole surrounded by a double fence of netting and barbed wire overlooked by watch towers. Outside the wire was bare ground extending to a hundred or more yards before the edge of the forest, and Richard guessed that most of it would be mined.

There was no office where details were recorded. He was simply marched through heavily wired gates into the central compound, taken to a hut and told that one bunk was his, and left in the dull-eyed company of ragged-clothed men of assorted nationalities.

No one else in the hut was British. But in the next hut was a grey-bearded man who introduced himself as Charles Campbell, a naval lieutenant who had been taken prisoner in Crete in 1941, who had slipped his guards in Greece on the way to Germany and had lived in the mountains for several months before being recaptured, and who had later escaped into Poland where he had joined an underground group before falling into German hands again late in 1943.

He said: 'It's a concentration camp by another name. Try to escape and they'll shoot you out of hand – or worse. You get chosen for this place when they want to lose you but can't quite persuade themselves to put a bullet into you. If you have a name here, it's because you remember it yourself. I suppose there are records somewhere, but there's no admin – just the guards, and they're mostly a brutal lot. What did you do to deserve it?'

'Stayed on the run in France for eighteen months,' Richard said.

Campbell raised an eyebrow.

'Is that all?'

'More or less.'

Campbell nodded.

'Okay. It's none of my business. I don't have to keep my mouth shut – they know all about me. But you can't tell who your neighbour is in this place. There are some odd characters around. As far as I know we're the only two British here, so I'm bloody glad to see you. We don't see the Gestapo here, as far as we know; but it's certain that it's one of their hell-holes. Anyway, we're alive, and they're not pulling off our finger nails, so we're better off than many – though I reckon we'll be lucky to get out. I've a nasty feeling that one day a firing squad'll march through the gates. But that's just instinct and a suspicious mind.' Then his mouth twisted into a grin and his eyes sparkled in his gaunt, bearded face. 'Tell you one thing you'll be glad to know, old boy. There's a radio under the floor in the hut next to mine. A Dutchman has it. They sent him here for helping some of your RAF types to escape. How the hell he managed to bring in the radio I don't know, and he won't say. But it's there – the only one in the camp. So at least we can keep up with the war news. Did you know there've been landings in France – the big show?'

Richard stared at him. He was thinking about Campbell's reference to the Gestapo. Now he dragged his mind away from the questions chasing each other across his memory of that last, tense meeting with Kurt Edelmann, and said: 'No. I didn't. What's happened?'

That was how he learned of the Allied invasion of Normandy on 6th of June 1944; and the Dutchman's secret radio also told him, a few weeks later, of the landings in the south of France, along the St Raphael beaches and around the Gulf of St Tropez, and then the collapse of German resistance in the Maures and the Estoril and the Ste Baume mountains; and a great surge of frustration wracked him, for he knew that if he had only been able to remain undetected for a little extra time he would now be free and on his way home.

But he was not free. Lisa was half a world away, and as the months dragged in alternating boredom and fear and hunger, he began to feel for the first time that, after all, perhaps he would never go home again. The camp seemed a doomed place, and the men in it were doomed; even the guards with their clubs and machine pistols seemed doomed, for theirs was a pointless, degrading task, and when they dragged a man away and beat him for breaking one of the petty rules it seemed to be without satisfaction or anger or even interest. It could not go on, and yet it did; and men died of illness or injuries and others were brought in to take their place, and only the war news encouraged those who were strong enough and lucky enough to survive through the savage cold of the winter.

Then, on a March day in 1945, the Dutchman's radio reported that the Russians had now swept almost unhindered across western Czechoslovakia as the German army fell back and tried to regroup within its homeland, and the camp inmates knew that they would soon hear the guns.

They also knew that they were nearing their time of greatest danger, for the guards might well kill their prisoners before they fled. Yet there was nothing to be done except wait and hope, and be afraid.

Ultimately most of them survived because of lack of discipline among the guards. One morning at the end of April it became obvious that they were pulling out, and the prisoners watched from the windows of their huts as trucks were loaded hurriedly with kitbags and boxes. Then an argument developed between two groups of guards, and Richard saw an officer snatch out his pistol and level it at a man standing on one of the trucks. Abruptly there was firing and the officer fell, and the man on the truck fell, and so did others. Suddenly a truckload of guards drove towards the nearest prison hut, the men leapt out with their rifles, smashed in the door and began firing inside; just as the other trucks were started up and were driven wildly out of the gates and away.

Richard was among the two hundred or so men who saw the open gates and ran for them, and then along the narrow mine-free road into the forest, while the guards shot indiscriminately at everyone they could find in the camp before they scrambled back into their truck and drove it out through the gates and away into the dark trees.

When the fugitives moved back cautiously into the camp, Richard found Charles Campbell's body among the corpses in the hut where the Dutchman had kept his radio.

Two hours later the Russians came.

They arrived in a motorized column coming out of the forest into the camp clearing; and when one vehicle left the road and exploded a mine close to the camp fence the soldiers began firing rifles and machine guns into the surrounding trees, and into the camp huts as well.

Then there was silence, and the prisoners in the huts climbed warily to their feet and watched the Russian troops approaching. There was no celebration, no shouted greetings or cheering; instead, one fear replaced another, for there was something in the attitude of the advancing soldiers which spoke only of cruelty and death.

For a time there were shouted questions from behind the pointed muzzles of the Russians' guns. But the language barrier was insuperable, and presently an officer bellowed orders and the troops climbed back into their vehicles and drove away.

Later more soldiers arrived and Richard saw that several were women and that some, of both sexes, appeared to be drunk. Again language defeated attempts to establish a relationship in the face of the troops' obvious suspicion, and it was not until late in the day that a better-disciplined detachment drove through the perimeter wire and the first conversations and explanations began.

Within an hour the prisoners were given spades and were instructed to dig a mass grave for the last victims of the German camp guards; and as he worked Richard saw that two Russian soldiers stood with levelled guns in their hands, watching with cold, hostile eyes.

By the time the grim task was completed the day had ended. The searchlights on the watch towers were switched on and the prisoners were ordered back to their huts for the night. No food was provided for them, although the Russian troops were seen in the hut which had been used previously as a cookhouse.

The following day a captured German lorry was driven into the camp, and a big man who climbed out immediately began to shout orders. He was a captain, the most senior officer to appear so far, and he quickly introduced order among the troops and the prisoners. Within an hour he had set up a table and chairs in one of the huts and the prisoners were brought in one at a time to give their names to an orderly who sat with him and who then handed out torn pieces of paper which became their identity forms.

When Richard's turn came the captain looked him up and down with hard eyes, and barked at him in Russian.

Richard said, in English: 'I am British. A British air force pilot. A prisoner-of-war. Do you understand me?'

Heavy lids came down over the Russian's eyes, almost hiding them.

'British? What is British?' Quieter; and suspicious.

'From Britain,' Richard said. 'From England. Royal Air Force. I don't speak Russian. Do you understand English?'

The Russian said: 'Speak German? Speak German, eh?'

Richard responded, giving his name and rank and repeating

221

that he was a prisoner-of-war. He addressed the Russian as 'Captain'.

The reply came in heavily accented but understandable German: 'So you are a pilot. What is an officer pilot doing in this place? Why are you not in a prisoner-of-war camp?'

'Because I avoided capture when I was shot down, and fought the Germans with the French Resistance. The Germans did not like me, so when they captured me they sent me here.'

The Russian turned and spoke to the orderly at his side, and the orderly wrote furiously in a notebook. Then the Russian turned back to Richard and stared at him. Again the eyelids lowered until only slits remained.

'So, British. You were in the air force, eh? But you are not in the air force now. You are in a camp where the Germans put spies and thieves and murderers. We know that some men in this camp have spied against Russia. You know that, eh? Some Poles have spied against Russia, and they are here. So why are you here? I don't believe you, British. I think you lie.'

Richard looked at the narrowed eyes and snapped: 'I am an officer of at least equal rank to yourself. I fought in the British air force for two and a half years before I was shot down, and then I fought the Germans for a long time in the mountains, with guns and explosives. I deserve your respect just as I give you mine. We have both fought the same enemy. I do not lie, and you know it.'

Without shifting his slitted eyes from Richard's face, the Russian spoke rapidly to the orderly, who again wrote quickly in his book. Then he nodded slowly, as if in answer to a question he had asked of himself.

'Go back to your hut, British. Take your piece of paper with your name on it. Keep it carefully. I will ask more questions.'

He waved a big hand in dismissal, but Richard stood still.

'Captain,' he said curtly, 'as a British officer to a Russian officer, I must ask for more humanitarian treatment for the prisoners here. We have had no food for almost two days. I am very hungry, and so are the other men. There is food in the cookhouse, even if it is not very good food. May we have your permission to feed ourselves?'

The Russian's eyes opened wide.

'If there is food in the cookhouse, and you have not had food even when the Germans have gone, it is because you have not gone to get it. Of course you have my permission to eat. I will place you in charge of all the prisoners. I will instruct my soldiers that you will arrange orderly eating. Now go.'

Richard nodded. He was suddenly beginning to feel more confident.

'Thank you, captain,' he said. 'I salute you, and the Russian army. I look forward to our next meeting.'

The heavy eyelids came down again, and the eyes were slits as they watched Richard leave the hut.

That night, with the prisoners fed on black bread and a stew made from salted pork and beef, Richard sat on the edge of his bunk and thought about the Russian captain and how long it would be before he obtained his own release. It was now May – he could not remember if it was the second or third of the month – and he guessed the war must be close to its end. But the Dutchman's radio had been smashed in the guards' final murderous orgy, and he did not know what was happening further west. So he thought instead about Lisa, and his home-coming, and how soon he might be able to marry her.

He slept soundly that night.

At noon on the following day he walked steadily around the central compound, as he tried to do for an hour every day; and then became aware of the big figure of the Russian captain watching him. The man stood beside one of the huts, a stained and battered greatcoat slung across his shoulders, his cap tilted back from his wide forehead. The sun was bright, and he wrinkled the skin around his eyes against it.

Richard walked among the scattering of other prisoners and approached the Russian.

'Good morning, Captain,' he said in German. 'I have eaten moderately well, and I feel better than I felt yesterday.'

The heavy eyelids were a shield.

'You do not look well, British,' the hard voice said in its guttural, stilted German. 'You are thin, and you have no colour in your face. Also, your eyes are troubled. That is either because you are a hungry man, or because you are a spy.'

Richard retorted: 'And if I were a spy, captain, on whose behalf would I be spying – and upon whom would I be spying?'

'Your grammar is better than mine.' The response was fast and

223

hard. 'How do you speak German so well if you are not a German spy?'

'I do not speak a German's German. And if I were a spy for Germany why would I be a prisoner here?' Challenge for challenge; and now Richard was chest to chest with the big Russian.

'Then perhaps you are a spy for someone else. There are Poles here who are spies for the imperialists. You say you are a British officer. So you are also an imperialist.'

Richard retorted: 'Why should I spy against Russia when I have been fighting Russia's enemy? I am a soldier, just as you are a soldier. I have fought Germans in the air and on the ground. And I have done it for longer than you have, captain. It does not matter what labels we give each other's countries. The only thing which matters is that we have fought the common enemy.'

The Russian leaned forward, lowering his head a little so that his eyes were on the level of Richard's own.

'I tell you something, British,' he said, and now his voice was quiet, so that a man at arm's length could scarcely have heard it. 'I tell you that I believe you. But some may not. There are men here who have worked against Russia and against Socialism. They may also have worked against Fascists, but that does not matter now, for the Fascists are beaten, and if these men go free they will work again against Russia. So they will not go free. Some will die. You have been their companion, and there are those who may believe you are part of them. I do not believe that. I like you, British. We are both soldiers, as you say. So I have a bargain with you. I will protect you, and you will teach your language to me. I speak good German and good Hungarian. I wish also to speak good English. You will teach me, British. And I will keep you safe.'

Richard took a long breath and, because he had no reasonable choice, he nodded.

'That's a bargain, Captain. But there must be another part to it – that you will also help me to return to my home. I have not been home, or seen my woman, for two and a half years.'

The Russian's eyes slitted again. He said: 'I do not have a home, British. It was destroyed by the Germans. I do not have a woman. She was killed by the Germans. So I do not care about your home or your woman. But you will go home, when the time is right. Now you will come with me. You will do what I tell you to do. That is necessary, for I think others may soon arrive here, and there may be unpleasantness. Come.'

He turned abruptly, big in his square-shouldered greatcoat and the peaked cap angled back from his face, and marched between the huts. And Richard followed him.

In the hut which had become his office the Russian said: 'I have other responsibilities. Now there is order in this camp I shall leave it. In two hours certain other people will arrive here. In one hour I shall go. You will go with me.' He swung round suddenly to face Richard, his cap tilted farther back on his head. And then he grinned hugely, his mouth wide and his teeth showing. 'You look dreadful, British. A sick man in ragged clothes. It will take time to give you colour and flesh. But at least we can give you clothes. Russian soldiers' clothes. Wait here.'

Richard watched the big Russian march to the door, then said tactfully: 'I will be proud to wear a Russian soldier's clothes. But tell me, Captain – what is your name? You know my name, so I should know yours.'

The Russian grinned again.

'I know your name, but I will call you British. My name is Josef Sokolov. You call me what you like, as long as you teach me to speak your language.' And he stamped out of the hut.

An hour later Richard climbed into a truck alongside Sokolov wearing the baggy uniform of a Russian private soldier, and they jolted out of the camp, along the dusty road between the minefields, and into the forest.

As they drove Sokolov said: 'When you meet soldiers, if they speak to you then you speak to them in English, and if they do not understand you speak in German. If you are afraid when I am not with you, you say "Captain Josef Sokolov". Then they come for me. Do not forget I am your friend who will help you to return to your home.' He looked sideways at Richard, and his thick lips parted in his great grin. 'But you teach me to speak English first, eh?'

So they drove on, to a Russian army command post where Richard was largely ignored as he stood beside the huge Sokolov. The tented encampment was the centre of frenzied activity, with tanks and armoured troop carriers rumbling in and out and, to Richard's surprise, large numbers of horses used for heavy haulage and also as personal transport by some of the officers. He sat with Sokolov for a rough evening meal in one of the tents, with other officers sharing the contents of the plates laid out on boards supported across the backs of two wooden chairs. Richard noted that three men who acted as waiters wore plain denims and, he thought, did not look like Russians; but he had no chance to identify their nationality, for as soon as the meal was over Sokolov poured two glasses of the fiery vodka which seemed to be the staple drink, and said: 'Now, British, you teach me. For one hour we speak only your language, hey? And you teach me well, British – otherwise I send you back to that camp.' And he threw back his head and roared with laughter at his joke.

And so it went on for five days; until one morning Sokolov thumped Richard's shoulder and shouted in his new English: 'Is finish, British. War finish today. Victory, hey? Germany dead. Hitler dead. We drink. We all drink.'

They did, throughout the day; so that by evening Richard thought there was scarcely a conscious man at the command post, and he had surrendered to the alcohol and the enthusiasm himself and fell asleep on the floor of the tent with Sokolov snoring beside him and several other Russians sprawled nearby.

But a week later he was still at the command post, acting as Sokolov's servant during the days and his English teacher in the evenings. And when he reminded the Russian that he wanted to return home his only answer was a huge grin, the offer of a cigarette, and a booming, laughing, meaningless promise.

Then, abruptly, he was ordered into the cab of the captured German truck, six soldiers climbed into the back, and Sokolov heaved himself into the driving seat and said in English: 'Today we go. That is good, hey?'

'Where to?' Richard demanded.

The Russian's shoulders moved in a great shrug.

'You will see. Nearer to Russia. That is good.'

'I want to move nearer to England. When is that going to happen?'

Sokolov crashed the gearbox and the truck jumped forward.

'You go to Russia first. Then you go home,' he shouted above the engine noise, and slapped the steering wheel in his enthusiasm.

So began Richard's journey east, from army camp to army camp: Sokolov was an engineering supply officer and spent much of his time checking the needs of armoured units and radioing details back to an unidentified headquarters. But always he demanded his English lessons every day, he spoke in English with Richard as often as he could and became angry when he had to resort to German to make himself understood; and by some mysterious means went on protecting Richard against inquiries from other Russian officers. It could not have happened in the British army, Richard knew; but there was little about the great Russian military juggernaut which corresponded, in discipline, behaviour or organisation, with any army he had ever imagined. And he knew that, whatever Sokolov might say to the contrary, he was as much the Russian captain's prisoner as he was his teacher and servant.

By June he was in Hungary, and now he demanded every day that he should be sent back home; until suddenly Sokolov's great grin faded and the lids came down over the eyes and he put his mouth close to Richard's ear even though no one else was nearby, and said softly: 'You go when I say, British. If you make trouble I say you are a spy. Then you never go home. You understand, British?'

It might have gone on for several more months, except for one minute of extraordinarily good fortune on the day Sokolov drove his truck back across the border into Russia and on to a minor military airfield where equipment he had ordered was being assembled.

As he stood in the entrance to a hangar, with Richard at his side, a twin-engined transport landed and taxied towards them. From the control tower next to the hangar three officers marched out to the aircraft, and Richard watched idly as they greeted several uniformed men who disembarked. A small guard unit was already standing to attention, and Richard guessed that the visitors were important.

And then, as they marched across the tarmac towards the hangar where he stood, he saw that one wore the uniform of a Royal Air Force Wing Commander.

Sokolov was twenty paces away, talking to a sergeant, checking papers and the contents of a wooden crate. Richard, standing alone, moved a step backwards; then another, out of the hangar into the sunlight, closer to the advancing group of officers. They were heading for the control tower, and their path would take them to within a dozen yards of the hangar entrance.

Richard moved another step; then saw Sokolov lift his big head

227

and glance towards him.

That was when he made up his mind.

He turned, faced the party from the aircraft, and marched straight towards them. He got to within ten paces before anyone seemed to notice him. Then two junior officers stepped out ahead of the group and Richard saw the Wing Commander looking at him and said, loudly and clearly: 'Sir – I'm Squadron Leader Haldane, formerly based at Hanford in 11 Group, Fighter Command. I'm an ex-POW and I'm being prevented from returning home. Please help me.'

The two lieutenants converged on him, one with a hand on the pistol in his belt. Richard stood still, drawing himself up, realising that the officer on the Wing Commander's left was a General and that the occasion, whatever it was, had some significance. He saw the Wing Commander's eyes looking him up and down, and anger on the General's face. Then the Wing Commander checked his stride, said something in Russian to the General, and paused, inspecting the shabby, thin-faced khaki-clad figure standing between the two hesitating Lieutenants.

For a long, long second there was silence. Then the Wing Commander smiled, stepped forward with his hand extended, and said easily: 'Squadron Leader Haldane – I'm delighted to meet you. My name is Moreland. I'm the British Air Attaché in Moscow, on my way to a reception being kindly arranged by our hosts.' He shook Richard's hand, then indicated the General cordially. 'But if you will excuse me for a moment I will explain to them in their own language why it is important that you and I have a conversation.'

Behind them, in the hangar's shadow, Sokolov watched; but Richard did not look back, for now he knew he was safe.

It was the 24th of July; the day when, in the church of St Thomas in the Devonshire village of Roxton, Lisa and Robert were married.

228

26

It was a sensation: a miracle in their midst. Few people had seen him, for he had not been into the village yet; but they all knew he was there. Some said he was at the Grange, others insisted he was staying with his mother in the new house to which she had moved when her other son had married. But the detail mattered little. He had come back from the dead, and they all talked about it and compared titbits of information and argued and wondered.

But none knew the agony.

Diane had been the one to tell him, in a small office at the Cambridge airfield where he had landed. They had sat together for a long time, and she had watched the thin face shrink, and the dark compelling eyes grow dull. He had been quiet about it, almost gentle in his questioning after the first awful shock. She had answered as well as she could; had tried to explain, to excuse, to reason. But there was little point, for Richard did not seem to understand; only that the source of all his strength for so long had been taken from him, and that the future which had been his sustaining dream was no longer there for him to claim.

At the end he said: 'I'll wait a few days before I come home. May I stay with you for a little while? Obviously I can't go to the Grange. But I'd like a rest. I need time to think first, though.'

After that he saw the Senior Medical Officer who put him into hospital for three days before he was pronounced under-nourished and suffering from severe nervous strain, but otherwise fit. Then they found him a temporary uniform and told him about the DSO and suggested he should be interviewed by the Press, but he refused. He rested for several more days, then they asked him how he would like to receive the medal.

The Group Captain said: 'I'm sure I can get you a trip to the Palace, if you'd like that.' But he had declined, so instead they arranged a special parade at RAF Hanford, and when they asked him whom he would like to be present he said: 'My mother. No one else.'

When the day came she stood beside an Air Vice-Marshal on a raised platform placed at the centre of the parade ground, and heard the band play and the Air Vice-Marshal's speech to the assembled ranks and saw her son receive his medal, and knew pride and thankfulness beyond belief.

But for Richard it was no more than a diversion; a discipline which helped him to school himself for what was to come; a touchstone at the edge of the real world with which he was not yet fully re-acquainted. He had wanted to see Steve Mitchell but was told he was in the Far East, so asked the station adjutant to send a message to let Mitch know what had happened. Then he telephoned Graham Telford and said cautiously: 'Graham, this may be a shock to you, so take a tight hold on yourself. I'm Richard Haldane.'

The next day he was on a train to London and a glad reunion. The Telfords prepared a room for him and he dined with them and talked through the evening, being careful not to refer to Nick until he realised that they had accepted their loss with quiet dignity and, indeed, that it gave them pleasure to recall times past.

He told them about Lisa and Robert coldly and clinically, and for a time they were silent, not knowing what to say to him; but he brushed the subject aside until, after midnight, Margaret Telford went to bed and her husband smoothed his silver-grey hair and fixed Richard with his shrewd eyes and said: 'I don't think you have finished, Richard. There is something else you want to talk about.'

Richard leaned back in a vast armchair and took his time before he said: 'You're very perceptive; although that shouldn't surprise me. I would have come to see you no matter what had happened, for the sake of all the things we have known and the friendship which I hope will go on. But I do need advice and it has to come from someone outside my family, and from someone I trust and respect. I want to tell you what I believe I have to do, and to know what you think of it.'

They talked for two hours then, and his dark eyes were no longer dull but hard and diamond-sharp, and his voice ice-edged. The next day he travelled to Exeter and stayed with Diane, and in the evening said: 'Mother, do something for me: telephone Robert and say I want to call on him tomorrow. Arrange a time for me, please.'

*   *   *

He had been there for ten minutes, and the resolutions they had

230

all made were forgotten as the bitterness surfaced and resentment surged and Richard's tongue lashed his brother and Lisa covered her face with tortured hands when he told her: 'You couldn't wait. You said you would promise me the world, but it took too long for you.' Again and again they said: 'Mitch told us you were dead. He saw the crash and said you had to be dead and you weren't reported killed only because everything was destroyed. And we waited until the end of the war and all the prisoners had come back –' But that only made it worse, for he savaged them: 'You waited? For what? To marry – yes. But marriage is for lovers. How long did you wait for that?' And then the words choked in him, for he remembered Yvonne and their hillside cave and this was all retribution by some dreadful god for he had betrayed Lisa and himself; and yet it was unjust, for his own betrayal had been instant, wild and unpremeditated, a reaction to fear and tension and relief, and just as quickly regretted, while theirs had been slow and calculated and discussed in comfort and safety. He knew he was unreasonable and that his vision was distorted, and once he wanted to reach out to her and heal the wounds and his mind cried out for her to come to him, but it was too late for she was Robert's wife and his bitterness came back and his voice cracked: 'Stop. I didn't come here for this.'

They stood then, in the quiet of the hall, looking at his gaunt face and the eyes shadowed by imprisonment and death, waiting until he said: 'I came to tell you that I'm pulling out. Half this estate is mine, and I want it.'

Robert nodded, weary now.

'I guessed it. We can make the arrangements. I'll either borrow from the bank or mortgage the place. We'll get it all valued, then we can dissolve the family partnership and I'll pay you out. The death duties after poor Ruth still aren't settled, but we can sort that out somehow.'

'We'll sell it.' The words slashed across the hall.

Robert hesitated, as if unsure that he had heard correctly.

'Sell it? What the hell are you talking about? We don't have to sell it. We just –'

'We have to sell it because I say so. Get it clear, Robert – I'll accept no valuation other than the auctioneer's hammer. Read the partnership deeds. I'm within my rights. I'll have half the value of this estate, and I'll recognise no measure of that value

231

except the open market. Agricultural land prices have been rising since 1939 and they're still rising. No valuer can decide what an estate like this might be worth on the present market.'

'Richard – please.' It was Lisa, ashen-faced. Involuntarily she stepped forward and reached for his arm, imploring. 'Don't do that. There've been Haldanes here for so long. Don't destroy that.'

'You have destroyed me.' His voice was like a whip across her face, and she recoiled from it as if it had been real, and she was like a hurt child fighting to cling to whatever shred of dignity was left to her and he saw the agony as he tried to turn away and found he could not move. Somewhere in his mind she was with him again in the magic of their first meeting and the warmth of their belonging to each other and the dream of their first time place, and he was holding out her hand as people applauded and he slid his ring on to her finger and said for all my life Lisa and now his life was over because Robert had taken it. His fingers clung to hers on his arm and then he was the child wanting to come home out of the darkness and seeing only the door closed and barred and all the strength which had carried him through the last dreadful years slid away from him and he whispered: 'Oh, Lisa, you were my world when I was afraid, and now it's gone.'

And the worst thing, as he dragged his hand from hers and went out of the hall and left the door swinging against the summer sky, was that they saw the tears running down his emaciated face.

27

The arrangements took four months. A senior partner from a distinguished company of agricultural auctioneers was commissioned to conduct the sale, and the event was widely advertised. Photographs were taken of the house, the home farm and the tenanted farms, and a catalogue printed. Then viewing days were arranged, and groups of farmers walked the land and talked to the tenants, while more than twenty serious contenders sought private meetings with Robert and his accountants.

But they saw nothing of Richard. He had taken two months' leave, part of which he spent in lonely holidays in the Lake District and in Scotland, walking the wild fells. He also visited Roxton church and the grave where Ruth and Nick lay, and stayed with Nick's parents. Then he returned to RAF service and was pronounced fit for flying duties. He flew a Spitfire again; but the fighter squadrons were being cut down rapidly and he was sent on a conversion course to learn to fly twin-engined Mosquitoes, and the family heard little of him.

The December day of the Roxton estate sale was cold and grey-clouded, with thin rain in the wind. The village hall was filled with chairs, and long before the sale began most were occupied. The principal of the local auctioneering company which had handled detailed arrangements stood at the front and said to his partner: 'It's a good crowd, John. Many spectators; but many potential buyers, too. Robert Haldane says he knows there'll be at least six people here who intend to bid seriously for the estate as a whole, and several more who want parts of it if there's no sale of the entire property. Four of the seven tenants will certainly try hard for their farms and there's plenty of interest from neighbouring farmers. We could see a lot of money change hands.'

The man at his side nodded thoughtfully.

'Maybe. But I think it's all a pity. They could surely have agreed on a valuation.'

'No. Richard's solicitors made that clear.'

'Will he be here, d'you think?'

'I doubt it. No one seems to know where he is. He could even be abroad. The impression everyone has, the family included, is that he doesn't care about any of it, except the final outcome.'

'What about Robert? Do you fancy his chances?'

'Yes. And he's confident. He knows there's a lot of money here, but he seems satisfied he can compete. He's well regarded by the bank, of course. I must say I hope he can retain it.'

Their talk was interrupted by the arrival of George Davenport, the auctioneer who was to conduct the sale. The entrance to the hall was a side door near the front of the building, and he stood there for several seconds looking over the assembly, noting a few familiar faces, nodding to acquaintances; then crossed to the local auctioneers.

'Afternoon John, Andrew. We're about ready, I think.'

The two men agreed, checking their watches.

'Five minutes.' They knew Davenport was a stickler for a prompt start. 'Robert isn't here yet, though.'

'He's outside,' Davenport said. 'With his family.' He turned and made his way up to the low stage and the table set on it, and the other two followed him, arranging themselves on either side and setting out their papers.

Then Diane came in, followed by Robert and Lisa, then by Harvey Roach, the estate solicitor, and accountant Conroy Jones. They took their previously-reserved chairs at the front, by which time every other chair in the hall had been occupied and there were people standing at the back.

The advertised starting time was three o'clock, and it was precisely that time when Davenport rose and the buzz of conversation died.

'Ladies and gentlemen, your kind attention, please.' He began all his sales like that, in a quiet, cultured voice which carried uncannily across a crowded hall without the aid of a microphone. He looked round at the expectant faces, re-checking the positions of the people he thought would enter the bidding, and said: 'I shall not take up more time than is necessary with preliminaries, for we all know the substance and detail of this occasion, and the conditions of sale are printed in your catalogues.

'The Roxton estate represents an almost unique opportunity for the acquisition of a productive, quality agricultural property of a type which rarely reaches the market. Through the war such sales were rare indeed; since the war there have been only two or three comparable occasions anywhere in the country. The home farm is an excellent dairy and mixed farm in extremely good order throughout and provided with a range of modernized stone buildings which you will rarely find bettered; the whole extending to some 500 acres. The seven tenanted farms, totalling 1,470 acres, represent a first-class investment yielding £2,500 annually.'

Davenport glanced across the assembly. There was some shuffling of feet and he waited for it to stop, looking over the top of his glasses, before concentrating on his papers again and continuing.

'I shall offer the property in eight lots, starting with the home farm including the house, followed by each of the let farms. I shall hold each successful bid and will then offer the estate as a whole In the event that it does not achieve a higher price than the total o the eight lots, the individual bids will succeed – all subject to the Haldane family's reserve. Are there any questions?'

He paused, studying his papers. The two local auctioneers looked expectantly round the hall, but no one spoke. There were a few coughs and chairs scraped, and Davenport waited until there was absolute silence.

Then the door opened, and Richard stood framed against the grey winter sky.

He wore uniform, his cap held under his arm, a lock of his black hair falling across his forehead. He had put on weight since he had last been seen in Roxton, and except for shadows lingering beneath his eyes he appeared almost fully recovered from his long ordeal.

For seconds he remained in the doorway, as heads turned and the crowd murmured its sudden excitement. At the front Robert glanced sideways and his mouth clamped into a hard line; then Lisa turned, and her hand crept to her throat and her apprehension communicated to Diane. Davenport rapped with his pencil and Richard closed the door and stood beside it, his back to the wall, his arms folded now.

Davenport said calmly: 'My final reminder to you is that the live and dead stock on the home farm will be subject to sale at a later date, arrangements to depend on the outcome of today's business, as will the disposal of the exceptionally valuable retail milk rounds which are a well-known co-operative enterprise between the owner and tenants of the estate.

'I start the sale by placing Lot 1 before you, including the magnificent house known as the Grange which must materially influence its value. What may I say to start the business? Twenty thousand pounds? Surely not less. Who will open at twenty thousand?'

Harvey Roach sat sideways so that he could see Robert and most of the occupants of the first three or four rows of chairs, and Richard who stared, his face expressionless, at the crowd. No one moved until Davenport's incisive voice said: 'Eighteen thousand, then. I will not start below.'

It began there, and Roach looked at the figures he had scribbled on the back of his catalogue. A good current market price for a vacant farm of this sort would be £40 an acre, although the house was an element he could not calculate. But £40 would yield

£20,000; and as he listened he heard that figure called, detecting a raised eyebrow from a neighbouring farmer as a signal.

Robert would bid in the first half of the sale only for the home farm and the house, and that just as a safeguard. His time would come when the whole estate was offered. Now he sat still, listening to the bidding until it stopped at £23,000, then nodding to raise it by a half. The bidder behind him came back with another £500, and Robert capped him again, openly and decisively, demonstrating his clear intention to buy. The farmer pushed it to £25,000, Robert nodded another £500 without hesitation, and it was done.

After that the tenanted farms were sold one by one, occupants buying three of them, the other four going as investments. But bidding was slow, for the post-war investment market in agricultural land was still uncertain, and the total yield for the seven farms was £34,000. It was a little disappointing, Roach thought clinically; but the big moment was still to come.

And then, with £59,500 on the table for the separate lots, Davenport said: 'All your bids will be held, ladies and gentlemen, and I will now offer the Roxton estate as a whole: a unique and profitable property, the like of which you will not find available again for a long time. Where may I start? Fifty-five thousand to get it going? Thank you' – to the farmer who had tried for the home farm.

Roach watched, fascinated; for this was the moment when the Haldanes would step down from Roxton after so many generations of ownership – unless Robert could succeed. He knew how far he could go: the ultimate loan he could service profitably, the point at which the bank would shake its head. It was all worked out.

'Fifty-eight thousand,' said Davenport, and Robert had not come in yet. Good tactics. Leave it late, then be positive. Lisa and Diane sat, eyes down, not daring to look or show anxiety. Richard was a statue, arms folded, eyes on Robert, face stone-carved. Fifty-nine, then a half, then the bids on the table for the individual lots were eclipsed at sixty thousand and a ripple of recognition crossed the crowd.

It hung there, and Davenport did not hurry it. Roach thought: Now, Robert; at the last moment, but then follow up fast. The opposition was at the end of the second row: an accountant or

236

solicitor, he guessed, acting for someone who might not even be there. He looked satisfied; until Robert nodded to sixty-one thousand.

After that it was five hundred, then another and another, until Robert's bid of £64,000 held and the contender sat back in withdrawal and Roach detected the smallest sign of relief on Robert's face.

'At £64,500,' said Davenport calmly.

Roach held his breath. There was someone else. Someone new. Robert responded instinctively; and straight away Davenport accepted another five hundred. The solicitor's gaze darted across the rows of faces; saw surprise, new interest. Robert went to £66,000, and the response was measured; not too fast, but fast enough to be decisive.

Everyone watched the auctioneer now, and the rapid shifting of his eyes above his glasses; trying to detect the direction from which the new bids were coming. Even Richard was watching him with his straight, hard gaze and expressionless face. Davenport looked at Robert and took a nod to £67,000, and then his eyes swept the room and he pronounced £67,500 smoothly, quietly, utterly without excitement, and Roach could not tell where the bid came from.

No one was moving, except Lisa and Diane who glanced nervously at Robert's tight face, and Conroy Jones whose bright eyes darted left and right, searching. Against the wall Richard was aloof, arms still folded, eyes on Davenport's face as the bidding went to Robert at £68,000. Roach wondered what he was thinking. It had been his doing, and he was watching his brother taken to the limit by an unknown rival. Sixty-eight was too high. It would mean a mortgage of well over thirty. That was more, a good deal more, than Robert had expected. Lisa whispered something to him, and Roach sensed desperation.

'Sixty-eight thousand pounds is my bid,' Davenport said clinically, and Roach turned his head, watching the tense assembly, looking for a flickering eyelid or a twitching finger which might betray the rival. Nothing. Still at sixty-eight. He looked at Lisa and saw her undisguised tension, then at Richard, motionless, unblinking as he stared at Davenport; not even a glance at his brother.

Then it came. 'Sixty-eight thousand five hundred pounds,

ladies and gentlemen,' said the calm voice, and a rustle stirred across the room like grass in a sudden chill breeze, and heads turned, questioning, wondering, as Robert leaned towards Conroy Jones and they whispered together, and Roach knew they were near the end for he had been a party to their calculations.

'I'll take another five hundred,' said Davenport easily. 'Five hundred may clinch the deal. Is it sixty-nine thousand?' He looked at Robert. 'Thank you. At sixty-nine thousand; now sixty-nine and a half. At sixty-nine thousand five hundred pounds for the Roxton estate.'

It was too much. The new bid had come too quickly. Whoever was in there had come to buy and would do so. Conroy Jones shook his head, but Robert nodded again and Davenport went up by five hundred; his eyes circled the hall and immediately he took seventy thousand five hundred and Robert sat back, glanced once at Lisa, and then nodded up at the auctioneer once more, but this time in resignation and defeat, as if he knew what would happen.

'Seventy-one thousand pounds,' said Davenport, looking at Robert. Then he glanced up, to the right of the hall, the centre, the left; and almost without pause for breath went on: 'And now seventy-one thousand five hundred. The offer stands at seventy-one and a half.' He was looking at Robert again, inviting the next bid; but then knew it would not come, for the colour had gone from Robert's face and Jones looked down at the floor, scowling; and still Richard was a statue against the wall as he watched the auctioneer, as if he had no link with the sadness so close to him, and Davenport's final questioning, and his sharp pencil tap as he said smoothly: 'The Roxton estate is sold.'

A wave of movement swept across the hall. No one stood up, but heads and shoulders shifted and the murmured question rose, repeated and repeated. Who? Had the auctioneer exercised a commission, bidding himself according to instructions already given to him by an absent client? Or was someone there, amongst them, who had conveyed repeated challenges so imperceptibly that not one person had detected them – except Davenport? People who had stood around the back of the hall began to edge sideways; three or four rose from their chairs; a newspaper reporter climbed on to the stage to speak to the auctioneer. Robert and his family remained seated, gathering their courage against the disaster.

Then Davenport tapped his pencil again, and somehow the slight sound carried, and everyone was still, waiting.

'Ladies and gentlemen, I am empowered to tell you that the Roxton estate has been bought –' he paused, looking slowly around the room, making the most of the moment '– by Roxton Holdings, the principals of which are Graham Telford Esquire, and Squadron Leader Richard Haldane.'

Voices rose; sharp, startled, as chairs scraped and Robert's head snapped round and the others turned with him, looking for Richard against the wall.

But he had gone; as if they had all imagined his motionless presence.

Robert's voice grated beneath the swelling rumble of the crowd: 'The bastard. He set this up, to get me out.' He looked helplessly at Harvey Roach who shrugged slightly, and acquaintances pressed around them, and then Conroy Jones slipped through the crowd quickly to the door and outside into the rain among the parked cars.

Richard was sliding into an elderly Rover and Jones moved quickly to him, catching the door before it swung closed.

Crisply he pronounced his verdict. 'That was revenge, Richard. Wasn't it?'

Richard looked up at him from the driving seat and cocked an eyebrow.

'Revenge? An investment, rather.' His voice was easy, almost indifferent; the Richard of old.

'Which ever it was, the price was too high,' said Jones tartly.

'Too high for Robert,' Richard said. 'He didn't have the confidence I expected.'

'The price was not money. It was your brother's ruin.' Uncharacteristically, Jones showed anger. 'I know it was revenge, whether you admit it or not.' Rain ran down the side of his face and dropped on to the collar of his coat. 'It's a sad day for the family, Richard.'

'You misunderstand the situation.' Now the hint of mockery had gone. 'Graham Telford wanted a share of Roxton as a memorial to Nick. If he'd lived, one day Nick would have been part of the business, through Ruth. He was fascinated by it. He talked of nothing else except how he would study after the war so that he and Ruth could contribute to it. This is his father's

remembrance. And mine, too – to Ruth. The rest doesn't matter.
And to save more questions I'll tell you where some of the money
came from – Graham's bank. It was discussed at a board meeting
last week. Graham had plenty to invest, and an exceptional
motivation, and the bank was the third, silent partner. They
authorised me to bid higher than I did. Robert didn't stand a
chance.'

Jones stared with his sharp, darting eyes.

'You were bidding? How? I was watching you. You gave no
sign.'

'I was looking at Davenport,' Richard said in his flat, cold
voice. 'I had instructed him that while I looked at him, I was
bidding.' Then he stared up at Jones, and the rain running from
his bald head and down his face, and said quietly: 'Let's shake
hands. I have too few friends. You have been part of all our affairs
for very many years. I don't want to remember only your dislike of
me.'

For a moment Jones hesitated; then his head nodded once,
quickly, and their hands clasped, before he turned back to the
hall; to see Lisa among the people now coming out among the
cars.

She came across to them, pulling a scarf close about her hair and
turning up her coat collar against the rain, and Jones glanced once
at Richard and then walked away.

For a moment Richard held the driving door open, watching
her. Then he eased out of the seat. She came up to him, quite
close, and said: 'Hullo, Richard. May I talk to you before you go?'

He nodded perfunctorily. 'Of course. Why don't we sit in the
car, out of the rain?'

For answer she turned aside, walked round the Rover and slid
into the passenger seat, closing the door. He looked down at her
for a moment, through the rain-splashed windscreen, then swung
himself in beside her. He sat still, watching her.

'Well? What is it?' Not hostile; just indifferent.

She said quietly: 'Maybe I won't see you again, for a long time –
if ever. So I don't want there to be any misunderstandings. Please
don't interrupt me. Let me say what I have to say.'

He nodded briefly.

'I won't interrupt. I promise.'

'Thank you.' She loosened the scarf around her head, pushing

240

it back. 'Do you remember, when we had that awful meeting, you said I had destroyed you?' She was tense, but her voice was steady. 'Well, now you have destroyed Robert. You have taken from him the most important thing there could ever be in his life; something much more important than me. So you are both destroyed; and I am destroyed with you because of it.'

He had promised he would not interrupt; and he could not have done so, for her words reached out to him across the bitterness and the agony. He waited; until she took a long breath and went on:

'There's something else. It's over three years since you went away. I never ceased to think of you or, in my own private way, to pray for you; even though they said you must be dead and I couldn't tell myself they were wrong. What happened was a terrible disaster none of us could foresee or control. But when you came back, the only time I've seen you since until now, you said that marriage was for lovers. Remember? Perhaps it is. But Robert and I were not lovers before we married. Never once. Because until time persuaded me there was no longer hope, I was your lover. And you are still my great love. Do you believe me?'

It was all so quiet, so gentle, with the rain drumming on the roof of the cocoon shielding them from the people outside; and it was easy for him to let his store of anger flow away and reach out to touch her hand.

'I believe you,' he said. 'Thank you for telling me. It was important to hear it.' And then he remembered Yvonne, and the memory stabbed into him because it was something he could never confess to her, and all this was his punishment. He drew his hand away and said stiffly: 'Now I think you should go back to – your husband. I hope you'll be happy, in time. And –' he checked, then added '– and tell Rob that I didn't enjoy today as much as I'd expected. And I won't enjoy tomorrow.'

For seconds she was still, and their eyes held on to each other. Then she pulled the headscarf forward, opened the car door, and said: 'I'll tell him. Take care of yourself.'

He watched her cross the crowded car park, through the rain and among the people, until she disappeared. Then he started the Rover and drove away, slowly.

28

The big hall of Roxton Grange was left with upright Jacobean chairs, the old blackened oak table which had been at its centre for so many generations, and a long sideboard. The deep leather armchairs and settee were gone; so was the carpet, and the polished maple floor was already dull. Paintings which had hung on the panelled walls were gone, too; stored, with furniture from other rooms, on the second floor in what had once been servants' quarters and, more recently, the temporary homes of Land Army girls. The kitchen had been left intact, the study alongside refurnished as a dining room, and two bedrooms retained; otherwise the house was a shell, closed except for the small living unit which was preserved so that Graham and Margaret Telford could enjoy their corner of the countryside when time allowed an escape from London.

Now, with January sleet pattering on the window, they sat in the dining room, drinking coffee and listening to Richard.

'We have no worries about Martin Calder,' he was saying. 'He'll be a sound estate manager just as he was a sound farm manager. And there are some promising candidates to run the home farm under him.'

'All we need now is to agree on capital expenditure for the first half of the year,' Telford said, 'and particularly whether the byre at Valley Farm is to be repaired or rebuilt. Have you spoken to the tenant?'

'Yes. I've talked to every tenant. I think they're all reassured. They respect Martin, and I think they trust me: I haven't quite ceased to be a nine-day wonder' – his mouth widened, but there was little humour there – 'and for a time they'll all be happy to let things coast along and see how the new regime functions. The Valley Farm byre should be repaired, I think: there'll be no trouble with the milk hygiene regulations and the tenant doesn't want to increase his cow numbers for the next couple of years, so we'll talk about a new building then. And I suggest we settle the capital questions when Martin joins us – we must involve him in every stage.'

Margaret Telford said: 'It's a new world to me, Richard, in spite of all the things Nick and Ruth used to tell us. But you don't seem to have forgotten much.'

Again the shallow smile: a gesture only.

'I never knew half as much as Robert, and I don't have the advantage of his technical education and his experience. But I was part of it once, and I grew up here. Even so, it's not going to be easy. But we knew that.'

'We did it for our own special reasons,' Telford said. 'And the investment is absolutely sound. Farming is in for a great expansion period. I'm only surprised that Robert's bank didn't back him further. But that's one of the differences between a merchant bank and conventional banking at High Street level.'

'Don't forget that Robert was by himself,' said Richard. 'There were two of us, as well as an enterprising bank. Our loan is much smaller and our interest charges correspondingly less than Robert would have faced. Granted, we have to divide the benefits; but since neither of us depends on Roxton for a living we can afford to see it as a longer-term investment than Robert could. And, like you, I'm certain land prices will double in the next ten years, and double again in the ten after that. Our job now is to make sure it's thoroughly viable in the meantime.'

Later they agreed with Martin Calder on the purchase of two of the post-war generation of tractors as soon as they became available, the sale of the last of the draught horses now that fuel supplies were easing, and the addition of new silage-making equipment.

The Telfords returned to London then, but Richard's short leave did not expire for another two days so he stayed on overnight, sleeping badly in the quiet house with its empty rooms. It was the first time he had spent a night there since the summer of 1942 and he thought he did not want to stay again. There were too many memories: he and Robert, quarrelling yet growing up together and feeling that they had a common destiny if only they could find the key; Ruth, and their undefined but unshakeable understanding of each other; and then Lisa who had spent so little time there but whose presence was in every room and every corner for him. As he prepared his frugal breakfast the next morning he saw her, laughing as she cooked bacon and made toast, then turning and catching his eyes and sending her secret messages to him. He walked across the drive to the white gate which led to the home farm and Martin Calder's house, and she was at his side again and her hand was warm in his, and he swore aloud and bitterly because once he had rejected her for a breath of time and the gods had decreed that he should pay the penalty for all time.

Yet he knew he had to forget. There was a new life to find after the years of danger and fear; new adventures somewhere, and maybe a new woman who would be his wife.

He just had to keep away from Roxton, and it would be all right.

*   *   *

A month later Steve Mitchell came back from Burma and India where he had been commanding a squadron of ground-attack Typhoons in the final months of the war with Japan and then had remained as an administrator while the RAF had packed its Far Eastern bags for the great return home.

They spent a riotous weekend in London with two WAAF Section Officers of Steve's past acquaintance, touring the Fleet Street pubs Richard had once known and buying their way into temporary membership of a night club where they drank a little too much and danced on the tiny darkened floor to slow body-hugging tempos. The girl with Richard was Andy, widow of one of the army's victims of the last defence of Dunkirk in 1940, who had assuaged her grief down the war years with the help of a series of male friends. Now she took little persuading into Richard's bed in one of the rooms he and Steve had booked at the Strand Palace Hotel with just such an eventuality in mind. She was skilful, inventive and passionate, and although Richard felt her talents beyond the bedroom might be limited he enjoyed the evening and the night, as well as their cheerful exhaustion over Sunday breakfast with Steve and his companion.

Later, when the girls had gone, he said: 'It was a hell of a night Mitch. I needed something like that.'

'That, and a few more,' Steve said. He and Richard had spent all Friday evening talking over the previous three and a half years and at one point he had said bitterly: 'It's all my fault. Everything's my fault. I shouldn't have been so bloody certain you'd bought it. But if you'd seen it, you wouldn't have believed –'

'Forget it,' Richard had said. 'It would still have been all righ

244

in the end if that damned Russian hadn't wanted a language teacher and a servant. You wouldn't credit it. The Russians are beyond belief. Paranoid, alcoholic, with no concept of the rest of the world after a generation of twisted propaganda, re-writing history to suit themselves; and with an army structure which gives the officer-corps the status of demi-gods as long as they worship the political commissars. Sokolov was never questioned about me because he was a prominent party member as well as an officer. He just acquired me as a sort of glorified slave. If I'd been awkward he'd have handed me over to the NKVD and said he thought I was a spy, and they'd have had the troops shoot me out of hand. Simple as that. I saw it happen to others. And the Embassy chaps in Moscow told me there are thousands of different nationalities who are just disappearing out there, either killed or sent off to the labour camps. I was lucky to get out at all. But it was too late then.'

'She should have waited,' Steve had grunted, but Richard had shaken his head.

'I was bitter. I said terrible things to both of them. But since then I've tried to see things as they must have seen them. I can't – yet. But one day I might. There's nothing truer than the old cliché about time being the healer. But it doesn't take away the scars.'

'You certainly left them with a few scars to contemplate,' Steve had said cheerfully. 'I wish I'd been there to see you take Roxton away from them.'

But then he had stopped, for Richard's eyes were suddenly warning him, and his face was tight.

'Shut up about it, Mitch. That's done with. I just don't want to see either of them again, and I don't want to see much of Roxton, either. I've got to start afresh. Maybe find the right girl. Then I can forget all of it.'

Now, on that Sunday, he knew that although Andy had not been the right girl she had helped, because for a whole day and a whole night he had not once thought about other things.

29

The farm was six miles from Dorchester: 400 acres of good land capable of producing almost anything except vegetables. Robert had bought it without stock and had started to build up a pedigree Friesian dairy herd alongside beef and a small sheep flock to dovetail with the arable rotation. The buildings were in good shape, and he was satisfied that he had put his money into a farm which would turn out to be highly profitable.

The house was less pleasing, especially to Lisa, for it was old-fashioned and neglected. But they had already called in builders and decorators, and their living room and bedroom had been the first to be altered.

Now, at the end of an August day in 1946, with half the cereal harvest in and the promise of a good day tomorrow, Robert stretched his legs across the hearth and said: 'I haven't felt so tired for a long time. But it's all going well.'

'How much more is there?' she asked. She took every chance to show interest, even if she did not understand everything he told her.

'Fifty or so acres, I guess,' he said. 'We're into the biggest top field now, and it won't need as much drying as I'd feared.'

She nodded. At least she did not have to be told the importance of that. She watched him massage his hands and thought it was all such hard work for him. At Roxton he had been the administrator, the manager, the adviser and the policy-maker. Physical work on the home farm had been left to Martin Calder and his men except in emergencies – although then Robert had always been able to show that he could tackle any job himself. But now he led his team of six men and their part-time harvest helpers in the field, and his muscles were only just becoming hardened to it. Yet she knew he enjoyed his new circumstances; which was more than she did, for he was out of the house for long days, including weekends, and at night had too little energy to turn to her in bed.

But one day it would be better, she told herself; once he had established the new place to his liking. One day.

He said: 'Next season it will be easier. Some of the machinery is nearly as tired as I am. The difference is that I'll recover, and it won't. I'll have to spend, as soon as we've sold the cereal crop.'

She watched him, sensing her chance to raise again a subject he had not welcomed the last time, and yet one which was never far from her mind these days.

'I could help, if you'd let me,' she said. 'The agency rang me again last week. It's nice to be remembered by old friends. And I could bring us in quite a lot of money if I got a good part for a time –'

'Go back on the stage?' He shook his head emphatically. 'We don't need money so badly. I'm just being cautious. I don't want to borrow, that's all. There's quite a lot of capital left from the Roxton shambles. I could buy tomorrow. I'd just rather wait and pay for it out of the harvest. Forget it, darling. I'd rather have you at home, every time.'

She said stubbornly: 'I wouldn't have to be away for long, Rob. It wouldn't hurt us. And it could bring in some useful cash. It could lead to other opportunities, too. There'll be a lot of money in television plays once we get a national service.'

'No, Lisa. Not at any price.' Sharp-edged words now. 'I don't want my wife to be an actress, and we don't need extra money: you don't even have to look at the books to know that.'

There was nothing else to be said; the danger signals were clear enough. But she was aware of her resentment. She had told Robert before their marriage that she still loved the stage and would enjoy an occasional return to it, and he had been indifferent. Perhaps in retrospect she guessed he had not believed her, and now she knew she had made a mistake. She should have made sure he had recognised that she was serious about it.

But had she been serious? Or was it only now that the question was becoming important? Certainly her life was not as once she had envisaged it. Yet neither was it radically different. She lived in the countryside, the wife of a land owner and a relatively wealthy man. They had to make new friends here in Dorset, and settle socially into a new environment. But that was not difficult; other people did it all the time. So why this secret, sad boredom?

She knew the answers. Robert was now a working farmer, with so much less time to give to the companionship she had hoped for. Already she could see changes in him: subtle, behavioural changes which edged him further still away from the Richard-image in which she had cast him. And, as a working farmer's wife, she had to change, too: yet could not. She ought to be more closely involved in the day-to-day running of the business, in providing meals for the farm workers and welcoming them under her roof and joining in their conversations. But she had not been born to that. There had been a big white gate between Roxton Grange and the home farm, and she would have been able to shelter behind it whenever she had felt the need. The estate office alongside the house had been the farm work centre; but now that role had been transferred into her kitchen. She was thrust into the centre of a closed, unique world she did not understand, among men whose conversations she did not understand. That was why she wanted to get away; to go back, just for a little time, to people whose language and interests and motivations she could share.

To excitement. And sympathy.

She got up and went into the kitchen to prepare supper. The cooker was old, the sink was stained and chipped, the cupboards were shabby: all temporary, all due to be renewed. And she had accepted the domestic inadequacies when Robert had bought the place. Yet now they irritated her. She resented them; and her own presence there.

And all the time she tried to hide from the truth: that once she had been so close to magic; and had lost it.

*   *   *

Diane wanted to visit Roxton; yet hesitated. She knew Richard would say she could go any time she liked. But she did not want Martin Calder to wonder if she was secretly reporting back to her son and his partner.

She pottered round the garden of the house she had bought when Robert had married Lisa, sweeping up a few early autumn leaves but thinking of the Grange and its ghosts. She had moved out just before the wedding, saying: 'Roxton will have a new mistress and everyone must know that. And I'll only be a quarter of a mile away.' They had protested that the house was big enough for all of them, with a lot to spare, but she had made up her mind. At first she had been lonely, but she had expected that and soon got over it, for she saw Robert and Lisa often and had many friends in the village. But now there were only the friends, and she felt drawn back to the big house and the farm, for the sake of her memories.

248

She saw Graham and Margaret Telford whenever they spent a weekend there. But it was four months since Richard's last visit, and she felt uneasy. Martin was a good manager; but being a manager was not the same as being an owner. Ultimately the estate would not do as well as it would have done under Robert, she felt; or even under Richard if he had lived there.

But Richard would never live there. He had no real interest in Roxton. She remembered the sale, and hearing his name announced as the joint purchaser, and her own silent distress that he should have turned so savagely on his brother; for she was under no illusion about Richard's motives. Her heart had ached for both her sons in their terrible, unsought conflict; and for the girl who, in her sadness, had unwittingly provoked it.

She hoped Robert and Lisa would be happy now. She had visited them a few weeks before, and she thought Robert was content enough although she knew he never forgot Roxton for a moment; his new commitment was a solace, but would never be a replacement. And Lisa? She supported him loyally in everything he did, yet the delight and the sparkle which had captivated them all when Richard had first brought her to Roxton seemed shadowed, and sometimes Diane had glimpsed a hurting deep in her hazel eyes; a secret pain quickly subdued when someone looked at her.

It's part of the Haldane tragedy, she thought; then shook herself away from memories and decided that, after all, she would go to see Martin: not for the sake of the past, but just in friendship.

*   *   *

The Roxton estate's new manager leaned on the white gate and watched his former employer drive away. Poor Mrs Haldane, he thought. She would never admit it, but it broke her heart to see the house shut up and neglected. He was not pleased about it, either.

He had been glad to see her, and was shrewd enough to recognise that his reasons went beyond her friendly concern for his well-being and that of her old home. For Martin Calder felt neglected, and a little lonely.

His new appointment had excited him. Next to a place of his

249

own he thought he could have wanted nothing more than to run the whole estate on which he had spent so many years of his life: to be not only the manager but the agent for the owners in all things. He was on a profit-sharing agreement and felt confident that by the end of the year he would have earned a handsome bonus. But there were two things missing: the satisfaction of meeting his employers, reporting his conduct and seeing their pleasure in his success; and the confidence which would have come from their endorsement. For Martin could only work within the constraints set for him; and he was already realising that, in the absence of the owners, it was not enough. Sometimes there were unexpected variables and the need to react to them speedily. He had to write long reports and wait for replies; and they did not always come quickly, for Graham Telford liked to leave most decisions to Richard who was now out of the country.

So he had been glad to see Diane, because at least it meant someone in the Haldane family was showing an interest.

30

The twin spires of Cologne's cathedral reached black against the fading day. The great Gothic bulk rose, grey stone darkened by age and smoke, the late evening sky behind; a scarred and jagged crown over the war-ravaged city, scaffolding and wooden support-beams climbing its side.

Richard stood in its shadow. The shattered, once-grand central station was at his back, twisted girders across its broken platforms. Four tracks only carried trains now; one had conveyed the train on which Richard had just arrived. It was nine in the evening and there should have been a car to meet him, for RAF Wahn was seven or eight miles away. But there was only the darkened city, and the young prostitute who sauntered across from the shelter of the cathedral. Her heel-clicks were loud in the street.

'I have a better place to go,' she said, in fractured English. 'You come with me, for a good time?'

She was about eighteen, with long dark hair and a short skirt and make-up which coloured her face even in the day's receding after-glow. Richard thought that in another time, and another world, she might have been pretty.

'No thanks,' he said in German. 'Go and look for somebody else.'

She came closer, surprised, smiling at him.

'If you speak German I can give you a specially good time,' she said in her own language. She tried to make her voice soft and seductive, but it was hoarse and her accent was harsh, from the depths of the city.

Richard said: 'Don't waste your time.' Then, as she turned away, sulking, he added: 'Before you go, tell me where I can find a telephone. I came in on what looked like the last train. There's nobody on the station now.'

'There aren't any trains at night,' she said. 'There won't be any more now, until the morning.' She looked at his uniform. His greatcoat was open and the brevet showed above his tunic pocket. 'Are you a bomber pilot?' No hostility; just a bored insensitive curiosity, wondering if he was one of the men who had shattered her city but not resenting his presence in its ruins.

'No,' he said. 'I flew fighters.' He did not tell her that he had been sent to Germany to fly Mosquitoes which once had led the bombers to their targets and had dropped the initial flares and incendiaries to illuminate them; nor that after seeing London and Coventry and Plymouth and his own city of Exeter he found the devastation in Cologne merely another symptom of the world's recent agony. Its extent was greater than anything he had seen at home; but the RAF had cut its teeth dropping harmless propaganda leaflets on enemy cities, and had only learned the meaning of total war from German example. Now, in the midst of one of the products of that lesson, he looked at the girl and said: 'I need to find a telephone. Is there one near?'

She shrugged, glancing up and down the street, then across at the dark mass of the cathedral.

'I don't know. There are some telephones. But none in the streets, like there used to be. Maybe there's one in the church. I don't know.'

'All right. I'll find one.' He picked up his hold-all, and in spite of the darkness knew she was sulking again. She turned and walked away without a word, heels clicking as she crossed the

251

square, and was swallowed by the black shadow of the cathedral.

He turned to his right, along the length of the station's shattered walls. A van rumbled across the square behind him, coming from the direction of the single-track Bailey bridge which had taken the place of the bomb-shattered Hohenzollern Bridge as one of the city's principal Rhine crossings. He followed its direction towards a wide street where an old Volkswagen jolted over the broken surface and, further along, another stood at a junction. There was no street lighting, but from the seemingly endless parade of ruined buildings whose jagged fingers were silhouetted against the sky, scattered lights came from ground-floor windows.

He walked slowly up the street, past a collapsed block of masonry, brick and stone piled high. He was the only person moving. But there were several vehicles now; and then he heard voices raised, a jumble of many voices, and crossed the street to a building. There were lights at street level, below empty windows and roofless rooms; he wondered how high it used to be, before the bombs fell. Then he pushed open a door and stared into a bar, crowded with faces beyond smoke, voices rumbling and glass chinking.

For a moment he stood inside the door, letting his eyes adjust, smelling beer and the cigarettes which cost a fortune on the black market. People, perhaps thirty or forty, were sitting around small tables on the left of the long room; the bar itself was on the right. Richard walked over to it, aware now that there was less talk and that eyes were watching him.

The barman was Richard's age and had only one arm. His pale face was expressionless as Richard said: 'I need to use a telephone. Do you have one here, please?'

The man's eyes widened fractionally. He had not expected to be addressed in his own language by a man in RAF uniform.

'We have no telephone,' he said. His eyes looked at the indications of rank on Richard's epaulettes. Then he turned away, busying himself with glasses.

Richard said: 'I think you have a telephone. Show me where it is, please.' His voice cut through the talk around him, and the noise level dropped further as more heads turned.

Without looking up the barman said: 'Telephones are scarce in this city.' He signalled with his one hand to a boy of fifteen or sixteen who walked along behind the bar and began to polish glasses.

Richard said to the boy: 'Where's your telephone?' His black eyes were reflecting the yellow bar-room lighting and the boy looked into them, licked his lips, and said: 'At the end of the bar. In the alcove.'

Richard moved along the bar. Everyone in the room seemed to be watching him. He shifted his hold-all across his body so that his right hand was free. He saw the alcove just behind the bar and walked round to it, stood so that he faced the room while he pulled a piece of paper from his pocket, and checked the number of RAF Wahn. Then, still watching the room, he dialled the number. Gradually the buzz of conversation rose again as he heard his call answered and said: 'Duty officer, main guard room, please.'

Within two minutes he was listening to profuse apologies and the promise of a car immediately. Then he said: 'I'm ringing from a bar. There's a bit of hostility here. How much do I pay them for this phone call?'

The voice in his ear said: 'Pay them? You don't pay the buggers anything. You could give 'em a few cigarettes, though. A packet's worth a week's wage to some people.'

Richard said: 'Thanks.' He replaced the telephone, picked up his grip and walked back along the bar. When he reached the boy he pulled a packet of Players from his pocket and threw it. The boy caught it deftly. Then he walked past the pale-faced barman and out into the street, letting the door cut off the rumble of voices.

As he turned back towards the ruined railway station he took a long breath and thought: Christ – what the hell am I doing here? I don't have to stay in the RAF. I must be out of my mind.

But he knew he was not; because this was home, and there was nowhere else to go.

*   *   *

The Wing Commander said: 'I understand you have very little experience of Mosquitoes.' His tone fell just short of hostility.

'No more experience that a conversion course,' Richard said coolly. He looked at the heavily-moustached, big-shouldered man behind the desk, and waited. He noted that the Wing

Commander was a navigator, and thought perhaps he did not like pilots.

'Spitfires, I see.' The Wing Commander was glancing at Richard's file. 'But a long time ago.' He stared at the ribbons beneath the pilot's brevet. 'You had a good war, by the look of it.'

That's it, Richard thought. I've a couple of gongs; he hasn't.

He said: 'If you can call losing your best friends, and your sister, and other things I won't bore you with, having a good war – the answer might be yes.'

'A lot of us lost friends and relatives.' The Wing Commander's voice was smooth. He looked at the file again. 'Shot down in '42? You spent a long time in the cage, then.'

'Twelve months. Before that, six months getting over my crash and a year with the Maquis before I was caught. Then my cage was a concentration camp.' Flat-voiced and hard-eyed.

The Wing Commander's eyebrows shifted.

'Quite adventurous. Expect you've found life dull since. You'll find it dull here, I'm sure. The only thing that livens it up occasionally is the Yugoslav guard between the admin. and barrack blocks, and the airfield. They're from the DP camp alongside. And they keep one up the spout. So stop when they challenge you. There are civvies employed here, and there'd be a lot of thieving from the airfield if the guards weren't trigger-happy. Watch out for them.' He shuffled papers on his desk to indicate that Richard's introductory interview was over, then added: 'The adj. will show you your quarters and introduce you to your flight commanders and to Baldwin, your navigator. He's been grounded since your predecessor was posted out on demob. so he'll be glad to see you – unless you try to fly a Mossie like a Spit. I'll see you at dinner in the mess.'

Richard left without knowing if the comment about flying a Mosquito had been a thin joke or a warning. But the next day, having met Alan Baldwin who had done over fifty operations navigating Mosquitoes in the final year of the war and who was now clearly excited about being flown by an ex-fighter pilot – 'some of these chaps are so bloody unimaginative, old boy,' he said – he decided to treat it as a joke. Besides, he had met the station commander who was himself an ex-prisoner of war and who had left him with the feeling that perhaps the new squadron leader was welcome after all.

254

He flew that afternoon, to check out his new aircraft. It stood outside one of the hangars of the ex-Luftwaffe airfield; great close-cowled Merlin engines with their huge propellers on either side of the slim torpedo-like fuselage. All streamlined power, poised. Not like the Spitfire which he still loved, of course. But if he had not converted he would have been out of a job now, for the fighter squadrons were being cut back even faster than the rest of the RAF, and those left were changing over rapidly to the new generation of jets. A thirty-year-old veteran who had had a fractured skull and a long time out of flying was not considered the best pilot-material for Meteors and the still-newer jet types on the way. So it had been Mosquitoes or a dragging, depressing office job and then demobilisation. And Richard knew that, at least for a time, he dared not consider that alternative.

Now he said: 'Come on, Alan. Let's see what she's made of.' He might have added, 'and you can see what I'm made of,' for he knew that he was on trial in his navigator's eyes: and in the eyes of the Wing Commander who, curiously, just happened to be passing and stayed to watch the take-off, and a number of the squadron personnel who were also loitering around the airfield to watch their new CO's first flight.

He struggled up the ladder and through the small entrance door under the fuselage, dumped his parachute and settled himself as Alan scrambled past and strapped himself into the seat slightly behind. Outside the ground crew primed the engines and waited with their hand fuel pumps, gave Richard a thumbs-up, and he pressed the starter and booster coil buttons. The port propeller started to turn, the Merlin banged as it fired spasmodically, then woke and roared. Then the second engine was started, the ladder retracted and door closed, and the exhaust thunder was muted. Richard checked instruments, exercised the flaps; opened the Merlins up to full power, reading their health on flickering dials; then throttled back, signalled the chocks away, and taxied slowly, testing the brakes as he reached the perimeter track.

At the end of the main runway he locked the brakes hard, opened the throttles quickly to clear the engines, closed them and let the brakes off with a hiss of compressed air. Then she was moving, and he advanced the left throttle well ahead of the right to counter the tremendous swing to port which the great engines would otherwise induce and gave full right rudder for the same reason. He held the tail down, waiting for rudder control before he lifted it. The Merlins thundered against his ears, so close on either side of the narrow cockpit, as the tail came up at 100 knots; and then he pulled the triggers on the throttles and gave her full power and she lifted.

His hands moved constantly then: brakes on, undercarriage up, throttles back but with the nose held down to build up speed without building up temperature, elevators trimmed, flaps retracted. He saw 200 knots registered, closed the radiator shutters and glanced over his shoulder at Alan who grinned back and gave him a thumbs up.

First test passed.

Then he synchronised the engines, eased the throttles forward and trimmed the Mosquito into a steady climbing turn, feeling satisfied.

They flew for half an hour. Only once did Richard allow exuberance to get the better of him and then – he considered afterwards – quite modestly. After that, they came back along the Rhine, checking landing instructions with ground control. He could see the expanse of the airfield, and the wide sandy area of scrub and woodland alongside still littered with the debris of the war's final battles: a Sherman tank, a German armoured car and a troop carrier, all scarred and tilted; a couple of anti-aircraft guns, their slender barrels still pointing skywards. The war had been over for eighteen months but nobody had taken them away, for there were more important things to do in this wrecked country.

He turned away, banking steeply, opening the radiator shutters, selecting the landing gear and the flaps, holding height on the downwind leg until he turned again and gave full flaps. Down below a thousand feet and the decision to land was taken, for Mosquitoes were intolerant at slow speeds. He feathered the propellers, came in over the airfield boundary at 100 knots, took the power off and, with the control column back, settled her smoothly, then saw Alan Baldwin still grinning at him.

As he taxied in to dispersals a Volkswagen drove away towards the control tower. He knew it was the Wing Commander.

Second test passed. And what had the other spectators thought of their new CO? He didn't give a damn. He knew now that his aircraft was in good shape, he had seen the countryside around Wahn from the air, had noted a few landmarks which might b

256

useful in the coming winter, he had a satisfied navigator and a squadron which looked good even if he thought there were a few disciplinary corners to knock off it.

Was that what life was all about now? He knew why he and the rest were there, and why other RAF squadrons were fully manned across the British Zone of Germany: the Russians were rumbling away to the east, there was no sign of a reduction in their immense forces in East Germany, and their anti-Western language was increasingly strident. Political and military evidence grew that the hawks in Moscow would have marched the vast Soviet army into West Germany several months before if America had not had the atomic bomb. Yet against the inconceivable might stacked on either side of him, Richard Haldane in his little Mosquito suddenly seemed superfluous. He was a sort of second-line policeman, kept for appearances.

He cut the power to the Mosquito's engines, and listened to the silence. God: how he wished there was somewhere, and something, and somebody else.

31

Christmas Eve was hectic. Diane had arrived at Robert's farm early in the afternoon to find the traditional domestic preparations for the next two days superimposed on a minor farm crisis. There would be one man short at milking that evening because of illness, and a cow had started to calve and was having trouble, so the local veterinary surgeon was on his way. To add to the pressure, Lisa had arranged a luncheon party for a dozen of their friends on Boxing Day and was preparing as much food as possible in advance; so Diane's presence in the kitchen was especially welcomed.

As the two women worked, they talked; and that was when Lisa asked: 'Do you think it's terribly wrong of me to want to get back to the stage, just in a small part in a short-run production?'

Diane concentrated on preparing stuffing for the turkey as she said: 'The way you ask suggests that Robert does. I can't adjudicate between you.'

'I'm not asking you to adjudicate. I'm asking you to tell me if you think I'm wrong.'

Diane chopped onions energetically.

'Yes. I do. It would mean you would have to leave Robert, if only for a few weeks. In the short time I had a husband, I would never have wanted to do that.'

The tawny hair fell forward as Lisa worked, hiding part of her face.

'I don't want to leave him. I want to leave here, just for a little time. But I couldn't tell him that, because he wouldn't understand and it would hurt him.'

'Leave here?' Diane's voice betrayed only mild surprise: a conscious effort. 'Why? The house is beautiful now. And Robert is pleased with the farm.'

'I know.' She brushed her hair aside with the back of a hand, but still she did not look at Diane. 'It's – terribly difficult to explain. Do you mind me talking about it?'

'I hope you will, if you think I can help.'

'No.' She carried a tray of newly-baked mince pies across the room, concentrating on it. 'I don't really think you can help. Not to solve it. Unless you can help me to understand myself. I just need – a change. I feel surrounded, by things I don't really understand. By people I don't really understand. I could have lived at Roxton. It felt – like home. I don't know why it doesn't feel like that here.'

Diane walked across the kitchen and began to wash up some of the used pans and utensils in the new sink beneath the shining taps. She knew why Roxton would have felt like home to Lisa, and the new house did not. Roxton was Richard.

She said: 'Do you mean you don't understand Robert?'

'No.' A quick response. 'Not Robert. His friends. He's made a lot of friends. And they're always here, for drinks in the evening or walking round the farm in the daytime and then staying for lunch, always talking about farming. I don't mind that. But I don't feel part of them. So I start to feel as if I'm not really part of Robert. He's so absorbed in the farm, and it's doing well, and I'm happy for him.' She hesitated; then added: 'That's it. I'm happy for him. But – it's like being a spectator. It doesn't do anything to me. I'm – cold inside.'

She turned away quickly to a wall cupboard and began to search for a dish, moving things about unnecessarily. And again Diane knew the answer. Roxton was Richard. And Richard was alive. Far away, unseen, unheard; a memory now. But alive. And thus a barrier, shadowy but impenetrable. If he had been dead the memory of him would not have been enough to hold Lisa back. She would have surrendered to her new life and her new man, for even if Robert was sometimes obsessive about his farm and could not understand why his wife was not equally absorbed and so allowed it to divide them, he was kind and he loved Lisa, and she would have been content.

But Richard was alive. And the awful, unbelievable, marvellous shock of his return had devastated her and had destroyed the new world she had begun to build so earnestly, and the years had not repaired it.

Behind her, Lisa moved more dishes in the cupboard; and then Diane heard them slide and the crash as two fell to the floor and seemed to explode, pieces flying.

And Lisa wept. She stood in the midst of it, her hands covering her face; silent, shaking.

* * *

Lisa's parents arrived on Christmas Day and stayed until the following afternoon, and it was a good Christmas, easy and light-hearted; but no one knew how hard Diane worked to make it so.

She was within two hours of her planned departure time before she decided what to do. Then she said to Robert: 'I've been here for two days and I haven't seen anything of the farm. Will you show me round before I go?'

So she followed her son across the great open yard behind the house and they went into the byre to see the dairy herd. The cattle shifted restlessly, heads raised, disturbed by their presence. But Diane did not look at them. Instead she touched Robert's elbow and said: 'Wait. I'd like to see the farm. But later. First I want to talk to you.'

He looked down at her, surprised; suddenly curious.

'Of course. What is it?'

'You may think this is just your old mother, interfering and not minding her own business. But I hope not. Listen to me, at least;

even if you don't agree with me.' Quiet, but not pleading, for Diane could still command attention when she chose.

'Old?' He stared. 'You're still a long way from sixty. And there is no business we don't share, even now.' He leaned against the concrete division between two empty stalls. 'I'm listening.'

She said: 'Lisa is very tense. She's fighting it. But it's slowly getting the better of her. Do you know that?'

To her surprise he nodded without hesitation.

'Yes. And I know why. Do you?'

She took a long breath, relieved.

'Richard,' she said.

He nodded again. His face was expressionless; guarded.

'I thought she would forget, in time. She never mentions him. This is the first time I've heard his name spoken for many months. We ought to be happy. I try to make us happy. What else should I do?'

'Understand what happened to her,' Diane said. 'She had been married for four days when she was told he was alive and on his way back. No matter how I try I don't think I can fully understand what that might have done to her; and I doubt if you can either. And then she feels she was responsible for the rest of it – the terrible family quarrel, and then you losing Roxton. She resents this place, because she knows it's only a substitute for what she really wanted.'

'It is.' He was matter-of-fact, as if he had finally accepted it. 'And I'm a substitute too. I always was. We both have to live with these things.'

'But she's finding it harder now, instead of easier. She feels she can't talk to you about it. That's why she wants to get away. But the stage is only an excuse. She thinks it would help to have a change of company and to get back to something she once enjoyed. It would be something new to think about. But a small part could lead to a bigger one. She might not come back. So you have to find something else for her.'

'Like what?' Very quietly.

She said: 'A child, Robert. Give her a child. Something that is totally, uniquely, yours and hers. Something that will dominate both your lives.'

'I don't think she wants to have children.' He sounded sad. 'We've talked about it. But she tries to avoid the subject.'

Diane said: 'Then cheat. Because it's what she needs – for both your sakes.'

But he shook his head.

'I can't. I know what you're saying. But I couldn't make myself do it. A child would have to be something we both wanted, from the beginning. I'll talk to her, though. I'll try. Because I think you're right.'

After that they began to walk through the buildings, looking at the cattle, the machinery, the extensions, the modernisation; until they turned back towards the house and he said: 'By the way – how's Richard?'

'All right,' she said. 'He's in Germany, in case you didn't know. He's very well.'

He said: 'Good. I'm glad to hear that.'

32

'In terms of capital, the investment has increased by twenty-two per cent,' said Graham Telford, 'which is at least as good as anything we hoped for and better than we expected, thanks to the rising value of farmland. And the let farms are yielding in line with projection in spite of maintenance bills we hadn't calculated. But the home farm's net profit is twenty per cent below forecast.'

He and Richard sat in his London office, papers covering the desk.

'Whose forecast?' Richard said. 'Not our original one – prices and yields have changed since then.'

'Martin's own.' Telford tapped a typewritten sheet. 'Just twelve months ago. And since then ICI have produced two reports which demonstrate that the country's better farms are achieving figures which he projected. What's wrong?'

'Don't know.' Richard shrugged. 'Germany's too far away. Now I'm here for a couple of weeks I'll see what I can find.' He lit a cigarette and eyed Telford. 'You having second thoughts, Graham?'

The sharp-eyed little banker shook his head.

'No. My personal commitment is yielding satisfactorily, and the bank's only interest is capital value, which is going up steadily. In any case, two years is too soon for judgement.'

'That isn't what I meant. I know the money's safe enough.'

Telford watched him.

'Why should I have second thoughts? And how about you?'

Richard contemplated the smoke drifting above his head and asked: 'Would you do the same again, if it had all happened now instead of two years ago?'

Telford settled in his chair. His smooth silver hair was bright against the dark-panelled wall behind him.

'I have a fascinating new interest, a base in a beautiful part of the country, and a sound investment,' he said. 'I expect I'd still want those things.'

Richard drew sharply on his cigarette.

'That isn't what I meant, Graham. But let's talk about something else, if you'd prefer it.'

Telford reached across the desk to the silver cigarette box at its centre. Richard watched. The banker rarely smoked other than his evening cigar.

'I know what you meant.' Telford studied the cigarette, then lit it. 'The answer is – probably not.' He was looking straight at Richard now, but his bright quick eyes were saddened. 'It was Nick's haven. After all the dangers, that was where he found peace and where he wanted to settle when it was all over. I thought I might keep something of him there. But everything is in the mind, Richard, and time changes that. I haven't found Nick at Roxton. We can't find people when they're gone. And a place like that isn't a memorial, it's a tough, commercial business, albeit in a beautiful setting.' He inhaled once from his cigarette, then stubbed it out, frowning at it. 'And you? Would you do it again?'

Richard said: 'No. I haven't found Ruth there, any more than you've found Nick. And I don't enjoy thinking about the other thing. I'm still in the air force, so nothing's changed for me except our occasional business meetings, like this one, and letters from Martin which I don't always answer as fully as I should. But everything changed for Robert – to what purpose? I was vindictive. Conroy Jones said it was a sad day for the family. He was right. Time heals, as I once told Mitch. I'd like to know how Robert's getting on, but I can't go and ask him. I'd even like to know how Lisa's keeping, although the thing is dead and I don't feel much any more. No, Graham.' He stretched, his arms behind his head, the cigarette smoke curling; and suddenly he was no longer interested in the past. 'I wouldn't do it again. Tell you what I will do, though: I'll slip down to Devon and find out what's happening to our revenue.'

                              *   *   *

After a day with Martin, walking round the home farm and dissecting the records in the estate office, Richard sat in his mother's home and said: 'The answer's where I expected it to be. Cereals are fine; but the livestock isn't doing as well as it should. Yet returns from milk are okay, beef and sheep stocking is up to the mark, the stock are fit and look good, and there's no better grass for miles around.'

Diane said: 'So it's either the way he feeds them, or the way he buys and sells.'

'That's right. And I'll give you any bet you like that it's buying and selling. Robert was brilliant at it. He could walk into a store market and buy young beef cattle as skilfully as any man I ever heard of. And when he sold them they were right to the day. The same with sheep. And he always knew exactly where to take his calves and cull cows to get the best price. You can't teach people that. It's an instinct. I shouldn't blame Martin because he hasn't got it – half the farmers in this county haven't, either; not like Robert, anyway. Martin's a good farmer and he's managing the estate well. But he's not as good as Robert in the mart. And it shows in the books.'

'So there's nothing you can do about it?'

'Not a thing. It's the product of absentee management – and Robert's absence particularly. While I'm in uniform it'll go on. And even if I lived here I couldn't pretend to be as good as Robert.'

'Are you going to stay in the air force?' She was pouring coffee, and trying to make her question sound casual.

'What else do I do? They're cutting down all the time; one day they'll tell me to go. But not yet.'

'Would you come back to Roxton then, and run it?'

He looked straight at her and said: 'No, mother.'

'So what would you do?'

'I don't know. Maybe try to restart where I left off when the war began, roaming around the world, for newspapers. There's television coming, too. Mitch is trying to get into film production, ready for the great TV boom everyone forecasts. I was a writer once: I could be again. And I could work with Mitch.'

'And you would have capital to put into a business – if you sold your share in Roxton.'

She said it so quietly that for an instant he was not sure of the words. Then his head snapped up and he stared at her.

'What on earth makes you say that?'

'Because you're not interested in it,' she said. 'You never were, and you aren't now. It won't go on, Richard. You know that.'

Then he sighed, and his shoulders relaxed against the chair. He reached for his coffee, adding a little sugar to it, stirring it slowly, watching the turning rings of bubbles.

'It will go on for a time,' he said distantly. Then he glanced up. 'And while we're on these painful subjects – how's Robert?'

'He's well,' Diane said. 'The farm's doing fine. He's worked very hard to get it to his liking. And the house is now a handsome place.'

'I'm glad. I have wondered, sometimes.' A reluctant confession. 'They must be very happy, then.'

'I think so.' Diane drank some of her coffee.

Richard said: 'But you're not sure?'

Just for a moment she hesitated. Then: 'I'm not sure. But it's not my business.'

'Nor mine,' he said.

*   *   *

She could not tell him the truth: that she who was his wife could bear to be his companion and his helper and to join her body with his; but that she could not bring herself to have his child, for he was not her soul-mate.

She knew no words to explain that. Nor could she hurt him so.

Yet he had become her jailer. She was captive in his world, among his friends and his workers and in the house he had made for her, and there was no escape. No, Lisa, he said, you may not become an actress again, it would be an insult to me and a rejection of the life to which you committed yourself when you married me; you would have to go away and our home would suffer and our relationship would suffer, and even if you came back after a little time you would never be the same again. She thought he meant that he was afraid of the stage and the men and women upon it and their imagination and the applause of the crowd and the sickening tension and the fantastic delight, because he did not understand it.

So she had said I want to be a nurse again. But that too offended him, because he wanted her all to himself and their house and the interests around which his life revolved, and could not contemplate that she was not captured by it all as he was.

Be satisfied, he said, to be my wife and to keep my house and share my success, and I will dress you in beautiful clothes and give you horses to ride and cars and we will have friends whom you will entertain. And now it is time we had children, that Robert Haldane became a father and Lisa Haldane a mother.

When she said no, I'm not ready, he became angry. But he would be both angered and devastated if she told him that when they lay in bed together he did no more than satisfy a physical need which had been woken in her so long ago and which remained, aching and demanding, in her body. He quietened it, for he was skilful; but it always came back, and the memories with it, and then she wanted to be by herself for a time.

Now it was becoming more difficult, for he was persistent, and several times he had tried to take her when she had not been prepared for him, and the fear had grown that one day their physical act would achieve its natural end.

She could not contemplate that, for even though there was pleasure and she surrendered to it, she thought it would be like having a child from rape. So now she kept away from him whenever she could.

For he was not her soul-mate.

But it could not go on like that. One day she would have to stop saying I'm not ready, and instead say I don't want to have children, ever. And she recoiled from that, for it would be a terrible lie and she would carry the penalty all her life.

Then there was a sad night when they had been careful as usual, and Robert held her afterwards and whispered: 'Tell me that it will be different, one day.' And she hid her face against his shoulder and pretended not to hear him; until he said the thing she had always dreaded he might say.

'It's Richard, isn't it? That's why it can't be right for us.'

She did not cry. She had never cried in his house except once, months before, when she had broken the dishes and the noise and the things she had said to Diane and all the aching had come together in a great suffocating surge that had been too much for her. So instead she turned away from him and said into the pillow: 'Yes. I've tried so hard. But I can't beat it.'

In a little while he asked: 'Do you still love him?'

She said: 'I don't know. I don't think so. He's been gone for so long, and I've never wanted to find him. It wouldn't make any difference, anyway. We both know he never wants to see either of us again.'

They were quiet then, lying side by side but not touching; until he said: 'So why does he still come between us?'

Suddenly she swept the bedclothes aside and stood up; then, to her distress, was ashamed of her nakedness and fumbled for her nightdress in the light of the small bedside lamp.

'It's not just Richard,' she whispered. 'It's – everything. It could have been right. It might have been right if he'd come back months after we married. But it was days. Just when we should have been so happy. I think of it, and it freezes me inside. And then all the other things, the dreadful things, and the bitterness –'

'We never stood a chance, did we?' His voice was quiet, almost gentle; and sad. He raised himself on his elbows, watching her. She was brushing her hair with quick, jerky movements. 'If he'd been more understanding it might have helped. But maybe not. The damage was done when your mother had the telegram and telephoned us. We were beaten then. And in a strange way I think I knew it.'

'That's hindsight,' she said. She looked at the hair brush and watched her hand shaking. He could see the whiteness of her knuckles in the subdued light. Then she put the brush down and stared at herself in the mirror. 'We talked about it for a long time. Remember? And we promised we'd try. But that was before we saw him. And the awful things that happened.' She reached forward, putting her forefinger on the glass of the mirror and tracing the outline of her image. 'I look terrible,' she said. 'Awful. How long have I looked like that?'

'Stop it.' He was sitting upright now, staring at her. 'You're beautiful, just as you always were –'

266

'No.' She turned quickly to face him. 'Not beautiful. Wasted.' She drew her finger ends down her cheeks, pulling the skin. Her voice was like a sound from a dream. 'Wasted. We're both wasted.'

Then she dropped to her knees beside the bed and rested her forehead on the sheets, like a child praying, and whispered: 'Such a waste, an awful waste, for ever and ever. . .'

33

There were changes coming, the Group Captain had said. RAF Wahn would soon be handed over to the German Government to become the civil airport for Bonn and Cologne; and in spite of the scare over the Russian blockade of Berlin and the mammoth airlift which had defeated it, the air force was being cut back further, with fewer aircraft and fewer men and women to fly and maintain and manage them. His announcement was followed by formal interviews with every officer on the station.

To Richard he said: 'You are a good pilot. As an officer and administrator you are efficient and hard – sometimes too hard, in my view, for a peace-time service, but you are respected. You are by no means as good at accepting discipline as you are at dispensing it, and if you are to stay in the service that is something you will have to think about. But if your commission is to be extended you will have to justify promotion, for which you are overdue. And I feel that your private commitments are taking too much of your time and energy. Before I decide what to recommend for you, I have to ask what you intend to do about them.'

It was a bad time to face the question, for only four weeks before Margaret Telford had telephoned to tell him that Graham had suffered a coronary thrombosis. The doctors thought there was every chance he would recover, as long as he retired. And, inevitably, he would have to reconsider his Roxton involvement before long.

Since then Richard had spoken to him and found him cheerful, confident and making good progress. He wanted to postpone decisions about Roxton – 'I don't see why, if everything goes well,

I should have to think about it for some time,' he said – but even via the telephone Richard detected reserve: a lack of the once-characteristic enthusiasm and aggression for which there was only one interpretation.

And then the Group Captain had issued his ultimatum: the RAF, or Roxton. 'Your financial interest in the estate is not my concern,' he had said: 'but I am anxious about the impact of your business responsibilities upon your commitment to the Air Force. Promotion is essential if you are to stay in the service; but it will demand your total attention.'

Resign, or sell Roxton. A healthy Graham Telford might have been able to handle the estate's business on his own, at least for a time, without too much harm befalling it. But now he was ill the situation was impossible. Richard could not become a sleeping partner in a business which otherwise depended on a sick man, and he knew without asking that Telford would not want to take another partner in his place. The Roxton connection was too personal, too intimate, for that.

Yet the RAF was his refuge from another world which he had rejected. He was housed and provided with friends and a familiar environment which appealed no matter how frustrating and seemingly pointless at times. He still enjoyed flying – as much, these days, as restricted operational hours allowed; and his initial disenchantment with life amid the wreckage of post-war Germany had faded into an acceptance of its depression and restrictions.

But how would he have reacted to it without the occasional release provided by the Roxton adventure and his association with the Telfords?

He knew the answer. So he sought another interview with the station commander and said: 'I need time to sort myself out, sir. I have two weeks leave due and will shortly have another week's entitlement. I'd like to take as much of it as I can, as soon as possible.'

'Take it now,' the Group Captain said. 'Take three weeks. If you need more time at the end of it, telephone me and I'll approve it. But when you come back I'll want your decision.'

So he scrounged a lift in an RAF Dakota transport flying to England and, early in June 1949, called on the Telfords.

Graham was at home and pottering in his garden. He looked well, but the sharp, bright eyes were quiet and he moved carefully. After half an hour of cautious talk he said: 'I'm dodging the issue, I've been warned by the medics – give everything up and be sensible and you'll live a long time: keep working, and you won't. And I have to admit I'm very tired, Richard. I'd love to be able to see Roxton, and stay there sometimes. But I can't contribute any more.'

'So it's over,' Richard said. He was neither surprised nor depressed; only resigned to the inevitable.

He spent the evening and the night with them, talking on into the small hours, taking care not to burden Graham with too many decisions yet unable to reach any of his own. So the next day he travelled across the country to see his mother.

But before he could talk about Roxton she told him, quietly and seriously, that Robert and Lisa had separated. It had happened four months before, and several weeks had gone by before she knew and was sworn to secrecy.

Now Diane said: 'There's no point in keeping it from you. I've seen them both, and it's finished.'

He stared at her, curious yet strangely unmoved.

'The fools,' he said candidly. 'How stupid. What went wrong?'

'They won't talk about it,' she said sadly. 'There's no one else, for either of them. It's a fundamental thing, I guess. I don't know where Lisa is, except that she's trying to get back to the stage – she had a part in a radio play last week. They're still polite about each other; quite civilised, really. But it's final. There will be a divorce, though I don't know what reasons they'll give.'

'I'm sorry,' he said, and was surprised to realise that he meant it. 'Sorry for them both. I haven't seen them since the Roxton sale, but I had hoped things would go right for them. What a wretched business.'

Then he shrugged, and the gesture was dismissive. He had more important things on his mind than the personal problems of a couple with whom he had had no contact for more than three years and whom he had consciously tried to forget. So he began to tell her about Graham Telford and the RAF and the decision he had to take, adding: 'I wanted you to know straight away. I still think of Roxton as partly yours.'

She sat still and silent, not knowing what to say to him; not knowing how to start assessing his problem.

'I don't know what I'm going to do,' he went on. 'The only

certain thing is that Graham will pull out. So the first option is to sell up. That would free me to stay in uniform, if I get the chance – which is by no means certain, the way things are being cut back, though I suppose there'd be some satisfaction in being called Wing Commander for a time. Or I could resign and try to run Roxton on my own, which would mean raising a lot of money. Or I could seek a new partner. But it would have to be someone I knew and trusted, and who had all the necessary experience. So that alternative isn't worth talking about.'

It went on for hours. But in the end all Diane could say was: 'It's your decision. It depends what you want to do with the rest of your life.'

He went to bed thinking about that, and the next morning borrowed her car and drove through the lanes to the deserted old house alongside the Roxton home farm. For a long time he stared at it, then walked through the echoing rooms, smelled the dampness and stood in front of the big stone fireplace in the cold silent hall and remembered his grandfather. This had been the heart of his dream: three children growing up through his old age, giving life to this house; the core of his hope that there would still be Haldanes at Roxton when he had gone.

There had been; but only for a little time. Now it was over.

They paraded in front of him. Graham Telford, converted from the city life and with a special memory of his own, but too late to help for long. Robert, with whom he could never agree yet who was still his twin and he could not break the tie even after so much time and so much grief; exiled now, on a lonely road. Ruth, who had been so precious to him; and the marvellous man she had married and who had wanted to commit himself to her inheritance. His mother, whose home this had been for more than a quarter of a century; content now, yet scarred so badly by the tragedies of two wars.

And Lisa, who had also been here, trapped by cruel coincidence between two men who looked alike but were not, and who was now another casualty.

He stared across the hall and saw his reflection in the window. He was also a casualty. The last casualty; yet the last warrior, too, for he was fighting when all else had been surrendered. And in his final struggle he would be the instrument which was to destroy Randolph Haldane's dream. He had fractured it almost four years before, in bitter revenge. Now he was going to shatter it beyond repair, because there was nothing else for him to do.

The choice was narrowing. If he stayed in the RAF, Roxton would have to be sold; but he did not think he would stay, for he recoiled from the prospect of years of uncertainty in a declining service. Yet he could not return here; there were too many unhappy ghosts in this house and he was not fitted to run the estate and the home farm on his own, especially with the burden of the enormous loan that would be necessary. In any case he had left it all before the war, seeking greater excitement than it could give. And he still needed that. His mother had been right: he had never wanted Roxton.

He had only wanted to take it away from Robert.

Yet where could he find excitement now? The post-war world was dull and utilitarian, and Britain was a declining nation under an ascetic administration whose vision of reform centred on restriction and humourless sacrifice which did not envisage the light of adventure beyond the tunnel. It was inevitable that people were subdued and dispirited, after the hopes which had nourished them through the disaster of war.

Most people. Then he remembered some who would never be subdued. He walked to the window and stared across at the summer green of the poplars and saw Paul Cardin among the cork oaks of Ste Baume and the Maures, and François and Marcel and Jean. And Yvonne.

Yvonne, with whom he had once yielded, and so invited the retribution of the gods.

Could that be true? Of course not. Unless she had been punished too.

Where were they now, those dangerous men and women who loved their liberty more than their lives? Where were the elderly Marchands who had nursed him in perilous secrecy from the very edge of death? Did they still remember him as he sometimes remembered them?

And where was Kurt Edelmann who had been Ruth's lover and, in the end, his own saviour? One day you will come to see me, he had said, and we will have much to remember for there is much that we have learned to understand.

There was much now that he did not understand, and so little time to learn.

34

The grey Nordkette seemed to rise up straight from the streets of
Innsbruck against the blue and white of the sky; just as it had
eleven years before, when Ruth had been alive and he had come
for her. No troopers now, with their hard eyes and their truncheons; no swastikas, and no fear. A clean town in the crisp air
coming down the broad steep-sided valley and across the silver-
grey river.

He drove his hired car through the traffic along the Maria-
Theresien-Strasse, and out into the suburbs to the chalet-style
house with the big trees still in the front garden where once Ruth
had been. The same knocker with its old man's face was on the
same door, and the woman who answered its summons was the
same; but much, much older.

He said in German: 'I'm Richard Haldane. I came here once,
before the war. I was a friend of Kurt's when he was in England.
Do you remember?'

She stared, struggling; then it came back.

'Yes. Of course. Richard Haldane.' Cautious, for his previous
visit had been frightening; but she opened the door wider. 'Will
you – would you like to come in?'

He thanked her and walked into the narrow hall and then into
the chintzy living room he remembered. He could almost see
Ruth with her bruised forehead, sitting in the chair from which
Kurt Edelmann's father rose now. He, too, was so much older,
and tired.

'Richard Haldane has come to see us,' his wife said warily.
'From England. He came before the war, when Kurt was here,
and –' she hesitated, searching for the name '– and his sister.'

'Ruth,' Richard said. He held out his hand to the old man.
'Hullo. I hope you don't mind, after all this time. I'd like to
contact Kurt again. Does he live here now?'

They looked at him as if they did not understand. Then the old
man cleared his throat and blinked rapidly.

'I'm sorry.' His voice was a faded sound. 'He – he doesn't live
here. Kurt is dead, you see.'

Somehow it had not occurred to him. He stared, letting the
shock sink in, absorbing it.

'I didn't know,' he said finally. 'I – I am very grieved.' He hesitated, then said again, lamely: 'I didn't know.'

So they told him, quietly, sitting with folded hands in their chintz-covered chairs. It was in 1944, just before the invasion of the south of France by the Americans and the French commandos. They had never known what happened; only that he was dead. Perhaps it was a bombing raid, or the dreadful bandits in the hills. They had not known where he had been buried, but after the war the International Red Cross had written to say that his remains had been reinterred in a cemetery near a village on the slopes above the Mediterranean. It had been a Christian burial, and they had been glad of that. The Red Cross had sent them a photograph of the grave. They showed it to him, and he looked at it for a long time, and lived again through so many years of his life.

Then they listened to his abbreviated story of the coincidence which had led to his meeting with Kurt in St Raphael, and how they had shaken hands and promised to meet again one day. But he said nothing about fighting with the Maquis, or Kurt protecting him from the Gestapo.

They questioned him eagerly about that time, and asked how Kurt had looked and if he had been well, and he told them he had been in good health and a brave and courteous soldier. Then he told them about Ruth's death, but not about Kurt's tragic involvement, and they were saddened. After that he had a small meal with them, and when he left he shook the old man's hand and kissed his wife gently on the cheek.

As he drove away he remembered their wistful eyes, and the photograph on the wall of the handsome Luftwaffe major whose courage and conscience had been his own shield, and the other photograph of the grave on a hillside. And he whispered to himself: 'Oh Christ. Does it never end?'

*   *   *

He drove back to Munich, then took a train to Lucerne and another to Lyon where he looked at the Hotel Terminus where the Gestapo had been. Then he hired another car and went north for a glad and emotional reunion with the Marchands before he turned south again and drove all the way down to St Raphael. But he did not stay long, for it had changed as the international sun-

273

worshippers had come back to the Cote d'Azur.

So he went along the coast, and his pilgrimage took him to the first slopes of the Maures above the Gulf of St Tropez, and to the cemetery near the eleventh century church in the shadow of the castle ruins where the seagulls screamed.

35

The celebration went on until the daylight came up out of the eastern sea far below. They travelled from miles away as the word went out that he was back. The Wolf had returned, and those who had known him and had fought with him kissed him on both cheeks and shook his hands again and again, and those who had only heard of him came to look and hoped for an introduction so that they could tell him how they had played their parts elsewhere.

It was a therapy, to feel their unquenchable spirit and share their excitement and their memories; to be with Paul again and hear his stories of the final months and the camaraderie and the courage.

And to be with Yvonne.

She was still dark, although he could see the occasional grey hair; still petite and slender. And he marvelled at this quiet, calm woman who had been so brave and so resourceful and, more than once, so deadly with the little gun in her handbag.

He marvelled, too, that they could look at each other so easily now, as if there had never been a cave high on a desolate mountain and the relief of passion after fear.

The next day Paul had to go to le Lavandou, and Yvonne said: 'Come with me down to St Tropez. We can have lunch there. You never saw it during the war. You'll enjoy it now.' So he drove her down the winding road and asked the question nobody had wanted to answer the night before: 'Do you know why they killed Major Edelmann? If you know, please tell me. It's important.'

'We know,' she said. 'One of the cleaners at the German headquarters was in the Resistance, and he heard soldiers talking and reported to us. Someone had told the Gestapo that the Major had captured you and had sent you away as a prisoner-of-war. He should have handed you over to them so that they could have forced you to tell them about us. They said he was a traitor, and tied him to a post in the yard behind the building and shot him. We heard a whisper that you and the Major had known each other before the war, but we did not know if it was true. Last night no one wanted to say that he was shot because of you, in case you had been good friends. But it was because he had tried to save you from the Gestapo, and he was perhaps your friend, that we buried him properly here, as soon as we could. And we asked the Red Cross to tell his family.'

He said: 'You are extraordinary people: all of you.' He was quiet for a few minutes as he drove, then went on: 'Now I understand why I was suddenly sent to the camp for special prisoners. I was lucky the Gestapo didn't come for me and shoot me too. Maybe by then, the way the war was going, they had more on their minds.'

'Why did he try to save you from the Gestapo?' she asked; and he realised that in the confusion of the night before he had not told them that part of his story. She listened, her dark eyes never leaving his face as he drove and talked, and when he had finished she said: 'There were many strange coincidences in the war. That was another. The gods must have been with you, Richard.'

'The gods with me?' He glanced at her. 'I doubt it. Just the opposite, more likely.'

She was still watching him. She said: 'Because of your lady Lisa?' He had told her, and Paul, about that.

He kept his eyes on the narrow road.

'In a way. That – and other things.'

He said nothing else, and she took the hint and did not question him. They drove along a road newly renamed Avenue du 15 Aout 1944, after the date of St Tropez's liberation; then into Avenue du 8 Mai 1945, when it had all been over except for Richard in his Russian cage, and parked the car near the Quai de l'Epi.

They walked slowly around the harbour with its fishing boats drawn up on the shingle and moored against the jetties in the bright sun, looking beyond to the first signs of the development which was to transform the little port in the next decade. The old town with its narrow streets and alleys was at their back, and they sat at a pavement table outside a quayside café and ordered wine and remembered other places, until he said: 'Do you ever think about what happened – what we did, just once?'

'I hadn't thought about it for a long time. Until yesterday.' Easily, without embarrassment; but her eyes were tender. 'And you?'

'Sometimes. That's what I meant about the gods.' He felt for cigarettes, uncertain now. 'Do you believe that people are sometimes punished for what they do? Not by men, but by – something else?'

She took a proffered cigarette without seeming to notice what she was doing.

'No,' she said. 'I don't. What are you talking about.'

'I don't know for certain.' He played with his wine glass; then took a quick drink and fumbled for matches. He was suddenly angry because he found the explanation difficult, and because he was uneasy with her. 'But I've always had the feeling that what you and I did was – a betrayal. And that what happened later might have been retribution.'

She accepted his match and blew smoke into the air.

'That's nonsense. You may have thought it was a betrayal. Maybe I felt that, too. But that was conscience. Everything else was coincidence. Thoughts of some mysterious retribution are just imagination. I'm surprised at you, Richard – you who were so strong and decisive and self-sufficient. What has happened to you?'

He said defensively: 'I changed when I got home. And I couldn't get away from the idea that, because of what we did, I'd brought it all on myself. That was why I was so bitter. I came to think of what happened as – as my punishment.'

She shook her head, her dark eyes searching his, trying to understand him.

'Then ask yourself why I was not punished also,' she said. 'I have two beautiful children. Paul and I are happy. Perhaps you and I should not have done what we did, but he does not know and he never will and he is not harmed. Our relationship is not harmed either. Our moment was the result of circumstances which were gone in the day.' She leaned across the table, closer to him, whispering urgently now. 'I remember what I said to you in that cave. I said I loved you, and other things, special things. I did love you, Richard. I still do; but not as I did at that moment when we

276

were one person because now it is my head which rules me and not my body; and not as I love Paul, because our love is untouchable and nothing could change it. I broke my promise to him, just once, but I did not harm our love. You and I did not sin, Richard: we yielded, but we were not scarred by it, and no one else was scarred by it. And there are no gods who choose some for punishment but not others.' She put her hand out and her fingers caressed his and pressed them, and he felt her courage as if she were transmitting it to him. 'Be brave, my dear friend. If you lost your lady it was because a German soldier put a shell into your aeroplane six months before you and I met, or because a Russian soldier kept you from freedom long after you and I had parted; not because of imaginary gods or fate or sin.'

He looked at her for a long time then; until he stubbed out his half-cigarette and stood up. She watched him walk away from her, across the road to the edge of the water and the boats at the quayside, and stand there, looking out over the harbour and the bay and the mass of the Maures rising blue-grey beyond. She made no attempt to follow him, but her mind reached out to him.

He came back presently, looking at her, stopping by the table and standing over her; then his mouth curved and was strong and there was the old hint of mockery and confidence.

'Thanks for the lecture,' he said. 'It was long overdue. And it could only have come from you, because I wouldn't have believed anyone else. Now show me the best place to have lunch.'

She did not move.

'Stop loving her, Richard. You only harm yourself.'

He raised his eyebrows, as if she had surprised him.

'Stop? I stopped a long time ago. I regretted, and still do, but there was too much anger for anything to be left except regrets. The curious thing is that I'm told she's going to be divorced and, would you believe, I'm sorry? I haven't seen her for three and a half years and that's all I am – sorry for her. I'm sorry for my brother, too. I hated him once. Now I'm just sorry for him.'

'Then it's over,' she said. 'Forget it. Now there's a new world. Go and win it.'

He put out a hand and she took it as she stood up, and he held on to her fingers as they walked among the people along the Quai Suffren. The blue of the bay stretched away in front of them beyond the mole, and the old town with its twisted streets and

277

coloured houses rose to their right towards the summer sky. And when he looked down at her he felt a peace which he knew would come back to him through all the years whenever he thought of her, and a secret sadness with it, no matter where he found his new world.

But he also knew that he had exorcised his ghost.

36

The rain had gone and the streets of Exeter were shining wet under the sun which forced its warmth through the receding clouds. He stood on the corner of High Street and Queen's Street, watching the traffic as his mind replayed his talks with accountant Conroy Jones and Harvey Roach who had remained the estate's solicitor after the post-war change of ownership.

He had landed in England from his Continental journey three days before, had telephoned the station commander at RAF Wahn and gained ten days' extension to his leave, and had then gone straight to London to see Graham Telford. After that he came to Roxton and spent several hours talking to his mother. Now the consultations were complete and the plan was agreed.

The Roxton estate would be put on the market in two months' time, with a sale dated ten weeks later if no private purchaser was found.

He had made the decision, and everyone agreed that he had no alternative. But he was deeply sad, for it heralded the end of almost two hundred years of family history. And Diane had been equally sad, for although she was not a Haldane, the Grange had been her home.

Now he shrugged it off. It was regrettable, but unavoidable. The only possibility of retaining Haldane control lay with Robert, but Diane had said decisively that that was now out of the question. Once Robert had been prepared to borrow to the limit to achieve sole ownership; but since then land prices had risen significantly and were now edging ahead of the profits graph, while City forecasts were that interest rates would increase to much higher

278

levels before long. The combination threatened an economic burden which would be unacceptable to any prudent man. If Robert had had more time to accumulate capital on his new farm, the formula might have been different; but he had been there little more than three years and had been spending rather than saving. Diane had said: 'Harvey Roach will let him know, of course; but in his position it would be utterly foolish to try to go it alone. And Robert is not a fool.'

Richard turned along High Street towards the ancient grey stone pillars of the Guild Hall. He would like to have known how Robert was faring, especially now he was by himself. But it would be difficult to find out, except second-hand through their mother. One day, perhaps, there might be a way to heal the rift, to satisfy two proud and stubborn spirits; but not yet.

Robert would be all right. And he, Richard, would be all right; when the estate was sold he would be a wealthy man. Yet he was almost indifferent to that. There's a new world: go and win it. He heard the words again. Whatever he did, he had to win. Money in the bank was only a comfort; it would not keep him occupied for an hour a week. So he would go out and look for his new world. He had already written to Steve Mitchell – Mitch, who was in America learning the tricks of the film trade and would soon come home to seek his own new world. Mitch had once said, 'You and I could work pretty well together, Rich,' and it had been more than a hint. Films needed producers, directors, writers: imagination and excitement, visual and aural. And the big television boom was round the corner. Maybe he would join Mitch in America for a couple of months, and talk about it. Maybe.

They were rebuilding Exeter. The shattered remnants of that awful night in 1942 were being cleared slowly, and temporary structures removed to make way for bricks and concrete and new designs. High Street was changing, and the weeds which had flowered in the ruins and lent their coloured tributes to Ruth and Nick had disappeared before the bulldozers. He stopped, the Guild Hall behind him now, looking at it all. Across the road was a new shoe shop. He needed a pair of shoes and he stepped off the pavement, dodging between two cars, crossing the street to the other side in long strides, and his shoulder nudged a woman who had just come out of the shop.

He turned, apologetic for his haste, saying distantly, 'I'm so sorry –' and Lisa said, 'That's all right – it was my fault too –'

They stood still; confused, wordless. He saw a blue suit with the newly-fashionable long slender-fitting skirt and a waisted jacket over a white blouse, and the tawny hair flecked with golden lights in the bright new sun after rain.

And her eyes.

He said: 'Hullo, Lisa. Isn't that a strange coincidence. How are you?'

She was looking at his dark lounge suit and grey shirt and navy tie. If she had ever expected to see him, it would have been in uniform.

'Hullo, Richard. It's – nice to see you. You're looking well.'

Two girls brushed past them, chattering about their make-up; then a man, grumbling to his woman companion about the traffic, and two elderly women struggling with shopping bags. One swung against Richard's legs.

'I – it's nice to see you, too. What are you doing in Exeter? I thought you were – I don't know – somewhere else –' Awkward, stilted words.

'I'm staying with my parents.' She was reserved, correct. He was a stranger, and she did not know him well enough for conversation to be easy. 'And you? Are you –' she looked quickly at his suit '– are you still in the RAF?'

He nodded, bracing himself against pushing passers-by.

'Just on leave. Though I'll probably be resigning soon.'

'Resigning?' Somebody jostled her and she half-turned. 'Leaving the RAF? I hope that's good news for you.'

A bus rumbled past and its brakes shrieked suddenly. He tensed himself against the sound, waiting for it to subside before he said: 'I hope so, too.'

Then they looked at each other, not knowing what to say next; passing strangers trying to find the key to yesterday. She moved as if to walk on, then checked and said: 'It's difficult, isn't it? I don't know what to say to you.'

The confession helped. He said: 'It's a shock. If we'd known it was going to happen we'd have had time to think of something.'

She tried to smile.

'There's so much, after all this time, that it's difficult to know where to start. Or maybe there's so little, because it's been so long and there aren't any links now.'

'Yes. Perhaps.' Amongst the people, and the traffic noise, he felt conspicuous and inadequate. He thought he wanted to go; to find an excuse to end it. But he could not think of the words, because he was so afraid she would think he was rude; so instead he said: 'Look – we can't stay here, being bumped by all these people. Would you – like to talk? Over a drink, just for a few minutes?'

She hesitated, as if wondering whether she could trust him; or herself. Then she nodded.

'All right. If you like.'

He said, 'Let's go down here,' and pointed to St Martin's Lane, narrow between the buildings, and she nodded again and they edged through the crowd.

It was little more than an alley leading to the cathedral close. But half-way down on the left was the sixteenth-century Ship Inn, where once Drake had swaggered and supped his ale beneath the great oak beams behind the low doors. They had been there often, in another life; but now the door was closed and he looked at his watch and said: 'Oh, damn. I'm sorry. It's after closing time. I've been on the Continent so long I'd forgotten for a moment.' He looked at her and said again, distantly, 'I'm sorry.'

'It's all right.' She glanced down the alley. 'We can go to the café near Mol's, if you like.' She paused. 'As long as you want to.'

'Of course I want to.'

They walked down into the close, side by side, looking straight ahead. The café was open, and he held the door for her and she said, 'Thank you.' Only half-a-dozen people were there and she went quickly to a table and sat down so that he did not have to move the chair for her.

He settled opposite and said: 'Coffee? And cakes, or something?'

'Just coffee, please.'

He turned to a hovering waitress and conveyed the order. Then they sat in silence until he said carefully: 'I'm sorry about you and Rob. Very sorry.'

'Thank you.' She was just as careful. 'That's – very generous of you. I'm sad about it. He is, too. It's been a difficult time. But perhaps it was inevitable.'

He said: 'I'm not being generous. I meant it. But we Haldanes are hard to live with, I suppose.'

'No. The circumstances. The whole miserable business.'

'That was my fault. I behaved very badly.'

'No, Richard. Don't say that.' She was obviously embarrassed, and it disturbed him. 'It was my fault, and Rob's. Or nobody's fault.'

'That's right. Nobody's fault. I wish I'd been able to see that, then. What went wrong between you? Or don't you want to tell me?'

She said in a small voice: 'I can't. It wouldn't be fair. But he was good to me. He was very patient. I was – ill for a time, I think. A sort of – breakdown. But I'm all right now. Just sad.'

'I'm sorry.' He said it awkwardly. 'I shouldn't have asked. I don't know why I did. Mother said you were trying to get back on the stage. Is that true?'

'Yes. I'm getting a little work. Two weeks with rep in Birmingham next month. And radio plays. Otherwise I'm helping father as a surgery nurse, which is nice. Why are you leaving the RAF?'

He shrugged. The waitress brought the coffee. He watched her set out the cups and the sugar and the spoons and was glad of the interruption. Then he said: 'Lots of reasons. I've just been in uniform long enough, I suppose.' He stirred sugar into his coffee, in slow motion, concentrating upon it, then added: 'The important news is that Roxton will soon be on the market again.'

It shocked her. She stared at him, her expressive hazel eyes wide.

'Richard – why? What's happened?'

'Graham's had a heart attack and has to retire. He wants to get out.' His voice was quiet, unemotional. He watched three women get up from a nearby table, chattering as they left. 'If I bought him out I'd be in hock to the bank for ever and ever. I'd be working just to pay the interest. And I know I'm not really fit to run the place. It needs a top-class, experienced agriculturist. Like Robert. Except, with respect to him, I guess he wouldn't be able to afford to buy it on his own now. The argument about me applies – too big a loan to make sense.'

She was still absorbing it. The memories came back, and she did not welcome them. She sat, tense and upright, as she said: 'What are you going to do?'

'Sell it. After that, I don't know. Maybe something to do with flying. Or have a talk with Mitch. You remember Mitch? Yes, of course you do. Sorry – I'd forgotten for a moment. He's in America studying films and television. I fancy that. Have you ever tried to get a film part?'

'No,' she said. But she was not thinking about it. She brushed her hair away from her forehead and he saw it catch the light from the window. She was looking at him intently. 'Do you know what you're doing, Richard? You must know. It's the end of the Haldanes at Roxton. When that – that awful thing happened to us, you were still there, so the family link went on. But not now.'

'I can't help it.' He was surprised to be giving her the impression that he did not care.

And then she leaned forward across the table so that she was closer to him, and her eyes held on to his, and he remembered a quayside table far away in St Tropez and a voice saying stop loving her and find a new world, and she said: 'May I ask you something? Please, please don't be angry. But have you thought that if you held on to your share and Rob bought Graham Telford out, you could work things so that –'

'No.' Softly, but like a small explosion. 'How the hell do you imagine we could work together? We haven't spoken for nearly four years –'

'You didn't work together before,' she came back at him. 'Robert did the work. You were the sleeping partner. But you sorted things out. You could again.' Then she stopped, and added slowly: 'Unless you're going to need the capital, of course.'

'I don't know what I'll need. Anyway, Rob has a good farm, mother tells me. He wouldn't want to move. And he probably hates the sound of my name.'

She shook her head urgently.

'He doesn't hate you, Richard. Not now. He's just – empty about it.' She waited for his reaction, and when it did not come, asked: 'Do you still hate him?'

'Hate him?' He looked surprised, as if he had forgotten how much he had hated, once. 'No. I think about him sometimes. And wish it could be – different.'

She whispered: 'Richard, this isn't for me. He and I are finished. Nothing can ever bring it back to life. But I owe him so much. Help me to repay him, by listening to me. It's true he has a good farm. He's worked hard to get it right. But it's been a shield.

He immersed himself in it, to the exclusion of everything, including me, so that he wouldn't have time to think about Roxton. But when he came to see your mother he always drove past it, and he always asked her about it. I'm sure he still does. You broke his heart, Richard. I've never blamed you; it was a terrible time for us all. But the way you chose to hit back was cruel. I don't believe you ever knew how cruel it was. Please, for your brother's sake, and your mother's, and your grandfather's if you like – even for the sake of all we once knew there – please give him a chance to come back.'

He wanted to be angry, to say that he had been the victim and had only hit back as a trapped animal would, and that she had been cruel to him because she had taken away his will to live; but there were tears in her eyes and she had said for the sake of all we once knew, and he could not fight that because he remembered it too. And then he wanted to hit back again, because he was cornered and she was getting too close to him and he wanted to keep her away even if it meant hurting her.

So he said: 'All right. Maybe if one of us has enough courage to try, something might happen. Though God knows if Rob will want to. But don't see me as the fairy on the Christmas tree, Lisa. And don't go too much about the thing we once knew. I threw it away.'

She had touched the corners of her eyes with a handkerchief, calming herself. But now she was still again; almost holding her breath.

'I don't understand you.'

Something was driving him; something he had to do, to clear his mind and cleanse his spirit. He said: 'And you will never understand. Nobody could, unless they were there. But it doesn't matter now, so you might as well hear it. Do you know what I was doing, when I was on the run in France?'

A couple at a nearby table got up, scraping their chairs noisily, and walked past, glancing curiously at Lisa's taut face and searching eyes. All the other tables were empty now and the waitress was out of sight.

'I don't know what happened to you. Your mother told me a little. But you told me nothing. What did you mean about – throwing it away?'

He straightened in his chair and said stiffly: 'I was with the

Maquis in the mountains. There was a girl, married to the leader of the group. We spent a lot of time together – working together. Then she was captured. Capture for the Maquisards, or anyone else in the Resistance, meant torture, then being shot. I got her out of it. We went up the mountains, with the Germans hunting us. We found a cave, and we knew we were safe, at least for the night. Then something happened. We just turned to each other; first to keep warm, then – we lost control of it.'

It was done. After so long. She had forced it. He waited for her anger, or her scorn, or her tears. Or nothing, because she did not care. Let it be nothing, then he would know and it would be easier. He reached for his cup and drained the last of the coffee, defiantly. Then, as he put it down and pushed it away, he felt her fingers touching his hand.

'Why have you told me now?' A breath of sound. No anger, no scorn or tears. And her face was beautiful to him.

'You had a right to know.' Not his own voice. Somebody else saying words for him. 'Even after all this time, when it doesn't matter.'

'If things had been different – would you have told me? When it did matter?' Gently, and so quietly; and her fingers still touching.

He was startled. It should not have been like this. It should have been the last, unassailable barrier; the final untouchable refuge for his new world. Yet she had not recoiled from it, and something was reaching out to him and it was more than he could face.

'I don't know. I expect I wouldn't have had the courage. Who can tell?' He was in a corner again, and he had to get out. Suddenly he pulled his hand away and said: 'I'm sorry. I should say I'm sorry, shouldn't I? For a lot of things. But we're grown up people, so perhaps you know. I'd better go.' He pushed his chair back, looking round for the waitress then realising the bill was already on the table. He picked it up. 'Maybe I'll find a way of getting through to Robert, and we'll see what happens. Maybe something might come right, in the end.' He stood up, moving his chair carefully, paying attention to it, adding pointless words. 'I've taken up too much of your time. Thanks for talking. And listening. I hope you – well, settle down again soon.'

He went then, quickly, without saying goodbye; touching her shoulder momentarily as he passed her. She turned, half-rising, saying, 'Richard –' but he did not look back and if he heard her whispered goodbye he gave no sign. He left money beside the till and was gone, walking beyond the window without turning his head.

For an unknown time she sat alone, looking at his empty coffee cup as if, somehow, it was a link. They had reached across the years of grief and anger and, for a moment, had been touched by a breath of the old forgotten magic. Then he had pulled back and now the door was closed and she would never know why. She had been with a stranger, a haunted shadow of a cavalier whose bridges had been broken and who could not find a new way across the divide. And she had failed him. If only she had had more time; if only he had allowed her more time to think, to search for words, to touch him with her spirit as once she did, to understand him and to understand herself. She raised a hand to her shoulder, wanting to feel again the parting pressure of his fingers; his last goodbye. Nothing now, nor ever again. No tears; they would come later. Just nothing, on this day which had been so ordinary at its beginning.

She gathered her handbag and walked quickly from the café.

The pavements had dried and there was sun on the grey cathedral and the grass was green. She stood for a moment, looking across the close, seeing people, focusing on them. Then she turned towards St Martin's Lane, past the tiny church at the corner, pushing the memory of him away, seeing the narrow pavement shadowed by the buildings pressing close on either side.

Seeing him.

He was standing at the other end of the lane, looking for her. She knew he was looking for her, down through the shadows to where she stood in the sun. She was still, breathless; and then she moved, and he turned, facing her, watching her, asking her the question, and she read it and answered it again and again as she went to him, until he held out both his hands and they were touching, seeing nothing except each others' eyes and the hope in them, hearing nothing except his whisper against the noise of the city.

'Come back to me, Lisa. Let's learn it all again.'

And it was the first day of the new world.

Fontana Paperbacks: Fiction

Fontana is a leading paperback publisher of both non-fiction, popular and academic, and fiction. Below are some recent fiction titles.

- ☐ THE ROSE STONE Teresa Crane £2.95
- ☐ THE DANCING MEN Duncan Kyle £2.50
- ☐ AN EXCESS OF LOVE Cathy Cash Spellman £3.50
- ☐ THE ANVIL CHORUS Shane Stevens £2.95
- ☐ A SONG TWICE OVER Brenda Jagger £3.50
- ☐ SHELL GAME Douglas Terman £2.95
- ☐ FAMILY TRUTHS Syrell Leahy £2.95
- ☐ ROUGH JUSTICE Jerry Oster £2.50
- ☐ ANOTHER DOOR OPENS Lee Mackenzie £2.25
- ☐ THE MONEY STONES Ian St James £2.95
- ☐ THE BAD AND THE BEAUTIFUL Vera Cowie £2.95
- ☐ RAMAGE'S CHALLENGE Dudley Pope £2.95
- ☐ THE ROAD TO UNDERFALL Mike Jefferies £2.95

You can buy Fontana paperbacks at your local bookshop or newsagent. Or you can order them from Fontana Paperbacks, Cash Sales Department, Box 29, Douglas, Isle of Man. Please send a cheque, postal or money order (not currency) worth the purchase price plus 22p per book for postage (maximum postage required is £3.00 for orders within the UK).

NAME (Block letters) _____

ADDRESS _____

_____

_____

While every effort is made to keep prices low, it is sometimes necessary to increase them at short notice. Fontana Paperbacks reserve the right to show new retail prices on covers which may differ from those previously advertised in the text or elsewhere.

FIVE MINUTE
FACELIFT

FIVE MINUTE
FACELIFT

Robert Thé
with Sally Riceman

Published By Blitz Editions
an imprint of
Bookmart Limited
Registered Number 2372865
Trading as Bookmart Limited
Desford Road
Enderby
Leicester
LE9 5AD
First published in 1997 by
Virgin Books.

A catalogue record for this book is
available from the British Library

ISBN: 1 85605 3849

Printed and bound by Lego, Italy

Photography: Antonio Traza

Models: Kitsa Pateras, Joanne Emma
Ray, Dolores Serrallé, Mercedes
Cabral-of-Smith, Sylver, Gemma
Godas Villaverte, Steve Young

Make up: Sally Riceman

For Virgin Publishing: Carolyn Price

Design: Paul Kime

This book is dedicated to Smita Joshi whose spirit is a
testimony to youthfulness.

A book is the product of many people's ideas and efforts, and
this one is no exception. I would like to acknowledge and
thank the following for all their time, ideas and creative input:

Carmel Dungan
Julia Ahmad Jamal
Smita Joshi
Paul Kime
Kundan & Narendra Mehta
Kitsa Pateras
Carolyn Price
Sally Riceman
Dolores Serrallé
Dorita Sheriff
Mercedes Cabral-of-Smith
Martin Stollery
Antonio Traza
Nadia Warner
Steve Young

Robert Thé
London, 1997

CONTENTS

INTRODUCTION

In the past if you wanted to take care of your face as you got older you were limited to two basic options. With option A you could spend lots of money on very expensive and highly dubious anti-ageing creams for which many extravagant claims were made but which unfortunately usually brought only cosmetic and temporary benefits.

Option B was more drastic: when you felt that things were getting out of hand, facially speaking, you could arrange to have a surgical facelift. By a nip here and a tuck here, magic could be created: worrisome lines, wrinkles and sagging cheeks vanished overnight. The catch with this outrageously expensive procedure was that it had to be repeated every few years, tucking a bit more here and a slightly more there. What had started out as a solution often ended up being a major problem in its own right, as successive operations rapidly diminished the credit balance and created a progressively more mask-like face, each one more rigid and unnatural than the last.

But now there is a third way, a way based on sensible, natural methods that aim to preserve your good features for as long as possible. This method is easy to learn and can be practised by anyone, anywhere and at any point in their life. It enables us to take positive steps through exercise, to discourage signs of ageing before they have an opportunity to develop in youthful skins, and, in skins where they have developed, to minimize their effects.

How to use this book

This book is divided into three parts.

In the first part we hear about 'Modern Day Skin Stories' and discover the secret world of our skin, what its structure is, what factors are instrumental in ageing it, what a good basic skincare programme consists of and how our thoughts affect the quality of our skin. In 'Your Best Asset' we learn about the structure of the face, discovering the individual major muscles, what they do, where they are as well as seeing how they work together as a team, helping us express ourselves.

The middle of the book focuses on three different facial programmes which are designed to ensure that as we get older our skin remains in optimum condition. In 'Basic Facial Fitness' we work systematically through each major muscle of the face so that the whole face becomes toned. This is followed by 'Turning Back the Clock', which includes exercises designed to troubleshoot a range of common problems that can be experienced as we get older. This section includes special techniques that work on releasing deep tension in the connective tissue, tension that is often responsible for hard-to-hide wrinkles and lines. In 'Facial Harmony' we include massage techniques – using both oil and oil-free moves – that can restore radiance to your face.

In the final part, 'Less is More', we look at how make up can be used in a subtle way to enhance your positive features and reveal your full potential.

To obtain the best results from this book –

- Read through 'Modern Day Skin Stories' first.
- Start the skincare programme recommended.
- Begin with the 'Basic Facial Fitness' programme.
- Read through each exercise before attempting it.
- Make sure you have short nails and clean hands before you touch your face.
- Apply a little moisturizer before you start.
- Use a mirror to see yourself as you do the exercises.
- Repeat each exercise several times until the individual muscle tires.
- Use your imagination as well to help bring about changes.
- Practise as often as possible.
- Be patient: changes will happen through time.

My personal recommendation is that you work through the book systematically, chapter by chapter. The exercises form part of a structured programme and will not make sense if you tackle them randomly. As you work through the book you should begin to notice small changes occurring, and the longer you continue the more pronounced these should become.

I hope that you will enjoy using this book for many years to come and that, as you begin to notice the benefits of this powerful program, you will get everyone around you involved and regularly practising the Five Minute Facelift. So dive in, enjoy and here's to your health!

Modern

Day Skin Stories

*I*magine for a moment that you really did wear your heart on your sleeve. It's a safe bet that you'd take good care of this precious, delicate organ and treat it with the respect it truly deserves.

But most people treat their skin, which is located on the outside of the body, as if it were unworthy of being cared for, paying it little if any attention. This is surprising because it is the largest of all the organs in the body, covering approximately two square meters (18 square feet) and weighing in at a hefty 3.2 kilos (7 pounds).

Your skin would be well within its rights to ask for compensation. It has a lot to contend with: regular exposure to the elements, filtering out harmful radiation and dealing with life's low life, such as dirt, grime and bacteria.

Despite everything the skin does for them, very few people take the time or effort to really understand it: how it ages, how to care for it and how best to listen to all the stories it has to tell. Understanding your skin is the first step in being able to care for it, of being able to lay strong foundations so that it remains healthy throughout your life. Practising preventative skin care on a daily basis, in conjunction with using the basic facial fitness programme and other exercises, will help you to maintain a healthy, glowing complexion and retain your good looks through the years.

No one could wish for a better bodyguard than the skin, which offers us head-to-toe protection, even when we sleep. And, like all the best bodyguards, the skin is not quite what it seems: outwardly supple and thin enough to allow complete freedom of movement, yet tough enough to offer a resilient waterproof barrier that stops life-essential water from getting out and undesirable things such as bacteria, infectious diseases and harmful ultraviolet radiation from getting in.

The skin is not just a simple surface covering the entire body: its thickness depends largely on where it is found, with the thickest skin occurring on the soles and palms and the thinnest around our eyelids. The skin is also a very busy place: in just one square centimetre there are approximately 3 million cells, 13 oil glands, 9 hairs, 100 sweat glands and 2.75 metres (3 yards) of nerves, 1 metre of blood vessels and thousands of sensory cells which allow minute differences of temperature, touch, pressure and pain to be instantly detected, providing accurate up-to-the-minute information about what is going on in the big wide world.

There's more to the skin than meets the eye. To begin with, what we normally think of as the skin is only the first or surface layer of several different layers. These first few layers form what is known as the epidermis, after that comes the dermis, then the subcutaneous layer containing fat cells that serve to protect the organs lying under it from damage.

The function of the epidermis is to offer a barrier, the first level of protection. The first layer, the stratum corneum, is made up of dead skin cells, which are continuously being shed. In fact, most household dust, when ana-

lyzed, is found to be composed of these dead cells! The epidermis also contains specialized cells that create a pigment called melanin. The amount of melanin in our skin is what determines our skin colour. Exposure to ultraviolet light stimulates production of melanin which produces the effect of tanning, the body's protective response against ultraviolet radiation. In geographical areas where sunlight is intense, the indigenous populations have a lot of melanin in their skin, giving them a dark hue. Equally, people who live in temperate, less sunny zones tend to have less melanin present in their skin. However, to call the skin colour of such people 'white' is incorrect: it is often more of a pinkish hue, caused by the blood present in the dermis.

The dead cells at the surface of our skin are generated five layers below in the stratum basale, which is in charge of producing new skin cells. Some cells become specialized, like sweat or oil glands or hair follicles, while the remainder become general skin cells and set off on a four-week journey upwards through various levels until they reach the surface as dead skin cells.

Living in the city can sometimes cause the skin surface to become clogged with grease and dirt, and develop a dull, lifeless appearance. In addition to regular cleansing, exfoliation or dry skin brushing can help clear the skin of dead cells, stimulate blood and nutrient supply, clear toxins through improved lymphatic drainage and allow the skin to breathe freely. But the removal of dead skin cells has to be done in moderation: too zealous or frequent removal puts pressure on the basale layer and makes the skin sensitive and raw, and susceptible to ageing.

The dermis is often known as the true skin and is usually much thicker than the epidermis. Its main function is to provide support for the epidermis and various structures found within the dermis. It is mainly made up of connective tissue that binds together, supports, strengthens and gives general shape to our flesh. Contained within it are two protein-based fibres, collagen and elastin. These offer the skin the twin benefits of stretchability (the ability to put on weight or get pregnant without ripping or otherwise damaging the skin) and elasticity (the ability for the skin to return to its original shape after stretching).

Embedded within the matrix of the connective tissue are other specialized skin cells such as hair follicles and roots, touch and pressure sensitive nerve endings, veins, fat cells, arteries and various capillaries as well as sudiferous (sweat) and sebaceous (oil) glands.

There are approximately three to four million sudiferous glands in the body and these are mainly located in the subcutaneous layer. Their secretions are emptied via a duct that leads directly to a pore on the skin surface, and is a vital element in helping to regulate body temperature by providing a way of reducing it quickly.

Sebaceous glands are small sacs with a duct connected to hair follicles. They are found nearly everywhere on the surface of the body, particularly the face. These glands produce sebum, an oily lubricant that prevents the hair from becoming dry as well as creating a waterproof mantle for the skin which helps keep it soft and supple. The level of sebum production largely determines our skin type, whether it will be dry or oily.

The skin is remarkably resilient, able to repair itself rapidly, often leaving no apparent mark of any damage being done. But with all its strengths, the skin needs to be taken care of and respected. The attention and care we give it can directly improve the quality of our general health and the way we look. And so, far from being a luxury, the skin's complexity demands that it is looked after and cared for. By working to keep our skin in excellent condition, the collagen in the connective tissue can remain well-organized and supple as we get older instead of becoming rigid, brittle and knotted. This means we will develop fewer wrinkles and retain a handsome face for many years to come.

If your skin is oily, count your-self lucky. Not day-to-day lucky, but long-term lucky. Unlike dry skin, oily skin tends to take a lot longer to wrinkle and show signs of ageing. The same contrast can be found in people with olive or darker complexions who generally age at a slower rate than those with pale, light skin.

However, apart from our skin type, there are other biological factors involved in ageing which can be prepared for, thus affecting how quickly we age.

The first signs that we are getting older generally occur around the age of 25. Expression lines, caused by the constant wear and tear generated by using our facial muscles every day begin to appear, usually around the mouth and eyes. And there are also changes in the natural elasticity of our skin as this daily wear and tear begins to take its toll on the elastin in the skin, causing it to break down. When combined with a general loss of facial muscle tone, the skin can become a little looser than previously. However, this process can be slowed down considerably by regularly practising good skincare and following a basic facial fitness programme.

The thirties and forties often bring a maturity to the face as life experiences and lifestyle choices begin to etch themselves into our features. Expression lines deepen, more and more wrinkles appear and the skin can begin to show the cumulative effects of gravity, leading to local sagging and bags under the eyes.

The sudden hormonal upheaval of the menopause not only has a dramatic effect on the body, it can also trigger major changes

within the face as well: the skin can become dryer or change its type completely; reduced circulation can lead to a paler complexion; collagen and fat cells in the face become reduced in size and number which, when combined with a general thinning of the skin, can cause the face to start to lose its natural plumpness, becoming slightly gaunt in appearance and triggering other signs of ageing to slowly develop: jowls, downturned mouths and turkey necks. Putting on a little extra as you get older is not such a bad idea, especially as it can help to counter the problem of natural shrinkage and collagen loss, plumping and filling out the skin. In addition, practising the basic facial fitness programme regularly and targeting specific problems using the trouble-shooting techniques shown in pages 46-60 will help to slow the effects of this change on the face.

Our lifestyle and environment also play a large part in determining how we age and how our skin responds. The principal environmental factor is the level of exposure to the sun's rays we experience throughout our lives. While limited protected exposure can be healthy, unprotected exposure and sunburn is most definitely not. Unprotected exposure to the sun can lead to the skin becoming dehydrated, the collagen within the connective tissues breaking down rapidly, and the appearance of wrinkles. So if you want to save your skin when out in the sun, always follow the Australian Slip, Slop, Slap rule: slip on a shirt or blouse, slap on a hat, and slop on the sun blocker. The higher the protection factor on the blocker, the better – even on cold, cloudy days.

In addition to the sun, the air that surrounds us and the air that we breathe plays an important role in the health of our skin.

Scientific findings show that smoking, whether active or passive, can age you just as rapidly as exposure to the sun, so is best avoided. Equally undesirable is the air conditioning and central heating found in most modern offices and homes. Although originally designed to make our immediate environment more pleasant, they tend to wreck havoc with our skin by drying it out. If your workplace or home has air-conditioning or central heating, make sure you regularly moisturize your skin and get plenty of fresh air, to counterbalance the effect of an indoor climate.

Eating poor quality, highly processed food such as convenience meals or fast food can also have a marked effect on our skin, because these often lack fibre and contain high levels of saturated fats, questionable additives and refined sugar, which the body regards as highly toxic, rejecting it often in the form of facial spots. Unsurprisingly, this type of diet often leaves your skin and face looking dull and starved of life. If your aim is to look as vibrant and healthy as possible, then include in your daily diet as much natural, fresh, unrefined food as possible. This will give your body the vitamins, nutrients and fibre it needs to keep you looking at your best.

Given that we are made up of 70 per cent water, what we drink has a significant effect on the quality of our skin and how we age. Drinks like tea and coffee, which contain toxins, are better avoided, as is alcohol, which has a negative physical effect on our body, causing it to rapidly dehydrate. The human body appreciates the intake of fresh water (between 1.5 and 2 litres/2-3 pints) every day to help the kidneys flush toxins from the system. This will leave the skin clearer and no tell-tale dark bags under the eyes to show that the kidneys are having a hard time dealing with all the toxins in your system. A regular monthly one-or two-day detox and system cleanse using just natural fruit juices or water also works wonders for your skin. Ask your doctor on how best to start.

The skin is a very accurate barometer of how stressed we are and will rapidly show when you are under too much pressure. If this pressure is sustained at too high a level for too long then, as many high-fliers often find to their cost, it can trigger rapid ageing, especially in the face. The antidote to stress is to make sure you manage it on a regular and continual basis, learning to relax fully. If you don't, then your skin is likely to suffer and wrinkles will settle in as long-term tenants. Getting regular, quality sleep should be a major part of your relaxation programme, because it helps the body to rest, recover and heal itself. Not for nothing do models hit the pillows early every evening: they know that it's the best way to make sure their skin is always in top form.

An optimum lifestyle doesn't happen overnight, it takes small constant changes and improvements: a nudge here and a nudge there to go in the right direction, and a sense of flexibility to forgive yourself for drifting off course occasionally. But, by making lifestyle choices that are kind to your skin, you will be doing yourself a big favour, long-term. And as the seasons change, your face will begin to show the benefits of all the positive choices you have made through the years.

A regularly followed skincare routine used in conjunction with the basic facial fitness programme is essential if you want your skin to look fresh and vibrant now and in the future. A basic programme involves: cleansing to remove excess make-up, dirt and grime, toning to remove the cleanser, and moisturizing which keeps the skin smooth and supple, discouraging wrinkles; exfoliation removes dead skin cells from the surface, and a mask detoxes and purifies the skin. Regular cleansing involves steps 1–4, which should be done twice a day. Exfoliate and use a mask twice a week, following the steps in this order: 1, 2, 5, 6, 3 and 4.

I Cleanse: Remove make-up and dirt build-up with cleanser.

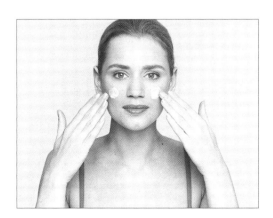

4 Moisturize: Use an appropriate mositurizer to hydrate the skin and help seal moisture in.

2 Wipe: Using a warm cloth, wipe face.

3 Tone: Using a toner on cotton balls, gently go over face, avoiding the eye area.

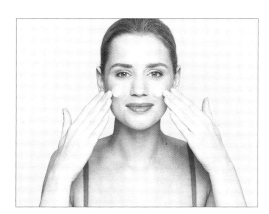

5 Exfoliate: Choose an exfoliant that suits you, and avoid rubbing harshly on cheeks and eye area. Remove with warm water.

6 Mask: Avoiding the eye area, apply a mask to dry skin. After the impurities have been drawn, remove thoroughly with warm water, tone and moisturize as usual.

THINKING BEAUTY

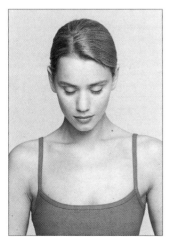 *T*rue beauty is not just about how you look on the outside, but how you feel on the inside. What's going on the inside is easy to spot, especially when we're upset or worried. The ability to take control of any thoughts that may push us off balance or which are less than positive is very important. Learning to release internal negativity can help us to release physical tension, especially within our face, and is the first step in learning how to allow our inner beauty to radiate outwards. So, let go of the strains of the day and think only beautiful thoughts as you try the following exercises.

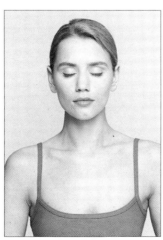

1 Sit with your head upright and very slowly lower your head.

2 Raise your head back up at the same speed, breathing slowly. Stop when your head is level again.

3 Finally, press two fingers just above each browbone and hold for a few minutes. These are excellent points to calm and centre you.

Your Best Asset

 Not everyone likes

the telephone. Those

who dislike it often say that

using it feels incomplete, like

half a conversation. Perhaps

this is because they are miss-

ing the vital visual cues that

we take for granted in face-

to-face conversations.

Without these cues, and relying purely on someone's tone of voice, subtleties of meaning can be very hard to pick up.

Basic facial expressions are pretty much the same the world over. An ecstatic Egyptian is as easy to spot as a delirious Dane; an angry Australian is as hard to miss as a volcanic Venezuelan. But our face is not just limited to expressing basic human emotions such as joy, anger, surprise and sadness, it can communicate dozens of shades of meaning in-between, everything from mild surprise to complete amazement.

The expressions on our face are clear enough to see, but what creates them is often a mystery to many of us. In the following pages we will explore some of the major facial muscles lying just beneath the skin, working continually to create a symphony of expressions, ebbing and flowing with our moods. We will also discover how single muscles work in harmony to create basic expressions.

Understanding how muscles work individually and in groups will help you to get the most out of later exercises and to turn what is a great asset into your best asset.

THE FACIAL LANDSCAPE: PART ONE

To find the greatest number and variety of muscles in the human body, you need go no further than the face. Nestling closely together, and often over-lapping for compactness and efficiency within a relatively small area, are dozens of agile and powerful muscles of differ-ent shapes and sizes. These muscles are on constant call to perform as we watch, listen to and interact with the world around us.

We begin our exploration of the facial landscape by looking at some key muscles in the fore-head, temples, eyebrows and around the eyes.

1 Place one hand flat against your forehead and then screw up your forehead. You should feel your hand being pulled up as the large *frontalis* muscle underneath it contracts.

2 Place two fingers in between your eyebrows and frown as if you were disapproving of something. What you are feeling is a combination of the *procerus* and *corrugator supercili* muscles located next to the eyebrows.

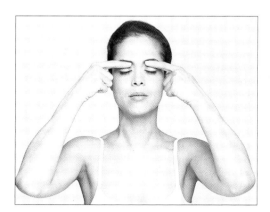

3 Close your eyes and gently place an index finger across the top of each eyelid. Then, keeping your eyes shut, try to lift the eyelid. The thin, delicate muscle you can feel pulling is part of the *orbicularis oculi* encircling the eye.

4 Place your fingers on both sides of your head, slightly above and in front of your ears. Now clench your teeth and feel the wide *temporalis* muscle ripple under your fingers. This muscle is responsible for closing your jaw and helping you to chew.

*Y*ou have to be pretty smart to make it as a facial muscle these days. Not only do you have to be able to handle simple routine tasks such as blinking automatically to cleanse and protect the eyes, but very often you have to track and simultaneously respond to what is happening elsewhere in the face.

To get a good idea of how flexible and well co-ordinated these muscles are, try talking, smiling and eating simultaneously and then for good measure throw in a surprised expression. Confused? Just think what it would be like if you had to consciously plan these moves all the time.

1 Place two fingers on either side of the bridge of the nose to feel the action of the muscles here. Try closing your nostrils with the *compressor naris*, and then – as though you are really angry – flaring your nostrils with *depressor septi*.

4 Place one finger slightly away from the corner of one side of your mouth and smile to one side. You should be able to feel the *zygomaticus major* muscle contracting under your finger.

2 Place your fingers on either side of your wisdom teeth and then let your jaw slowly open. You should feel a muscle bulge outwards as you do so. This is the *masseter,* which is a key muscle involved in chewing.

3 Try pursing your lips and feel with your fingers the circular muscle called *orbicularis oris* that surrounds the mouth, without which speaking and kissing would not be quite the same.

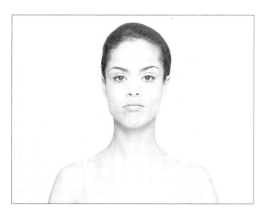

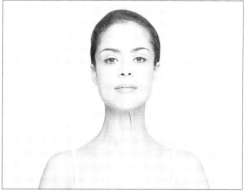

5 This is the muscle that everyone uses when they want to sulk, pout or are about to burst into tears. Simply pull up the muscle at the front of your chin, the *mentalis.*

6 Tense the whole of your neck as if you are just about to explode. A sheath-like muscle, the *platysma,* will stand out and temporarily give you the appearance of a bodybuilder.

$\mathcal{W}$e've already explored some basic individual muscles, so let's now see how they work in tandem by running through some basic facial expressions. It's a good idea to use a mirror to help you see how different muscles work together, but while you practise try to also become aware of how they feel as they flow from one expression to another.

If you do this exercise often enough, your muscles will begin to remember other possibilities. You might notice a sparkle return to your face as you shake off your habitual and perhaps tired facial expression and allow a freshness and vitality to flood in. So go ahead – express yourself.

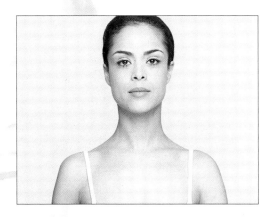

I Start by creating a neutral expression – a fresh canvas, if you like. Breathe slowly, relax your facial muscles and clear your mind so that you can create the following faces.

4 Everything has a beginning, middle and end and joy often follows sadness. Think of a really joyful moment in your life and let your face radiate the pure joy of that experience.

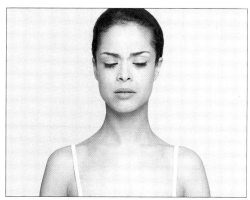

2 Someone has bought you a wonderful, unexpected gift or perhaps you've heard some fantastic news. Let your face show how surprised you are.

3 Sometimes the news we get isn't so great, or things don't turn out quite as we'd hoped. Let your face flow into general disappointment or sadness.

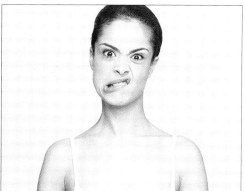

5 OK. So maybe people aren't perfect all the time. What's the one thing that other people do that always makes you really angry? That's right. Show your mirror what you really feel.

6 People who laugh enjoy life more, and if you can't laugh at yourself, this one is definitely for you. Do what you have to, but get silly in front of the mirror. Afterwards return to Step 1.

Basic

Facial Fitness

$\mathcal{G}$eorge Orwell once remarked that by the time we reach 50 we have the face we deserve. Poor George, if only he'd regularly practised a basic facial fitness programme!

Fifty years ago skin care regimes and methods of keeping young were in their infancy. Today we have many wonderful techniques for making sure that our skin remains in optimum condition throughout the years and that our faces are as toned as the rest of our bodies.

The basic facial fitness programme is a simple system of exercises, starting with a general warm up, tension-releasing exercises, and then moving on to a series of specific exercises targeting each area within the face, systematically working each major facial muscle, before concluding with an invigorating facial re-energizer.

Some of these exercises may take a little time to get used to and the results may not show immediately, but facial muscles are very responsive and with regular practice your face will start to benefit, giving a more healthy appearance and a glowing complexion as well as a firmer, fitter and more youthful look. It doesn't matter how old you are when you start: the big advantage of this programme is that anyone can benefit at any time of their lives. The important point is that the sooner you start, the sooner you will notice the wonderful benefits the programme has to offer. Practise these basic facial fitness exercises consistently and the vibrant and fresh face you deserve will be yours.

The first step in any physical programme is warming-up. Although the basic facial programme is a gentle pro-gramme, we can benefit from loosening the upper body, specifically the neck and shoulders, which stimulates the circula-tion, to prepare us for what is to follow and make the facial exercises more effective long-term.

Choose a comfortable chair that also gives you support as you carry out these exercises and the ones that follow. Ensure too that the surrounding environment is well-heated, because muscles relax and function better when they are warm. Finally, make sure that you are wearing loose, comfortable clothing that allows you to move freely as you work through the programme.

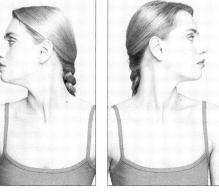

1 Start your warm-up by loosening your shoulders. Place one hand on each shoulder and start to draw clockwise circles with your elbows. Draw these circles progressively larger.

2 Then, keeping your head vertical, slowly look across to your left shoulder and then over to your right. Repeat ten times.

3 Bring your head back to the centre and then gently tilt your head slightly to the left. Bring back to the centre and then repeat on the other side. Continue until you reach a tilt of 45°.

4 Finally, raise your shoulders up to your ears and then allow them to drop down again. Repeat this invigorating movement ten times and end by shaking out.

RELAXING THE FACE

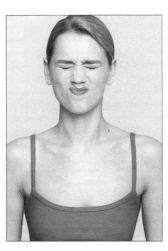

How tense is your face? My bet is that like most people, myself included, your facial muscles are surprisingly tense and longing for some TLC.

I Squeeze your face up as tightly as you can and then let it all go. Repeat ten times.

One of the surest ways of ageing faster than we should is to ignore the tension that builds up in the facial muscles as a result of everyday living. Tension creates blockage and pollution in muscles which can cause more and more lines and wrinkles to form as the surrounding tissues become increasingly stagnant and lifeless. Relax your face, enjoy the surge of energy and feeling of vitality and the rest will follow naturally.

2 Place your hands on either side of your skull, just above your ears and use all your fingers to work the *temporalis* muscles.

3 Now look straight ahead. Let your jaw drop as wide as you can, breathe slowly and create the biggest smile you can. Hold for as long as possible. Relax and repeat ten times. This exercise releases tension from deep within your face.

4 Finally, use your fingertips to explore your face, searching for any remaining tension spots that need to be soothed away. End by gently resting both hands over your face.

The appearance of worry lines on the forehead is not usually a happy occasion because it marks our eligibility for promotion as one of life's veterans. While some people look forward to promotion, others would prefer to choose when they would like to accept the post. If you feel that promotion has come a little too soon for your liking or you want to put if off as long as possible, then use the following techniques. These can help to banish unwanted worry lines while encouraging extra blood flow and vitality to the whole of the face. So without further ado, let's take it from the top.

I Place the pads of your fingers firmly on your scalp and massage in small circles, releasing any tension wherever you find it. Tension within the scalp is a great cause of worry lines.

2 Place your index fingers flat against the centre of your forehead. Begin a gentle sawing action up and down, working slowly out and then back in again. Repeat ten times.

3 Place your hand against the top of your hair-line and look down. This should create a strong stretch that helps to reduce wrinkles and tone the muscle. Relax and repeat ten times.

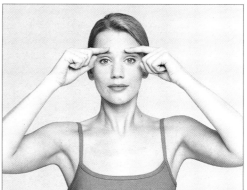

4 Place your index fingers over your eyebrows and try to contract the *frontalis* muscle while keeping the fingers firmly against the brows. Relax and repeat ten times.

The eyes are the focal point of the face. Stress and tiredness can soon take their toll and leave the thin, delicate skin of this area vulnerable to the first signs of ageing. In use all day, and even pressed into service while we dream at night, our eyes need to be regularly looked after. Use these exercises to keep the eyes and surrounding areas well toned to avoid those first tell-tale signs of advancing years, such as drooping eyelids and crow's feet.

 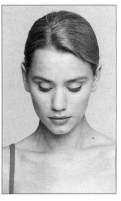  

This ancient yoga exercise is excellent for stimulating and relaxing the set of muscles that control eye movement.

Slowly look straight up and down. Next look out of the corner of your eyes, first to the left and then to the right.

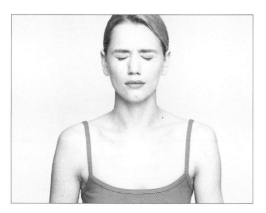

2 Screw up your eyes tightly. Hold for five seconds and release. Repeat ten times.

3 With your index fingers, press on the inner corners of both eyes. This is a powerful acupressure point which disperses tension and is good for bags under the eyes.

4 Place the index and middle fingers by the outer edge of one eyebrow. While pushing up towards the hairline, look at the tip of your nose, then shut your eye. Relax and repeat ten times before repeating on the other side. This tones the *orbicularis oculi* and is good for droopy eyelids.

5 Most importantly, rest the eyes. Simply close both eyes and place the palms of your hands over them for as long as you like. You will find the darkness and warmth of your hands produces a rare and delicious sensation.

Open your lips slightly and then slowly raise one side of your mouth upwards in a snarl. Hold for a few moments and then release and repeat on the other side. Repeat five times on each side.

$\mathscr{P}$lump, rosy cheeks are a sign of a healthy appearance. However, gravity can begin to make its presence felt as the years roll by, with our cheeks slowly beginning to lose their fullness and starting to sag. The following exercises are designed to reverse this process by stimulating and toning the muscles that support the cheeks. Practise this regularly and you will soon begin to experience the full benefits of keeping gravity in check with stronger and more youthful-looking cheeks.

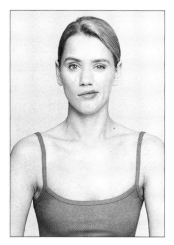

2 Grasp your upper lip and pull down slightly. Now apply the snarl movement, slowly lifting both sides of your mouth. Keep your hold on the lip and feel the cheek muscles being worked.

3 Place your index fingers at the top of each cheek. Open your mouth and slowly move the upper and lower lips away from each other, forming an oval. Smile and feel the cheek muscles being worked under your fingers. Repeat ten times.

4 Now, try to wink one eye without actually closing it. You should feel the cheek muscles rising as you do so. Repeat several times before doing the same exercise with the other cheek.

SEALED WITH A KISS

The mouth is one of the hardest-working parts of the human body, with eleven muscles helping us to shape our vowels and words, giving form to our ideas. We also depend on the flexibility of our mouth to highlight what we feel – smiling, laughing, even kissing would be very different if we couldn't use the muscles around our mouth. At the same time, our mouth is at the frontline of the digestive process, keeping food in while we chew it well. If you want your mouth to retain its flexibility and look good through the years, try these exercises to stimulate and tone it.

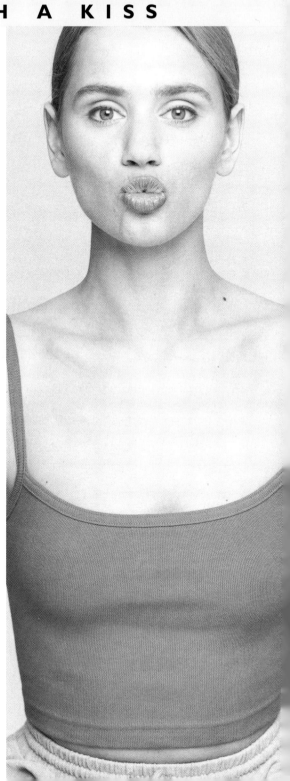

1 Some vowel exercises to start! Say 'A' loudly, shaping it clearly with your lips. Follow with the big vowels: 'E', 'U' and 'O'.

2 Open your mouth halfway, curl your lips inwards. Tense and hold for a few seconds, relax and repeat five times.

3 Stretch both sides of your mouth outwards, as though you were saying 'Eeee'. Hold for a few moments, relax slowly and repeat five times.

4 Now for the big moment! Pucker your lips for the world's biggest kiss and let fly. Repeat five times or more.

Place your fingers on either side of the jaw and hook your thumbs just underneath it, by the ears. Let your thumbs slowly sink in, feel the tissue soften, release your thumbs and move along slightly and repeat.

𝒪ne of the most common anxieties about appearance occurs when the jawline suddenly starts to lose its definition and becomes a little vague about where it thinks it is meant to be. If your jawline is beginning to migrate south, don't panic! Left to continue its travels, it might well decide to sign its emigration papers and develop into a double chin, but if you take positive steps now, you will probably be able to convince it to stay put.

2 Curl your lips over the upper and lower teeth and close your mouth gently. See if you can make a seal-like puckering noise by opening your mouth slightly and sucking in some air briefly before closing.

3 Take a slow, deep breath. Then contract the *platysma* muscle in your neck for three seconds. Relax and repeat ten times.

4 Gently tilt your head back and let your mouth fall slightly open. Keeping your head in this position, bring your lower lip up to meet the upper lip. This move will tone both your neck and jaw.

RE-ENERGIZING THE FACE

*A*fter doing the exercises in the basic facial programme, you'd expect to look like you've always lived on a health farm on top of a mountain. But you don't just want muscles that have been toned and stimulated, you also want a full recharge! This is where the exercises below will come in useful. So let's re-energize and go for the tingle!

1 Use the pads of your fingers to gently drum all over your face. Start at the chin and work your way up and come down again. Keep going until you can feel your face starting to tingle.

2 Continue up onto your scalp and keep drumming all over your head. This feels great and is wonderful for releasing stored energy in your body.

3 Breathe out through your mouth, stretch your tongue out and down, roll your eyeballs upwards and roar loudly like a lion. This ancient yoga exercise is a powerful toner for your entire face.

Turning

Back The Clock

*T*he basic facial fitness programme is a great way to make the most of your face, ensuring that your muscles receive regular attention and remain well toned and healthy.

Unfortunately, not all areas of the face are equal: some need a little extra help now and again in order to firm up in line with the rest of the face. Perhaps your own cheeks are full and rosy, but you'd really like to do something with that second chin. Or maybe you don't mind the odd line here and there, but you really want to pack those bags under the eyes and send them as far away as possible.

This section includes specific exercises to tackle the major problems that the face experiences as it ages. These include: pale skin, loose flesh, wrinkles and expression lines, low eyebrows, crow's feet, bags under the eyes, a downturned mouth, poor jaw definition, a double chin and a lined or 'crêpey' neck.

Some of the exercises, especially those involving the connective tissue in the face, can bring noticeable results if they are practised regularly and with sensitivity, helping you gently to turn back the clock. If any of the above problems are of concern to you, include the specified exercises in your general basic routine. Alternatively, this section can serve as an advanced workout, allowing you to systematically work through the exercises as part of a preventative programme and encouraging your face to look its very best for as long as possible.

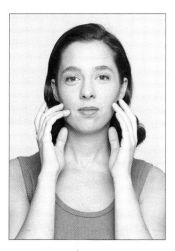

Our skin type can change greatly as we get older. With the arrival of the menopause, changes in the circulation within the face can also occur, making us look drawn and as if we spend a lot of time indoors.

Like any other part of the body, the muscles in the face need to be well supplied with blood. This not only brings fresh oxygen and nutrients, but can also take away toxins so that the tissues remain vibrant and healthy. By following these simple exercises, we can keep the energy flowing throughout our face and restore the colour to our cheeks.

❚ Begin by using the pads of your fngers to tap your face. Make sure you tap the whole face several times.

2 Use the fourth fingers of both hands to gently pinch or pluck your cheeks and surrounding the areas.

3 Move onto your ears and give them a thorough massage with your fingers.

4 Finally, gently slap your face with the inside of your hand, pushing the flesh slightly upwards as you do.

LOOSE FLESH

𝒯he physical effects of gravity begin to make themselves more apparent as the years go by. This is especially true for the face, where previously well-defined features cast off their anchors and one-by-one set sail due south.

In addition to regularly using the basic programme to benefit your whole face, it's worth trouble-shooting and toning any areas that you think might need extra help. If you practice these exercises regularly, you should see the muscles slowly toning up and become firmer and more defined.

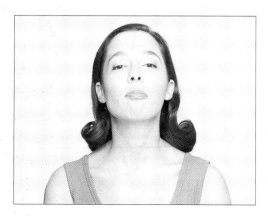

1 Tilt your head back, push out your chin slightly and bring your lower lip over the upper lip.

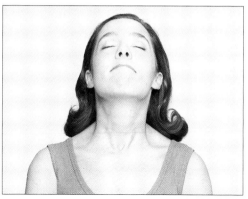

2 Slowly smile in an upwards and outwards direction. Repeat five times.

3 Grasp the upper lip and gradually lift the cheek muscles in the direction of the eyes, then release. Repeat five times.

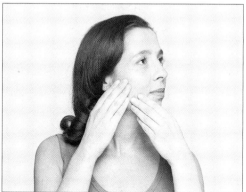

4 To end, use the pads of your fingers to gently caress your face in an upwards direction.

Use two fingers to press gently between the eyebrows. This powerful pressure point helps to release deep facial tension.

$\mathscr{W}$rinkles and expression lines rarely get good press. Consequently, as soon as they appear, they are often resented and wished far away. In truth, they are a natural by-product of life itself, a physical diary of our experiences through the years, signs of who we really are.

However, if you'd rather live without them, try the following exercises. As you work, wait patiently for the tissues between your fingers to soften or warm up, because this shows that wrinkle-causing blockages or tensions are being released. Through time, practice and repetition, the lines will slowly become less etched and noticeable, and the skin smoother.

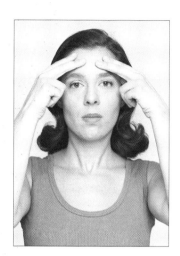

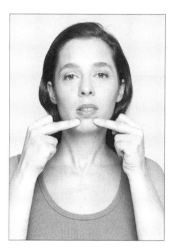

2 Place two fingers slightly apart on the forehead, and bring them slowly closer as you feel the space in between warm up and soften.

3 Use the same technique on the upper lip, slowly working your way around the mouth, releasing tension as you go.

4 Continue in the chin area, working in as many places as you can.

L O W   E Y E B R O W S

$\mathcal{S}$ooner or later, low eyebrows or drooping eyelids will appear in most people's lives. Gravity and the relative thinness of a few muscles that can easily lose their tone through the years are largely to blame for this. Sagging in this area can be particularly worrisome because the face depends on the eye region to help lend it definition. If the shape or size of our eyes is affected, and especially if they are made to appear smaller, the face can 'age'. The way to help prevent this is to exercise the eyebrows and upper eyelids regularly, as shown.

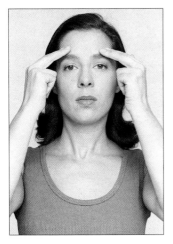

1 With your fingertips, tap backwards and forwards along the eyebrow several times to release tension.

2 Raise your eyebrows as high as you can. Try to do this in four stages. Stretch your eyes as wide open as you can and then bring your eyebrows down slowly, look downwards and then relax. Repeat five times.

3 Create a 'V' shape with your first two fingers and place them on either side of the eyebrows. Now try to squint with both eyes while using your fingers to resist the movement. This is very good for building up the muscles here.

$\mathcal{O}$ne of the first tell-tale signs that we are getting older is the appearance of lines around our eyes. Many people are sent into a tailspin by this, checking obsessively for new lines every time they pass a mirror. Bags or puffiness in the eye area, which can make us look somewhat tired and world-weary, has a similar effect. If you want to reverse this process, try the exercises below. These will help to release the congestion that creates new lines and deepens existing ones.

1 Grasp the skin on either side of your eyebrows and roll it between your fingertips. This breaks up a lot of the tension that causes crow's feet.

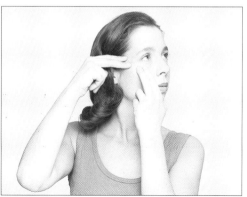

2 Place two fingers on either side of a wrinkle you want to smooth out. Wait for the area between your fingers to warm up and soften, letting the crow fly away!

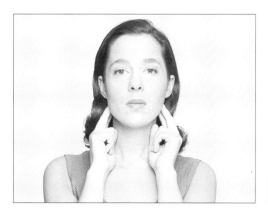

3 Use two fingers to massage free any congestion that has built up immediately behind the earlobe. Congestion in this area can contribute to bags forming under the eyes.

4 Use the same technique as in Step 2 to soften and release congestion below the eye. The skin here is delicate, so be very gentle as you work.

*A*fter many years the smiling muscles on either side of the mouth (*zygomaticus major* and *minor*) can start to lose their tone, causing the corners of the mouth to turn downwards, creating an appearance of sulking or frowning. No one wants to look perpetually frumpy, so the answer is to make sure that these muscles are regularly exercised properly to restore tone and lift the corners so that the mouth is level once again.

With your mouth slightly open, bring the corners of the left side of your mouth out as far as possible. Then work the right-hand side of your mouth. Repeat five times.

2 Close your lips and with one side of your mouth, smile broadly up towards the ears. Work the other side and repeat. Once you can do this successfully, try both sides at the same time.

3 Repeat Step 2, but this time extend the smile up towards your eyes. When you are ready, work both sides simultaneously.

4 Finally, place your index fingers on the corners of your mouth and tense the corners into an upward smile. Use your fingers as resistance and then relax. Repeat twenty times.

DOUBLE TROUBLE

These two exercises are designed to help you keep a well-defined jawline. This is essential if you don't want little folds of flesh to appear and give your face a loose, even droopy appearance. If the muscles underneath the chin also begin to lose their tone and fall under gravity's spell, then they too can begin to sag, encouraging the development of a double chin, which can look less than flattering. If you practise these techniques regularly, you can help chase away the spectre of loose folds and unwanted chins, creating well-toned muscles and smoother, tauter skin.

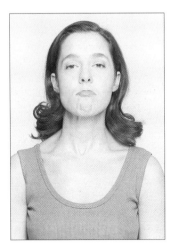 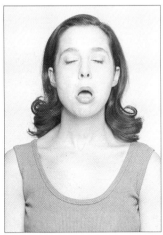 

1 Open your mouth and pull your lower lip tightly over the bottom teeth.

Then open and close your jaw as if you were trying to scoop something up with it. Make sure you really work your jaw so that you tone the muscles. Repeat five times.

2 This is a classic move for toning slack muscles. Use the back of your hand to tap or gently slap under your chin. Repeat with the other hand and increase your speed.

WORKING THE NECK

𝒯here are some lucky individuals who weather the passing years with hardly a line or fold; the only place that gives away their age is their neck. The skin in this area is very thin and its natural elasticity and smoothness can slowly change, drying and becoming crêpe-like as we get older. In addition, lines can easily appear on the neck itself, slowly deepening into creases. If you want to preserve the smooth quality of your neck or return it to its former glory, then spend some time investing in these exercises.

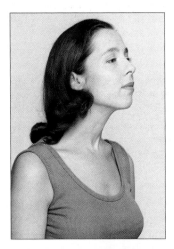

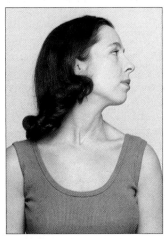

1 Tense your neck muscles and stick your neck out slowly and bring it right back like a turtle. Repeat five times.

2 Keeping your muscles tense, turn your head from side to side five times. This is excellent for toning the neck muscles, preventing slackness.

3 Place your hand on your forehead and push forward with your head, resisting with your hand. Repeat by putting the hand on the back of the head and pushing backwards.

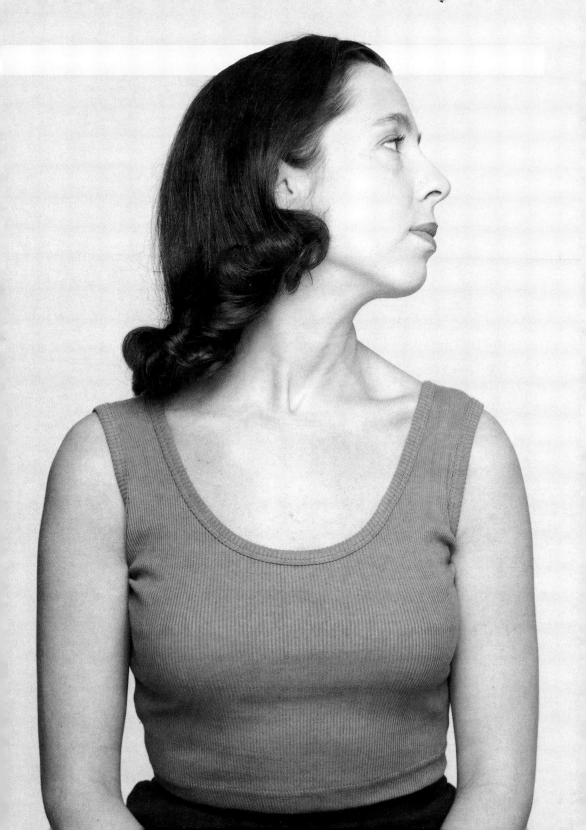

Facial Harmony

If you feel that your facial muscles are over-worked, tired and truly in need of a holiday away from it all, then pamper yourself and get your partner to give you one of the following fabulous facial massages.

While it is important to make sure that you follow and practise the basic facial fitness programme and regularly target any specific areas that need special attention, it's also a good idea – if you can find the time – to receive a soothing facial massage.

The results are always quite beautiful to watch: the face slowly relaxes, deep-seated tension is unlocked and caressed away and the years gently rolled back, leaving your face looking softer, fresher and years younger.

Regular massage is an extremely powerful tool because it successfully disperses the tension that builds up in the muscles and tissues, thus preventing the formation of lines and wrinkles. It also helps to restore circulation and clears out any harmful and ageing toxins trapped in the tissues.

In the following pages we will look at two types of massage. The first is a wonderful relaxer and general tension disperser which requires a tiny amount of oil mixed with lavender to work its magic. The second uses no oil at all and releases tension at the deepest level, smoothing out long-term wrinkles. These sequences are suggestions, ideas to be explored, so encourage your partner to develop his or her own intuition and creativity in their search for facial harmony.

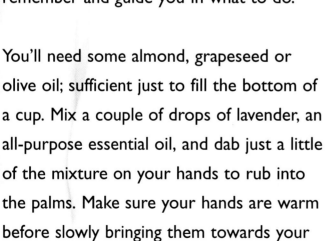

I Place your hands on either side of your partner's face at the base of the neck and slowly stroke upwards towards the forehead. Repeat three times.

If you've never worked with oil or given a massage before, don't worry. Massage is one of our most ancient skills and once you get started, your fingers will begin to remember and guide you in what to do.

You'll need some almond, grapeseed or olive oil; sufficient just to fill the bottom of a cup. Mix a couple of drops of lavender, an all-purpose essential oil, and dab just a little of the mixture on your hands to rub into the palms. Make sure your hands are warm before slowly bringing them towards your partner to start.

2 Gently caress underneath the chin, using alternate hands in upward sweeping movements.

3 Position your thumbs in the middle of the forehead and slowly move your thumbs away from each other to the sides of the head.

4 Using the underside of the little fingers, create a light friction between your partner's eyebrows.

*G*ently encourage your partner to breathe out all their tension. Once you begin to work, make sure that all your attention is completely on them. Losing physical connection can be very disconcerting for your partner and can stop them from fully relaxing and enjoying the benefits of the massage.

Keep your movements small, the pressure constant and the speed even. Don't rush any movement; if anything, slow down and repeat the same one several times, because this will help your partner to relax deeply and really let go. Focus on releasing any tension and smoothing out any lines you may find: you might be surprised to see real changes happening as you work.

1 Place your third fingers just underneath the brow bone and press upwards and then repeat, moving outward until you reach the outer edge of the eyebrow.

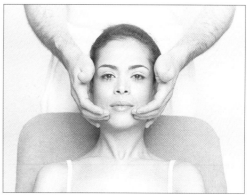

2 Use your fourth fingers to create small upward circles around the chin.

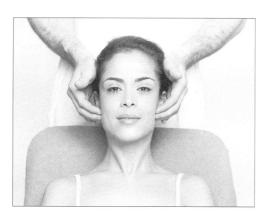

3 Find the chewing muscles on each side of the face. Make some slow circles with the pads of your fingers.

4 Grasp the ears and gently pull outwards. Finish by covering your partner's eyes for a few moments.

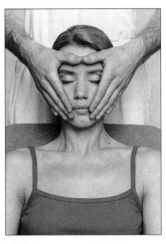

Gently place both hands over your partner's face. This will feel good and is very calming.

*A*lthough oil-based facials are very pleasurable to receive and help release general tension, nothing beats working without oil when you want more detailed, close-up work.

The aim when you work is to release tissues, some of which may be trapped together in small pockets. This requires the lightest of pressure upon the skin and the patience to wait for the tissue to slowly release. If you place one or two fingers on either side of such a pocket and wait, you will slowly begin to feel the area warm and soften. When it does so, move your fingers slightly closer together and repeat until the tension has completely disappeared.

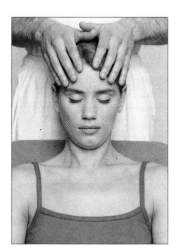

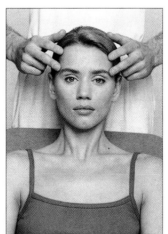

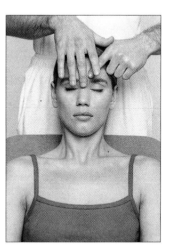

2 Spread your fingers and place them very, very lightly on the forehead, then begin to move towards the hairline, feeling for subtle restrictions.

3 Place your first two fingers on either side of the forehead and wait till you feel a slight warming-up or release. Move the fingers a little closer and repeat.

4 Put one finger on the bridge of the nose and hold it there for support as you run the index finger of the other hand down the nose.

HOME AND DRY: PART TWO

This approach works on the connective tissue, the flesh that is not muscle and which binds everything together: skin, muscle, tendons and organs. When a kink or blockage occurs in this tissue, it can mean the beginning of wrinkles. By working directly on the connective tissue, we can see even quite deep wrinkles fade and disappear.

The other technique to develop when using no oil is to work an area in several directions, repeating the same movement over and over again. Connective tissue has many layers and working like this will guarantee success.

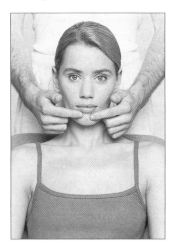

1 Begin by searching for any restrictions on the upper and lower lip. Again, move the fingers closer when an area softens, then repeat.

2 Repeat the process, this time working around the chin. Don't forget to try different directions.

3 Place your fingers under your partner's chin and wait for a warming-up, softening or pulsation in the area between your fingers.

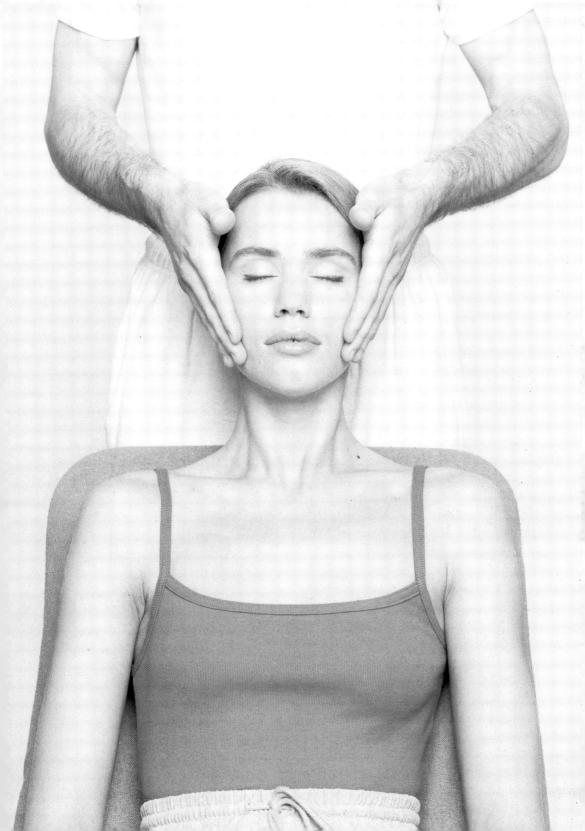

$\mathscr{L}$ess Is More

$\mathscr{L}$et's face it, the last thing you want to hear as you get older is how great your make-up looks. Wouldn't you much rather be told how great you look?

But if you want to keep looking your very best throughout the years, it's important that you adapt to change. As you blossom into sophistication and wisdom, you probably won't want to go on wearing the same clothes you did as a teenager. Many women, however, stick to the same make-up ideas first learnt as young girls. Unfortunately, the brash colour schemes that once impressed your friends will probably fail to keep up with the changes in your face or skin tone as you mature. Rather than complimenting you, vibrant colours can often make you look considerably older than you are.

At the first signs of ageing it's easy to fall into the trap of applying more and more make-up in the hope that no one will notice that you're getting older. But it's hard to fool anyone when your make-up enters a room before you do.

It takes only a subtle shift of focus – accentuating the positive, enhancing your eyes rather than hiding your crow's feet – to look ten years younger. By updating your techniques and colour schemes, adapting to changes in your face and being subtle in your use of make-up, you can make the most of what nature has given you. Whatever your age, you can look fresh, radiant, attractive and confident. It really is true: less is more.

*B*eing a 30-something is not easy. It's a time when we get on with the serious business of settling down, developing a career and building a home and family. Any one of these is a full-time job in itself: juggling all three successfully sometimes verges on the impossible.

Foundation: Use a light base and cover face and neck. Then gently press in translucent powder to fix your foundation.

It's also a time when we start to notice the first subtle signs of ageing, with lines and perhaps a change in our skin appearing. Gone are the days when we could do exactly what we wanted to our body. Now we really need to look after ourselves and learn how to use make-up in a way that naturally enhances our beauty.

Eyes: Using a cream colour, highlight the lower eyelid and just below the eyebrow. Then use some brown on the crease between the browbone and eyelid to create a contour effect and blend. Apply eyeliner to the upper and lower lid and blend once more.

Lips: Line with a soft pencil and then use a moisturizing lip colour to cover lips.

Colour: Whereas a blusher is used to bring out pale cheeks, a bronzer can be used to bring colour to the whole face. Gently bronze the face and highlight the cheek bones to give a healthy glow.

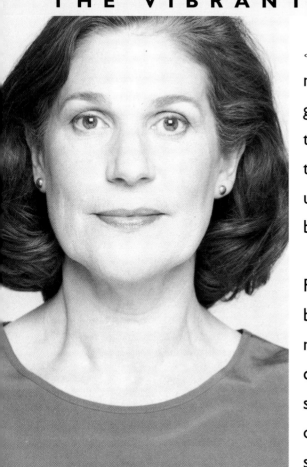

*L*ife does begin at 40, with many women experiencing greater energy and drive. On the other hand, they also have to cope with the great physical upheavals that the menopause brings.

Facial skin often changes, becoming less plump, looser and more lined and skin type can change dramatically. Using the same make-up techniques will only add to the ageing process, so it's important to update and learn how to accept and adapt to the new you. This make-over will show you some ideas, but any cosmetics sales assistant will be more than happy to spend time discussing appropriate colours, techniques and products to suit your personal needs.

Foundation: If dark bags have settled, you can use a cover-up before you apply your base. Don't go too heavy as this will make the skin appear older. Gently powder with translucent powder.

Eyes: Cover the eyelid with a non-metallic cream/white shadow and add contour shadow just above the socket line as described in page 75. Blend. Then pencil the outer third of the eyes lightly and blend using a Q-tip.

Lips: If you have fine lines around your mouth, use a dry lip liner. Any other type of lip liner may tend to bleed up the lines. Then apply colour. If you want your colour to last, blot with tissue, powder and apply lip colour again.

Colour: Just for the final touch, apply a small amount of bronzer all over your face to give a hint of colour.

Foundation: On a well moisturized skin gently apply your base, carefully blending the hair line and the jaw and neck. Try not to get any in your hair especially if your hair is light or grey. Then gently powder by pressing with a power puff.

$\mathscr{T}$here are many mature women who could give their younger sisters a run for their money. What they have in common is a graceful acceptance of their age and the determination to use all their resources intelligently to help them look like a million dollars.

They take consistent good care of their skin, recognize and highlight their best features, regularly revise their make-up, and embrace any physical change as an integral part of themselves. And, if their eyesight is less than perfect, a magnifying mirror helps them to put their make-up on accurately and to keep it light, refreshing and natural.

Eyes: Using non-metallic shadow, cover the eye area with a cream right up to the brow. Then lightly blend a brown shadow above the socket line which is where your eyelid dips in. Then blend. Apply eye pencil to the outer third using gentle strokes.

Lips: Apply a tinted lip moisturizer. This is sometimes better than a colour if your lipstick tends to bleed.

Colour: Whereas a blusher is used to bring out pale cheeks, a bronzer can be used to bring colour to the whole face. Apply a bronzer all over your face using a big brush and light strokes to create a healthy glow.

INDEX